Praise for

"*António Lobos Antunes é, na atualidade, um dos mais pródigiosos e fascinantes mestres*" (António Lobos Antunes is today, one of the most prodigious and fascinating masters.)" —Claudio Magris, *Corriere della Sera*

"One of the living writers who will matter most" —Harold Bloom

"Lobo Antunes, one of the most skillful psychological portraitists writing anywhere, renders the turpitude of an entire society through an impasto of intensely individual voices." —*The New Yorker*

"He's been compared to Faulkner, Dos Passos, García Márquez, Céline, Cormac McCarthy, Malcolm Lowry, Proust, Woolf, Canetti, Gogol, Camus, Cortazar, and Nabokov. The real challenge for reviewers is coming up with a new Master of World Literature Antunes hasn't been compared to." —*Quarterly Conversation*

"Considered by many to be Portugal's greatest living writer, António Lobo Antunes' relative obscurity in the English-speaking world is something of an enigma . . . The author of 23 novels, and still . . . turning them out with unerring industriousness, Lobo Antunes is quite a big deal in Portuguese-, Spanish- and French-speaking countries. He has his illustrious champions too: George Steiner calls him 'a novelist of the very first rank . . . an heir to Conrad and Faulkner;'" —*The Millions*

"A living grandmaster of literary modernism." —*Full Stop*

"Antunes is definitely a writer worth reading for his literary talent and his insights into Portugal's history, geography, and national character." —*Publishers Weekly*

"His themes are reminiscent of Faulkner's and Celine's, and his style is as complex as Proust's." —*Library Journal*

"Lobo Antunes's interweaving of thought, memory and dialogue, both inner and outer, creates as close an experience to the chaos of thinking as is possible on the page. His characters leak trauma while remaining outwardly composed and bland. The inner self is Lobo Antunes's ultimate preoccupation, especially the exploration of neuroses and phobias." —*Times Literary Supplement*

Other Work by António Lobos Antunes

Act of the Damned
By the Rivers of Babylon
Commission of Tears
Elephant's Memory
An Explanation of the Birds
Fado Alexandrino
The Fat Man and Infinity: And Other Writings
The Inquisitor's Manual
Knowledge of Hell
The Land at the End of the World
The Natural Order of Things
The Return of the Caravels
The Splendor of Portugal
Treatise on the Passions of the Heart
Until Stones Become Lighter Than Water
Warning to the Crocodiles
What Can I Do When Everything's on Fire?

MIDNIGHT IS NOT IN EVERYONE'S REACH

by
ANTÓNIO LOBO ANTUNES

TRANSLATED FROM
THE PORTUGUESE BY
ELIZABETH LOWE

DALKEY ARCHIVE PRESS
Dallas, TX / Rochester, NY

Deep Vellum | Dalkey Archive Press
3000 Commerce Street, Dallas, Texas 75226
www.dalkeyarchive.com

Deep Vellum is a 501c3 nonprofit literary arts organization founded in 2013 with the mission to bring the world into conversation through literature.

Text copyright © 2012 by António Lobo Antunes
Translation copyright © 2025 by Elizabeth Lowe
Originally published in Portuguese as *Não é Meia-Noite Quem Quer* by Dom Quixote, Lisbon, 2012.
Published through Arrangement with Agencia Literaria Carmen Balcells, s.a.
First English edition, 2025 | All rights reserved.

Support for this publication has been provided in part by grants from the National Endowment for the Arts, the Texas Commission on the Arts, the City of Dallas Office of Arts and Culture, the Communities Foundation of Texas, and the Addy Foundation.
Funded by the DGLAB/Culture and the Camões, IP – Portugal.

Library of Congress Cataloging-in-Publication Data
Names: Antunes, António Lobo, 1942- author. | Lowe, Elizabeth, 1947- translator.
Title: Midnight is not in everyone's reach / by António Lobo Antunes ; translated from the Portuguese by Elizabeth Lowe.
Other titles: Não é meia noite quem quer. English
Description: Dallas, TX : Dalkey Archive Press, 2025.
Identifiers: LCCN 2024058700 (print) | LCCN 2024058701 (ebook) | ISBN 9781628976120 (trade paperback) | ISBN 9781628976212 (ebook) Subjects: LCGFT: Novels.
Classification: LCC PQ9263.N77 N3513 2025 (print) | LCC PQ9263.N77 (ebook) | DDC 869.3/42--dc23/eng/20241212
LC record available at https://lccn.loc.gov/2024058700
LC ebook record available at https://lccn.loc.gov/2024058701

Cover art and design by Nuno Moreira
Interior design and typeset by Douglas Suttle

Printed in the United States of America

MIDNIGHT IS NOT IN EVERYONE'S REACH

TABLE OF CONTENTS

Translator's Note — ix

Friday, August 26, 2011 — 13
Saturday, August 27, 2011 — 203
Sunday, August 28, 2011 — 399

TRANSLATOR'S NOTE

The title of this novel comes from surrealist poet René Char's "Entraperçue" in *Chants de la Balandrane*. "I sow with my hands / I plant with my water / Silent the fine rain / On a narrow path / I write my secret / Midnight is not in everyone's reach / The echo is my neighbor / The mist, my companion." The line has been translated as "midnight is not within every man's reach." I chose to substitute "everyone's" for "every man's." The midnight in the poem alludes to the hour of midnight that the Romans established as time zero, marking the start of a new day. This is the moment to which the story leads us: the suicide of the narrator, which releases her from her torments. René Char described himself as a poet who intended to bring the dawn of hope to a difficult life. He used images of light to counteract the darkness of despair. The action of Lobo Antunes's novel occurs over three days, from Friday to Sunday, August 26 to 28, 2011, when the protagonist, a 52-year-old woman, returns to say goodbye to the home on the beach at Alto da Vigia where her family spent summers. The book is divided into three parts, one for each day, and each part has ten chapters, designated by numbers. Like many of António

Lobo Antunes's works, it is a polyphonic novel, in which the voices of the characters are interwoven, often indistinguishably, from each other. It reads as if there is just one voice, however the narrator's psychic space is splintered into many fragments: "if I only could communicate in as many voices as mine divides itself into." The character's memories come from the important people in her life, and the voices in her head echo back to her in the beckoning sound of the pines and the ocean waves. By hurling herself off the same cliff where her brother jumped to his death, she hopes to return to the authentic life that was stolen from her, a place where "the waves move without hurting me."

The corrosiveness of time and the treachery of memory are twin themes in António Lobo Antunes's works. The voices in the novel speak to each other in a stream of dialogue that mimics the indirect speech, which is the core narrative technique of most of Antunes's works. The dialogue requires close attention because often it is not clear who is speaking, and the spoken lines, marked by em-dashes in the original and the translation (using the Portuguese convention for punctuating dialogue) come from different people from distinct points in time. The spoken lines are often followed by commentary from the main character, who argues with, cajoles, scolds, and mocks her interlocutors. Portuguese has many more forms of past and conditional tense than English, which shade the narrative with temporal nuance. To capture this grammatical complexity, I resorted often to the gerund, and to switching from past to imperfect to present in the same paragraph. His phrasing has been compared to jazz, with improvisations that interrupt the narrative flow, and refrains that mark the melody. I strove to capture some of this cadence, which marks the ebb and flow of memory.

The African wars are a dark presence in many of António Lobo Antunes's works. A practicing psychiatrist during his professional life, he served as a medic in Angola and witnessed first-hand the physical as well as psychological ravages of the war. In this novel, the collateral damage is in the home country. The protagonist's beloved older brother commits suicide to avoid the draft into the Angolan war. The middle brother returns with post-traumatic stress and retreats into muteness, in ironic counterpart to the youngest brother, who is deaf from birth. The wars drain the country of resources and many, like the narrator's family, live in deprivation. Images of death and destruction are compounded and magnified in her memory: a distant embittered mother, an alcoholic father, rejection by her best friend, a miscarriage, a failed marriage, and breast cancer.

In the next to last chapter, a young version of the protagonist wakes up in the house and sees her whole family around the table, and her smiling older brother. Time is internal, suspended, and as ephemeral as sea foam. It is expressed throughout the book in the forms of diary, dialogue, and interior monologue. The 6:40 on a Sunday of her suicide is the arbitrary time she chooses to die, when she can be reborn, the midnight that is within her reach. "The house is quiet, and I am calm." This is perhaps why the last chapter, consisting of two words, is in the voice of the deaf brother, who repeats the phrase of a tongue twister from his speech therapy that echoes throughout the novel "Sheee saaills . . ."

Elizabeth Lowe
2024

Midnight is not in everyone's reach
René Char

# FRIDAY, AUGUST 26, 2011

I.

I awoke in the middle of the night certain that the ocean was calling me through the closed shutters, I turned my head in the direction of the window and I felt it looking at me just the way the sound of the pines was looking at me and the voices of my parents, at the end of the hall, looking at me, everything was looking at me in the dark repeating my name, I asked
—What did I do?
and there was silence, the ocean and the pines disappeared from the window, where did you go, all of you, and my silent parents, if we lose the ocean and the pines there will be almost nothing left, a few roof tiles, the reeds, the sand, without the tracks of the gulls, early in the morning, just the garbage from the tides that the lifeguards had not yet swept, driftwood, oil cans, I was five, my brothers were seven and nine, I won't speak of my older brother, we don't speak of him, there he is, smiling at me
—Hey girl
riding his bike to the beach with me on the back which hurt a little, happy, and frightened
—we won't fall I promise

and we didn't fall, when I got off the fender I was still a little sore but it would pass, they had placed a green flag on a post in front of the waves, from time to time a ship passed in the distance, my father would be sleeping, a newspaper folded on his chest, on the sofa, that is it looked like he was sleeping because his mouth was open, he didn't have gray hair and he wasn't sick, he had not died, my mother was talking with the next door neighbor

—Do I have to keep telling you not to ride with the girl on the bike she'll break a leg you never stop

my not deaf brother and my deaf brother threw things at each other and my deaf brother, you'd shout his name, and he didn't turn toward us, he started to cry, my hair was already not black like my father's, dyed blond, my mother to the neighbor, cleaning off my deaf brother's face with a towel

—Do you see what I put up with?

at the far end of the beach, on the rocks leading to the lake, there was an abandoned building with the sign Alto da Vigia Shellfish and Drinks fading into the limestone walls, where after dinner the gypsies would get together to plan to rob us, mother said

—I hope they rob all of you, so you shut up about it

Although you couldn't see anyone with a wooden leg and bags to put us in, I saw them do it with kittens and the bag wiggled, they lowered the bag into the laundry sink and it stopped wiggling, they buried it in a hole in a corner of the yard and ordered us

—Go away

only my deaf brother stayed, trying to kick up the dirt with his feet, I said to him

—Don't be upset

and a blackbird sang two notes in the pines, why get upset about a bag that dripped blood and the mother cat sniffing around, I didn't have children, I, that is I had one and I lost it, where did they bury it, my husband said

—They didn't put it in a hole, and it wasn't a baby yet

while the bike slowly made its way up the hill to the house, I remember the sound of the bell, the mailman rang it loudly, I arrived in the morning to say goodbye to the house, the week we turned in the keys, the trees were offended with me, one notices those feelings

—How mean of you to leave us

they won't look at me tonight, they'll pretend to forget who I was, rooms stripped of furniture, a piece of paper to the right and on the floor to the left, remains of mattress stuffing where my bed was, the same ants as before in the kitchen but the shelves missing pots and pans, a package of sugar, closed with a clothes pin, alone in the pantry, and the memory of my father looking for a bottle in the pantry, I responding to his haste that had ceased to exist, his shaking fingers letting go of my memories

—there are no more bottles, father

and my father stubborn, looking through a chest, opening a box, giving up looking at my untidy hair, I can't get used to being blonde, he died years ago, why do you want to come back here, sir, today of all days, to torment me with your thirst for booze and the handkerchief you used to wipe your forehead and you don't bother with your face, you wave a shaky goodbye to nobody in particular, pause for a moment, and end up hiding your hand in your pocket, like a cat in a bag, soon to be still, a hole opens up in the yard and you disappear forever while the rest of you trips in the living room, my mother to the next door neighbor, pointing to us

—My kids are worthless

the cross I bear, Miss Liberdade, a deaf son, a useless daughter, a kid that kills things, another crazy one, not to mention the husband who reeks of alcohol

—Get the spiders out of my clothes

a bunch of thieves, girlfriend, up there in the Alto da Vigia Shellfish and Drinks it seemed to me like one more vandal, looking more closely, a twig blown by the wind from the ocean, two or three skinny donkeys that the gypsies forgot, stepping on the ground with fragile hooves, in silence like the ocean and the pines, looking at me mournfully

—Are you really going to leave us?

my deaf brother let us know he understood by the way his eyebrows moved, a spoon banged against a saucepan and my deaf brother remained aloof, we grew silent thinking of him, measuring each syllable

—Maybe

he found out before the others, I don't know how, that I was going to get married and he pushed me down the hall

(fewer gulls than when I was little why?)

in a little whisper

—No

many fewer gulls, no robbers, the Alto da Vigia nonexistent, not a wall, or even a patch of orchard, weeds swaying endlessly, one of the donkeys fell when a rock got loose and the scrawny dogs swarmed around it, I would wake up in the middle of the night certain that the ocean was calling me through the closed shutters, who told it my name, I turned my head in the direction of the mirror and felt it looking at me, the donkey turned its bloated back, its legs sticking out straight, just teeth, my father, also looking bloated in his pajamas

—Have you seen a bottle anywhere, girl?

his feet having difficulty walking, his voice seeming to drag itself up a difficult climb, my mother

—Do you want to kill yourself like your oldest son did?

I returned to this house to say goodbye to it, the lifeguards covered the donkey with a tarp and took it to the slaughterhouse, the echoes of the pines in the echo of my footsteps, which of us is the trees and which of us is me, a crow flew to another branch in a frenzy of pages, the rooms grew larger, it seemed to me that a piece of Esmeralda's dress, a doll of mine, and at the end the sun in a shard of dishware, if I could communicate in many voices my voice divided itself, my mother

—Can't you stay still?

buttoning the blouse that pinched my back, the only thing that annoys me about growing up is that my older brother doesn't take me to the beach on the fender of his bike, starting next week, when I turn in the keys, I will not be able to look at the house from a distance, the pages of the newspaper slipped to the floor while my father slept, from time to time he would go to the pantry to sneak a drink

—Cough medicine, my girl, cough medicine

with a different color on his ears and his forehead, tell the pines not to look at me, it's not my fault, we would arrive in August, we would leave at high tide, when the gulls were no longer at the beach, poised on the chimneys, the waves reached the ocean wall and took the sand with them, not to mention the summer and my mother's voice, my brothers and I on the back seat of the car which was loaded with suitcases, they faced the front and I was facing the back, on my knees, watching the vacation grow smaller in the distance, the kiosk, the café with the foosball table, the last trees and then the highway, the gas station where they made us pee even if we didn't have to go, my brothers at the door with the silhouette of a man and I at the door with the silhouette of a woman, where my mother didn't go with me anymore

—Wash your hands well

and I was proud to go to the bathroom by myself, where there were always traces of perfume, in spite of my face at the lower rim of the mirror, it took centuries for me to see myself squarely in the mirror, there was a third door with a silhouette of a wheelchair which to this day I look at with curiosity, we arrived in Lisbon in an instant, tiles were missing on the building next to the Thebes Bakery

—What does Thebes mean, Mother?

and my mother, as always, had no idea

—So many questions

with a dark look directed at my father, rummaging where the bottles were after we emptied our suitcases, smells of a closed-up house and absence, which lingered for weeks, until the smell of food and people became stronger, if you ran your finger across any surface there was dust, I didn't tell them we were out of toothpaste so I wouldn't have to use it, I had the sensation that the ocean and the pines were coming back and they didn't, although there was a little bit of sand left on my feet and I was happy to find it, a lost gull crossed the porch but there was no donkey and no robber on the neighboring rooftops, when they wrote they didn't mention if my older brother talked about me, one day, if I can muster the courage, I'll talk about it, my deaf brother started to protest, demanding to sleep with the elephant that protected him from the trap doors of the world, hidden in the middle of the dirty clothes in a knapsack that hadn't been opened, my mother shouted in his ear

—You're seven years old, aren't you ashamed to sleep with a stuffed animal?

I didn't need the elephant, I had a hippopotamus on my night table, its name was Ernesto, he took care of me without my needing to hug it, I didn't mind putting him in the sheets, but Ernesto preferred the night table

—I'll stay here, and you stay there

just as I preferred to keep Ernesto's name a secret

—Don't tell anyone, hear?

and I of course obeyed, my grandmother was very old, she was at least forty or seventy

—What's your hippopotamus's name, dear?

I didn't answer, don't tell anyone, Dona Alice, almost as old as my grandmother, with a defect on her thumb, helped my mother three times a week, at the end of the month they got together to do the accounts, with pencils, on the back of an invoice, getting the numbers wrong, the nephew with the floating kidney, what is a floating kidney, you don't tire of boring people, girl, Dona Alice stuffed the pillows into the pillow cases, my mother, who was interested in illnesses

—How is your nephew's floating kidney, Dona Alice?

Dona Alice holding the pillow half out of the pillowcase

—Some days are better than others, they want to do an open stomach surgery

and for a few moments the idea of dying terrified me, death meant a lot of people standing around us and whispering

—Don't they respect the dead anymore?

my father in a black tie, more industrious in the pantry, my mother sobbing at intervals, no longer so irritated by us, announcing with resigned solemnity

—It will be over in a minute

that was a lie, the days were very long, for an example it was an eternity between lunch and my father getting up from the couch to take us to the circus after a trip to the pantry, my deaf brother, nervous because of the spotlights, hung on to us to yelp at the elephants, not me, I was enchanted by the woman on the trapeze, who was blonde like I am now, the certainty that if we met each other we would become friends and I would lend Ernesto to her for a night or two, even with the ocean calling me through the closed shutters and the robbers in the yard advancing toward me, around the tent the cages with sleepy lions, their pelts just like the tattered rugs that they leave on the street waiting for the garbage trucks, and a clown, pulling his bulbous nose to his hat, intending to scold his son with the enormous mouth, gigantic words that I wasn't able to hear, confused with the music of the band, I saw Dona Alice's nephew but I didn't see the floating kidney, I walked around him to investigate observing that he looked just like us on the outside, my mother

—Did you think the floating kidney would be suspended in the air?

the kidney was around somewhere and Dona Alice's nephew trying to catch it the way you try to pick up bath soap, he'd close it in his hand and it would escape, a blue spot if we stay still, without a trace if we swish the water, why do soap bars get smaller, don't be mad, mother, it wasn't a question, imagine, the girl in the circus never came to my room, how old would she be today and also it's not a question I just want an answer since I didn't meet her, I turned my head toward the window to feel them looking at me, everything looked at me repeating girl, I remember the afternoon when my mother's face changed

—You'll have to wear a bathing suit that covers you up there
where, in my opinion, there was nothing to cover up, two little nuts that had begun to bother me and that's it, the rest was the same, the hippopotamus was worried
—Are you going to throw me out?
and I got out of it by saying
—So many questions
immediately feeling guilty
—That's not what I wanted to say, I'm sorry, of course I won't throw you out
that was when my older brother was still alive
—Of course, I won't throw you out
and I lay down, I needed the night table for pictures of movie actors and the box for my bracelets and earrings, besides wanting to avoid the teasing from my friends
—Do you have a rhinoceros?
no rhinoceros, no hippopotamus, I don't forgive you for not being with me when my older brother, when the waves, when many people were whispering in the sand and it wasn't a donkey that fell from the rocks, when a policeman brought the bike that was left on the wall, my father not hiding in the pantry, a bottle in his hand, my mother lifted her eyes from the mask of her hands
—Do you have a question?
I who don't bother anybody, came to say goodbye, I don't understand the reason
—You'll have to wear a bathing suit that covers you up there
why the house doesn't belong to us anymore, feeling that the ocean is different, the pines are different and standing on ceremony with the empty rooms, walking lightly and hesitating at the doors

—May I come in?

Where there used to be a sugarcane plantation there was a house, two, and a boy hitting a tennis ball against a wall, next to a broken irrigation system, I went into the street to put Ernesto in the trash, between two bags, burying him as deep down as I could, you could see one of his legs, I took a bag from the bin next to it and Ernesto ceased to exist, when an ambulance came down the road, the bike had gone down in the direction of the beach, my father locked us in my deaf brother's room

—Don't leave

you could hear people in the living room, a man saying to Father

—Sign next to the X in pencil

the donkey was just teeth, and its legs were sticking out, while he signed my mother, in a voice that exists inside handkerchiefs

—He always swore he wouldn't go to the war

A blackbird adjusted its feathers next to the window frame, observing us sideways, continuing its grooming, we were leaning against each other, afraid, which of these hearts is mine, the man to my father

—Write your name clearly since it's not typed in

and a hammer, doves, the gate sounding like a long tear, as a nail lacerated the cement, everything alienates me, today, everything wounds me, my mother, staying inside her handkerchief

—I'll go in the back with him don't try to stop me

the ambulance leaving, now not in the direction of the beach, along the avenue where I never saw anyone, a chapel, olive trees, my deaf brother held the elephant to his stomach, my not deaf brother saying

—I'm hungry

the blackbird disappeared in a twisted flight and for the first time in my life, how dumb, I missed a bird, not a wave or a pine tree, the three of us sitting on a bed holding one of their hands, moist with terror, squeezing my arm, and I didn't understand if my blood belonged to me or if it was being exchanged with the others, perplexed, nervous, my older brother smiling at me
—Don't worry girl
or rather
the man accepting my father's signature
—It's ok
a disguised reproach
—He's a drunk
then footsteps, first on the clay, then on the steps, then inside the house, on the window frames a cactus with a red flower vibrating explaining everything, I heard a few random sentences, the rest not, something caught my interest
—What?
the cactus
—You're too young to understand
and she grew silent, something about a body with stiff legs, only teeth, on the beach, the footsteps, inside the house, approached the door in a way that only the floor existed, not the walls, or the furniture, the lock jumped, another jump, the lady next door, solemnly
—I'll stay here a few days until your parents get back
I was too young to know that my older brother had drowned, the cousin of the next-door neighbor in the kitchen couldn't figure out how to work the stove
—I can't get used to this one
opening and closing closets, yanking open drawers

—Where do they keep things?

my husband eating yellow plums, his fingers stained with juice, inquired

—Are you going to say goodbye to the house?

I wasn't eleven anymore, I was fifty-two, or rather here I was eleven and fifty-two, with black hair and blonde hair over my white hair, not understanding that my brother had drowned, I understood the teeth, the stiff legs sticking out and the tarp, I didn't understand death, the circling of the gulls over the pantries, and a dozen of them on the roof of the Casino, my husband wiping his fingers on the napkin, with the tip of his tongue at the corner of his mouth, which used to make me feel tender because it made him look younger and for centuries he hasn't made me feel tender, I'd appreciate your putting your tongue back in your mouth, thank you

—Go where you like but I need the car

so that I arrived on the train and the bus, at the station's old buildings with shutters that were boarded up, a child, looking at me from a tiny orchard, waving goodbye endlessly, not a goodbye for a person, a goodbye that a doll makes when the wind-up mechanism stops, if it were just the tongue sticking out, the arm slowly became immobile, never

—Did your older brother drown?

never had I seen such serious eyes, the orchard started to walk backwards and I lost sight of it, I gained a cemetery, that I also lost, where a group of people lowered my older brother to the ground with the help of ropes, my mother wasn't in their midst and my father wasn't talking with a bottle hidden in the pocket of his coat, my not deaf brother reached for the can of cookies

—I'm hungry

the next-door neighbor grabbed the can from him and set the table, mixing up our places and our napkins, I hated sitting in a chair that wasn't mine
—Settle down, dinner is almost ready
my older brother's chair empty forever, my mother would put her hand on the seat
—I will carry this cross to my last day
my father returned from the pantry tripping on the rug, then catching his balance
—Don't upset the kids, enough is enough
the black dress on the return from Lisbon, hopefully the gypsies won't abandon any more donkeys in the rocks, if a piece of rock breaks, they'll fall into the ocean and it could not be my older brother, it could be my deaf brother, it could be me, he always swore he wouldn't go to the war, which war, mother my father
—Haven't you ever heard about the history of Africa?
and we could hear the waves behind his voice, one afternoon when I thought they weren't looking I found my father in front of my older brother's bike, in the garage where there was an accumulation of cribs, broken objects, when he noticed I was there
—Go take a walk, girl
my husband
—So how are you going to say goodbye to the beach house
I hated the yellow plums, the pieces of fruit inside his mouth distorted his cheeks, my father and I walked down the street to the beach, the houses, the grocery store, the café with the foosball table where my father ordered a glass, and something inside him, which I understand and don't understand, stopped him from drinking
—Later

the expression on his face almost made me scream, I inherited his nose, his hands, and my mother said to the next-door neighbor

—She looks just like her father

at the end of the road the inn with walls encrusted with shells and from there the sand, she's just like her father, people with baskets were harvesting mussels and small crabs that were almost transparent in the rocks, my father sat me on the wall holding me by the stomach, the spray from the waves stung my skin, the flag on the mast was not green or yellow, it was red, I wanted to ask

—Please don't hold me so tight

but I understood that he had to hold me that way, not for my sake, but for his, I didn't say

—Don't talk about my older brother

knowing he wouldn't talk about him and the proof that he wasn't was that I could hardly move, the many times we should have said

—Father

and we didn't, the Alto da Vigia Shellfish and Drinks was already destroyed, families eat their lunch from dinner pails, two or three dogs, their heads down, without finding even a morsel of cheese worth their while, I came here to say goodbye hoping to find a morsel, a scent that was worthwhile and not even the pines answer my question, my father's throat making sounds of someone locking up their life with seven keys, I came to say goodbye to the house, and yes, I don't need the car, I don't need you, what do you know of the eyes in the shutters at night, of the voices that repeat my name, I need a child to wave goodbye to me in an orchard until the train forces me to lose it, I need my younger brothers, the crows, Ernesto who returns to the night table and waits for me, my father and I on the steps where people shook their shoes before putting them on, my deaf brother in front of my older brother's room not daring to enter, they emptied the drawers and took his clothes, my mother

—I never want to hear his name again

while my father and I kept walking along the tar road, he feels like a bottle, he doesn't feel like one, sir, do you want me to get it for you and he remains silent

—No

he is silent

—Are you ashamed of me too?

and he wasn't, I assure you, even when he remained in bed without being able to get up, he wasn't, I saw him in the hospital and he smiled at me

—Do you remember the wave, girl?

when we walked on the beach the next week, and the next week, and you hardly reached my waist, I didn't drink did I, I behaved myself, I was proud of myself, the doctor

—Take a look at these awful test results, they're all purple, not one of them reads blue

no vestige of the place they found the body, I was thinking if I'm still they didn't have that son, when visiting hours were over, he turned toward the wall so he couldn't see me leave

—Girl

and one or two days later I was at the wake and the burial, unknown cousins who squeezed my hand murmuring condolences, ladies I didn't know, my mother seated, in front of the urn and the candles, accompanied by severe creatures, the coffin leaving the hearse under umbrellas, the wreaths under the rain, I was standing in the rain, the priest, his glasses wet, hurrying the prayers, my deaf brother not greeting anyone, if you touched him he'd run away, he was the one who slashed the bike tires, broke the bell and twisted the saddle, water ran down his nose, not from his eyelids, he went to a school where they talked with their fingers and made sounds in their throat like my father in the sand, the last thing I remember of him is his head turning toward the wall, with all his tests showing purple and an IV in his arm, without saying goodbye, who says goodbye in this family before dying, we leave and that's it, my husband

—When are you coming home?

and I didn't answer him, I'll probably not come back, I fall like a pinecone from a tree and stay on the porch, the poplars in the cemetery heavy with the rain, the teeth of my older brother very heavy under the earth, this in winter with all the lamps lit and dark just the same, I liked to write other things and I can't now, I wave to you like the child in the orchard until the wind up mechanism stops, my husband, as I put on my coat

—The father drinks until he drops dead, and the daughter decides to say goodbye to the house where she never sets foot how did I get mixed up with people like this?

and while I waited for the elevator I heard dishes breaking but what was happening beyond the doormat didn't concern me, in the mirror was a woman with blonde hair it took a while to recognize as myself, if I had a son I hadn't brought him with me, I had forgotten him, and with this the thought of the hippopotamus losing its stuffing came back to me, my mother sent me to fetch cotton from the medicine cabinet and she put a piece of it into the hippopotamus, she asked for the sewing box with that awful pair of nail scissors, she sewed him up and while she was sewing, it could seem strange, she sat me on her lap without asking

—How long has it been since you took a bath?

I leaned against her neck and the rain of all the funerals stopped, my father and I came back from the beach a different way, circling the neighborhood, his shadow always arrived before mine on the uneven ground, from time to time we stopped for my father to adjust his lungs in his ribs, breathing heavily, and the waves were ever distant, my mother cut the thread with her teeth and gave Ernesto back to me, she closed the sewing box

—How does he look?

she tapped the tin with the cotton and gave the two things back to me

—Go put these away

that is the sewing box on top of the ironing board and the cotton next to the first aid kit, I was sad that I didn't have a scrape on my knees to put one of them on and earn the respect of my brothers by limping, the cold water spout with an H engraved on it while the hot water spout had a C, it dripped constantly even though we twisted it tight, my father

—One of these days I'll replace the washer

if we reminded him weeks later

—It slipped my mind

and he disappeared into his paper without any cartoons, only words and pictures of old gentlemen who were all called Minister, when she returned to the living room my mother, distracted, picked up Ernesto and rocked him, when she noticed me, she handed him to me

—I must be crazy

and her lip was a kind of tear, we noticed that in her head a carousel with giraffes and wooden horses and shaky boards were exploding, while a booming voice on a loudspeaker

—Travel on the eight and you'll travel better

and the guy from the Well of Death, wearing a motorcycle helmet, accelerated on a dais

—Do you remember the carousel, Mother

her memory, happy, full of giraffes if my older brother hadn't invited me

—Girl

the two of us got on board, fascinated by the animals, radiant with fear, whirling around in shaky circles, I remember her father coughing into his sleeve, I remember her mother, very fat, leaning her cane to get off the sofa, I asked

—Do you want me to loan Ernesto to you for a night or two?

and my mother hesitating, I accept, I don't accept, looking at the hippopotamus, looking at me, holding on to the wooden giraffe that was starting to turn, my mother growing tall suddenly, folding the glasses she used to sew with, putting them away in their case, depositing the case on the armrest of the sofa and ordering

—Get out of my sight

while the guy from the Well of Death, who I was in love with from the time I was twelve, ignored her smile as he accelerated on the platform

2.

Death is when there's one space too many at the table and the chairs have been spaced out to hide it, one notices the discomfort of absence because the picture on the wall is off-center and the sideboard is further away, especially the picture that is too far to the left and there's a hole from the first nail, where the frame used to be, visible, one speaks differently waiting for a voice that doesn't come, one eats differently, leaving a portion on the tray from which no one helps themselves, the elbows of our dinner partners don't get in the way of ours and we miss the obstruction, my mother to my not deaf brother, who had not yet gone to Africa and was affected by the war, slapping the back of his hand

—Do you think that's how you're supposed to hold your fork?

my father tearing apart a piece of bread on the napkin without noticing, he was paying attention to the place that should have been next to his and the neck of the wine bottle vibrating against his glass, we didn't hear the ocean, we heard a pneumatic hammer pounding on the floor of a house behind us which made our floor jump and altered the peace of the water in the carafe, my mother said

—If I had only

and she stopped talking when my father's expression signaled

—Enough

my deaf brother, in front of a tray with little cows printed on it, his napkin at his throat and grains of rice on his chin, the motorcyclist who accelerated on the Wall of Death platform appeared and disappeared, a wooden giraffe peeked out of the shaking windowsill, blinking its eye with immense lashes, the loudspeaker was off, the music more tenuous than the pines, my not deaf brother couldn't manage the cutlery and the fish slid off his fork, my mother balancing tears inside her eyelids, squinting

—An eighteen-year-old boy, my God

the giraffe abandoned the windowsill to the shaking, ever since I married you, I haven't been happy, the alcohol, the unemployment, the debts, it's impossible that the children don't understand, I said to her, also to myself

—Understand what?

and the piece of bread that my father was breaking up quickly, some fingernails longer than others, his shirt stained, pupils that saw and then didn't see, saw me

—Girl

and the features from before came back, that passion for his daughter, sir, my father who didn't kiss me, I don't deserve to kiss her, I was sure that my deaf brother noticed everything, discovered mute voices that don't stop, don't stop, so many people talking inside themselves, wanting to cover my ears with my palms

—Leave me alone

only my older brother was still although he was at the table with us, the presence of someone who isn't there frightens me, his chair against the wall, and there he would occasionally gesture to me

—Don't worry

even though the waves pulled him to the beach, now an arm, now another, his torn pants, my mother picked the grains of rice off my deaf brother's chin with the corner of her napkin

—Where did this unhappy child come from?

and the floor in peace because the workers with the pneumatic hammer were taking a smoke break, when the father of my mother was not a portrait, I rubbed my chin vigorously to rid myself of the mustache even after checking in the mirror that my chin was clean the mustache kept irritating me, the only kind thing he would say to me was

—Smartypants

he had to cross immense tufts of hair, that smelled of cigars and soup, until he reached me

—Smartypants

that a pair of brown teeth slurred, he left pushing hinges that needed oiling, not joints, that got stuck in the middle of the road, like the wooden leg of my not deaf brother, who came back wounded from the war and was living I don't know where, the leg moved toward the chest of drawers, determined, slow, it scraped, fell, and in spite of having fallen walked on in the emptiness, the mother of my mother sighing inside her fat body

—I had a blind dog when I was little

and I don't remember other things that were said, I remember the ring impossible, looking at the ocean calling me, to take off my finger and the wristwatch, with its Roman numerals, that wouldn't wind, stuck at eleven twenty, the kitchen clock, also stopped, six fourteen and the other, in a glass dome, with a pair of bronze angels holding up the face, fixed at two fifty eight, how multiplied time is, the mustache and the blind dog

—He was in my lap when they gave him the injection

they stunned me, when were they alive, when am I alive and what was my age when I was there, my mother

—Try it on

a woman's bathing suit that I refused to put on

—I don't want to wear this even when I'm grown up

the pines were for me

—You're a teacher, aren't you?

on the scratched lid of the cookie tin that had a picture of a carriage with a princess, or rather the girl on the trapeze, wearing a crown, guaranteeing me

—We're friends, I swear

and although I felt like refusing the cookies so she would have something to eat when she felt hungry at night and so she wouldn't find the tin empty, I to the pines, admitting, ashamed

—Yes, a teacher

certain they didn't believe me, there are no twenty-eight year old teachers, or six and fourteen, or two and fifty-eight, with a kitchen towel around their neck

—I don't know how you do it, but you always make a mess of yourself

my grandmother's cane scraped the floor taking her along with effort, I should kiss the cane, not her, my grandmother was an enormous thing that the cane used, death is when there's a place too many at the table, disguised by the wider distance between the chairs, and we waited for my older brother to appear and ask in astonishment

—Where do I sit now?
there are times when I set his place at the table, my husband
—Do we have guests?
I say
—We do
without listening to the pause that becomes anger, or the plate flung to the floor, my husband sweeping the cutlery and the glasses off the table
—Do you mind telling me who you invited?
and I knew perfectly that it was the older brother who I didn't come in time to take care of, I offered work to the deaf one, I'll pay the rent of the crazy one, I send my mother money every month, the older brother who threw himself into the ocean centuries ago because of the war in Africa, and if he already belonged to the family there was no other solution than to pull him out of the waves, I support the relatives and my wife thanks me with nonsense like this, a plate for the dead one and I pay for everything because a teacher's salary is miserable, what did I discover in her when we married, her clothing askew, her mania for talking to things, even when she got pregnant she put the child in the wrong place, after the operation the doctor said
—You can't have any more children
I
—You can't have any more children
she was dozing in bed and the only thing I heard her say was
—Is it eleven twenty or six fourteen?
turning her head
—Not with your mustache
and now alone on the beach saying goodbye to an empty ruin, looking for the past in the pines or rather a drunken father whispering

—Girl

a hippopotamus that was lying in the garbage and I, with no obligation, enduring the family, a cheap beach house on the hill over the village, with the bicycle of said brother, she

—He used to let me ride on the fender

rotting in the garage, my mother suddenly bigger, holding a pair of blue handlebars

—Put on the bathing suit and shut up

I was afraid that my father, happy with a bottle in the pantry, would stop paying attention to me because I was big, while he, at the door of my room, recognizing me and I was happy, for you I'm still a girl

—A woman fierce girl

while the sink that needed a new washer, kept dripping explosions in the bathroom, my mother

—If we had the money, I'd have gotten it fixed months ago

suddenly a horrible suspicion

—Are we poor

like the people who paint their shoes instead of polishing them and eat, defending themselves with their elbows from the greed of others, a little apple in the shelter, seeds and all, I teach Portuguese in a school, looking around afraid they'll steal it, the apple eaten to the core, which I also chew, and the inspection of the pan, tipping it to one side and another, hoping to find leftover soup, if they lost interest in the can with the trapeze lady, they would eat it and the trapeze artist for me, the students don't respect me

—If I wake up in the middle of the night, what will I do?

if I wake up in the middle of the night, not mentioning Ernesto, noise the whole time, they get up, sit down, the trapeze artist, dying lions, and clowns without noses scolding, when I get old I will put her, bedecked with bracelets, in the ticket booth or help the magician who pulls out doves from his empty hands, smoothing their heads with the tips of his fingers, until the pneumatic hammer begins to work again, scrambling my thoughts, and the world jumping around me exchanging my memories of place, my not deaf brother on a boat to Africa, with hundreds of fellow soldiers in green uniforms, still without big teeth and stiff legs, in January, in the cold, the grey Tagus river tossing garbage, I remember a wicker basket and corpses of gulls, if it were just getting up and sitting, they imitate animals, laugh, I couldn't find my not deaf brother on the wall, I don't know if it was because of the fog or a tugboat pushing a freighter, my mother sent him chocolates, preserves, in the case of the next-door neighbor

—Do you see the cross I bear?

a breezy morning in Alcântara until the river just, my not deaf brother does not exist, the water and the birds exist, most of them sheltered in the recess of the storeroom, the people on the dock went away and I am single, there was a picture of my father, if they asked to go out with me, he'd change the subject, burdened, he would answer

—We'll talk about it later

in an album, an inscription, In Tomar, with a date that you couldn't see since there was a thumb smudge on fresh ink, two guys with him next to a door that said Infirmary, my father

—This one is Fernandes and that one memory fails me, it will come back to me

the next day at dinner, an exclamation of triumph

—Osório?

until the album pulled out of the drawer, pinky finger on the photograph

—It's Osório

and a story, full of tributaries and ramifications, in which we got lost, about how Osório wounded a phalange on a shooting range, they amputated his ring finger and got married with a ring on his pinky, my father, victorious

—His bride Cândida and his godfather Abel

asking pensively

—What has become of Osório?

Osório's life, his fate, the very Osório installed in the middle of the tray of lamb, uncomfortable, timid

—Excuse me

wanting to dissolve into the album to hide the missing phalange with the other hand, the album, open on the table, covered several plates, my mother

—There's a dead mosquito on that page

and Osório becoming smaller on the page while my mother got up scraping her chair

—The bug took away my appetite

Osório was embarrassed and in fact, with every gesture, you could see he was missing a finger

—A mosquito from Tomar?

the people left and we were still on the docks, convinced that the boat was coming back, or at least my mother hoped it would

—There could be a malfunction in the engine

my father transported Osório and Fernandes to the drawer, with Tomar and marriage in his head, Fernandes and he were asked to leave during the toasts, pushing each other down the avenue, now best of friends, now enemies, Fernandes vomiting on his knees in the park, promises to stay united after they left the army and they never saw each other again, he wrote months ago and the letter was returned, Addressee Unknown, my father examining the envelope suspiciously

—He gave me the wrong address

and then my mother, and the children, and then the jobs, comments from superiors, comments from clients, fierce bosses banging their pencils on desks

—Aren't you responsible for this?

a more modest job, another job, when my daughter was born, they told me it was a daughter, I swore that, here Fernandes never replied, there, memory calls up those things, the head is fickle, in a while I know, for two months I didn't drink three, two months and a few days, not many, two months and six or seven days and a feeling of unease, thirst, I talked with my daughter in her cradle convinced that she could hear me even when she was sleeping

—I can't do it

I ended up taking a bottle to the travel agency that hired me as a clerk, just so I could look at it, I opened the drawer and closed it right away, one afternoon I took off the seal, another afternoon the plastic wrapping around the top, another afternoon something happened with the telephone operator, the director planting the bottle on the desk

—You piece of shit

the telephone operator was with him, her hair pinned up and what seemed to be a tear in her blouse that revealed the skin underneath

—Didn't I tell you

the waves in the background, apologizing for my older brother

—It wasn't our fault

I don't care about having children, what's important is the voice of the pines, I have the impression that the crows, my mother agreed to return to the table after changing the tablecloth and Osório to my father

—If you had warned me, I wouldn't have bothered anyone

death is when there's one extra place at the table and the place at head of the table for my father deserted, alone, now I understand why you turned your back to us, sir, nobody was with you taking a mosquito out of an album and a couple of soldiers that time erased, the conviction that the crows were in the well because a bush was moving, as a child I heard conversations upon conversations, now they just shake, once a snake whipped through the grass, its tongue moving in and out like my husband on certain nights and I was afraid of him

—No

looking at the ceiling

my father

—Girl

Just my husband grinding into me, embraces, groaning, the headboard crooked, one of my shoes on

—Wait

without understanding the reason for the flowers still in the vases, the dish with my still necklaces, the groaning louder, knees pinning mine, an earring popped out of my ear and where is the back, I thought I saw it in a fold of the sheet and I lost it, the lips, I hadn't given permission

—Don't cripple me

surprised in their conversation, the snake not whipping the grass and afterwards not in me, on my side of the bed, my older brother threw a stone at it and brought it balancing on a stick, I didn't throw a stone, looking for the earring back on my knees thinking my eyesight keeps getting worse and the doctor telling me to make out capital letters in an illuminated rectangle, lifting up pillows, examining the bedspread, things can disappear out of spite, reaching for the lamp that out of spite, gave shocks, after looking under the mattress, dust, a cockroach with its feet in the air, a pen cap with teeth marks which intrigued me because I don't bite, the earring back finally in the bedframe, it had taken refuge there while I was looking on the floor, I discovered that at the beach house my deaf brother spied on me when I got undressed, I felt his breathing, I opened the door suddenly and he ran away, after that he looked at me in a perplexed way, either I am more than her or she is less than me, sticking his fingers in his pants to compare himself to me, which of us isn't normal, my mother threatened him with the scissors, and my deaf brother, bristling, on his knees, every time a bitch in heat on the beach was followed by the rest of the dogs, wanting to see, even when the album was closed we could hear Osório, my father

—It's true that Osório
excusing himself
—I didn't notice the mosquito, dear
my father, in a friendly tone of voice
—It wasn't the poor thing's fault

I've come to say goodbye to this house, or to my older brother, or to myself, it was on August twenty-eighth that he or the donkey went into the ocean, the seedbeds in disarray, the laundry tank with a broken leg, how many years has it been since I've heard the pines and haven't heard them since, only the students in Lisboa and you are on the third floor, Senhora, talking to myself about the miseries of life, that once in a while the twin sister visited, with a little hat and a package of cakes, suspended from a finger by a string, continuing to argue over the parents' silverware until the one in the little hat turned away furiously, twenty eighth of August, once she gave me the package of cakes that couldn't get rid of her finger

—Eat them, girl

my father trying to help her with the string, making it worse, the neighbor left her house on Tuesdays, also wearing a hat and carrying sweets

—How are you, Alfredo?

and the husband, his right eye enormous, studying her with hate, he doesn't walk, he doesn't talk, he lifts his eyelid in silent combustions, I never imagined there could be such rage, an attendant gave him his lunch and maybe my not deaf brother lives in some kind of hovel, one of these days I'll run into him on the walk waiting for me, the husband jumps and the neighbor and I recoil shocked, the silverware

—I'd rather die than put up with this

half a dozen tarnished pieces of silverware in a chest

—The wedding present from the Secretary of State to my parents

I try to imagine what the Secretary of State meant, the neighbor pointed to a distinguished gentleman on the wall

—Portugal has gone downhill since he died

and the gentleman agreed with her, August twenty-eighth, despite the kid, I didn't forget the date, in a thin voice that was still full, authoritarian, that before had swelled the country

—It's true

the cutlery wasn't even real silver, it was pewter, how would the husband be doing, who according to the neighbor couldn't be an engineer because of a black fingernail, before his eye swelled up, I came to say goodbye to myself, the first time that, when

I was twelve or thirteen, I buried my underpants in the sand so my mother wouldn't notice, and she did notice, she locked me inside the bathroom with her, and I thought
—She's going to give me a sermon
and she
—Where did you put your underpants?
no
—Girl
just like my father
—Where did you put your underpants?
the next morning, I dug on the beach, at the place I had left them, and they weren't there, inside my stomach something was churning, not pains, but prickles and the fantasy that my bigger bones, who I am now, if by chance my father
—Girl
what do I say to him, I don't have the courage to say it, he must smell it because it smells, my deaf brother avoiding me, I was being chased by dogs down the beach, I felt like not being me, I felt like hiding, if by chance my father
—Will they notice when we sit down at the table?
my older brother left a letter, propped up on the vase, a month later he was drafted, the mailman delivered a receipt to my mother
—You must note the time of receipt, Senhora
she spent eternities reading it, report on October seventh at nine a.m., rolling a curl on her little finger, my mother hesitating to trim it
—The time that he left?
not my mother's pen, the one that was attached to the mailman's lapel by a string, if I don't say anything it was the cap of

that pen I found under the bed, death is when there's one place too many at the table, after school my older brother
—What is this?
Even moving the chairs to pretend one notices the absence because the picture is too far to the left and the sideboard is father away, my older brother
—I'm not going to any war
especially the picture farther to the left and the hole from the first nail, on which the frame did not hang, showing, my older brother turned his head toward me for an instant and returned to the draft notice, sometime before an acquaintance of my father's, who worked at a mysterious job, making people be still at the Thebes Bakery, predicted
—If your boy continues to conspire against the Country, we could start to get annoyed
my older brother blushing
—It must be a mistake
with the papers under the clothing in the drawer, a friend in a jumpsuit waiting for him on a corner, a quick phone call, my older brother
—I'm coming
and a car waiting for him in the square, my father on his way to the pantry
—What are you up to?
and the bottles stacked up, a box crashing, a jar of jam on the floor, my mother
—Aren't you ashamed?
the certainty that everyone knew what was going on with me and that they were talking about me, observing me, if I put on perfume the smell got stronger, one speaks differently waiting for

a voice that doesn't arrive, you eat differently leaving a portion on the tray that nobody takes, the elbows of others don't knock against ours and we miss that, I smelled my mother and Dona Alice and didn't find anything, Dona Alice to me, forgetting to arrange the sheets in the washing machine, smelling something as well, the apron, the arms

—Do you smell something strange?

the cousin with the floating kidney parked on a bench because walking made him tired

—They won't operate on him in the hospital

my older brother tore up the draft notice and my mother

—Are you crazy?

my father, back from the pantry, watched knitting his eyebrows, he didn't carry on with us, he read the paper, looked at the ceiling, or crumbled up a piece of bread on the table without eating it, my deaf brother stopped eating out of the pan and articulated a sentence, in a tone like a doll's, monotonous, slow

—Sheee saaills seeea sheells

he said this straining his throat and ending up breathless, my mother in a low voice, in a tone that preceded tears

—My God

struggling to keep them from climbing, eating them with the stew, we noticed the tears because she was chewing water, the lost carousel number eight, the guy from the Well of Death abandoning the platform and the dead motorcycle

—The bike conked out

not a strand of hair when he took off the helmet, my mother was disappointed

—He's so old

he was missing a canine, he accepted sandwich from the food cart, he declared to the owner of the tent of mirrors

—You can only laugh

that deformed people

—I'm screwed

my mother became distorted there, her head enormous and her torso minuscule or all of her very thin while a recording of laughter without happiness played, in the end all the same, like when they tickle us and we twist around, it kept playing terrifying the customers, hold on to grandma, mother, hold on to her legs

—Do I look like that, Senhora?

grandmother, also stretched out, embracing her in turn, they had to bring them to the street, where they palpated themselves to reassure themselves how they really were

—Did I really become what I saw in the mirror, seriously?

the owner of the tent at the entrance, indifferent to the suffering of the clients

—All you can do is laugh

with an enormous head and a minuscule trunk, what the profession made him, my not deaf brother didn't send word about Africa, my mother went to inquire in a military building and they consulted registers

—At least he's not on the list of the dead

After five or six months a letter arrived, and on the page Sheee saaills seeea sheells, no signature or date, my mother looking at my deaf brother who excused himself immediately in his uniform wandering, not articulating, writing letter by letter with his tongue, how intriguing a voice that transforms itself into a pencil

—Listen to the loud laughter, lady

I was already engaged then, already a teacher and still bothered by the smell, escaping the dogs and the men with bigger eyes, not just one, the two of them, the husband of the neighbor and my deaf brother

—The cats don't catch the crows

I took messages in an office carrying documents from one secretary to another, my mother disappointed with how old the guy from the Well of Death was, pulling on the sleeves of the adults

—I want to leave

around the fair too much night as always when we walked away from the lights and probably some giraffe, escaped from the carousel, in the bushes, my not deaf brother did not repeat the news, my mother was convinced one of the giraffes was coming toward her, loping along the uneven boards that shook, besides the giraffes buffaloes, zebras, a worker that jumped from animal to animal collecting the tickets and the cackling of the mirrors mocking her until we got home

—All you can do is laugh

when the empty lots transformed into buildings and streets, our door kept the animals from approaching, now leaning forward, now leaning back, with thick eyelashes, with an iron rod through its throat so we could hold on and another through the stomach to support our heels, garlands of lights colored the tone of our skin, I'm green, I'm lilac, I'm blue, I'm green again, when it stopped I turned lilac, another meter and I was blue, my father was thinking about the bottle

—Do you still remember that?

my daughter is a teacher, my hearing son is in therapy because of the war, we left him the tray on the table when he came to eat when nobody was in the room, we couldn't speak to him or see

him, he stopped up the keyhole with paper, he didn't answer us, Dona Alice was forbidden to come in and my mother
—Do you see the cross I bear?

the ocean and the pines stopped looking at me, a gull flew to the room dissolving into the trees, I remember one of them on a telephone wire with a fish in its beak, what happened to the gypsies, in this moment for example, I smell the stink on me, I am certain that if I dig in the sand I'll find the underpants, the windows are dirty, I'm dirty, the students spying on me over their notebooks, discovering the difference like my husband discovered the difference

—There's something here

my mother

—You're going to have this for years and years

and wanting the gypsies' donkey or me, death is when there's an extra place at the table, even when you separate the chairs to disguise it, you notice, if he fell from the rocks, my older brother
—Girl

trying to teach me what I didn't understand, the certainty that he touched me on the shoulder before going down to the beach, the certainty that a phrase that he formed with a finger on the garage door, there was the crib, the crooked bike, garbage, there was my daughter coming to the garage door, there was the goodbye of my oldest son and I didn't need to decipher it because my daughter looked at the finger marks and announced
—Sheee saaills seeea sheells

while the older brother or she, and it hurts to say this, disappeared into the ocean.

3.

I hardly know anyone here, people have sold their houses or gotten old and changed, where Senhor Franquelim's bar used to be there's a pharmacy, where there was a shoemaker is now a handicrafts store, full of clay and wicker objects, the Italian's home is still there but uninhabited, without curtains, the sunflowers in the garden are dead, I used to talk with them and they would answer me, I confided so many secrets to the sunflowers
   —Don't scold me
  about my family, about what was happening to me, one of the lifeguards from when I was little sitting on a bench, at the entrance to the café with the foosball table, his crutches next to him, foreign newspapers in the kiosk, postcards in English on a metal Christmas tree and Senhor Manelinho's wife at the counter, with white hair, not recognizing me, an adult now, what happened to your dog, always lying in the sun, chin in her paws, I never saw it move, it looked around about to make some kind of statement, and thinking twice, gave up
   —What for?
  and I thinking all afternoon about what had come into my

head, I hate it when people don't finish sentences or regret what they've said, don't give excuses

—It wasn't important

leaving me hanging to imagine things, not discovering anything

—What happened to your dog, Senhora?

and Senhor Manelinho's wife was searching for my real face under this one, in case a light went on in her head to clear up her confusion

—You lived up there past the engineer's house, right?

past the engineer's house and the summer camp with sad looking kids in smocks behind the garden gates, they'd take them to the beach in a line walking two by two, with the same straw hats and sandals, herded by people who were always counting them

—Is Rosário missing?

dipping their feet in the water as a group and squatting in the sand, my mother saying to the next-door neighbor, watching my deaf brother who put everything in his mouth, shells, cigarette butts, pieces of glass

—They must be orphans

while she stuck her index finger in his mouth and pulled out a screw, displaying it in her palm

—Even rusty screws, can you believe it?

while my deaf brother tried to steal it back from her, the next-door neighbor

—They're all like that my godson ate paperclips for lunch and today he's a vet

although, if he has a break, he still eats clips for lunch between consults, there are addictions that don't go away, if we don't teach our kids early, they develop obsessions, I had a thirty-year-old cousin who went to sleep holding on to a diaper, the woman confessed

—I can't sleep any other way, sorry

the dry sunflowers made no comment, they don't expect consolation or happiness, besides the sunflowers, the tiles of the façade were visible, bottles from our pantry that a delicate spiderweb wove together, oscillating lightly, I imagine the tresses of witches look like that, one of the bottles is intact, with the ocean, which didn't have time to make my father happy, Sheee saaills seeea sheells, Senhor Manelinho's wife looked at me sideways, searching, perhaps, with an expression that made her look younger, and no light went on in her head, the fact that no light was blinking annoyed her

—There's a bottle here, did you know?

not even the noise of a newspaper folding, or greedy footsteps moving faster

—Seriously?

It wasn't about chairs hiding absences, nobody in my family was here to eat, what remains of your family eats in Lisbon without thinking about you, even though you laid down shells, cigarette butts, bottle shards, including a screw in your mouth, they didn't come, why do people grow apart, what creatures have we turned into, the lifeguard with the crutches chased away a kid with one of them

—Tell your mother it's still early

arranging his dead buttocks on the bench, he lived from the bellybutton up, from the bellybutton down there were just thick socks and useless sandals, on the other hand, in the butcher shop, Senhor Leonel hadn't changed, his hunchback was identical, the enormous knife hacking the animals into pieces, maybe a bigger double chin when he butchered the bones, it bothered me that my father, if I am the reason he doesn't talk, didn't take care of the bottle

—Was I rude to you?

he turned to the wall, taking a long time to accept his death, death for me, is a question that I've asked for forty years, what do dead people do, how do they do it, why do they take off their clothes, remove their wallet, their watch, all their belongings, a pair of shoes was saved, that came back from the shoemaker after the funeral, put in the closet for months, Dona Alice afraid to touch them

—dead souls are creepy

my deaf brother put them on one day and paraded around the house, my mother

—Where did you dig those up?

shoes that turned up the rugs, the laces untied, things you wear become forlorn when nobody is inside them, the clothes in the closet disembodied, collars that don't swell or shrink, the absence of hands in the sleeves, where the hands end up, my mother

—The shoes

in a tone I preferred not to hear, or rather, I heard it but I won't talk about it, why not give my father's jacket or pants to the carcasses hanging in Senhor Leonel's butcher shop, auntie tied it up, some swear that it's good luck to touch a hunchback, with a chronic spinal disease, I have never met such a circumflex person, I felt like trotting like the gypsies' donkey through what is left of Alto da Vigia, rocks and a remnant of a storage shed where the water didn't reach, to the outcropping of rocks, the ocean, in the shutters, on the beach with me, waiting for me, my father didn't come with us, he stayed at home to think in the pauses between slugs from the bottle

—What are you thinking about, father? he looked at me seriously and stayed serious in spite of the smile, a tenderness like the folds of paper that the wind, in passage, lifts up, they take flight for a little while, give up, lift up again, and fall, they don't change place again, what a mystery, we find them stuck to the wall, in the middle of the moss, or not stuck to the wall, they disappeared, I don't remember seeing my deaf brother happy, he whirled around the rooms in a rage without direction, he noticed the slightest movement of objects, he would pull himself up my father's knee and I would get furious, if you pat his hair I'll stop liking you, my father offered me the other knee and I

—I don't feel like it

distancing myself on the tips of my toes to make myself taller and I turned away, went to my mother's purse to put on her lipstick, I walked past my father and my deaf brother dismissing them with a gesture

—I'm too old to sit on your knee

and I squatted on my heels when I got to the yard, eight years old again, time is so unjust, what's the point of such a slow childhood and now life goes by so fast, the daughter of the lifeguard came back with the kid

—It's still early the wastrel is letting the soup get cold

the useless sandals scuffing along following the crutches in the direction of the house, before he used a whistle to call us, authoritarian, severe, now his armpits carried him along, time is so unjust, Senhor Franquelim's tavern with the men in berets, playing dominoes and spitting on the sidewalk, replaced by a drugstore where the woman at the counter lined up bottles, my father appeared in the yard and I stood on my tiptoes

—How old do you think I am?

while my older brother oiled the bike without noticing that I was an adult, turning the wheels that today have no tires, I run into a schoolmate and she is old and I'm not, what's happening to you, I discover in the mirror that I am just as old as she is, what's happened to me, they removed one of my breasts, I won't go on about that, the arm on that side doesn't move as well as the other one, I lost the strength in my hand, I can't forget the tubes, the catheter, nights and nights waiting for the morning that didn't change whatever it was, at six o'clock

—Open that little mouth for me

and a pill on my tongue under the cruelty of the florescent light, what happened to the bike, where is the garage, I took care that the pines, I took care that the ocean, it wasn't my mother taking my temperature, and bringing the food

—So much fuss about a cold you're fine

applying Vicks on my ribs with her ring scratching me and a sticky syrup for the cough, the spoon in the package, also sticky, if I touched it I had to lick my fingers and they stuck together even if I dried them on the sheet, my mother put on her glasses to check the mercury in the glass tube, my father torturing his lip without thinking of the pantry

—Isn't the fever going down?

my not deaf brother and my deaf brother forbidden from coming in

—They won't stay still until they catch it

and I floating in the covers like my older brother in the water, I like to think it had been that way, the water not the ground, a scintillating canopy where shadows, vague forms, elastic stains, slowly, and he happy, I don't know a single person here, where

the shoemaker was is a crafts store, the sunflowers didn't console me in front of the Italian's home, in spite of the chain, a half open door from which a cat escaped, the lemon tree in agony
   —I'm not good for anything anymore
   its roots adrift, look at the lemon tree, father, say something that helps, my not deaf brother put a caterpillar in my dress and I nearly fainted, I felt the itch of its legs on my stomach, from my stomach it went down to my leg and when it reached my sock it fell off, my mother caught me putting down rat poison, store out of reach of children, in my not deaf brother's cereal, she washed the pan with bleach
   —Have you gone crazy?
   she wanted to take away the medicine that I held on to with force
   —He doesn't deserve to live
   she found me on the street where a truck carrying soft drinks braked almost on top of me and the driver got out of the cab, walking unsteadily, wiping his face on his shirt
   —That was a close call
   with the crucifix in the rearview mirror still swinging, my father, who did not touch me, appeared from I don't know where, not from the pantry, not from the living room, he materialized there, smacked me on the bottom, and his hand made me more indignant than the caterpillar, he finished the
   —Girl
   finished the passion, I hope he explodes from the drinking
   —I don't like any of you
   I refused to give back the rat poison to kill all of you, my older brother stole it from me
   —Girl
   and I, of course

—I don't like you either

　　capable of biting the world, kicking on the ground, they took me to the house under the pines that didn't say my name for example, not to mention the accusing eyes of the ocean, that is my father carried me, holding me with outstretched arms because of my hitting, my kicking

　　—You're all bad, I hate you

　　why were there so many horrible people in my family, I'll grab Ernesto and leave tonight, my mother dumped the rat poison into the toilet

　　—A month with no dessert

　　she burned the packaging in the yard and threw the ashes into the dumpster, in a while, when the rats find out, dozens of animals making nests in the roof and tearing out my eyes, I'll take the bus to Lisbon and a train to another country, my mother, the rats learned from the truck carrying soft drinks to show up suddenly, caught me putting my shells and a dozen cookies in my backpack

　　—What crazy thing are you up to now, you stupid girl?

　　and instead of hitting me, she embraced me shaking, I had seen her express sorrow, I had never seen her tremble, my older brother, in the doorframe

　　—Get ready tomorrow I'll take you on a special bike ride, girl

　　and my mother's shaking intensified, blowing her nose by mistake on my skirt, not on hers, and to be honest, that pleased me, they did surgery on my breast, it should have blown its nose on me, I won't go abroad, I won't leave you, the palms on my face, the nose almost touching mine, the eyes, so close, just one, curious about me, a breast

　　—Is it brown or black?

my father tried to calm down the truck driver with a bottle, both sitting on the kitchen step where you could hear the ocean, the crucifix on the rearview mirror, rattled, still dancing back and forth, a breast and the armpit, I put a prosthesis in my bra and adjust it when it slips, my elbow raised, over the clothing, my mother has two eyes again, brown, my older brother examining the waves that once in a while forget themselves and start up again, guiltily

—Sorry

beyond the bushes, the houses, the anesthesiologist, and I naked and conscious that I'm naked under the sheet, I won't go on about that

—Are you allergic to anything?

not on your account, Madam Doctor, I could be any naked person, I collected the shells, I ate a cookie that tasted like dust, I could have gone to Tunisia and I gave up Tunisia, the order of the shells on the table was wrong, and I was moving them around without finding their positions, as far as I know I'm not allergic unless, my mother's features still haphazard, if you could imagine how this is difficult, daughter, and the cackling of the mirrors

—All you can do is laugh, just laugh

mocking me, the enormous head, the minuscule trunk, you were born when I was too old and didn't have the strength, your brothers spent me to the bone of my soul, when I found out my son was deaf, I accepted God's punishment for my sins and still they told me

—You're pregnant

I didn't answer your father for a month, not because I was mad at him, because I was ashamed, his body rigid in the bed and knowing what I knew

—All you can do is laugh

   I felt pity for my husband to have to pay for my part and his, despite his being on the other pillow

   —It doesn't matter

   or rather I wanted silence and, on his pillow,

   —it doesn't matter

   wanting to nullify the other and make it up to your father, you inside me, I don't know anybody in the neighboring houses, I remembered the morning sand, before the tracks of the gulls and the footprints of the people, my father accompanied the truck driver to the gate, we always called the garage door a gate that was missing two boards, with the loose lock, to say goodbye to the man, and I don't know why, my father moved me, sometimes, when he looked at us, his face

   —Have pity on me

   and how could I feel pity when I was only eight years old, what pity could I have at that moment even though I was still alive

   —Are you allergic to anything?

   and I only noticed the movement of the lips that moved with the sentence, taking away its meaning

   —Are you allergic to anything?

   A foreign language that I don't know, the anesthesiologist waiting for a reply, and I was waiting to understand the question, where are the pines, where did Ernesto go, bring me my older brother back please, with the wrench to adjust a wheel and a lump on his chin

   —What's going on, girl?

   waiting for the clerk to leave the post office, on the street beyond ours, telling me to go home

—What are you doing here?
with the Alto da Vigia in the distance and the donkeys grazing on thistles that were resistant to the ocean breeze, not just
—Are you allergic to anything?
a foreign language, and
—What are you doing here?
an equally foreign language, my older brother did not squeeze my hand, he did not smile at me, he gathered his courage with the hurry of someone who gathers blankets that protect him from the cold, with the intention of asking the post office clerk
—May I walk with you?
the post office clerk, goddaughter of senhor Manelinho, annoyed to see me
—No
The features of my older brother appeared, he was wearing a starched shirt, new pants, a few drops of my mother's perfume on his ears, I
—You're wearing mother's perfume, aren't you?
the post office clerk, softened by the perfume
—Just to the grocery store
and the back of his neck was so red, his hands multiplying themselves
—Your hands are enormous, brother
anxious to fill the silence
—Your name is Idália, isn't it?
a ring, worth little, on her finger, wanting to whisper to her friends
—The brother of the deaf guy went with me to the grocery store
suddenly the fear of deaf children, Sheee saaills seeea sheells,

digging in the dirt looking for caterpillars, he shouted like the crows, not like the blackbirds or the gulls, a sound coming from the depths of a grotto, he would grab our wrists, shouting, until we saw a lizard or a frog that he was trying to stomp on and that escaped him, my mother trying to shake him off

—A lizard congratulations, that's enough

and running into my father who looked at her without resentment or censor, my older brother returned levitating from the grocery store, if you didn't tie him down he'd levitate, once the post office clerk gave him her arm and I roiling with jealousy threw a piece of roof tile that had come off the lawyer's office and they didn't even see it, travel on number eight and travel better, any day a giraffe, the screws loose that were holding it to the board, fall, be careful, senhora, in case of an accident I won't be born, being born at the same time, it's a supposition, we would be friends or not care about each other, if you told me

—I'm your mother

at school recess, smaller than I, weaker, knowing fewer capitals and fewer verbs, trying to order me around

—Don't take off your coat, it's March

I didn't even hear her, my mother was always with a mulatta friend in a corner, talking about me

—Do you see the cross that I bear?

full of herself for sitting on the beach, with a ridiculous straw hat on her head and sun cream on her nose

—The sun is making me look so old

talking with the next-door neighbor who was wearing a baseball cap with a New York logo embroidered on it, the neighbor the mulatta friend who was befuddled by the multiplication tables

—Carry one or two?

an eye on her crochet work, one eye on us, vigilant, bitter
—My husband
the next week the post office clerk was alone, my older brother fixing the saddle that didn't need fixing and a guy, in a helmet, pushing a motorcycle to the grocery store, riding circles around the post office with seductive bellows of smoke, with the front half of the bike in the air, I hope it impresses you, he drove past our gate unsettling the dogs, my older brother ran five or ten meters and returned, beaten, surrounded by the sniffling dogs, or was it he who was sniffling, or were all of them sniffling from hurt pride, the only difference was that the dogs turned back, after pensive circles, to the tiny supermarket, while my older brother slammed the door of his room and a funereal silence settled over the house, where you could hear the murmurs of the dead and the solitude of the pines, the post office moved to the neighborhood where the pool was and the clerk disappeared, Senhor Manelinho's wife tried to remember me since you could see her thumb leafing through old pictures
—How many years has it been
the prosthetic breast different from the other one, my husband
—This won't change anything between us
and it did change things, both of us staring at the emptiness of Sunday mornings, if my leg brushed against his he pretended to check the time on the night table to move away from me, if I took off my nightdress, he turned his head without realizing he did it and when he turned his face toward me on the pillow I saw the affliction, the nausea, without his needing to say anything
—I can't, I'm sorry
only in the dark when
—Come

a condemned person, my face in the pillow, listening to the bushes that we didn't have in Lisbon
—I'm not forcing you to do it
not even the ocean in the shutters
—Poor thing
the backs of my earrings intact, a peck on the cheek
—I think I have a stomachache
my older brother pointing to the bike fender
—I promised you a bike ride, girl
my husband
—Don't move now
and he and my husband pedaling in unison, with difficulty on the hill, me thinking about the catheter and my mother applying menthol ointment, shouting like my deaf brother when he found himself alone, stroking my arm and the arm hardening under my fingers, if my next door neighbor touched me and I was like this, thinking
—When will this end when will this end?
the bicycle pedaling between old houses, on the patio of one of them a maid was hanging clothes on a line, lifting her elbows because an invisible gun was pointing at her, I waved to her and she waved a handkerchief in response, my older brother and my husband, it doesn't matter, I think it was my husband
—You like it, don't you?
the houses were not just old, I like it, thank you, but sad, the gables were collapsing, a broken lock moaned, no pine tree, no ocean, I don't know anybody here anymore, people have gotten old and turned into something else, the lifeguard with the crutches was on his to eat his soup, Senhor Franquelim weeding a little garden in the provinces, uninterested in the gulls, an unlit

cigarette always hanging from his mouth and I never saw him light it, the same one through all the years, I bet, my father scolding himself as he took out the bottle

—You'll never stop being stupid

and the crumbs from the piece of bread, that the fingers tore apart, stuck to the sleeves, when I was little, I'd crawl under the table, surrounded by legs, and how weird to see legs with no body on top of them, there was no relationship between them and the voices on the other side of the tablecloth, maybe my mother's sandal slapping the rug

—You won't rest until you send me to death's door

I'm not allergic, make a note on your pad, how humiliating to be supine in front of a standing person, it must be good to walk, make noise with your heels, to hear

—Your breast is fine

on the twenty-eighth of August plus two days, when the guy on the motorcycle went off with the Post Office clerk, instead of walking to the grocery store, he went by our gate looking at us out of the corner of his eye, first going to the house up the road, then back down, and my older brother, with an open book, pretending he didn't see, put a chair ten meters from the wall and sat, turned toward the road, without turning a page, a competent young man sawing planks on the cover and the title *Manual for the Perfect Carpenter* in an ostentatious calligraphy, on the weekend the Post Office clerk didn't come by, on one of the last times she asked me

—What's your name?

my older brother immersing himself in the *Manual for the Perfect Carpenter* and I stayed still, not the pines, envying her earrings, while she noticed my not deaf brother spying through the curtains, watching me pick up snails and lining them up on the wall, on Sundays my mother carried a shopping bag to the store, she was going to buy a piece of cork with more than ten thousand pins stuck into it, I'm not exaggerating, she and my father ate them from a casserole

—What's your name?

that reeked of garlic, how can you take pleasure in putting something so squishy in your mouth, thinking about what my name really is, the Post Office clerk with a voice that was like a knife scraping a plate until even your nails shriveled, it could be I'm exaggerating, I exaggerate, I envied her ring, the attention my older brother gave her, what a moron, without asking me

—May I walk with you?

incapable of noticing who was scolding him, I don't want hands on my shoulder, how stupid, I wanted, for example

—You're pretty

when I walked into the room with a bath towel wrapped around my head like a crown, my mother's slippers, and her robe on, pinned at the neck with a safety pin, behind me like a train, instead of a sigh

—You'll trip on that and hurt yourself

as if there were princesses that trip there aren't, the palms say thank you with their chin, a wave bigger than the others on the beach, leaping across the sand to the mast where a cork float was beyond the flag, and taking with it, when the wave receded, lunch boxes, meatballs, babies, what I wouldn't give for the Alto da Vigia to be there still with the dog of Senhor Manelinho's wife, always in the sun, on the newspapers, her chin in her paws that I never saw move

—Poor thing, she's eleven years old

so that when I'm eleven I won't move, I'll stretch out, my eyes closed, thinking on top of foreign magazines and the Christmas tree with the English post cards, the idea that Senhor Manelinho's wife was about to recognize me but didn't, the lamp of her memory was extinguished, I used to hoist myself up to see the porcelain figurines, a fisherman, an exuberant girl, a dolphin, I turned to my mother
—You don't seem to like them
my mother replying immediately
—I don't like anything
that's a lie, she liked to mend my father's shirts one after the other and swallow the buttons, you're the one who's allergic, she stuck the needle and thread into the little holes, took them with water and then pulled the thread slowly while she felt a tickle down her esophagus, my mother hit me with a slipper and one of us cried, the other one liked to swallow the entire sewing box, the empty place at the table insisted
—I'm here
like the bike
—I'm here
my older brother's undershirts in the drawer
—We're all here
now when I needed him to let me ride piggyback, took a turn around the garden and I was happy
—Faster
I was so happy
—Faster, bro
jumping over a flower bed, two flower beds, the letter propped on the vase and the ambulance with the drowned person inside, leaping over people at the gate, the conversations in low voices

—Go fast, bro

the Post Office clerk leaning against the front wall, just shock, and after we leaped over the shock the road was full of sun where nobody, except for us, were so fast that grief couldn't reach us or exist

4 ·

There are times when I feel so defenseless, so fragile, so unworthy of you, my shadow to my left and I needed you to walk on my right side, so I change directions in the yard so that you walk on my right, close to my heels, and then I think the shadow is you
—Girl
who I saw leaving one afternoon without saying goodbye, not pedaling fast, but slowly, from one side of the street to the other, I wanted to tell you that the front tire was almost flat but you knew that the front tire was almost flat and what did it matter, all you had to do was leave it against the wall, my deaf brother, entertained by an anthill, rose quickly to look at you, moved by an instinct that let him anticipate things before they happened, for example, at the table, he'd stare at my father's glass, forgetting to eat, and he returned to his fork an instant before a shove with an elbow knocked it over, or without an elbow shove, it fell over by itself, my mother
—What are you doing?
sweeping up the broken glass into a dustpan
—Don't walk barefoot here, it's dangerous

my deaf brother who anticipated everything, one day he started to look at my father the way he looked at the glass, there are times, he didn't stop him from going to the pantry, he just observed him, and I feel so defenseless, so fragile, I feel like going to bed and covering myself with the sheet, not existing, not being, August twenty-sixth, too early not to be, I didn't have a bike and if I don't say anything I can't climb the rocks, my mother, anxious about my deaf brother who didn't stop staring at my father

—What's wrong with him, Holy God?

what would the world look like from the Alto da Vigia, tell me, remains of the gypsy bonfires and the appetite of the gulls, they made their nest in the roofbeams that were left over, they threatened me with open beaks, protecting their young, and so much wind there, if I raised my hand I'd touch the clouds and change their direction, there were still tables, chairs, a dismantled coffee pot, another beach in the distance, or rather spans of beach that disappeared and reappeared under the insomnia of the waves and a goat, with a broken rope around its neck, on a cliff, my father understanding my deaf brother, looking at him in turn

—Not much longer, right?

and my deaf brother agreeing, not even

—Sheee saaills seeea

his mouth digesting a scream, not throwing it up, just like the goat digested it without throwing it up, why are the gulls acting so fierce, how do they hold that much anger in their body, my father almost reaching for my deaf brother's shoulder and then withdrawing his gesture, my mother

—What are you two up to?

we're not up to anything, I'm preventing his death, ma'am,

and his face against the wall, I'm remembering his past, the father of my father
—How did you put on so much weight, boy?
proud
—He's solid like lead
the pains that I didn't complain about, why, nobody can understand a pain that isn't theirs, what's the use in feeling sorry for myself, it was with my deaf brother that he talked, not with us, the father of my father put him on the floor
—You made my arms go to sleep, you rascal
in muffled voices, I know you're not my son, I'm your son, I know that you don't have my blood and the father of my father
—You're going to be quite a man
I have your blood more than the others do, sir, don't pay attention to what my sister says, I stole it from you, when is the glass going to fall, boy, not now, Tuesday, sir, and none of us here, focused on the weak goat that slips and the ocean opening its jaws to swallow it, a foot, no foot, the snout, no snout, you must be able to hear it bleat at night, your daughter so defenseless, so fragile, reuniting with the shadow, as if the shadow protected her, wrapped around her, your daughter in the hospital
—Take the pill, I don't have all day
thinking of the breast they cut off her, my older son hanging reasons outside of himself, leaving them on the vase like the sack of bread on the door handle, we didn't notice the baker, we didn't hear his footsteps, we didn't imagine that the pines would cover the entire spectrum of sounds except that of the bike tires going down the street, what design did they embroider on the sack, a watermill, a mill, and I so defenseless, so fragile, now it's noon, at the entrance of the room with no shutters or curtains, my deaf brother not saying

—Sheee saaills seeea sheells

my deaf brother

—Sis

in a voice that began well before his lips, and got lost in his gums, and even so he was able to say

—Sis

without inflection or ownership, that the teacher took eternities to practice with him, putting his left hand on her throat and the other hand on his throat until the vibrations were

—How did you get so heavy, boy?

and the father of my father, very proud

—He's heavy as lead

alike, the two at the same time

—Sis

and the teacher kissing him, happy, she didn't smell like my mother, she smelled like a young woman, like pleasure, like laughter, starting in June she carried summer on her skin, ladybugs, grasshoppers, buzzing, because of the summer my deaf brother, whose beard was starting to grow, squeezed her throat hard and the teacher recoiling

—What are you doing?

losing her balance on the cliff of the chair and the ocean taking her, this didn't happen on the beach, in Lisbon, tile façades, the Thebes Bakery

—What does Thebes mean, Mother?

getting angry at me because she didn't know

—So many questions, be still

while Thebes was eating at her, she should have studied instead of going out with my father, on her last year of high school there he was at the gate, he worked in a solicitor's office

—What is a solicitor?

he paid for my car ride, at two months he talked with my parents, flowers for my mother who was vacillating, a bottle for my father that made him stop vacillating, they drank it on the first Sunday, my father taking another shot

—Gas prices aren't bad

ever more optimistic

—Contrary to what he had thought, life wasn't so bad

my oldest son for my daughter

—Thebes is the name of a city in ancient Greece

I was waiting for

—What is ancient Greece?

and instead of prodding

—What is ancient Greece?

my daughter, enlightened, the curious about

—What is ancient Greece?

and enlightened, my older son who left a letter on the vase and a bicycle against the wall, when I met your father, at seventeen, I was ignorant about the world and because I didn't know anything about the world it punished me, me in my deaf brother's room, next to my parents' room because they informed them

—He'll need help

so that we married him to a relative of Dona Alice who takes care of him and we have to sit at the table when she visits us, the letter from my older brother, that I never read, I'll open it tomorrow when I go to the beach, now, that I can see you, there aren't any dolls in the kiosk, there are packs of cigarettes and boxes of cheap cigars, how this house has shrunk in size, without space for any echoes, even without rugs there's no echo inside it, the post office building in the neighborhood where the pool is but I didn't see the clerk at the balcony, substituted by a man who, along with the stamps, sells lighthouses made of shells and ashtrays with mermaids printed on them, one of them with only one breast, like me, that the artist forgot to add, tests every three months, the next in October, I can't forget, if the results are good we'll remove fat from your abdomen and reconstruct the breast, you'll not even notice the difference, you'll see, sometimes Senhor Manelinho's wife spread her fingers across her belly and placed a pill under her tongue, taken from the little box in her apron by fumbling fingers, she waited with eyes closed before coming back from far away

—Would you mind repeating your order?

still pale, without strength, surprised by the kiosk

—Am I here?

they transformed my childhood into moribund ruins, just Senhor Leonel who keeps on going with his enormous knife but leaving the butcher shop his leg gives out on him, a blackbird on a cactus ignores me, certain that my husband is on the phone, in Lisbon

—Nice news for us I'm free until Sunday

you're not free until Sunday, you're free starting Sunday, I've kept the goodbye note from my older brother in my desk and I didn't open it, why, if it hadn't been the draft notice it would have been some other reason, at night I discovered him seated on a stone in the yard while the ocean came and went in the dark, he didn't come up here to look through the shutters, he limited himself to a few reflections and a whitened fringe that was always moving, there were moments when my father sat next to me, starting when just a pinecone dropped, Thebes is a city during the time of the ancient greets, like Dona Helena, who knew nothing

of the Greeks, remembered that name, my mother gave money to Dona Alice's relative, wanting to ask
—Do you know Thebes?
and instead
—How's he been behaving?
facing Dona Alice who pocketed the bills
—Calm as a cucumber
and my deaf brother staring at them expressionless, walked among us like a stranger, picking up an object to then abandon it to chance, my older brother
—I swear I won't go to war, I'd prefer
and the ocean, tame now, on the rocks, Dona Alice's relative patted down the banknotes again and buried them in her sleeve, Senhor Manelinho's wife, astonished to be alive
—Do you mind repeating your order?
just to listen to herself, relieved to find she had a voice, not for me to hear her, the image of the dog, with its nose in its front paws, came back and then disappeared again, they said Senhor Manelinho had another wife, other children, when I started to grow his way of looking at me changed and I, even though I was dressed, was without a blouse or a skirt, feeling ashamed and wanting to cover myself with my hands, everything was changing in me, I lost the sharp angles, gained a kind of round majesty that confused me, my older brother didn't know me that way, he knew me squatting in the yard poking a snail with a twig, if the creature turned in my direction it would escape me, one Sunday or two they took us to the mountains to have lunch, I liked boiled eggs and today I gag on them, leaving the kiosk, already close to home, I continued to feel Senhor Manelinho glued to my back, whispering flattery that the pines diluted and for the first time

something in my body made me afraid, it went limp, consenting, a shiver in my shoulders, a kind of sigh emptying me, I was angry at myself and in spite of being angry, how do you say this, accepting it, I saw my mother pruning the dahlias in the flower bed, I looked back and there was no Senhor Manelinho, he had gone back to the kiosk in a flash, my mother plucking corollas

—Did something happen to you?

I remained silent since instead of words I had spoken a sigh, annoyed at my legs that threatened to buckle, my father

—Girl

but my deaf brother noticed because he made a gesture as if to throw a stone at me the way he threw them at the dogs that sniffed at each other, once I found him in the garage playing with himself, he threw a piece of wood at me and ran off, my older brother

—What did he do to you?

that was during the time of the Post Office clerk when I still didn't understand my body, I understood it because my mother looked like that, in Lisbon, with the guy who came to fix a pipe in the kitchen, kneeling under the sink

—We have to change the siphon

and my mother, leaning on the refrigerator, the vein in her forehead pulsing, the next day I saw her again, wearing perfume that wasn't for going shopping, she wore it when we had Easter dinner at Thebes Bakery, her hair done with a hairpin, that she never wore, of blue bakelite with yellow flowers, not sandals, her Sunday shoes, her apron hanging on the nail with the oven gloves and their little bears holding on to pots and pans, she ordered me and my not deaf brother

—Get out of here so you don't breathe in the dust

she locked the kitchen door and at a certain point the hammering stopped, objects that moved with pauses at intervals, what seemed like bodies leaning on the kitchen counter and then metal objects being adjusted, hammering again, a sink opening and closing

—It's done

a debris of fabric, the pop of a button, a mysterious odor mixed with the perfume, objects that moved stiffly, my mother saying something I didn't understand, I didn't hear, I heard without understanding, I understand but I won't say it, the man arranging tools in a metal box

—I don't know

the key turning and the man in the hall, at the entrance, on the stairs, I don't remember his face and even if I did I couldn't remember it, my mother running to the bathroom, her hair comb out of place and the zipper of her skirt not in the back, on the side, the endless shower, her sandals on again, her hair the way it usually was, her clothes in the basket with white spots of paint, my mother to me and my not deaf brother

—You didn't see me, did you?

and I felt sorry for her without understanding why, suddenly so pitiful, so, I don't know how to explain, so guilty, not guilty, I really don't know how to explain it, my father, my brothers, the next-door neighbor, the Thebes Bakery, a Greek city with worn umbrellas and the coffee pot dripping, my mother to the owner of the bakery

—Do you see the cross I have to bear?

the owner of the bakery maybe saw but as for me I didn't see it at the time, now I do the way I see the goat wavering on the cliff, its hooves together, its mouth open, the pardon, the eyes not focusing on the world, the gulls, not seven, not eight, dozens of gulls that skim by each other screeching, she gets dressed quickly before my father shows up, ma'am, it's six o'clock, defrost the fish, start the dinner, and my mother looking at the footprints of the man on the floor tiles next to a pencil stub, she throws the pencil stub into the garbage, she doesn't put it in her apron, she pulls out the scrub brush and cleans the vestiges of the mud, the rust, the lead pipe, years later I found the pencil stub in the pocket of her apron, under some clothes pins, and I wrote Sheee saaills seeea sheells with it, I wrote on an old invoice, I wrote Thebes, I wrote mother, I scratched it all out, I threw the invoice, by chance, into the disorder of my bag, if you want I'll smooth it out, show it to you, the owner of the bakery

—You're paler this morning

the man didn't come back, he had, he certainly won't read this, he's as old today as the lifeguard with the crutches, he had a snake tattooed on his arm

—Hey you, did you forget my mother?

and he cupping his ear with the palm of his hand

—Sorry?

taking the sun in a doorway, pulling out one of those pocket watches with a cover to check the time without understanding what he was looking at

—Ten to three what?

if you mentioned my mother the palm cupped the ear

—Sorry?

I was hopeful because, guessing by the wrinkles, he had a shred of rationality, after the wrinkles smoothed out and I lost my head

—I haven't eaten anything today, not even a cup of soup

with an iron wrench that I'll never forget

—I need to change the syphon

that's what sticks with me and what do I do with it, the blue comb is broken, I found the pieces in the chest of drawers and I could swear that my not deaf brother stepped on it on purpose, my father, who also noticed it, spent more time in the pantry, the pieces of bread crumbled one by one, another man before this one and I hadn't been born yet, you were the one who killed him, mother, it wasn't the bottles, you killed him and I can't get angry, Senhor Manelinho to his wife

—Bitch

with the lock to the kiosk in the air, his brother-in-law embracing him

—Calm down Manelinho

Senhor Manelinho's wife crossing the street to the cane field

—He's gone crazy

Senhor Manelinho, without the lock

—Just one minute you bitch

I thought that the dog would lift her nose from her feet but she kept on sleeping, at night it would follow its owners home from a distance, carrying its aloofness and its sleepiness, it didn't bark, it didn't snore, it didn't get excited about cats, they waited for her at the door

—Pirolita

and the invisible dog in some corner of the dark scratching herself, if there were steps between the yard and the entrance, she would lie on the ground refusing to climb them, her jowls hung loose, her ears hung down, everything hung down, Senhor Manelinho's wife

—Manelinho

the next day she was missing teeth and one of her eyelids was swollen, covering the pupil, Senhor Manelinho answered for her

—She tripped

while the wife sold newspapers muttering angrily under her breath, Senhor Manelinho asked attentively

—Do you feel like tripping again?

a black knot on her leg, a bruise on her arm, one day it came out without my noticing

—Why a wrench?

and my mother's needle missed its mark, my older brother set up a swing for us on a branch, maybe we were happy, it's hard to say, my not deaf brother didn't hit the blackbirds with a slingshot, my older brother pushed us one by one, I got double the time, very high, until we brushed against the pines, we were happy, I think, my father to my older brother

—Be careful with the girl

I had a friend next door named Tininha, two months younger than me but that didn't offend me, I taught her how to swallow buttons and put petals on her nails to look like nail polish, it doesn't cost anything, you moisten the petal on your tongue and for a while, if you don't move, it stays on, while the silver plate of the chocolate tray comes off right away, we tried to paint them with colored pencils but the tips kept breaking, Tininha's mother

—What nonsense are you up to?

looking at my older brother, who at first didn't notice her, like my mother didn't notice the worker, or he noticed because she hardly ever appeared on the terrace my older brother at home with the *Manual of the Perfect Carpenter* back and forth not being able to read it, I remember the chapter How to Build a Folding

Table, with the guidance of drawing A, A1, B and the schematics C1, C2, and C3, I asked him
 —What's happening, brother?
he looks out of the window
—Nothing
Although he peered out again caught between vanity and panic, what one does, how one does it, what am I saying, an elegant lady, with dark glasses in a gold frame, the husband all day long, in shorts, skinny legs and sandals with big toes, each toe as big as my wrist, washing the car with a broken hose that flooded the gravel, drying the fenders with cloths, shaking the rubber mats, kneeling down with the battery operated vacuum, vacuuming the upholstery, Tininha's mother to me, armed with a lounge chair and a magazine, lowering her dark glasses and instead of the glasses, not eyes, but eyelashes
 —What's your brother's name?
while the husband extracted dust from the sunroof with his pinky finger, large toes and tiny fingers, looking at his pinky and rubbing it on his shirt my deaf brother caught flies, trapped between the curtain and the windowsill, he closed them into his palm to feel them buzz, Tininha to me, with flowers called princess earrings in her ears
 —If we pull of the wings on this side, they'll fly crooked
and we tore of the wings on this side, and they flew crooked, hitting the furniture, the wife of Senhor Manelinho talked with a handkerchief in front of her mouth, ashamed of her missing teeth, she bought dentures that hurt her gums and Senhor Manelinho, distracted, tried a
 —Idiot
that the dentures made difficult, Tininha's mother in the

lounge chair, face down, butt up, on a towel, pedaling in the air surrounded by creams, shaking her hoop earrings which were decorated with little bells that tinkled musically and my older brother flying crooked against the furniture, now the hanging plant, now the closet, or a couch with broken springs that nobody used, I said to Tininha
—How do we reattach their wings?
while my older brother buzzed around all over
—Caramba
anxious to open the lock on the window and incapable of doing it, I kept the princess earrings and traded them for a squashed piece of candy, a fair trade, I asked my mother
—Do you like my earrings, ma'am
My mother, without moving her eyes from a defect on a towel
—Lovely
Tininha's father went away Sunday night and returned the following Saturday, honking so they'd open the gate, with shoes that hid the size of his toes, Senhor Manelinho's wife insisting
—Idiot
with a sloppy spit, Senhor Manelinho, suspicious, replied
—What?
and she, counting change,
—You must be hearing ghosts
we saw the light in the dining room and Tininha's father eating alone, we saw the light in the living room and Tininha's mother stretched on the sofa, in a black robe, plucking her eyebrows, we saw the light in Tininha's room, each of them lived separately, they didn't come together, Tininha showed me her Ernesto, which wasn't a hippopotamus, it was a lion named Rogério, we introduced them to each other, at the wall, while

my older brother flew here and there hurting himself all over, incapable of learning how to build a folding table in spite of the assistance of the drawings and the diagram Indispensable Precautions, Ernesto and Rogério didn't fall in love with each other, one-eyed, stupid, not even a polite smile, not a bow, a very ugly iron ring, if it were my mother she'd make him take it off, Tininha disappointed

—They're not getting along

so we left them for days on the wall, in time-out, and when the time-out was over they stayed in the same place, puzzled, the gulls flew toward us, during high tide, in cruel circles, and swooped down toward the beach, faster than my older brother's bicycle, with an endless scream making the waves shiver, in the intervals of Sheee saaills seeea sheells my deaf brother imitated their sound, my not deaf brother

—You're a bird

and my deaf brother, who translated mouth movements, looking for a corner of tile to throw it at his head, still today, in spite of the wrinkles and white hair, that expression in the case of Dona Alice's relative who upset him, in March he had a thyroid problem, the doctor who treated me at the hospital

—Let's wait and see

and we continued to wait until November even though he kept squeezing his throat with his fingers, Tininha's father changed his jacket and tie for shorts and sandals and Tininha's mother made a face of disgust that clearly said

—Don't touch me

the princess earrings all day long and a flower stuck in our hair always falling to the ground, Ernesto stayed in time out but in my bedroom drawer, at the bottom, behind the clothes, until he learned some manners, I showed Tininha a wart on my thumb and she studied it with respect

—Can I catch it?

Tininha contemplating her own skin hoping, that out of friendship for me, one would sprout on her, not just friendship, the desire to possess useful things that you can pull off with your nail, what happiness, for example, the hard feces of the blackbirds crumbling to dust, they moved yards for lack of a *Manual of the Perfect Carpenter* to keep them still, my older brother, tired of being a fly, peeked through the curtain for hours on end, I'm not sure if this was before or after the Post Office clerk, I guess before, around the time that Senhor Leonel plummeted to the floor of the butcher shop, foaming at the mouth, they called the fire rescue, took him away on a stretcher and he came back very thin they relieved his head of a wart that was inside it, if he was still they opened him with a blow of a large knife, and Senhor Leonel not getting the cut of the meat right

—What a spike

not with his whole face, out of a corner of his mouth, it will be night soon and the house is dragging along in silence, Tininha's house is deserted, the roof is broken and half of the gutter has fallen into the daffodils, maybe in the silence the bottles in the pantry are getting together, my father wandering around there

—Girl

with the heavy footsteps of a deep-ocean diver, of bronze, that people have in the dark, although they are directed at people who never arrive, my older brother with them and I

—Bro

without seeing him, the hope that it was a donkey that

belonged to the gypsies, not you, falling down the rocks, the hope for tomorrow with Tininha waiting for me, scolding me
—You took a long time
and I did take a long time, I'm sorry, I couldn't come earlier, I got married, lost a child, suffered with this thing in my breast, or rather I discovered a lump that I didn't believe was a lump
—It can't be
I waited awhile, convinced I was mistaken, and there it was under my fingers, even though it couldn't be, even though it certainly wasn't, the certainty that even now it isn't, I thought
—It looks like an inflammation
knowing it wasn't an inflammation, I made an appointment and didn't show up
—It will go away
I didn't torment my breast to give it time to get better, when I persuaded myself that it was better, I made the appointment again, the doctor
—Well
and tests, exams, biopsies, the
—It can't be
frightened inside, get rid of the defect on the towel and take me on your lap, mother, let me stay for a minute, a minute is enough, staying for a while with my face in your neck with my eyes closed, or rather forget what I said, don't pay attention to me I've become ridiculous with age, they shaved half of Senhor Leonel's hair and he did a comb over thinking it would hide the scar and it doesn't, part of his skull is sunken in, my older brother opened the window suddenly, with the *Manual of the Perfect Carpenter* in his hand and the middle finger holding the page open, Tininha's mother put down her magazine and turned

toward him, her skin so brown, her hair so black, the music of the little bells, one of her straps slipping down, at night, Tininha waited for me

—You took so long

and I, guilty, I took a while but I'm here, we're both here with princess earrings, petals instead of nail polish, pin cushions inside our blouses to grow up faster, we're here with Ernesto and Rogério and I let you pull up my wart a little if you don't make it bleed, if I could get you one

—We're friends, aren't we?

word of honor, I'd get you one, maybe Senhor Manelinho's wife sells them, Tininha's mother lowered her sunglasses and the *Manual of the Perfect Carpenter* fell to the floor, Tininha's mother's eyelashes asking what does the folding table matter, what do drawings A, B, and C matter, not to mention diagrams C1 and C2, the lashes of Tininha's mother asking

—What does my husband matter?

my older brother, with all of his wings, took flight, without touching a piece of furniture, and flying over us and the wall, flying over the last bush to the sunglasses to land on the eyelashes

5.

And when the wind shifts, the pines and the ocean grow still, I am alone, my parents and my brothers disappear in a puff of smoke, the blackbirds are immobile, not just birds, things, the gate swinging into the deserted road, some voices still but they don't pay attention to me, they talk amongst themselves, I am fifty-two years old and wear princess earrings waiting for nobody, how old would Tininha's mother be, in a widow's apartment, forgotten by the fly that had landed on her, it didn't land on her, I don't think it did, how does it do it, the *Manual of the Perfect Carpenter* with no instructional drawings, the body this way, the body that way, after they say this, then they say that, then they ask

—Do you love me?

inside an ear that runs away without escaping, dilates unhurriedly, vibrates, Tininha's mother, without vibrating anything, nails without polish and the hoop earrings with the little bells in a box with useless necklaces

—At least do you remember the way you were?

the husband, in pajamas, cheating at cards, without remorse for tempting fate

—And your husband washing the car?

a kid about fifteen or sixteen looking at me through the window, his sister, with a hippopotamus under her arm, always with my daughter Clementina, the name of my mother who died giving birth to me, I don't remember if it was the kid looking at me or I was looking at him, it was centuries ago, my husband shuffling the cards again, he didn't open the newspaper in the intervals

—I don't understand the world anymore

the father of my daughter's friend hid a bottle in the flower bed, the bottleneck sticking out, convinced that bottlenecks flowered, his deaf son bothered me, it seemed that at any moment he'd stand on his tiptoes and he was capable of floating, look at the deaf boy leaving with the gulls and screeching like them, thankfully the pines were back and I was not so alone

—What's your name Tininha?

she, embarrassed

—Clementina, it's so ugly

hating the picture of my grandmother that my mother had in her room, in a frame with a little bow under it, not a woman, a frightened girl

—Am I really going to die in childbirth?

and she died in childbirth, really, without realizing she was dying, just faces that receded, she wanting to call out to them and not being able to, and after the last face, as shocked as hers, announcing

—I don't believe it

the light out and the waters converging over her head the way they did over the head of my older brother while the goat bleated without anyone hearing, my not deaf brother, with a hammer, looking for snakes in the well, the only one of us who wasn't afraid of the dark, we waited for him at the docks when he returned from Africa, and he didn't let us kiss him, in the taxi he was interested in the streets instead of being interested in us, he said

—Thebes

with what seemed like a smile and wasn't a smile, it was a burning hut, the next day my mother found him packing

—I'm leaving

he didn't have a hippopotamus, he had marbles, but who talks to marbles, he needed a light on to sleep, he always appeared before my parents at dawn, his pajamas on backwards, dragging his pillow to their bed after traversing the minefield of the hallway, dripping water in the dishwasher, creaking boards, the breath of the cafeteria full of teeth

—I'm going to eat you

and the certainty that they held us with hands that we felt and didn't feel, we felt them without feeling, they wanted to grab us, they were there, how many times did we hear pained complaints, my mother turned on the lamp, which looked like the monsters in the hallway, the blue hair, the eyes popping out of their sockets

—What do you want now?

and how to express what you want when you don't want anything specific except that they let us climb under the sheets with them, the monster with the blue hair and my father's back, without a neck or arms or legs, stirring up pebbles in the well that his cough turned over, in a thunder of defeat from which were born fingers in despair

—My God

that went out right away resuming their mineral state, into which you were transformed sir, a complete collapse, a dizzying fall

—Seriously, you don't think Clementina is an ugly name?

and I don't think Clementina is an ugly name, I think it's original, it's like a photo album, the stains of dry glue are not white anymore, they're dark, that the photos deserted, I remember cola bottles with a hole in the cap, destined for the bushes, that gave off a smell, not just the smell but the taste, I tried them

—Did you tell Rogério?

and Rogério's only eye was distracted, his back was losing hair, sprawled on the bedspread, Tininha, pushing him away to save him from Clementina

—No

and in pushing him away Rogério was twisted like a corkscrew with one of his limbs asleep on his bellybutton

—No

and I sometimes crossed my legs to make it seem that I had only one, I liked to hold on to the table to stand up

—I'm lame

I liked the pinpricks afterwards, when my leg started to come back to life, to tap the sole of my foot on the floor to wake up my ankle, the first insecure step and my mother to my not deaf brother

—Are you leaving?

with the third step, all of me envying Senhor Melo who from the knee down wore a metallic prosthesis, a cylinder with a rubber tip, because he slipped in front of a locomotive changing tracks and my mother right away began to warn us of trains that would cross our yard by fluke

—You see?

when he worked at the station, Senhor Melo would slap the cylinder

—It feels like my leg is still there
my not deaf brother
—I am
not just the pines now, the blackbirds, doves in the olive trees behind the chapel, what are they doing in the air if they eat creatures on the ground, the chapel had a granite cross on top of the spire, with dots of mica that the reflections of the sun lit up and turned off, from month to month the sacristan opened the door with an enormous key and inside was as humid as a cave and a statue of a saint was on a wooden column that looked something like my mother in a photograph on her identity card from ten years ago, a lip extended to my not deaf brother
—Why?
straw pallets burning, chickens escaping, an old man with a pipe in front of a supine woman, my not deaf brother getting into a bus at the edge of the city, dragging the pillow of his rifle, identical to ours, finally you're afraid of the dripping water in the dishwasher, the creaks of the floorboards, the breathing of the coffee pot, those who peer at us from the doorways, I remember my parents' alarm clock and its tin heart that could never rest, ready to explode, my not deaf brother
—A grenade
pushing down on to the mattress springs, Tininha said into Rogério's ear
—My name isn't Tininha, I'm Clementina like the girl in the album
waiting for an acknowledgment that didn't come since Rogério didn't make a single gesture on the bedspread, disdaining her with his silence, showing his annoyance with his silence, if you liked me I wouldn't sleep alone like Ernesto doesn't sleep

alone, she threw him against the wall and the animal disappeared on the other side of the bed, where there's a hole that ends up in the grinding wheels of the center of the earth, with God forcing the handle to turn, that makes the day turn, is it really God that operates the machinery and makes the years go by, before I thought so, today I'm not sure, they said I lost a child

—You lost your child

and I'm not even sure, a gull in the garage that arrived and left and my not deaf brother to my mother, dragging a suitcase

—Look the hallway is burning don't pay attention to the old man with the pipe and the woman on the floor?

and not even the pillow of the rifle and not even my parents were important to him, we got up from the bed and a mine was going to kill us, a little blind man with an accordion tapping his way along the path

—One of these days when you least expect it, I'll regain my sight

sitting in the sand, in front of the waves, wearing a jacket even in August, listening to the goat on the rocks, not the ocean, while the donkeys, on the Alto da Vigia, approached the surf with a gypsy startling them, I never saw a gypsy on the street, with their black hats and their carts, if I am still they will live in Thebes with the Greeks, I consoled Tininha

—You don't need Rogério, I'll share the hippopotamus with you

my mother in Africa, unsettled by the old man with the pipe and the woman lying on the floor, my father with his fork suspended on the way to his mouth, surrounded by offspring that ran away, stepping not on the floor, but on debris and bits of crackling

—What is this?

the first time I touched my breast and didn't find it I thought

—I'm ten years old again

so that I find a pin cushion and hide it in my bra, I put on princess earrings, and I'm grown up again, I thought, in the hospital

—Tininha will come in here

one summer when we arrived, her house was closed up, the flower beds were full of weeds, the lock was on the gate, her mother's lounge chair was absent from the garden, she didn't live in Lisbon, she lived in Cascais and Cascais swallowed her up, a cat jumped out of the bushes and without paying attention to me, evaporated into a crack in the wall, even though the cracks are narrow the cats are able to get through them, they stop having a body on this side and they find it again on the other, the nurse saying to me

—Your child wasn't where it should have been

like I was probably never where I should have been, in school with the students, in the living room with my husband, waiting here for Sunday in the deserted rooms and if there's no Sunday what will I do, my not deaf brother saying to my mother

—Let me by, ma'am

with the suitcase and the chimney sweeper they gave him as a child in his hand, realizing he was holding it, he didn't drop it on the floor, he propped it on a chair adjusting its legs and straightening its head so it would be comfortable, how old are you, brother, twenty-three or seven or twenty-three and seven or are you an old man with a pipe, gripped with terror, I bet in Africa you thought more about the chimney sweeper than us, how many times did I ask you

—What's the name of your chimney sweeper?

and he covered his face to keep him from answering pretending he didn't hear me, he thought that it had been thrown out and there it was in the closet

—Why do people abandon us and toys stay, mother?

I thought of my mother

—Even with a boyfriend you're still a child?

—I don't know

opening the night table, not the drawer, the space with a little door underneath, and showing me the torn rabbit that the slippers covered, everybody in this family holds on to their childhood in secret, not just this family, in fact, you'll see that Tininha's mother has a bear, her father has a tin truck, you'll see and God has a reindeer sleigh with a button that bleats when you push it, while on the other hand I didn't find my older brother's childhood in any trunk, he hid it under a board in the attic or took it with him to the rocks and a rogue wave took him away from the beach, it's not just my not deaf brother, what age are we all, if we returned my father to the father of my father of my father and raised him in the air and delivered him to the rug, content

—I can't stand him

my father happy too

—He can't stand me

proud of himself, forgetting the bottles

—I'm made of lead

taking out his liver, which wasn't made of lead, it crumbled quicker than the bread on the tablecloth, don't mess with his liver, sir, don't turn it into crumbs, my mother shaking it on the porch to feed the sparrows

—What a waste

while my father, on the sofa, palpated under his ribs, concerned that his father would think him a lightweight, my father

—I didn't want to embarrass you sir, I'm sorry
hating his father to think less of him
—This doesn't weigh a thing
taking a bottle from the pantry to empty it in the sink, apologizing to the sink
—It's the last one
a small sip, timid, nervous, firmly pushing the cork into the bottleneck with his palm
—I've given it up
and ten minutes later digging out the cork with a knife, more nervously still
—Don't be mad, Daddy
the pines and the ocean returning to the shutters, everyone in this family hiding their childhood, the blind man tripping, discouraged
—I thought I could see, imagine
Senhor Manelinho's wife to Senhor Leonel's wife, showing her the glasses with one of the temples held together with duct tape
—I can't see worth shit with these
the big letters of the newspaper were out of focus, her own face was blurry in the mirror
—What do I look like now?
Senhor Manelinho, who held on to grudges
—You old hag
Senhor Manelinho's wife
—Have you ever tried to look at yourself?
so I ask myself how old we are and do toys console us, my father in the yard with his own father on his mind, wearing a hat even in the house, I liked to watch him shave in the morning stretching the skin of his neck and the blade moving up his neck

leaving a wake of foam, his father invited him to rub his fingers on his cheeks, checking the perfection of the shave
   —It's like a baby's bottom, don't you think?
and it did seem like a baby's bottom, father, so soft, the last bits of shaving cream removed carefully with a folded piece of toilet paper, father applying aftershave with slaps on his face that smell of violets from the herbarium, the scent redolent of spring
   —Ready for the day, my boy, ready for the day
with violets on his face, my father, envious
   —How long will it be until I can shave?
and the years passed, very slowly, and he didn't grow any facial hair, tell me how old we are, a hand full of gulls over my head and the pines are back, my father moistening the shaving brush, turning it in the box of soap, spreading it on his mustache, taking one of the blades from
   —How old are you?
the first aid kit for the blood on his lip, his mother looking for cotton in the box, she applied antiseptic to the wounds
   —You're always doing stupid stuff stop crying
father at the dining table, how old
   —Did you cut yourself?
are you, afraid mother would tell him, without daring to look at her, and the spoon rising from the soup tureen, saving him
   —It's nothing it's better now
wanting to jump on her lap, kiss her, call her tender names, there's nothing better in the world than relief, life is full of colors, a carpet unrolling in front of him and he'd have to float over it's better now what happiness, it's nothing, there are no more beautiful words, the mother of my father winked at my father while the father of my father folded his napkin with ecclesiastical deliberation

—What are you smiling at, father?

and a boy's voice, coming from the mist that preceded me

—Old things, girl

when there weren't bottles yet and mother stood between him and death, I just do stupid things, mommy, you're right, I'm sorry, in the backyard that looked over the beach, where I was looking at a grasshopper, the slow, sad voice of the mother of my father, and why was it slow, why was it sad, I don't understand, what happened to you, ma'am

—Unfortunately, I can't help you, son, I'm sorry

the green grasshopper was just elbows, exchanging one leaf for another, in the middle of the path between the leaves transparent wings grew out of it, when it landed he lost them, how do they appear and disappear, tell me, there's so much mystery on Earth, so many surprises, the memory of the older son's letter hurrying the bottles, if at least I took pleasure in drinking and I don't, if at least it would make me happy and it doesn't, I lost my feeling of being made of lead, I crumble my liver at lunch, Sheee saaills seeea sheells, mixing it with the, on the seeea shore, bread, the doctor smoothing the lab tests on his desk

—You should be dead

the grasshopper spreads its wings to reach another leaf, in a few minutes I'll turn toward the wall in the hospital not to escape my family, to escape myself, mother, to gather, to rise from the soup tureen, which won't save me anymore

—Don't worry

I turn toward the wall so they will help me to fly, with my nose in the plaster I should be able to learn how to fly, my not deaf brother pushed my mother with his knee

—I said to let me pass, Ma'am

the way he did with the Blacks and the suitcase his adult pillow helping him walk in a hallway that didn't end, he noticed the water dripping in the dish washer, the creaking of the floorboards, the breathing of the coffee pot, full of teeth

—I'm going to eat you

that held him with hands he didn't feel, or he felt without feeling, they were there, near his mother, the burning huts, the chickens running away, an old man with a pipe before a woman stretched out on the ground and therefore my not deaf brother

—I said let me pass, ma'am

pushing her the way he would push anyone who got between him and the truck at the edge of the village keeping him from getting on, I can't remember Lisbon anymore, the buildings, the streets, there must be a boarding house where he stays during his leaves from Luanda, there were always couples on the stairways, the ocean has come back with the pines, there he is looking at me, the grasshopper of the mother of my father landed on my head, the fear that it would get trapped in my hair and lacking courage to pull it off, I can't get it, my older brother

—Don't move

freeing me from it

—So much drama because of a little bug

a little bug moving its hairy legs and the tiny points of its eyes in the minuscule head, always couples on the stairs, always loud conversations, music, and laughter, a mestiza girl coming in his door with a towel on her head and a sheet around her waist, her feet were so ugly

—I'm sorry, wrong room

the man laughing

—Where were you going, you naughty girl?

cheap cologne, I'm missing a breast, you know, a second mestiza for the first, pointing at me
—If you don't want the soldier, lend him to me for awhile with features just like those of the woman lying by the burning huts, more cheap cologne, more uncurled shells, more nails without petals, not princess earrings, little glass spheres, the second mestiza to my not deaf brother
—Pay first and I don't do anything nasty
she didn't do anything nasty, she didn't do anything, the father of my father, for whom the napkin was a ducal accessory, raising it to his mouth in pompous gestures
—What I wouldn't give to see you turn into a man
and he didn't see him, something in his aorta, as he howled his surprise
—Do you think I deserve this?
as if we got what we deserve and we don't get it, the blackbirds, in the mating season, chasing each other in the branches, you couldn't tell the females from the males, at least I couldn't, my older brother could, there was nothing he didn't know, Thebes, for example, my not deaf brother was incapable of it, the second mestiza
—Can't you get it up?
and my not deaf brother thinking that if I stay still I can't, I lost it between the huts when we arrived with the flame thrower before dawn, the attendants at the funeral parlor shaved the father of my father, at the end my father stroked his cheek to assess the perfection of the work and the baby's bottom was humbug, stubble everywhere, I went to find the brush, the box of soap, the basin in which you mixed the soap with the water and the box with the blades and I started to shave him again, the way you

should, until the baby bottom came back, I didn't forget the slaps with the liquid from the bottle that smelled like violets from the herbarium, I dressed him, shined his shoes, knotted his tie at my neck before transferring it to his, I announced, satisfied

—Ready for the day, ready for the day

and he didn't look like a corpse, it looked just like him, violets all over the house, my mother's smile

—I think he left feeling happy

wanting to proclaim to the relatives, radiant with herself

—That one puts me in a corner

and my mother's pride hurt me, I'm a drunk, don't believe him, ma'am, a big tear in a small smile

—You're lying, aren't you?

I'm not lying, mother, it's true, mother's double chin trembling, the handkerchief at her nose, the question

—What life deals us!

getting herself ready to disappear, she has the house to herself and the moldy silence that grows, she can always lift her spirits by contemplating the shaving blades in the box, but she doesn't disturb them because of the knocking, my not deaf brother to the second mestiza

—You'd better go

why don't I do what my older son did, for what deluded reason do people stay here, the female blackbirds are smaller with fewer colors, besides they don't sing but how to figure out who's singing if they aren't far from each other, my not deaf brother locked the door, turned out the light and even with the light off his eyelids burned, a boy took three steps and fell without a word, my hearing brother's companions in the cafés of Luanda with their eyes full of the bush blocking the view of the bay, the

island, the white birds that followed the trawlers and before the plane back the scrawny dogs and the warehouse with the crates, the little blind man
　—If I could see, what would I see?
the ocean and the beach were the same, the same algae, the same garbage, the stop for the Lisbon bus, the newspaper kiosk
　—It really does feel like a baby's bottom, you should be proud of the gift they gave you, father
the ability to make the cheeks smooth, Tininha, when she left, could have stuck a note in the hole in the wall where we kept our treasures, a clipping about a movie actor, a copper medal found between two stones, the notebook where we wrote our diary, sharing the pages, her penmanship had flourishes on the capital letters the way the teacher liked it, my not deaf brother thinking
　—I lost the action
the mail came on Wednesdays, maybe a letter from mother, sometimes nothing, a fellow soldier asking him
　—Don't you write to your family?
he who didn't remember his family, if he remembered anything, it was his older brother going to the beach without waving to anyone although he pedaled in a different way, looking at things as if he was devouring them, the little fountain made of shells attached to the stone wall, the store of the Italian, the crates of merchandise outside, grapes bananas plums and the price on pieces of cardboard attached to pieces of wood, Tininha's mother lowering her sunglasses with her index finger
　—Don't you want to come over?
the *Manual of the Perfect Carpenter* open on the rug, with the pages turning by themselves without his touching them, the first chapter, Indispensable Tools, full of crowbars, saws, and tubes

that he didn't know what they were for not to mention the description of various types of nails, screws, wrenches, and planes, what would he do if he approached the lounge chair counting his steps to take longer the way he counted his steps between the gate and the house

—If there are forty-seven, I'll last for centuries

or between the gate and the fountain

—Three hundred twelve

without ever getting it right, one day two hundred twenty, on another two hundred fifty-six, possibly the fountain had moved although it pretended to stay where it was, things move away and return, the world is elastic, after all, he calculated the length of the dining table

—Thirty palms length

and twenty-eight or twenty-nine, it was consistent, to the table, one calculates, he tries to guess the last numbers of car license plates, parked cars didn't count, it said nine zero, it said three five, the same with the makes, the same with the colors, the Post Office clerk took a while to leave he decided

—I'll count to one hundred and one and if she doesn't come out it's bye-bye

she didn't show up and he was at one hundred and one, resigning himself, at ninety she was closing the door and my older brother was twisting his toe cap in the dirt, sullen, so many numbers for half a dozen minutes to the grocery store, the crates with the crooked price tags, on top, a quick order, in a low voice

—Get out of here, fast

and he walked up the street again, defeated, no longer hearing her heels on the pavement, I searched for Tininha's message in the treasure hole by removing the stone and the hole was empty,

not empty, a shard of a mirror, and what messes with my head is that I could swear Tininha was around there
—Clementina is so ugly
she hadn't lost a child, her husband paid attention to her, gave her trips, bracelets, not a teacher like me
—A teacher how trite
enduring the bad behavior of the students for pocket change, a lawyer, or a doctor, if she were a doctor, I'd show her my breast
—Do you see?
and she without pausing
—We were friends a long time ago I forgot about you
despite the princess earrings and the petals on our nails, I was shy about telling her about the pin cushion, confessing
—I've missed you
Clementina a name that smelled of albums and remnants of old glue, Tininha, in a doctor's smock, with her pocket full of pens and a stethoscope around her neck
—I didn't miss you
and so cold, my God, instead of becoming indignant I was upset, trying to understand where I'd gone wrong
—How did I offend you?
without discovering whatever it was, I lent you Ernesto, it was me who opened the nuts on a rock and hurt my fingers, I allowed you to ring the bell on my older brother's bike and never accused me
—It wasn't me it was Tininha
I never made fun of you
—Don't tell anyone
I didn't tell anyone that your name was Clementina, on the contrary, I guarantee it

—I didn't like my name

and I didn't care, what is the importance of a name, people have the name they want, I wasn't able to tell you what I chose and what I call myself when I talk to myself even when, with an impulse of the wind, the pines and the ocean grow silent and I am alone, my parents and my brothers have disappeared in smoke, the blackbirds aren't birds anymore, things, some voices in the ocean don't talk to me, they talk among themselves, what's left is my father as a child in front of my grandfather who wears a hat shaving in the morning stretching the skin of his neck and the blade gliding in a wake of foam, in the end my grandfather invited him to touch his cheek to confirm the perfection of the shave

—It's like a baby's bottom, isn't it?

my father to me, as small as he was, proud to show me

—See how my father's skin feels like a baby's bottom?

and it does feel like a baby's bottom, father, so soft, a baby's bottom that you could stroke for hours on end.

6.

I came to say goodbye to my older brother, and through him, to myself, I don't know, the woman who I, I mean a co-worker of mine, said that she wanted to accompany me, and I answered
—No
and she slowly let go of my arm, each finger, independent of the others, loosening, going and staying, there are people who take a long time to leave us, the body goes but the eyes stay there, just like dogs who are abandoned in a remote place come back, not angry, humble, you open the door and they don't dare come in, wet from the rain, my not deaf brother did not return to come back in the house, we heard he was in the provinces, we heard he was in Lisbon, once I thought I saw him near the Thebes Bakery but he turned his back and walked quickly down the road, why he wasn't carrying the pillow of the rifle I don't know, my co-worker
—It's probably not him
because everything about me before I met her leaves her uneasy, there are the eyes full of questions, I am intimate with every pine and the changes of the ocean that doesn't accuse me or give its approval, it's there and that's it, if it weren't because of

Sunday I wouldn't even notice it, when I was little, yes, when it decided to greet me, I supposed that my not deaf brother walked around the bend of the trolley car and I lost him, when I visited my mother she

—Your father

and then she grew still, demurred, my not deaf brother would come back because he missed us, he was taking a while, maybe at night he stopped at our door and peered at the stairs, who can assure me that he'll come in today and when he sees me

—Girl

doorknobs, it's been years since my mother ran after me around the table, one shoe on and the other in the air

—Don't run away from me, you demon

once I stopped and she didn't dare beat me, she stopped in turn, the two of us facing each other, who will give up first, my mother didn't complain to the next-door neighbor

—Do you see the cross I bear?

feeling, like I did, the bottles in the pantry, forgetting her shoe

—Do you think she wants to kill herself like the other one did?

my not deaf brother also going from room to room, surprised at hearing the blackbirds or picking up a forgotten rag on the floor, smiling with his mouth in his palm, we were happy, the rag stayed on the floor and in that I understood what a lie it was, my not deaf brother didn't come, I doubt it was him next to the Thebes Bakery, we didn't talk and nevertheless there were times when I'm certain he wanted to be with me, he almost said

—Sis

and catching himself in time, from the beginning each one of us was a stranger to the others, my older brother called

—Girl

he put me on the bike fender and right away, my mother complained, what children did they give me, they don't care about each other, when the older one died the three who were left were indifferent, and you are mistaken, ma'am, the crow-like voice of my deaf brother in the reeds

—Sheee saaills seeea

the cries that they give during the equinox, surprised by the ocean, my not deaf brother escaped in the direction of the olive grove behind the chapel, trying to cut down all the trees of the world with a toy hatchet, not steel, plastic, I think for him the huts started to burn that day, to whom the distaste that gave the idea of not happening yet still present, my mother said they don't have feelings, their hearts are made of stone, what sins do You want me to expiate, I am a weak woman, I run around the table behind my daughter, and she stops, waiting for me, I also stop, incapable of hitting her, if my not deaf brother were with me in this house, even if we didn't talk and what would we talk about, I would be better, my husband meeting him, still not my husband, offered his hand and my brother did nothing, I can't forget the outstretched hand and my not deaf brother with his in his pockets, my mother

—Won't you greet your future brother-in-law?

and he didn't greet him or sit at the table with us, he decided

—I'm not hungry

and a door slammed, to this day I wonder whether it was the door to his room or to the street, I remember an ambulance siren stopping me from hearing it and a broken lamp downstairs preventing me from seeing him, Senhor Manelinho, against whom my not deaf brother fought, dragged him by the arm

—He said that after he cut down the trees, he was going to kill the ocean and at the back of the yard my deaf brother shouted sounding like a crow

—Sheee saaills seeea

tirelessly, my co-worker from school

—Promise me

and still shrinking, silently, I took off the princess earrings and the petals from my nails, I didn't pay attention to Tininha calling me not even to the voice of the father of my father

—Baby's bottom, baby's bottom

so many times in me beyond the waves on the rocks, almost as strong as the silence of people, if I were grown up I would be bigger than the world, I would take giant steps and the relatives, what choice would they have, would obey me, only the crowing of my deaf brother's voice would continue, put your right hand on my throat and the left on yours to talk like me and he didn't, Dona Alice's relative

—That's my fate

my father exchanged a bottle for the smallest flask that he could fit in his jacket, the mourning tie uncertain around his collar, his palms rubbing together without rest losing his fingers, finding them again, losing them again

—I'll be made of lead yet

one finger finding the other and suddenly the rain, drops in the leaves of the flowerbed that waved without falling off, shrinking and spilling out to the edges of the petals with a little light inside them, when the people who bought our house come for a week perhaps they will tear down the walls and take advantage of the land to build a bigger dwelling, into which other children will drag the pillows of their insomnia on a trip lasting weeks, a guy in the pantry

—Why so many bottles?

and now the afternoon was bending its shadows, a sound of farewell in the notes of the blackbirds, sparrows in disorder, the lifeguard with the crutches doesn't pick up tarps anymore, they gather guys in berets for us, my co-worker bought identical rings for us, the one she gave me was too big, we had to have it sized and I couldn't get used to it, I was always taking it off and putting it on, my husband

—Where did you get that

I

—At the school fair

thinking how easy it is to lie, the insects of the day substituted by the insects of the night, now present now absent, trying out their wings, Tininha in a doctor's smock in the hospital, with her pens and her stethoscope, remembering slowly

—It happened a long time ago

slowly recovering Ernesto, Rogério, unbuttoned memories and I didn't have the courage to address her with the familiar "tu"

I

—Doctor

and the princess earrings, the crush on movie actors, her mother's eau-de-cologne shared at the wall and aren't little girls silly, doctor, she took my pulse in the morning as she looked at my chart, promise you won't tell my name to anybody and a name tag Doctor Clementina on her lapel it wasn't me who put it there, it's Tininha to whom I promise not to tell anybody, now, as long as I don't tell about the petal nail polish and Rogério's one eye, Tininha let go of my wrist and her heels hurt me as she walked over me thinking she was walking through the ward if my not deaf brother saw her he wouldn't shake her hand, if my older

brother wasn't around the sunglasses her mother didn't lower with the tip of her index finger and not eyes, eyelashes
—What's this one's name?
while her husband washed the car with the hose, you're right, Doctor, it happened a long time ago, if you don't mind please walk over me again so I can accept that we died, I am a school teacher, not a lawyer, not a doctor, as girls we were so silly, no daytime insect today, the ocean transparent, with a dark bird connecting two rooftops sticking itself in a hole of Tininha's chimney, the pines and the waves have a somber tonality, it's something of my older brother's, the change purse or a picture of us with our parents, left on the beach and taken off the beach by the arm of the wave, my father sleeping inside the newspaper and not stones like in one's sleep at night, just pebbles, my mother
—What a fool
and nevertheless, she would swear, and nevertheless it's enough
—What a fool
enough, the father of my father guaranteeing
—This boy will go far
and in fact, with the years that he's been dead, he must be walking in the antipodes, what a lovely gift, grandmother, divine the future, it's just that I don't understand, with so much cleverness, how come he didn't get rich, two tiny rooms where his baby's bottom would shine, once my father
—If he had known you
and his eyes wrapping themselves around each other, I didn't know it was possible for eyes to get mixed up in a face, and returning to their place as soon as the mouth scolded them
—Enough nonsense
my father taking refuge in the pantry, with the remains of one

eye still to the side where these matters take a while to compose themselves, returned with more colors
  —Girl
  his palm almost on my head without touching me, my mother with the iron not saying
  —Fool
  with eyes growing closer together that the nonsense contaminates and tugging his handkerchief because of an itch on his nose, her voice growing distant
  —We could have been
  and we could have been what, let go of the fantasies, we weren't and today it's too late, it's over, she's walking hunched over, complaining about her bones, treat the stones in your bladder at the clinic and don't bother me with an old woman's complaints, an enormous bird in your chimney, Tininha, why didn't you sell the house, your father was an engineer, I was the daughter of a drunk, that was a long time ago, Doctor, she said to the nurse
  —The dressing is for bed eighteen
  and we're done talking, be well, goodbye, the color of the beach was brilliant, my not deaf brother
  —What if the ocean comes up to here and we drown?
  attentive to the sound of the rising waters, you were near the Thebes Bakery, weren't you, you were here today, smiling with Ernesto in your hand, why didn't you take him, he could be your pillow as you dragged him, in the days ahead, in the hallways that are missing, the co-worker I mentioned offered me a ring when I agreed that she, not when they introduced us, she was in the Ministry before
  —If I could dream, I would come back sooner
  the hand on my knee resting there too long, the thumb raising

my skirt, my husband, and then from the skirt my thigh, at the point that the skirt ended, my husband examining the ring
—There's a date engraved in it
and I
—it's the year the school was founded
thinking how easy it is to lie, my husband
—I've never seen such an ugly ring
and it wasn't ugly, it came in a package with a pink ribbon and a box and a card, my husband, who after three months of marriage put his wedding ring in the drawer
—It's not that I don't want to wear it, but it's the idea that my hand doesn't belong to me
not just easy, simple to lie, my older brother, coming down the street for the last time
—I'm coming
without hurrying, saying goodbye to things, they surprised me with a new nightgown, shoes from Lisbon, not beach sandals, the creased pants, I thought
—The Post Office clerk has come back
I thought
—And Tininha's mother is waiting for him at the pool
but his face wasn't sad or tense, just normal, he greeted the owner of the café with the foosball table, he greeted Senhor Manelinho who was fussing with one of the tire rims of his ancient car, kicking them to check its resistance
—This piece of shit only gives me trouble one of these days I'll send it to the junk yard
and the gulls didn't fly to us because there was a serene ebb tide and a tongue of sand before the breakers, that is light waves, translucid, how long will my not deaf brother's huts burn, how

long will the old man with the pipe stay in front of the supine woman, in the burnt rubble of the village, in the midst of the terror of the chickens and so how do you lie down with them, the quartermaster called him from the truck
—Hurry before they come
afraid that the blacks would ambush them when they returned to the wired enclosure, despite the dusk a last blackbird, one afternoon, many summers ago, a magpie appeared in our yard, we had barely approached it when it left laughing, not the laughter of a person, a circus mockery and we
—Are we ridiculous?
he passed the chapel, when straight to the olive grove, evaporated, he looked like the priest who came to lead the processions, the jowls, the nose, Senhor Leonel, on his knees
—What do I lose with this
hoping that God would send him a cure with an unexpected generosity, he listed to the rosary on the radio
—It doesn't do any harm
because when you least expect it, a miracle happens, my deaf brother felt the music in the vibrations of the floor the way he felt the wind when the windows shook, the supine woman didn't let go of my not deaf brother whenever someone else drew near him, the only magpie I'd ever seen, I think, mocking us and with reason, my friend, we're not worth much, the woman lying there saying to the rest of them
—Are you all dead too?
bullets in her belly, her legs, a piece of shrapnel in her side, the quartermaster
—What's wrong with you?
and an ox doesn't walk by, they died, even my mother and

my sister are dead, I don't dwell on them for a minute, when my mother wanted to kiss him when he arrived on the boat he turned his head because the lips of the cold corpses, with crusts of blood between their noses and mouths and flies in their eye sockets, burrowing, burrowing, the dirty disheveled old man with the pipe and his ribs poking out, it's a good thing my father didn't see him on the dock, my father who had shaved even though he wasn't able to make it as smooth as a baby's bottom, who had once done it except for my grandfather, he stuffed himself into his Sunday clothes that barely fit him, in spite of the vest not matching the pants, the only time I saw my father wear hair pomade, shiny with grease, my not deaf brother also avoiding him

—Did you forget your pipe?

My deaf brother and two chickens waiting, my not deaf brother in a corner of the taxi not answering the questions, forced to travel with an African village that pursued him relentlessly, not even the pillow of a rifle to protect him from us, the Thebes Bakery confused him

—Where am I?

with its awning, the counter, the women returning from shopping with their carts next to them, because there were no Thebes bakeries in Africa, there were wooden barracks, a barn, the mortars on their tripods pointing at the night, my husband pointing at the ring

—Are you going to wear that?

I hesitated, remembering my co-worker, the box, the letter, the way she put it on my finger and kissed it, my hand in hers, I absentmindedly

—Yes

surprised by the

—Yes

and insisting

—Yes

in a tone that broke, gained strength, repeated

—Yes

and under the

—Yes

a flickering indecision

—Why am I doing this?

a woman almost my mother's age, the same fold in her chin

—Do you see the cross I have to bear?

the same alert unease as if old bottles vibrated in her memory and nevertheless her eyes, and nevertheless her mouth, something of Tininha, not of Doctor Clementina, in the way she walked, in the manner of her gestures, in the absence of Rogério and at the same time

—Do you promise you won't tell anyone my name?

my not deaf brother going down the stairs not to the street, to the army truck that was waiting for him, I'm not in Lisbon, I will never be in Lisbon, dozens of old men with pipes, dozens of supine women and the magpie laughing at us, my father

—Your grandfather

and our grandfather in the cemetery, what grandfather, trees and grass and oblique flights of creatures, don't toy with me, father, don't try to deceive me, remember the goat on the rocks, remember it falling, I regret not leaving a bicycle leaning on the wall or having the chance to tell you I'm sorry with a letter on the vase, my father going down the steps behind him, giving up, pushing us the way my not deaf brother pushed us in the direction of the pantry, the father of my father addressing my father with care

—This one is going to leave us in the lurch
   and he didn't, he ended up sitting on the sofa and repeating
   —Sheee saaills seeea sheells
   with pensive slowness, my father to his past
   —What lurch?
my not deaf brother far away from us, setting fire to a hut in Lisbon while the blacks tried to save themselves, imagining the Thebes Bakery in flames, the awning, the counter, the women with their shopping carts, my not deaf brother who we didn't see again and I with the ring from, I with the ring from my co-worker, the first time they kissed me I didn't understand the ecstasy of movie actors, it was wet and sloppy, it was like meat and a kind of worm fighting with my teeth, it made me want to wash out my mouth and get rid of it, I didn't understand it at the time and I still don't today, my husband sometimes, at night, my co-worker almost every time and what I see, with my eyes closed, is an old man with a pipe supine in front of me, I hear the cracking of the burning wood, what seem like gunshots, voices that call
   —Hurry
   I hear the distress of the chickens, I came to say goodbye to the house or to my older brother, and through him, to myself, I don't know, what the reason is for what happened so long ago and continues to happen, Senhor Manelinho's wife and Senhor Manelinho hating himself unceasingly, Senhor Leonel not getting the cuts right with the knife, admiring himself
   —My goodness
   Tininha not talking to me all morning until she crushed me with the burden of her inner weight
   —Do you think God exists?
   she with a basket of clothes to iron

—Do you think I have time to do this?

and if God doesn't exist what will become of us, I don't hear the ocean and therefore I don't hear my older brother or the donkeys on the Alto da Vigia, I hear the bleating goats with their muzzles together on the rock, without God the earth would fly off its orbit and crash into the comets, worse than the electric carts at the fair crashing into each other, do you remember the colored lanterns, those poles holding up the mesh top of the tent, throwing off sparks, and the workers who jumped from car to car to collect money, young Senhor Manelinho, before the kiosk, worked there, his hair still not styled and dyed blond, really blond, the woman with the carts in ecstasy

—How beautiful

while the waves came and went on the beach like the hands on the cloth of the pants of the blind man with the accordion, patient, eternal

—I don't see black I see gray with blue dots

while if I closed my eyes, I saw gold hoops and between them the smile

—Girl

my older brother lowering the saddle

—Can you already reach the pedals?

I pedaled but I was afraid, I didn't want to, the ground was far away, and the thing threatened to lean over and tear up my knees, luckily my mother called from the window

—Don't force the girl to do it

on certain occasions I must admit it was useful, ma'am, thank you, she secretly gave me a candy

—Don't tell your brothers because I only found this one

and doubt about who was sticky, the candy, or my gums, and

who got stuck to whom, I got tired of pulling it off the roof of my mouth with my nail and my nail got sticky too, stuck everywhere, my not deaf brother

—Do you suck your fingers like a baby?

and I didn't suck my fingers, I tried to get rid of it, if I touched it whether or not it was stuck to me, let go of me, with the arrival of night and the echoes of my footsteps was greater, one foot here, the other in the whistling of the pines, I will miss the tears of resin in the intervals of the bark, not tears like ours, solid drops, heavy, if you pulled them off with a shard of glass they became viscous

—Are they also candies?

my deaf brother tried my name without getting it or a gull pronounced it in its language

—Instead of a deaf brother did you have a bird, ma'am?

my mother raising her arm, sorry she had

—God willing, you

and hiding herself in her sleeve while her features fell down her face, eyebrows, nose, lips, if at least someone would encourage her, inviting her to stroke her cheeks with her hand

—Baby's bottom baby's bottom

consoling her while she

—God willing you won't have a son like mine

and I revealing what I didn't know

—It's not worth wishing me whatever because I had a son and I lost it

and my mother's face catching my arm

—My girl

I pushed her away let me go, old woman, you're an old woman, in a little while what happened to my father will happen

to you, turning to the wall without anyone's company because he doesn't deserve to have anyone of us with him, with respect for my son, if it was a son, if I was able to almost have a son, I don't feel sadness or pity, I am almost as bad as you, my co-worker
—You're not bad, my lovely
convinced that I wasn't bad, imagine, convinced that I liked her, in spite of the padding that smelled of a coat that had been in storage for many months, a piece of furniture on it a clock without hands, if the clock is without hands does time not exist, with shepherdesses and nymphs, I never could tell, substituting the hours, there are six shepherdesses and three nymphs at this moment, almost night, therefore there are two days for my older brother, for us to be together, I on the Alto da Vigia fighting the wind, how do you get up there, there must be a path between the rocks, pools of water, pebbles, if a bison is still it could be a gypsy, it could be a donkey, the idea that my father, before he turns to the wall in the hospital, a wave
—Girl
just one more wish, he didn't wave, he didn't say a word and he didn't say a false word, I said
—Get out of here
I took my mother to the hall full of people, machines squeaking on their wheels, a couple whispering
—Father said to get out of here
and I'm not angry, ma'am, I pity you the way I pity myself, we are so weak
—Do you think God exists, Mother?
she with the laundry basket of clothes to iron
—Are you sure you have time to do that?
always baskets of clothes to iron, always the thirst of my father

in the pantry, how many times does he fall and lie there on the floor, incapable of getting up, talking to himself, if you come close you hear a voice that is his but doesn't belong to him, interrupted by little chuckles, a gasp, more chuckles

—This one's going to beat all of us with his sandal

and my brothers and I incapable of anything else looking at him, we were so small, my older brother to my deaf brother

—Don't cry

my not deaf brother biting his fist among the huts that burned so he wouldn't cry and nevertheless if you asked me

—Were you happy?

I'd answer yes, of course we were happy, we had pines in August, we had the waves, a hallway where we dragged our pillows on the difficult night when the coffee pot

—I'm going to eat you

and the waves agreed

—It's going to eat you, run

the lamp on my parents' night table was on and under the rumpled hair and the shoulder blade that was sharper than I thought, poking out of the night shirt, an order between indignation and sleep

—Go back to bed quickly

as if it were possible to go back to bed, sleep with so many gunshots around, so much panic of the chickens, so many dogs limping, so many women stretched out at the feet of so many old men with pipes, so many trucks leaving abandoning us between the ashes and manioc conveyor belts, my husband examining my hand

—And why do you want this ring, may I ask?

while the night wasn't just the pines and the waves, the

agaves near the well touching the leaves of the leather one after the other, insisting

   —Sheee saaills seeea sheells

   I came to say goodbye to the house or my older brother, and through him, to myself, I don't know, the remains of the bicycle in the garage under the little shutters where a timid clarity not of the sun and yet not of the moon, from the light on the ceiling of the hospital where they took my, where my father, where my mother one day, where I again, the woman I, or rather a co-worker, said she wanted to accompany me, I said

   —No

   and she let go of my arm slowly, each finger, independent of the others, letting me go, going and staying, there are people who take a long time to leave us, the body moves away but not the eyes, just like the dogs abandoned far away who come back just as they abandoned me far away and I returned here, I don't know why I hoped to find my not deaf brother waiting for me in one of the rooms of the house, we knew he was in the provinces, we knew he was in Lisbon and if you find yourself in the living room don't go away, we need each other, you know, I'm sure we need each other, the hallway is so complicated if we're alone, each one of us with our pillow, in our pajamas, looking for a mattress in the dark that we'll never find but it doesn't matter, bro, it doesn't matter, you always have an old man with a pipe and I have the waves on the beach, grab your rifle, point it at me, and order me to walk to the edge of the cliff where, contrary to our older brother, someone helps me jump.

7.

Since the waves only start to get bigger in September I should have taken note of the high tides on Sunday and chosen the last one, when there are fewer people on the beach, almost only fishermen but on the other side of the rocks and one or another beggar surrounded by dogs in search of leftovers, almost all of the cars are going towards Lisbon, there are a half dozen people at the bus stop next to the closed kiosk so they might not notice me, now on foot now crawling looking for a path between the rocks, my mother didn't let us go up there

—You must all be crazy

declaring to the next-door neighbor

—With their father the way he is I had to raise them myself

while the sun disappeared in the water, first red, then pink, then a pale strip from the horizon to the beach and then dispersed layers, as soon as the layers disappeared a slow breathing in the dark, mixed with the steam from the soup

—Time for dinner, kids

that my mother brought from the kitchen with a plate in each hand, blowing the strands of hair from her forehead with her protruding lower lip, as soon as the lower lip was in the place of the strands of hair they fell again, if one of my brothers lifted his spoon my mother took it away from him, threatening him with it

—How many times do I have to repeat that you start when we all sit down at the table?

the porcelain fruit bowl, looking like a basket with one of its handles broken

—I'd give anything to know who broke that handle

looking around in the expectation of a silence that was more tense than the others, tomorrow I'll buy a newspaper from Senhor Manelinho's wife to check the tides, normally they are listed at the end between the temperatures of the cities of Europe, Tirana, Belgrade, Oslo, and the two drawings with the seven differences that my older brother surrounded with a bubble, one button too many on a shirt, a bigger cloud, I turned over the paper and there they were in tiny letters, a high tide at seven o'clock, with nobody at the bus stop and the beggar and the dogs having given up on scavenging on the beach, it suited me, my mother returning the spoon

—Now you can eat, Senhor Bad-Manners

the lampshade was twisted on top and straight at the bottom, the lady wearing a dress with a vine design in one square and without in another, something in the flower vase and at the moment when I was going to guess my brother, high tide at six forty-five, almost seven, what peace, I feel peaceful in the waves until the next morning, the bubble was older

—Five forget-me-nots in this vase and four in that one

they notice everything faster, they get to everything first, I'm not smart, I'm dumb, my co-worker pulling me toward her

—Who made you think you're not smart?

high tide at six forty, the sun was pink, I think they don't notice me . . . who has noticed me in the past years, men don't, my father
—Girl
was perhaps the only one, my mother
—He adored that girl
I don't know if I believed her, he didn't put me on his lap, he didn't touch me, he was
—Girl
ever more distant, there were times when he passed through my mind, how stupid, that he was afraid to touch me when he was still it was because he was ashamed that he didn't hit anyone with his sandal, my father to my grandfather
—I'm sorry, Father
I think I heard on one occasion that he thought nobody was in the living room, he lowered the newspaper to look at the ceiling,
—I'm sorry, Father
convinced that the baby's bottom was near the lamp, an old man with a hat peeling a pear, not with a knife, with a pocketknife, he must have been born in the provinces, that way of speaking, his manners, there were pines where he came from like here, sir, there was the ocean but I don't believe it was the ocean, a stream if anything, maples, oak trees, the father of my grandfather in the well
—I drowned
and when they pulled him up
—What could I do, tell me?
the pink sun dissolved in the waves, if on Sunday at six o'clock you climb up to the Alto da Vigia, don't pay any attention to

me, who's paid attention to me these past years, few men said anything whatever to me on the street, they were interested in the others, I'm not smart or pretty, my co-worker pulling me to her

—Who put it in your head that you're not smart or pretty

the proof that I'm not pretty is that Tininha

—the dressing for bed eighteen

without softening, thinking

—How could I be friends with that one?

my co-worker caressing my neck

—I noticed you right away

few men said anything whatsoever to me on the street, did you know, my husband at first, and I was so grateful

—I'll wait for you here tomorrow

—That dress looks nice on you

—I'd like to hold you

but he forgot that quickly, after my son when the king has a birthday, in the dark

—Come here

and no more words, a sigh

—Caramba

looking like he was about to cry and protesting in the shadows of the pillow if I drew near him

—It bothers me when you breathe on my neck

no carambas, weary, in the gray of the slats of the shutters the volume of the night tables, the volume of the chest of drawers, moving my head so you don't push me away, let me stay with you I won't bother you, I swear, I just wanted to and without saying what I wanted, I would just like to and you don't let me, you find me repulsive, long dinners with strangers, bitter weekends, sad holidays, I pretend I'm reading, I think I hear

—I wouldn't mind embracing you
that's a lie, of course, if I approach you turn your mouth away
—Can't you let me be for a moment?
and I sit on the other side of the sofa
—I'm sorry
trying the seven differences in the newspaper puzzle, I don't discover any, but tomorrow I will discover the tides, the gray clarity of the spaces between the shutters the hands of the clock in an impossible position, we lived through times that don't exist, they say, and they keep going without end, I spent centuries awake while my husband was in the coded language of dreams that nobody has the key for or a sigh of disappointment
—Where does the whistle stop?
and I was moved by the whistle, I touched his foot with my foot and his foot moved, heels are monstruous when you don't see them, the spine transforms into a rosary, the hair of the other person suddenly on the pillow
—Who are you
and in the seconds almost
—That dress looks nice on you
almost
—I wouldn't mind embracing you
and nobody came, it was not my co-worker that I wanted to see, you were, on some August a cousin of, you, Tininha had been at her house for almost a week until her parents came to pick her up, the mother of Tininha's cousin to the mother of Tininha, lowering her sunglasses with her index finger and looking at my older brother
—Who is that one?
whispers I didn't understand and a smile joining them on

the lounge chair, Tininha and her cousin, both wearing princess earrings and petals on their nails, not paying attention to me in a corner of the yard opposite the wall, collecting lizards in a can and sharing Rogério, the mother of Tininha's cousin distracted from the magazine, her skin darker and her hair blacker, to Tininha's mother

—You've got a piece of eye candy there

while my older brother pushed me on the swing, awkwardly, the father of Tininha's cousin helped Tininha's father wash the car and only after the cousin left and the mother of Tininha's elbowed Tininha's mother

—If you let that piece of eye candy go, you're stupid

in a car that the two of them also washed, with enormous shorts and toes in the scandals, Tininha calling or before, Tininha warning

—Rogério is calling you

bending the stuffed animal to the right and to the left

—Can't you hear him?

with one of the princess earrings lost without noticing and I pretending that I didn't hear Rogério and I didn't hear her although Rogério's voice was clearer, they talk louder than people and a way that you understand better, they don't get colds and they don't cough, even after a whole night forgotten in the rain they get soaked but they put up with it, you squeeze them and the water comes out and they are still alive, their eyes are glass spheres, in Ernesto's case they are blue and there's a pin to stick them into the felt, I showed him to my mother, she dried him in a sheet, and Ernesto was stretched out, it's true, but healthy

—Even here I'm smaller

the jealousy while Rogério called, what did my older brother have that excited the neighbor ladies, fortunately the *Manual of the Perfect Carpenter*, the red flag wasn't necessary because there wasn't anyone on the beach, protecting him from them, me to Tininha

—What's your cousin's name

and Tininha hurt me walking on my body along the ward

—Nita

at six forty the rocks were lower and they stopped existing and the foam rose in an angry cloud, if my son were alive he'd be fourteen now, the age of my not deaf brother, squatting, cruel to the frogs, sticking wire into them and my deaf brother on his knees, watching, at seven to seven, my deaf brother saying something that didn't come, he lifted his tongue and it coagulated until a

—Sheee saaills seeea sheells

emptied him of sounds, at twenty to seven on Sunday I was on the goat rocks, my legs together like Senhor Manelinho curled his fingers

—What a woman

then an English woman who was returning from the beach, Senhor Manelinho's wife piling change from the cigarettes on the counter

—Not even enough for the collection plate at home and he feathers the nest of the rich

a public phone, near the kiosk, where no one made a call, you put in the coin and it swallowed it, its old receiver, in a rusty deglutination, Senhor Manelinho, without turning to his wife, molding the ever-receding figure of the English woman with his long arms, he couldn't imagine hands capable of reaching that far

—What's gotten into you, bitch?

they boarded the bus, went on to Lisbon, and Senhor Manelinho, both hands crippled

—What a woman

how do you manage to eat, if I entered into the seven differences I would soon figure it out, a man with arms in the square above, a man without arms in the square below, and I in a triumphant ball, the high tide of Sunday shrinking the sand and when it reached the sea wall it expelled the gulls, from the Alto da Vigia tiled roofs and tiles that the pines hid, my mother to the neighbor next door

—He loves his daughter

as if anyone were in love with me and my co-worker squeezing my ear slowly

—Ingrate

I, stubbornly jealous, to Tininha

—I don't feel like playing

my not deaf brother with a cast on his elbow, I was piqued with the cast and my mother's scarf held it with a knot at his throat, his gait more solemn

—I'm wearing a cast, watch out

they cut his meat for him, they cut his fruit for him, he stopped taking a bath, how lucky, my mother brushed his teeth stopping him from turning on the faucet, wetting the toothbrush, and sticking it in the plastic cup that he tore the Pluto sticker off of

—I don't like that dog

in the secret diary of the wall, written by Tininha

—I'm sorry

and my co-worker blowing her nose

—Sometimes you're so unfair

when that happened to my older brother my father stood in the middle of the living room not bothering with excuses for

the pantry, they greeted him and he was distracted, they talked to him and he didn't answer, his jacket was too big at the shoulders because he had suddenly lost weight, you've aged since they brought him father, if my grandfather put his hand on your cheek
—Baby's bottom, baby's bottom
his palm inert when I
—Father
his gaze sweeps over me without noticing me, he didn't see anyone except the girl, a bother, he saw his older son, elegant, on a stretcher being taken away by the firemen, my deaf brother squeezed his knees together
—Sheee saaills
and he putting him on
—Even though you're not my son
his lap, the only one he put on his lap, I swear, what does he mean by you're not my son, the voice of the plumber through the closed door
—We've got to change the syphon
and my mother locking herself in her room feeling like dying, for weeks she didn't scold my father about the bottles, the plumber with the iron ring, ma'am, who never came back, what would the other one have been like, before I was born, there must be a secret hole in the wall to write I'm Sorry and certainly she heard me because after a few days she delivered an envelope to my father which I found after his death by opening the drawer, she served him the best slices of meat at the table, fixed her hair, she took off her apron after locking the door, we didn't have time to talk, sir, why didn't you abandon us, what were you thinking, my grandfather saying when he visited
—That boy will go far

my father, in what appeared to be a type of sarcasm, but wasn't sarcasm, imitated him

—Far

from time to time returning from the pantry mocking without mocking

—I went far

and my mother buried in her sewing as if she couldn't see with her glasses, I had my nose in a magazine as if I couldn't see out of my glasses, my husband

—Are you blind?

and you can't even imagine how right you were, it's true, I'm blind, do you have an accordion you can lend me, as soon as I put the ring on my finger I went blind, my co-worker when she said goodbye

—You don't see me, right?

of course I don't see you, I'm blind, the same way I don't see my mother in the kitchen talking with the plumber, I see, how does one understand this, her guilt, imagine, and the man standing up slowly, I see the closed door and me and my not deaf brother closing the latch, my deaf brother who never stopped was still

—Sheee

two women talking in the boarding house on the first floor, with little faded flags of countries on the porch, the guy with the painted face and dressed like a woman to whom the police said

—This isn't carnival

and he arguing

—That's how I am

and he was that way, he had a husband and nobody made fun of them, they lingered at the Thebes Bakery where the guy

knitted little jackets, a fan on the table to relieve the heat and here on the beach the still of the beginning of the night, before the insects and the whispers of the dead praising the power and the glory of God, when the pines haven't yet gotten used to the dark, thick, so big, we think
   —We aren't the same
   and if I am still there's a reason, where is my pillow so that my parents will comfort me, I wrote in the secret diary, under Tininha's entry, we'll be friends forever and my pinky will be hooked to yours, my co-worker never hooked her pinky except at lunch when it was with my older brother, it took me a while to notice, too many people, too many firemen, too many neighbors, conversations far above our heads and therefore sentences we couldn't reach, if a syllable fell one of us picked it up examining it from side to side without discovering its meaning, my mother with little time for me, my father none
   —Girl
   I was offended by him, they told me that my grandfather worked in a store, surrounded by sacks, doing accounts all day, he climbed a staircase to the street and facing him was the Tagus River, if the boss didn't agree with the numbers he mumbled into his hat
   —Look out, I'm a man from the north, watch it
   I know little about my other grandfather, we'll be friends forever, Tininha, you and bed eighteen that needs the dressing, the rest heels that walk on me and a faded sky in the window, until then I thought the sky was smooth as a baby's bottom and I was wrong, with each step I took in the house a dozen accompanied me, farther away, closer, who is with me, who is spying on me in the dark, solitude is terrible not when we have nobody

left, but when another is with us who doesn't answer and hides, not gypsies, not donkeys, the creatures we were and that pursue us, blame us, if I could find princess earrings I would wear them, if my deaf brother were with me I'd put his hand on my throat and order him to

—Squeeze it

please squeeze it because the high tide scares me, at night it scares me, all these footsteps confuse and frighten me, when my husband got up at dawn I spied on the noise of the soles of his shoes in a panic thinking I'd never see him again, fortunately a faucet, fortunately a cup on the counter and the soles returning erasing them, I would put the hand of my deaf brother on my throat and order him to

—Squeeze it

lamps along the way, the clock hands on the night table at the same impossible angle, will it move and make time so that I will get old like the others, the lifeguard with crutches, Senhor Manelinho's dyed hair, more shells, blonder and wrinkles without hope underneath, my husband in pajamas, the buttons misaligned with the buttonholes, lying down in a windstorm of sheets with one slipper on, his arm searching for the slipper for the bare foot and giving up on it, disappearing with the room when he pressed the light switch that seemed to have separated from its wire, I wanted to help him and he touched me at last fingers shaking and a spark flew out in the dark, one of these days one of us will be electrocuted holding on to that thing, dead, the waves start to grow in September but they are yet to arrive, I don't break apart on the rocks, they bring my intact body to the beach in the morning, the co-worker strokes my thigh, I didn't believe that, the swing, which you can still see, since my older brother died

quietly, one of the ropes on a wire, I didn't believe there were such patient caresses but there are, murmuring in my ear
—Don't say sad things because they upset me
hiding my ear because of the shivers that, the slippers of my husband, made me itch, the memory of my husband's slippers, I don't know why it bothered me when I arranged them under the bed, I felt like kissing them, one of them had a hole in the toe, kiss it, kiss the toe too and then I began to hear the pines and the ocean, not like during the day, but slower, sweeter, the wind touched them in such a soft way and the ethereal halo of the water rose to me, it was an elderly man, accompanied by a woman who appeared to be his daughter but wasn't his daughter, and fortunately my older brother couldn't appear, who bought this house, if he did appear there would be more lounge chairs, more long earrings, more sunglasses lowered with an index finger and the *Manual of the Perfect Carpenter* I don't know where, Senhor Leonel substituted by his nephew, a blond whose hair was unruly, in the butcher shop, not to mention the pimples bursting out all over his face, the slaves of the woman who accompanied the elderly gentleman bothered me too, if Tininha's parents hadn't left two creatures, one on each side of the wall, smiling at each other and my not deaf brother an old man with a pipe, standing before their stretched out bodies, between chickens and burning huts, no bottle in the pantry, a packet of powder for the cockroaches and a forgotten can of preserves, smelly oil, curdled, my mother to Dona Alice's relative pointing to my deaf brother, the hair of the blond nephew also a hut, how many huts are there in Africa in round numbers, pointing to my deaf brother immersed inside himself, when we pushed him on the swing he was happy, when we didn't push him he hung from our sleeves trying to pull us to the swing, my mother

—Has he given you any problems?

the menu of Thebes Bakery on a rectangle of paper glued to the balcony, Dona Alice's relative

—He needs clothes

and my mother

—Do you see the cross I have to bear?

my mother

—Again?

they lived in a room two streets down, in front of a park where I never saw a soul except a beggar crumbling cigarette butts on a piece of newspaper, rolling up the paper and smoking the news, when we went by him he straightened up in his rags

—My respects, mademoiselle

and I, fourteen or fifteen years old, stopped to ask myself

—Could he be a prince?

a room filled with images of saints and paper flowers and my deaf brother unshaven, so mistreated, gentlemen, why don't you cut his nails or take him to the slide in the park, in spite of his age I'm certain he'd like it, you told Ernesto not to play with him, to speak in gestures, I didn't think that Ernesto could move his legs and he did, if I caught him at it, he'd stop, pretending to be made of cloth, why do toys pretend they are toys when we're with them, my schoolmate

—Sometimes you're so strange

the clock with the shepherdesses and nymphs disapproving my strangeness, my husband looking at the bed

—Explain to me why you have to sleep with that rotten pillow?

and I answering him, silent, you never had to walk down hallways in the middle of the night, you never had to protect yourself from drips, explosions, the coffee pots that were going to eat you, a difficult silence between us and in the silence the voice of my older brother

—Don't dream that I didn't think of our parents, don't dream that I didn't think of all of you

climbing up to the Alto da Vigia scraping himself on the rocks, my grandfather recognized him

—The rascal takes after my son and he's heavy as lead

my mother fearful that they would drop him

—Don't pick him up that way

while my older brother hung on to the weeds and the protrusions of the rocks, there must have been a path here, if I am still there will be stairs, if I am still there will be a handrail to reach the shellfish and the drinks instead of spiders and feces of feral cats, once in the big pine forest I saw a feral cat running with a bird in its mouth, which disappeared into the bushes, here they call them *ginetos*, I never walked so fast as on that day and when I got home, why the hell do they call them *ginetos*, I couldn't speak, my father

—Did something happen, girl?

of course I thought of all of you, new shirt, and creased pants, in tatters, the shoes from Lisbon ruined, even if I wanted to go back, and I thought of going back, I couldn't, I always said I wouldn't go to the war, it was me, I couldn't see the sense of it even in the meetings against those, you were too young to understand, who delivered letters to people, received messages, distributed pamphlets all of this from strangers to strangers, they didn't open up to me, they didn't even say thank you they didn't confide in me, they extended their hand without raising their head, take this, take that, wait in such and such a place with this book under your arm and the certainty, although I didn't see anyone, that they were watching me before they approached, one day we'll go to a gathering of friends and we didn't go, you have no idea what was at risk, there are whistleblowers everywhere, we have to learn to trust you and they didn't learn to trust me, Dona Alice's relative to my mother

—He's obeyed so far but who knows in the future

caution is necessary, we need carrier pigeons that the police can't detect, by chance I saw her at the movies embracing a guy who reminded me of Senhor Manelinho and something stung me, that is after the Post Office clerk, Dona Alice's relative to my mother

—Sometimes he makes me furious, he's already broken one of my saint figurines

a feral cat with a chaffinch in its mouth, almost yellow, big, embracing a guy and something stinging me, I felt like calling the police, not to going to the war and calling the police, after two or three days I called from a haberdashery far from the Thebes Bakery, I reported the places where I waited, the letters, the messages, the girl, before this summer a guy in front of the house and therefore I can't give up now in spite of these weeds that I'm slipping on and these angles of the rocks that threaten to break, in spite of you, on the Alto da Vigia a lame donkey that escaped, with a wound on its croup full of flies and larvae, look at the waves down there, the tide about to

—Tell me why you have to sleep with that rotten pillow

rise, I could have brought my pillow to this hallway full of drips, explosions, mouths that don't stop warning

—I'm going to eat you

I should have brought the pillow or asked to borrow Ernesto, so much wind here, so many fallen walls, so much noise that I can't hear you, so much sand in my eyes, the damp shirt, my bones are damp, the bleats of the goat that chews on its terror, not carousels, or rather what I also chew on, her eyes looking like mine, no, her eyes are mine, not pupils, white, her hoofs mine, the wavering of bodies is the same, the father of my father lifting me up

—The rascal takes after my son and is heavy as lead

and therefore, I will not stay afloat nor will I go to the beach, I'll drown, maybe the bones, one day, many years from now, when they free themselves from the lead, a feral cat without hurry, not scolding me, with yellow skin fur or brown and a thick tail, striped, the time I took to be able to breathe, my mother

—Did something happen to you, girl?

dozens of little shepherdesses, dozens of nymphs, and I incapable of saying a word, it could be

—Sheee saaills seeea sheells

if they put one of my hands on my throat and the second on the throat of someone else and relearn the sounds, look at the toothless donkey convinced that there were plants in the ground, the walls on the Alto da Vigia were crumbled, fragments of wooden boards, a table to which, Dona Alice's relative

—Until now he's obeyed but who knows in the future

was missing a leg, my mother brought a lemon toddy because everything is solved with lemon toddy, isn't it true

—Drink it while it's hot

if something happens to you your father will kill me and when the police asked my older brother, who was speaking, he hung up the phone convinced that everyone on the street knew, the guy on the front sidewalk slowly smoking an interminable cigarette, if I don't say anything the police, one of those who stretched

out their hand without lifting their head, wait in such and such a place with this book under your arm, the *Manual of the Perfect Carpenter*, I said to my mother, a cup close to my mouth
—A feral cat in the pine forest, ma'am
my not deaf brother, wanting to find it
—What's a feral cat like, Sis?
an animal with a chaffinch in its jaws that could have been me, taking it to a den where its kittens waited to chew me leaving only feathers, even the princess earrings, even the petals on my nails, Tininha's cousin scorning me
—That's your friend?
and Tininha, entertaining herself by planting weeds in the weeds, with a transparent glass necklace with elastic showing between the beads, almost offended
—Do you think I have friends like that?
she talked with me because there wasn't anyone else there, her house was better than ours, her father's car was nicer than my father's my mother was plainer than Dona Alice compared to hers, if she knocked on their door, and there was no reason to knock on the door, but I suppose there was, my mother called her ma'am and Tininha's mother without greeting her in the same way my mother did not greet Senhor Manelinho's wife, one doesn't kiss the poor, they say
—Good day
and it's everything or not even
—Good day
they say, they say
—I want this, I want that
and they do it, Tininha's mother, from the porch
—Do you want something?

and my mother retreating to our gate
—No I don't want anything, ma'am, sorry
the same way that Senhor Manelinho's wife would do, submissive, embarrassed, not my mother's name, of course
—Madam
Senhor Manelinho's wife
—You forgot the bag of fruit in the kiosk, Madam
and my mother without thanking her, why thank her, it was only her duty, sending me to pick it up, I thanked her for my mother
—Bless you
a thrill of recognition that made me feel bad
—Look at that girl
and everything done correctly, everything as it should be between us, my older brother becoming indignant
—Shameful
and nevertheless, he called the police because he saw a woman grinding her hips against some guy, not him, my older brother
—You'll pay for this
and putting down the phone sorry and not sorry, my older brother a table without a leg, a donkey, a goat, an insignificant thing sliding down from the Alto da Vigia, trying to catch his balance, giving up, and that a distracted wave caught him unawares, not caring about him.

8.

My family's picture became the most prominent absent rectangle on the living room wall, a space with a bent nail where voices hung, not a landscape with boats, I look at them the way my father looked at the frame calculating its position, I correct them, I refuse to see, I correct them again, the confused voices are in an oblique frame, all the syllables are clear in the horizontal frame, my mother

—How many times do I have to tell you to put your hat on your head

she with a Panama hat on her noggin and cream on her nose making it difficult to obey such a comical creature although my mother under the Panama hat and the cream, the question, in doubt

—Seriously, is it you, ma'am?

my brothers also had cream on their nose and caps of different colors so she could see them from a distance, the brims of the hats erased their faces and therefore my brothers could be identified up to the neck, from the neck up you could only see their ears, if you took off their caps they were creatures you could recognize or not, my father having the same thought

—Who are those guys?

the ocean seemed like it was from another year, I assumed they substituted it every summer so there would be a new ocean in August and when I returned there were the old waves that I already knew from their cadence and form, what an old beach, this one, it's enough to observe the oxide in the screech of the gulls and the same garbage in the sand, the basket, the shoe of an eternally drowned person, the foam dirty with oil and very complicated to clean in the water, nothing is altered except we have more wrinkles

—Soon we'll be old people, can you believe it?

and my clothes were too tight, my mother scolding me

—Won't you stop growing?

and I wanted to so I wouldn't find the clay lizard in the toilet, hiding until then, that started to emerge with the threat of what was about to drop as I strained, just the point of its snout but when you least expect it a terrible five dozen, my not deaf brother smashed it with the hammer and it's a good thing

—That thing was going to kill me

my father forbade my mother to hit him

—You're right

a terrible half dozen and I admired his courage, the remains in the garbage and even in pieces the bits of the lizard kept moving, or was it I who was moving, or were we both moving, he is preventing her

—Wait a minute

and I closed the lid of the toilet and sat on it

—You won't take me with you anymore

while its tail and legs, my co-worker's face rising from my belly

—If I could have your baby

they faded quickly, I lifted the lid a crack and the creature was dead but the ocean was the same, the kiosk was the same, just the people, I said to my co-worker
—I've had enough children
only people changed, I shouldn't have hung the voices the way one is supposed to because she kissed my bellybutton
—I was joking
instead of the lizard
—I said it's over
with a pipe on his belly Gualdino Ceramics and therefore the lizard wasn't made of clay, of porcelain, Senhor Gualdino put it in the oven and painted it later, who will assure me that there isn't a mold for lizards and children, I say to my co-worker
—Do you have a mold?
and my co-worker had a horizontal nail on her forehead, the rest of the creatures had a vertical nail, hers was lying down
—What?
disillusionment, coming from the small boat, of people who will never understand, it had been a long time since walking alone had stopped being difficult for me, these pines are the same ones that were here before I was born, more worn than the ocean, the big bird that roosted on Tininha's chimney walked across the yard in the direction of the olive grove, not just the empty walls, almost no furniture, one of the living room windows hanging by its hinges and the night insects around me, the blue cap of my deaf brother, the yellow cap of my not deaf brother, my mother offering the tube of sunscreen to the next-door neighbor
—Would you like some?
since the next-door neighbor didn't want any she applied a

centimeter to my nose, I was embarrassed to walk on the sand in front of the next-door neighbors

—I bet her father is a clown

a guy we'd forget if it weren't for the noise of the bottles or a question to the depths of the newspaper

—How long has it been since you gave up thinking that you'd hit us with your slipper, sir?

his voice thicker than ours, if there were two of us capable of, if he could count, the nurse

—Would you like me to bring a mirror so you can see the scar?

if he were alive he'd like me and if he liked me in spite of my mutilated body, I don't want to see the scar or feel the absence of fingers, this is someone else with my name, this one, which by coincidence feels what I feel or I think I feel, I've changed, sir, I'm not a girl, I'm a donkey that's about to fall down, that falls down and they don't bring it to this house because the house is gone, there's no stove, no chairs, there's not one person who speaks except for me who speaks with the trees and nevertheless everything is familiar as if you were all close to me, here on the X-ray there's a little knot in the bone that doesn't look right to me, I was distracted from the doctor thinking of the clown's nose or a small crab in the bucket, moving its legs in two fingers of water, the crab got out and scrambled to the waves, as fast as I was on Sundays, my older brother takes me for a ride on his bike and informs me

—I'm sixty years old now

all I have to do is take his voice off the nail of the picture for him to come back alive, all I must do is take the chorus of voices off so that a crowd of people will be around me, my mother's aunt, whom we visited at Easter, served us slices of cake on a plate with a fork and I would eat it with my hands

—Didn't they teach you any manners?

they never took the top off the piano keyboard, her lips were stretched apart revealing missing incisors, the remaining teeth carried an extra exposed nerve that protested, the rugs hiding secrets in the fabric

—We're poor

although my mother's aunt to my mother

—They exaggerate, don't listen

soup tureens fixed with wires, the sugar bowl without handles on the lid, a dirty mop that they forgot to put away when we rang the doorbell, my mother reassuring her

—All rugs exaggerate

leaving a note under the sugar bowl so that the aunt would notice, pushing it with her fingers against a dead gnat on the napkin, I remember Mother, you looking for money in your wallet and bringing it wrapped up in a handkerchief, if there were time, and there is no time, I'd ask you to show me that trick, your expression ordering me

—Keep quiet

you're a good person, did you know, if my father didn't weigh like lead maybe we'd have been happy despite ourselves, I blew on the gnat that fell in your lemonade and you, heroically, drank it, my co-worker

—Your mother after all

and I

—Shut up

because it's none of your business, those are family matters, in any case I'll give you some free advice, never lift the top of a keyboard to save yourself pain or put a fork in a slice of cake because they jump, I miss us, if I could find some sun cream

I'd put it on and we'd be together again, sometimes a touch of nostalgia colors me purple inside, you and father were happy, mother, we were happy, and I forbid you to contradict me, I don't feel sad, I swear, we continue on the nail of the landscape with boats and the frame the way it should be, each syllable clear, in a little while

—Sheee

My deaf brother on the swing that one of us pushes, my mother's aunt's husband is fatter in the picture, whoever believes in the principles that pictures don't change is wrong, they put on new ties, gain color, get sick, I always thought that grown-ups secretly gave them food, wiping their mouths roughly the way they did to me

—Two or three spoonful's more, sit still, and then you'll see the picture

my mother praising him

—He keeps growing

my mother's aunt agreeing

—Thank God he doesn't lack an appetite next week I'll buy him a shirt with a bigger collar

the kind that come in a cardboard package full of pins that prick, there's always one left that you don't see, and it pokes us in the ribs, me on the stairs, at the door

—What about the gnat, mother

running an exploratory finger down my neck

—It's gone down

my family is not just in the brightest rectangle of the absence of the picture on the living room wall, it lives on the beach too, it doesn't take long for my father to be restless in the pantry

—What happened to my bottles?

so that after Sunday I stay at home with you and look for Tininha with two princess earrings in my hand, the seagulls are in the ocean because of the ebb tide, an albatross, other small birds, that come at night, whose names I don't know, hopping on the rocks picking at mussels and those water fleas, they seem like fleas to me that hide in the stones, my not deaf brother fights with my deaf brother because of the swing, my mother from the window
—Leave the boy alone, son
while aunt's husband keeps growing, sometimes you must buy bigger frames because they don't fit in the other ones, smiles that widen, glasses they didn't wear, a mark on the cheek that we hadn't noticed, my co-worker stroking my skin
—I see a little scar here
from when I tripped in my room and hit my leg on the chest of drawers, the nurse put cotton on it, tincture of iodine that burned, more cotton, adhesive, I didn't think my eyes could hold so many tears, when we are happy we don't even notice them, they are waiting inside our eyelids or behind what we see, in fact I don't know if they are tears of drops of iodine, the nurse to my mother
—There might be a scar
and there was a scar that in time I stopped noticing, it probably faded, my co-worker's index finger brought it back and with it a stretcher, a tray of objects designed to maim, bottles of curative liquids that gnawed at people Tininha in the hospital
—Hurt the one in bed eighteen
tweezers and scissors to remove my stitches and a furrowed brow lamenting
—I think the idiot in the mall didn't get my glasses right
my co-worker also wore glasses

—The idea of losing you traumatizes me when you get to my age, understand
   phone calls at night and I pretend
   —Wrong number
   notes in my locker with petals of perfect love, jealousy, the married son in Belgium, the husband, a solicitor in the provinces, who exchanged her for the maid with exuberant lacework
   —The help is cheaper, and he was always cheap
   Chinese objects here and there, we got rid of one and we tripped over the next, a halo of November even in April and May, the son with a blond creature and a blond baby on his lap, with features diluted in the shade of a tree, where does the shade of the pines go at night, I know that the ocean continues because of a mote or, when the wind turns, the sound of a wave announcing
   —Sunday
   and silence again, my co-worker
   —It was enough to think you would call me and I couldn't sleep
   my deaf brother abandoned the swing to chase a cat next to the laundry sink holding an upside-down basin, so many animals in the world without mentioning the breakfast coffee mugs, except that in the mugs dressed like us was a kangaroo in suspenders, an ostrich with a neck scarf, my older brother's had a dancing panther dressed like a Tyrolean, the son of my co-worker sometimes sent a postcard with a doll peeing into a lake, so many animals, my God, centipedes, mules, lobsters, a mule pulled the old hawker's cart full of desks and trunks that nobody bought, the old hawker wore a beret, under the beret an unlit cigar and a tiny dog walking between the axels when the cart stopped the little dog stopped in the middle to reflect, without scratching its ear with its hind leg to smooth its hair, one afternoon I saw

him walking down the road alone as if the cart were still rolling along over him and they told me the old hawker was found dead in the pine grove, sitting on his bench, but the mule had been stolen, they realized he was dead because the unlit cigar was on the bench, they also stole his beret and after a time the cigar was seen on the chin of a second beggar, not just desks and chair, mattresses, pillows, a stuffed hedgehog, everything a person needs, a little while ago, five minutes or so, I thought I heard the wheels turning and the treasures fighting among themselves, once in a while he pressed the bell and shook it asking people to come, that is, just me at the gate admiring him without a look of gratitude in exchange, Tininha refused to go with me

—He must be full of lice

in the pine grove, near the cart, the covers under which he snored and a half-eaten chicken, feathers scattered around, the little dog joined the other strays on the beach although he was more polite, more distant, he ignored the garbage, if I stay still, the old hawker could have been an engineer or a count in another time, there are royals who turn into monsters and sleeping beauties in books, you don't even have to read them, it's enough to look at the pictures, monsters talking with girls, almost August twenty-eighth and the donkeys, the wind, on the Alto da Vigia, if I stay still, there may be snakes, I don't know, monsters talking with girls and sleeping beauties, in glass boxes, in a forest clearing, my co-worker to me

—My sleeping beauty, my everything

I wanted to keep sleeping

—Five more minutes don't open the shutters

you pull a string and he rises out of the sacks to fill us with what we are and he is so heavy on top of us, sleeping beauties in glass boxes in a forest clearing and in the corner of the watercolor a terrifying witch walking away cackling, my co-worker gathered material from the whole world, esplanades, churches, jumbled together in her room, that on the weekend my husband was in Madrid at a meeting and the picture of the son, the Chinese knickknacks that who knows why remind me of my mother's aunt and the sick piano of her gums, the clarity of October in July, intimate, sad, the suspicion that my mother was with me while I convalesced from the flu without my mother, of course

—My sleeping beauty, my everything

a thermometer and syrup

—Put the thermometer under your arm and open your mouth quick

a spoon hitting my mouth and a taste of sugar running down my chin while my co-worker, in a robe, stretched out at my side

—You're so lovely

looking for the breast I have left and lingering over it

—You're so lovely

a fifty-two-year-old body so lovely and I have to hide it in a larger dress since it is not only the dead who get fat, a leg against mine, a bone bothering me and with this the certainty of finding myself in the pine grove instead of the old hawker with all the branches brushing sobs, I taking shelter in the cart because of the humidity, the cold, and the little dog surrounded by feathers while it tasted the chicken, the bell called the clients in endless rings, anyone, my deaf brother, my older brother, my father who will go far away and continue to distance himself between roots and the earth, cutting the mule's reins and taking it, my not deaf brother an old man with a pipe in front of me and the huts burning, the big bird on Tininha's chimney staring at me from

the dark that revealed his frozen pupils against my frozen pupils, if we release the animals on the mugs into the wild what space will be left for us between the kangaroos in suspenders and the ostriches with neck scarves, my father
   —I see rats
      shaking them off his body with desperate fingers, my mother
   —It's the alcohol
   —Drinking yourself to your death
   until the sweat calmed down becoming dull drops that a towel dried, the fear let go of my father substituted by a peace that had no features, my mother unfolded a blanket on the couch, which warmed us when we had colds, the body began to dissolve in warm drops and under the drops was new cold skin, not just the frogs, it's us, my mother to my father
   —Are you going to sleep there all night
   unless a man in a hat gets him up
   —The boy keeps getting heavier than lead, I say
   and he carries him to a crib I don't recognize, one of those you see in caves and where improbable ancestors who don't even exist in the albums lay one day, not just so many animals in the world, generations of strangers draining out of me and I will never drain out of anyone, the trip is over, my friends, I've lost my son, let's dry out, from now on a beach house will transform into another house and any house therefore will be like any building in the place of ours even those ghosts are lost in there
   —Where is the collection I can't find it
   of course, you can't find it, it isn't there, other walls, another floor, the disillusioned cortege of dead who leave and when they leave, they weren't, my father waking up under the cover, taking care of himself in the bed

—What happened to my lamp?
and the switch with the sparks, my mother
—You were seeing rats yesterday
and he didn't believe it, traces returning to his face
—Rats?
while my co-worker
—Tell me you like me
in a syrupy voice, with the taste of sugar, running down her chin and my father's fingers outside of his hair meditate
—What rats?
trying to sit up without being able to, look at the bell clapper in the chapel and my mother
—Slowly
holding him at the waist, one of his shoes on the foot with his foot inside it and hollow, another shoe less hollow but firm, the trembling of the fingers that he didn't want us to see, the pupils dancing under his eyelids, the doctor
—What a lamentable liver
my belly swelling like my body
—So lovely
it swelled, my skin was like that of the suitcases in the closet, I said to my co-worker
—Don't I smell like mushrooms?
a blast of cardboard breath on me, all these pagodas and dragons have made me old, my co-worker, grateful
—It wasn't so hard to say that was it, my pearl?
in a voice that heightened the October of the room bringing night early and rain with it, I'm on the beach in August, not in a Lisbon apartment
—You kiss me now

feeling the pines that grow silent and return, in front of the brightest rectangle of the absence of the picture on the wall of the living room with my family with me, my father in a painful equilibrium

—I don't get tired walking anymore

Tininha with her lame foot between the lounge chair and the wall, slower than me but she managed it with her two feet and I could only use my right, sorry, my left, I just did it and it was my left, life is so inexplicable, the portion of mysteries I leave behind me, in fifty-two years I haven't understood much and after tomorrow the waters will close over my head without hurting me, if my son were here he'd be twenty-seven, my father with his nose against the window of the living room that didn't look out on the beach, it had a view of an empty lot with rockrose trees and willows and then a school

—I don't have much time left

in a voice that wasn't his but when he turned around

—Girl

with a smile, all that was missing was a ribbon for him to give me at Christmas and perhaps a few months are part of the not much time left, and they were, my mother bringing her soul from I don't know where, I know it wasn't from her throat

—Do you want to frighten the little one?

when it wasn't the little one who was frightened but her, my deaf brother banging a toy locomotive on the ground, each bang jolt that dented it, and a wheel came off and rolled under the table, nobody will see me fall off and if they do they'll think it's a donkey or a goat, Senhor Manelinho's wife

—It looks like something's going on at Alto da Vigia

organizing magazines on the counter, in one of the English

postcards a girl with an out of fashion hairstyle waved with an inner tube, she was also wearing an out of fashion bathing suit, I remember the photographers with tripods who took pictures of people on Sunday and dried the negatives on a line, they arrived wearing black jackets and bow ties

—Lighter and quicker, doll

and with boots in hand, they carved a display case in the sand with soldiers, couples, a guy with fists at his waist defying the universe, a kid on his mother's lap, twenty-seven, how awful, with a seriousness in which you could anticipate future disappointment, debts, diabetes, divorce, the landlord reluctant to fix the roof, my father kept his smile in an invisible door and it's also October here, at times a Chinese plate, with its hooks, in the place of the landscapes with boats, the shepherdesses and the nymphs transformed the hours into a time before we were born the remains of which are morning coats and gaiters in the pantry, my co-worker

—My grandmother left this for me

and a woman in mourning giving her the watch inside a kitchen cloth

—For you to remember me with

and she got it right, ma'am, even I who never saw her, remember, how she was your grandmother, my co-worker thinking

—She had a tube in her throat after the operation on her larynx

where the sounds leave from in a whine of a drill, words that are not as small as ours, gigantic, in school calligraphy, one waited an immense amount of time until the sentence was complete, covered with a gauze square that the tube sucked and blew with her respiration, she didn't move her lips, it was the tube and the gauze that formed her sentences, she died when they put me in Leiria and on Saturday afternoons, when a simple hour lasts for weeks I kept hearing her, I didn't take the watch from there so not to upset her because when she got irritated her conversation grew slower still, if you mess with the nymphs she appears right away and I see that it's her, before going into the room, because one of the sandals is louder than the other, on my mother's side, starting at a certain age, I never found out why, women become sandals and I asked my schoolmate to shut up since I thought there were people in the yard and nobody except the roots of the pines talk to me, not just the treetops, once in a while a branch falls in the dark and even if it were a needle I think I could find it, the sounds amplify at night, not more intensely, they are more delicate, precise, my father

—Rats what nonsense

and after the rats he became distant, crumbling the bread at the table out of inertia, during a dinner, in the middle of the fish course

—My mother

he was still for a moment and then began to sing rock a byebye baby on the tree top when the wind blows the cradle will rock, he went quiet again and placing his silverware down

—Every night before turning off the light

—and when they forced him to shut up, now I lay me down to sleep, I pray the Lord my soul to keep my son is going to bed, he lingered at the door before leaving and you could distinguish his profile against the light door, then it was just the light door, afterwards the dark door when they turned off the light, her voice and my father's cradled me, I didn't understand what they were saying but they took care of me, I bet that you, in the hospital, be gone bogeyman, father, I bet that your mother looked in on you from the door, he turned to the wall not to escape from us, but to talk with her, you started drinking before I was born and because of my deaf brother, it wasn't because of my mother, it wasn't, why didn't you hit him with your slipper instead of the others, it wasn't, he didn't get angry, he didn't blame anyone, he pretended not to notice, right, just like my mother, look at that big wave in the cove between the rocks, just like my Sunday, not noticing that you noticed and nevertheless when you were upset it was at yourself, not her, that my deaf brother hugged your knees, you were incapable of consoling him, so upright, so rigid, wanting to put him on your lap and hate him at the same time, my mother tried to remove him from you, and my deaf brother

—Sheee saaills seeea sheells

trying by force

—I

repeating

—I

and locking herself in the room where she came out of to cook without answering people, we could eat the soup without all of us being at the table, we could not have manners that she wouldn't notice, she with her forehead in her plate without any manners, once asking my father in a soft voice

—Is it you or me that you want to kill with your drinking?

and my father crumbling the bread hoping that his fingers would come apart too, when I say

—We were happy, weren't we?

you can't imagine how much it pains me to lie, my deaf brother at your side on the couch leaning his head on you and your hand on his shoulder, he never did that with me or my other siblings, my mother

—I would prefer for you to kill me rather than accept it

and he didn't accept it, to punish her, with the bottles in the

pantry, he humiliated himself, to humiliate her, accepting jobs that were progressively lower paid
—Nobody's going to make dough with him
humbler, small odd jobs, I remember him wearing uniforms—a chauffeur, an usher, a doorman—I remember you on Sundays with a bottle in your lap, I remember saying
—Daddy
and he didn't look at me, intoning go away bogeyman, get off the roof, to a silhouette in the doorway, giving himself courage to not have courage, if his friends from bachelor days sought him out, he'd make us tell them
—He's not home
forcing himself to cough so they'd know he was alive, and he saw his nails squeezing his arms the way he saw his shoes hurting him, hurting him, when the doctor
—What a lamentable liver
instead of happiness the sensation that my father was almost happy
—Finally
But I was probably mistaken, they talk so much crap, the drunkards, without realizing what they're saying, for example stupid little verses, childish nonsense, now I lay me down to sleep, I pray the Lord my soul to keep, I think my son went under the bed, for example
—What do you talk about with Daddy, Mother?
for example
—You can turn off the light, I'm not scared
and he alone in his room, terrified, as was the case in the hospital, with a tube in his nose and a tube in his intestines, alone in his room, terrified, in the dark because even though the lights

were on it was dark, even though my mother took his hand it was dark, even though
    —Father
    dark in spite of knowing that my
    —Father
    not
    —Father
    under father
    —Daddy
    my deaf brother
    —Sheee saaills seeea sheells
    my father's arm incapable of moving and wanting to find him, my father's arm almost
    —Son
    my father's arm
    —Son
    my mother in the hallway
    —I can't take it anymore
    only a mouth out of control instead of a woman, incapable of an exclamation, only insisting
    —I can't take it
    asking me, fighting with her handkerchief
    —Can't you do anything for us?
    and instead of listening to her I was interested in the plumber
    —We must change out the syphon
    the kitchen door closed, my brothers with me and in the lightest rectangle of the absence of the picture on the wall of the living room my father returning from the pantry
    —Girl
    and smiling at me.

9.

Words begin to lose their connections, for example when I say night I want to say night and refer to its other meaning which I can't recall, when I say mother I want to say the first day at school and I am afraid to go in, extending my arms to a woman who is saying goodbye while a second woman prevents me from, blocking the stairs, running to her, ordering her to go away
 —You've dropped her off, relax
 and I am among strangers who don't know my name, a coatrack full of jackets that don't belong to me, drawings that I didn't do on the walls, a room with small tables, another girl crying refusing to let them hold her, the woman leaving who looked like my mother, hesitating at the gate, the second woman to her
 —Standing there won't help
 and the first woman walking on the sidewalk, along the fence, quickening her pace, very upset, stopping suddenly, the second woman ordering her to disappear with a hand gesture and she running to the corner, softening, looking at me again, then disappearing, I bet she was stopped behind a tree thinking
 —I can't go back to get her

with a blue skirt on that I'll never forget, every time she wore it, I was convinced she didn't like me and if I called her, she wouldn't come, offended, my co-worker
—Don't squeeze me so hard, you'll suffocate me, my beauty
and I was convinced I hadn't even brushed by her, I let her touch me, I didn't touch her, it's hard for me to touch people, I inherited this from you, father, it's not that I don't want to, there are times I do but if I touched someone I'd dissolve into them and wouldn't be me anymore, once I took the blue skirt off a hangar in the closet and hit it in the laundry basket, my mother when she found it there said
—Who put this here?
observing my brothers, observing me, thinking, lifting my chin
—Don't worry, I won't wear it again
her face full of small tables and looking like a little girl about to cry, words that didn't reach her lips, coming from a distant past when her godmother said
—You're going to live with us for awhile
footsteps descending stairs waving goodbye and my mother on the landing in silence, a different bed, toys that didn't care about her, chocolates she craved but refused to eat, when mother returned from the hospital
—What's a hospital?
and she descended the stairs, this time with you, they had already forgotten her, she walked through the rooms of the house recognizing them with difficulty, she remembered the red glass and the copper pheasant, she had an idea of the smells but it wasn't really her mother, she was stiller, thinner, and had the impression father was not as tall, what did they take away from

me, what has changed, what did they take from her and what has changed that is lost forever, mother weighing herself
—I gained half a kilo, my goodness
looking more like the person called
—Mother
inside herself and nevertheless something was missing that she wasn't able to explain, father slowly returned to his former size and gestures, however in spite of the same jackets and cough he wasn't exactly father, a wrinkle between his eyebrows, more mixed-up words, more silence, he hardly bathed and when he did he was more careless with the soap, he didn't return to inhabit that place, he merely accepted it, from half kilo to half kilo her mother returned and nevertheless
—Are you sure you're my mother?
she opened a smile that was part happiness and parts that had none
—I was sick, you know?
and the sickness robbed pieces that made a difference, she stopped singing in the kitchen, she didn't pick me up to dance with her to the music on the radio, she didn't teach me how to imitate animals
—What does a rooster say?
she sat, palms on her cheeks and absent, if you tugged her sleeve, she'd come back trembling
—You scared me
my mother threw the blue skirt in the garbage
—I'm done with this
while a tendon in one of her cheeks stretched and shrank, the harmonica of the knife grinder played at all hours the notes in harmony with the cart, in pieces, full of broken umbrellas

opening bat wings incapable of flying, that exuberance of junk was rendered immobile, he pedaled a bike wheel with his toecap and held knives and blades against a moving wheel that let out sparks like a lighter, so that my mother and I stood at the window mesmerized, one not older than the other or rather I was the older one, what a way to earn a living, gentlemen, blowing on a harmonica the alphabet of the music, the knife grinder wiped the spit off on his pants, I always wanted an instrument like that when I was a child and to this day, my co-worker in the middle of her Chinese knickknacks her October, feeling tender

—Promise you won't grow up, baby

I don't grow up, words start to lose their connection, for example night means night but there's also another meaning I can't recover, I understand half, half is missing, the most important one, it is diluted under the rustling of the pines that don't talk to me anymore, they talk among themselves without paying the slightest attention to me, the Alto da Vigia is invisible and nevertheless the donkeys, if you pay attention, in the rockrose, soft little shells, cautious, choosing the earth without hurry, I'd like to dance with you mother, with the walls and the furniture swirling around, the radio is still now, the stains on the walls are still, the mother of my mother suspended in the middle of a cleanliness spreading in my kidneys without complaint, only the wrinkles on the sides of my mouth are deeper, when the wrinkles disappear the feather duster asks

—What's it like to be sick, ma'am?

the scale consoling her

—A half kilo more, my goodness

the hands of the clock on one of the fine lines that separate the numbers, on the numbers there are lines but they are thicker, the

clock hand vibrating before deciding on one of them and mother looking down fearfully
 —Don't torment me, scale
 she took off her shoes to get on the scale and the alienation of the shoes irritated her, what we are not doesn't suffer, they limit themselves to waiting like objects of the dead wait to be offered to the living, the pin box for this one, the pen for that one, the chrome triton that you liked so much for the cousin who helped you in the end, she gave you drinks with straws, she emptied your urinal, she wiped, bless her, your anus, hopefully nobody from the courthouse will appear one day on the threshold with shepherdesses and nymphs
 —The deceased insisted, she wrote it in her will
 my husband after I unpacked it
 —What is that?
 and I with the clock in my hands, my surprise as big as his was
 —I have no idea
 shepherdesses and nymphs that don't care what we have in our house, they are concerned with teapots with distorted landscapes and creatures in tunics painted on cups, they pay attention with gray clarity to the embroidered pillows, a damask bedspread like the ones in the sacristy, and an insecure little voice turning off the toaster which I never trusted
 —It's the two of us forever, right?
 because everything that's electric is treacherous, the drier that eats my hair, the vacuum sucking the carpet along with the dust, if I am still the pines will turn their backs to me because it's Sunday, and when a tree turns its back you can't hear it anymore, there is no more definitive emotion, everyone knows this, than the

disdain of plants, my husband examining the clock and handing to me as if it burned his skin

—It still smells of camphor who sent you this beast?

I repeated for months when I went into my schoolmate's house

—There's an obnoxious smell in here

The source of the smell didn't come to me and finally I realized it was camphor, an aroma that sticks in your nose and turns our gestures into ancient ones like the chests where the past piles us, letters tied together with pale ribbons, cufflinks with the crimp only, without the malachite on the little silver claws, keys to open the past that time has changed the locks for and open dusty voids after turns and turns, you stick in your hand and a cousin is in a wheelchair, shriveled legs tucked into a blanket, lifting a class of anise

—It's been a long time, you rascal

or a steamship trip to the other shore because of a whale breeching and you see the size of its head, all of you would fit inside it, today or tomorrow, when you least expect it, you do well to stay asleep and it swallows you without your noticing, there were dozens of lodgers in there, if you don't believe it ask the person ahead of you, it's in the Bible and the person ahead of you trying a fin

—It's a fact

maybe this whale also has lodgers, if we cut it open we find them having lunch, napkins at their necks, offering a chicken wing

—Do you care for some?

keys, keys, keys that open dusty voids after turns and turns of the key, you stick in your hand and an elderly lady that they shut in her room when visitors came

—Just a little while, Aunt

asking for silence with a finger on her lips, whispering assurances in my ear

—I'll tell you a secret did you know I'm a grand duchess?

holding the clock in my palms, without a place to put it, afraid of a sudden October in the apartment, vague rain, drab clarity, tame desires to die still, not all at once, member by member, lightly, this arm, an ear, the spirit abandoning my body in a leisurely hyperbole, returning out of politeness

—I almost forgot to say goodbye to you

and disappearing in the camphor, the great past of Tininha's chimney watching me with long nails, the wind came from the olive trees and vibrated on the roof, they should light a lamp and stay close to me, if my mother came from Lisbon to keep me company the woman from the school would slap her with her hand

—Standing there isn't helpful

thank God that the blue skirt is in the garbage, my mother comforting me

—Don't worry, I won't wear it again

she who never sang or danced again, alert to the bottles in the pantry, removing the chairs that got in the way my father and the sofa so he wouldn't lose his balance on the rug

—Won't this ship calm down?

throwing a disapproving look at my mother suddenly without alcohol

—You

while the syphon in the kitchen was perfect, not a single drip, a spot of paint on the mosaic that mother covered with a slipper to clean later, ashamed of us, shaking my not deaf brother

—Haven't you ever seen a stain

haven't you ever seen a stain on my sheets, my underwear, in the fabric of the bedspread that doesn't come out, doesn't come out, or rather I can take it out of the sheet, the clothing, and the bedspread, I can't take it out of me, people see it and discover it right away

—Did you see that?

my daughter not another man, another woman

—Doll

and in realizing it I died, and she didn't understand that I was dead, we died, and they didn't notice, we stopped existing and they thought we were present, the neighbors answer for us

—She's just worn out

the pines with their backs turned, echoes of their footsteps, my daughter and her co-worker in the empty house, not on a floor with Chinese knickknacks where the light didn't enter, it stayed in the little boxes and faded slowly, at nine in the morning it would soon be dusk, you pulled up the shutter and not a sound came through the windows, grumbling outside while it went away, my schoolmate in an apologetic tone

—I didn't have the money to rent anything else

few blouses, private lessons on Sundays at the dining table with a chandelier that imitated candles, two of them burned out

—I wish I could show you a palace

and she showed me a second floor in a neighborhood with modest little stores and people without color, how do you stand living here where the trolleys make things wobble like turkeys, a wave, another wave, and no ocean watching me from the beach or receding with the tide beyond the rocks, the elderly lady back without my turning the key

—I'm a grand duchess, girl

extending her hand to nobody, in Tininha's mother's room there were pink silk curtains and silk pillows, in the open closet transparent blouses undulating endlessly, my older brother

—I won't look there

wondering

—What's going on with me?

surprised at his body inside the pajamas, Senhor Manelinho suddenly next to him

—What a woman

and disappearing right away, my older brother explaining

—I'm only sixteen

but Senhor Manelinho was installed in the kiosk to settle accounts with the newspaper truck, he wasn't even eighteen when he climbed to the Alto da Vigia, seventeen, he had started to shave, his voice hadn't changed completely yet, from time to time the high pitch of a child would derail his sentences, my co-worker

—When my husband was alive, we lived better

another neighborhood, another apartment, more dresses, a week in Spain in the summer, her husband holding a corner of the sheet, ready to kick her with his heel

—Can't you see I'm trying to sleep?

and my co-worker, disconsolate, respecting his sleep knowing he was awake thinking of his assistant, when she was in the bathroom he made a call covering his mouth with his palm, if my co-worker appeared suddenly he hung up, flustered

—Shit going on at the office

unable to place the receiver on the phone while a tiny voice insisted on the receiver

—Are you still there, Alberto?

until the phone shut up after

—Sweetheart?

hovering there for a time, their noses avoiding each other, now on the ceiling or on the terrace where the lounge chairs were in the sun, my co-worker with a sarong tied under her shoulders, conscious of her too-large thighs, the doctor

—You don't look more than twenty

or thirty or forty, in fact, the son has gone away but the stretch marks from my pregnancy have stayed, not even my feet were like that, the thick ankles, so many toes, not five like before, seven or eight that the shoes had deformed, the feat of cutting her toenails with her knees to her chin supporting her feet on the bidet, they cut them for her at the hairdresser after soaking them in a basin of warm water between women of her kind that time defeats, her husband smoking in bed while the

—Sweetheart?

and the

—Alberto?

they came and went between them altering the tone of life, the curtain no longer was white, the ceiling no longer was cream-colored, the breakfast tray with the toast ready to eat and the ruins of the brioches a perpetual accusation, the pot of orange marmalade a message that neither of them wanted to hear I want to hear the opinion of the waves in disagreement with mine, we almost never think the way the others do, the pines have an opinion that satisfies me but now they are mute, Tininha's mother closed the shutters with gestures that cried out

—Fool

to my older brother who defended himself

—I'm afraid of you

Tininha's mother couldn't hear him because of the closed

shutters although you could see a dark shadow behind them, then only light, then no dark form, my older brother
    —I'm going to get dressed jump the wall and throw a stone at it
and continuing in his pajamas sitting on the mattress, if only Senhor Manelinho could encourage him
    —She's waiting for you, buddy
but Senhor Manelinho wasn't in the kiosk, in one of the little houses, later in the cane field, on the other side of the road, with his wife and the dog, or in the café with the foosball table where men were at the worn counter, the owner took the cognac off the shelf, attentive to the line in the glasses and the sick niece with the bad lungs, ready to go into the back lot with a client but needing to call the owner to a side to negotiate the price, after a few minutes you could hear coughing in the bushes, what do the waves want, the client returning with a distracted look, adjusting his trousers, a few minutes later the niece was in her corner covering her cough with her arm, my older brother, what do the waves want anyway, admitting
    —Even if Tininha's mother were the niece of the owner I wouldn't have the courage
what do the waves and the pine trees and the wind that rises and wanes want, a beetle hitting the walls, missing the window, it insisted, missed again, brushed the back of my neck, lost, evaporated into the hallway if my mother were with me she'd say
    —I can't stand those bugs
with eyes closed because when they were closed the beetle was inoffensive, the wind wants me to go away, there's no doubt, it doesn't want me here, it wants me at the Thebes Bakery with my mother or my co-workers between laments, Chinese knickknacks, and kisses, how to leave her

—Shit at the office

without threats or tears or perhaps not threats, just tears, sitting at the dining table and the private lessons with her head on her elbows

—You're going to kill me

and she might kill herself, why not, what are we doing here, I'm happy that after tomorrow the Alto da Vigia and no possibility of hurting myself on the rocks, water, and I won't feel the water, my older brother standing still in front of the shutters

—Tell me what I should do, Senhor Manelinho

and Senhor Manelinho lingering his gaze over Tininha's mother

—What a woman

the niece with the cough not even sitting, squatting in a shapeless skirt, on certain afternoons I would see her picking up garbage on the beach with the beggars and the stray dogs and looking so much like them, the bones salient on her face, I didn't think there were so many bones in a face, a torso, legs, I didn't notice if she spoke or, like my deaf brother

—Sheee saaills seeea sheells

just ordering her

—Come here

and she obeyed, they ordered her

—Go away

and she obeyed again, not the way people obey, the way animals obey, the owner of the café with the foosball table feeling no pity

—Her lungs are failing little by little

and it was true, what a shame, she closed things that came out of her mouth in a handkerchief and on her dirty apron that was covered with grease spots, Senhor Manelinho to my brother

—What a woman
Senhor Manelinho's wife
　　—You asshole
not to her husband, to the rack with the postcards, Mr. Manelinho's wife was heavier than he was, vaster but kept in line by the lock of the kiosk that hit her in the buttocks, the wind wants me to go away, we've known each other a long time, if by chance I thought there were thieves in the kitchen nabbing the wooden spoons or the jam pots I'd cover my ears and there wouldn't be any thieves, I'd uncover my ears and a shutter would be off its hinges, banging, my co-worker's husband studying his cigarette
　　—If I say there's shit going on in the office there's shit going on and that's the end of the conversation
　　the phone, sounding so serious, seemed to support his story, my older brother started taking off the shirt of his pajamas with the idea of a nightgown, jumping the wall and knock knock on the shutter, he stopped at the second button, gave up, buttoned it again, unbuttoned it to the middle thinking
　　—What if I'm mistaken and she calls my parents?
　　the beetle returned from the back and pestered me again, when it decides to rest I'll take my sandal and kill it but the thought of the smashed beetle nauseated me, who knows what's inside its shell, viscous things, guts, a lilac paste running out of a chalice, the words start to lose their connection, for example when I say night I want to say night but there's also another meaning that I can't recall, there is so much time until Sunday, Sweet Jesus, get through the rest of Friday, make my way through Saturday, I thought of my not deaf brother in this house but there were no food scraps, no ashes in the bucket, no mattress in the room, the relative of Dona Alice to my deaf brother

—Slug
    pointing to the bed
    —Get in bed, slug
    —Sheee saaills seeea sheells
my co-worker's face, interminable
    —Did you leave me?
myself to the pines
    —What did I do to you for you to turn your back on me?
my older brother in the mirror
    —I can't jump the wall I have a pimple on my forehead, and she'll send me away
at the same time, he was surprised by the pimple and relieved because of it, rationalizing, in the direction of the kiosk, as soon as the pimple disappears, Senhor Manelinho, I guarantee you I'll, wishing that the pimple, in addition to getting bigger, would be eternal, a pimple, if possible, that would last until vacation was over and he was grateful to the pimple
    —What luck
my co-worker's husband arranged vests in his suitcase
    —I'm not leaving you, I just need some time alone to think
the wheels of the suitcase put tracks in the carpet, he stopped every three steps
    —this thing is heavy
thank God for the elevator but the car was on a steep ramp, it will take me a half hour to get to the car and then who is going to load the suitcase in the trunk, his assistant waiting on the sidewalk, in a neighborhood of new houses and streets without names for now, scaffolds, workers, vans that unloaded crates, and a blond girl, prettier than his assistant, with a ring on her thumb in a guard house with the sign Sales, my co-worker's husband assessing the girl

—And if I hooked up with that one?
   his assistant without any ten, the ocean, derness
   —It's about time you got here
   her eyebrows arched
   —You've barely left one and now you have an eye on another?
so the blond could hear and hide in a corner full of floor plans, forms, prospectuses, in the building with unfinished stairways, pipes sticking out, black workers hauling tiles, the suitcase was hard to take out until the assistant
   —Give it here
suddenly it was easy, objects can be so malicious, what treachery, and this, without approaching the window, the ocean, a section of beach, the tin roof of the kiosk at the top of the ramp, the bird on Tininha's chimney adjusting its wings to screw them on better
   —I'm not drinking anymore
   and the moment I was going to answer him I lost him, my co-worker's husband walked defeated behind his assistant who carried the suitcase with aerial energy and comparing his body to hers he felt so humiliated, so old, short of breath, sensitive to cold, discomfort in his spine, which was getting stiffer, it wasn't the healthy teeth that bothered him, it was the number of false ones, I run my tongue on them and there's increasingly less of me in my mouth and then this knee on certain days, for no reason, is more painful to bend than the right one, his assistant he had hired as a file clerk and let him kiss her against the metal file cabinets had no false teeth, a mouth, that belonged to her entirely, smiling, fingers on his cheek, a caress that turned into a bite
   —Smartass
   escaping from under his arm and still smiling
   —We have to work, don't we?

not father, just mother in the place where the train had come from and wearing cheap clothes, smelling the tiredness of the passengers and behind on the payments for the dishwasher, ate lunch from a bag brought from home, she was wrong about the processes but what difference did it make, what make a difference was

—Smartass

what was missing, my father, who didn't drink anymore, if he was still in the café with the foosball table, with Senhor Manelinho pointing to him

—This friend doesn't drink any more

and now nobody got hit by a sandal and weighed more than lead, the doctor saluted him in returning the blood tests

—A liver like that is priceless

so that as I always told you mother, you don't have to blame yourself, we are happy, we will be happier on Sunday when my older brother finds me in the water

—Girl

not just

—Smartass

the final pinch, the energy, late letters get resolved, everything gets resolved, girl, lunch at mother's house with mismatched plates, father a corporal in the Guard that diabetes took

—Don't act sad, I didn't know him

in the bathroom, a sink under a skylight with a gasket made of boards and a bucket to help her swallow and draining directly into the center of the Tagus because it gave it the impression of hearing siren songs, mother looked at both of them, moved, superimposed blouses, not very clean, spreading her breast on the oilcloth with a few squares in the fiber, the deceased in an enamel locket at her throat, one can't recall if it was an oval or heart-shaped

—You'll treat my little treasure well, won't you doctor?
while my co-worker's husband thought
—who took a loan to buy that piece of junk?
not just the ocean, a section of the beach, for the first time my existence is clear, not to mention the olive grove beyond the chapel where the flocks, huts, my past, and my time now, what is left until Sunday at seven in the evening, the blind man with the accordion
—I can see everything
not needing a cane, his hair will grow, Senhor Leonel, relax, we, those who endure, are eternal, Dr. Clementina without stepping on me
—Good morning
not
—Back when
Dr. Clementina
my mother stirring memories
—you put on airs like your childhood friend Tininha
bringing up too many memories, the father of my father offering her his cheek
—Baby's bottom, baby's bottom
the first day of school and I was afraid to go in, stretching my arms to a woman who walks away while a second woman blocks me from running to her, ordering her to leave
—Relax, you've handed her over
the knife grinder's harmonica taking me with it, charmed, everything I need to sleep here, not even Ernesto is missing, everything I need to be comfortable, my co-worker's husband
—I'm cooked
and you're cooked, sir, all you can do is put up with it the

best you can, while you can, if you can, with a little laugh mocking him

    —Smartass

and the knee that starts to tremble, in a few months he won't be a smartass

    —Fool

and no laugh, only at the front door

    —Don't wait for me

my co-worker's husband not waiting for anyone, pulling his jacket up to his neck because of the cold in March, a treacherous rain in the window, a draft of air, without origin, blowing over his false bones, all his false teeth hurt, the real ones are still, that's why we are not what suffering begins, not illness, ideals of illness, not sadness, the idea of sadness, wake up, sir, your feet still work, not too well but they work and what's the advantage of their working better, nod off until two in the morning dreaming of Chinese knickknacks and a chandelier with two bulbs out, breathe in the perfume of the assistant who remains in the living room, and be satisfied, coming awake, knowing you exist, until there's a key under the doormat

    —Are you still there, jerk?

and a dog eyed look to beg her, resigned, to stay here, to abandon the couch working pulleys that he didn't think he was capable of, he lifted one buttock, let it fall, almost answered

    —I'm here for good

and why answer, he was there for good like I'm here for good until Sunday, brother, like your bicycle is here for good until they tear down the house and build a big house over it, maybe the pines and the blackbirds will stay, maybe there will be wind in the eves, maybe the well will be filled with rubbish so people can't drown in it, my father returning from the pantry thinking

    —I'm better
    my mother cutting the meat and potatoes for my deaf brother, bringing the bowl
    —Let's eat, kiddos
    while the pieces of bread crumbled one after the other at the head of the table and a man in a hat praised my father
    —He'll outlive us all I'm not usually wrong
    my older brother, feeling left out, smiling at me
    —Girl
    and I wearing princess earrings and petals on my nails reaching for my fork, my mother
    —Hold your fork properly
    and I pick up the fork the right way, relax, I am a schoolteacher, I have manners, I'm not afraid of Sundays, I swear, and I won't abandon you.

10.

I liked you the first minute I saw you it's just that I didn't know what to do after my husband exchanged me for, after my husband left, I was dead, see, dead, everything was dead inside me, when our divorce was finalized, I thought, without sadness or happiness, because inside I'm not sad or happy, just indifferent, now I'll have to put up with classes again, kids in front of me who will not make the effort to listen to what I say and what I can say doesn't interest them, they go to school because they have to, they don't listen, they don't learn, they don't know how to talk no matter how much they write, whispers, nudges, and I alone in front of them the way I'm alone at home, I didn't even see them, take my word, I delivered the curriculum while matters in relation to work and without relation to each other appeared and disappeared in the measure that my mouth continued to move, the gas bill, for example, that I forgot to pay and now I have to go in person to the company and put up with hours in line before they close the counter in my face, a tooth in the back of my mouth is bothering me, my stepmother, years ago, you were the one that disappeared, Bambi, and it was the arm, without wanting to, that expelled it from the chest of drawers, the Bambi from the time of my mother and I was so upset, my God, forcing it to die again, beyond the Bambi little remained of her, my stepmother got rid of whatever belonged to her, my father silent and I crying with rage, not with pity, in my room maybe from the habit of having her there without talking to her, I never talked to her, that is my mother didn't talk with me, she looked out at the street from the verandah, so thin from pancreatic cancer, before the cancer there were no words either, the only word I remember was eat and I had my mouth full, forgetting to swallow, remembering my grandfather kicking the donkey that his daughter-in-law was riding, my grandfather, to me, look at that useless beast and the water rising slowly, me, to my stepmother, don't kill my mother, ma'am, let her stay with us, the sewing basket, the apron on the hook, a comb lost under the bed that my stepmother pushed with a broom, on her knees, what a mess this place is, the comb with hairs still in it, which my stepmother plucked out with two fingers, her hands away from her body, as if it were about to attack her and she threw it in the trash, I wasn't crying for my mother, incapable of explaining what I felt for her and didn't even feel whatever happened, I think I was crying for myself although I didn't know why, my grandmother said there's no way you'll grow and my grandfather, at the other corner of the kitchen, murmured tender things to the dog that brought in the wild doves in its gums, as stubborn as the donkey, my grandfather said one day I'll tie her to my daughter-in-law and make her pull it and then he felt bad, and later he let me play with his penknife that he dug out from the depths of his pants, pulling one of the blades out and saying take it, and my grandmother pulling the knife away from me, indignant, you won't rest until the little one hurts herself, the Bambi in pieces on the floor and my stepmother, her hands held high, don't lie, going to my father and lowering her hands, your daughter broke the Bambi and my father was distracted, he hardly eats he never gave me orders, he left prison, and returned to prison, men came in civilian clothes to get him, you piece of shit Commie, they pushed my father into a car and he spent time in a kind of fort by the ocean where they took me a dozen times, my mother first and my stepmother later after showing papers, a uniformed guy rustled around in the lunch pail of food we had brought, what are you hiding here, lady, a second uniformed guy groped around more thoroughly with echoes and clanks of metal, proclaiming you're trying to destroy the country, traitors, I remember other visitors with other lunch pails, and they stuck a knife into a meat pastry, let's see what you're hiding in the dough, I remember more echoes and more clanking iron, the birds, the salt of the waves, once in a while a pause, and I with my heart in my mouth, waiting for the next time he'd take a long time to return, why do you suspend your motion, you, why does the ocean stop before it starts again, the birds themselves were immobile, the very wind was immobile, a hallway, a room, a second hallway, a second room, iron chains noisier than the water, I remember people waiting at a long table and my father standing, one eye swollen, dark spots on his shirt and a uniformed guy saying ten minutes, the swollen eye a big eyelid and a pain in his ankle that made it difficult for him to move his body forward, he stayed behind and if my grandfather helped, your knee is in shambles, my father couldn't go beyond a line in the floor two meters away from us and a gull on a post was laughing, I didn't think gulls were capable of mockery, the claws, the beak and something in its beak that stretched its throat up and down to devour it but didn't enlarge its body, the uniformed guy finally gave our lunch pail to my father, stuff yourself, for ten minutes a dark humidity, the wind, the waves without any lift, so quick and my heart beating to their rhythm, my grandmother put the penknife in the pocket of her skirt declaring my grandfather to be a mangy old fool, the guy in the uniform said the visit was over and the knees that were mush disappeared after my father, someone tapping him us on the shoulder, let's go ladies, more irons, more hallways, more rooms, a kind of loading ramp, where they delivered a man in a van, one of his hands dangling, a small bird that the caprices of the ocean confused the way they confused me, they still confuse me, I always felt like a myopic crab on the beaches, walking at random, obstinate, what would you be doing at this moment, you said I'll be back Sunday and it's still not certain you'll find the way, people with machine guns, I ask myself if they're made of plastic like the one that the boy upstairs had, the gate, and not made of plastic, if I am still they'll be real, outside of the gate there's nobody, dust, pebbles, I think of father I forget and besides this what does it mean to think of father, the bus stop is in the sun, Lisbon far away down a road in which villages, alleyways with bells ringing and a couple of lights that blinked at random, following the train for centuries, the face of a woman in a window, I won't forget her face, and the bells were suddenly interrupted, in their place was silence, a deafening and inaudible noise, I liked you from the first moment I just didn't know what to do, I saw you in the teacher's break room and I didn't approach, I saw you at the meetings and forced myself not to look at you, when they freed you and the fort was empty and my father's knee always mush, you could hear where he was because of his dragging foot, in the afternoons he'd fill the pockets of his jacket with bread crumbs and install himself in the park, next to the lake, talking to the fish with crumbs, round mandibles that rose from the mud and sank again, he didn't play cards with the others, he didn't talk with them, once a lady opened her wallet and gave him money, and my father, startled, the coin in his palm, ended up giving it to the fish, when I visited him I had the impression that a sentence was between us, his or mine but I can't say which, if we are together I almost can't remember, when you left, I lost you, all the lost sentences even if I pronounce your name, I give the sentence to the fish, father, what do I do with them, looking at your wedding ring in the café next to the school, with a soldier between us at the counter, wanting to die, I smile a greeting that wasn't a smile, it was skin tearing and when you smiled back, inside a piece of toast, the wish to die attenuated a little, your smile, without your realizing it, burned in my blood, my body leaned toward yours bothering the soldier, he stepped back and I, saying to my body, what is this, while the chains in the fort didn't stop clanking hiding the sounds of the gulls and the waves, what harm did you do, father, whom did you offend, what does communist mean, what does Country mean, once I found a wig and a pair of glasses in your drawer, put on a mask, sir, and my father, who didn't give away small change, drop that, that is his mouth moved but it took me awhile to connect it to drop that and when I understood it was he I was amazed, look, he talks, and then I was happy to have a father with a voice, the owner of the café to you saying the bill is paid pointing at me with his chin, you, blushing, thank you and I was happy that you blushed, so uncomfortable, so timid, you ran off to school, I'm late, sorry, and the way your hair bounced made me feel tender, in spite of having read in your file that you were fifty some years old an adolescent my God, at my grandfather's house there were rats at night, lying in bed I heard them gnawing in the store, any day they'll get to our fingers and eat us, that and an owl on some roof, you can't calculate the number of noises that a night in a village is made of, not to mention the trees and the anguish of the rocks, during the day they chant but at dusk their torment impresses me, many diverse languages and the wings of the insects joining them sewing them together into dozens of different cloths, my grandmother's sewing machine had the same fierce noise, after a week had gone by I waited two hours for you to finish your classes while my grandfather, examining the well, one more year if that, looking at the animals with an expression of farewell, calculating the sheep, the goats, the two or three larger animals, one more year if that and we have to sell the calf to buy another daughter-in-law, he didn't get to sell the calf, the attack came first, he was sitting at the hearth and he turned into plaster, he didn't double over, he became a thing, bubbling a thread of speech, my grandmother, not understanding, called the others useless and falls asleep like they do, after two hours I saw you leave your classes and a dizziness, a feeling of well-being, an ant hill, the rats, I was a sack of corn in the store that a thousand incisors lacerated and my grandmother, raising a shovel in her hands as she came down the stairs, I asked would you like to have a coffee and chat before you go home, you could hear the shovel hitting the sacks and one noticed the beams from the oil lamp to the middle of the stairs, not light, yellow nodules that came apart and turned not just on the stairs, on the walls too, my grandfather, containing a laugh, I run into that old woman and I laugh with disgust, pride, here we are the two of us, you looking at me as if between the movement of lips and sound the same pause that separates lightning from thunder, lingering, looking at your watch, I don't have time, accepting out of politeness to compensate for what was already paid for, according to the owner, you and me at a table with the napkin holder between us, how do they do that after you take out the one on top the other one is sticking out part way, I to you, with the mystery of the napkins in my mind, I'm not very social, you know, but I liked you and you, looking for the packet of Kleenex in your purse, your hand, that wanted to caress me, feeling sorry for yourself in spring and autumn it's always like this, the pollen, while you blew your nose, I liked you from the first moment, you pushed the Kleenex with your pinky finger and you can't imagine how much I wanted to kiss it, there were one or two women before you, two more out of loneliness, friendship, for, because a person has times when, but not for love, I swear, the nurse to my grandmother I'll ask my brother-in-law to take your husband in his car to the Lamego hospital and my grandmother starting to understand it's not because he's useless, my grandfather bubbling for a week in Lamego, that is in winter and the streets are so sad, without people because everyone is dying of cold, a tree branch breaking, a gutter in the ground that the water kept from hearing it fall to the ground, it seems my grandfather spoke one afternoon to talk about the calf and the daughter-in-law or to take an interest in the rats in the store, I don't know, my grandmother swore that he asked did you kill a lot of rats yesterday and on the weekend instead of plaster, limestone, he didn't buy a new daughter-in-law, he didn't sell the calf, a long time later I looked for the penknife and I couldn't find it, the many things you cut with it, sir, the sausage, the strings that were wrapped around the vegetables, the necks of the roosters, the sacristan's ear, me to my grandmother, what happened to the penknife, grandmother, and my grandmother put it in his vest because he'll need it under the earth with roots around him trying to keep him from coming home, who doesn't know that the poplars are mean, I had two women out of loneliness, for friendship, because when a person thinks about themself it takes up a lot of memory, but not for love, I assure you, I saved that for you or before I didn't even save it, I didn't imagine I had it, the two of us in the café next to the school, my hand on yours and yours escaping on the pretext of finding the Kleenex, after the hand episode you avoided me for weeks, a nod of the head, a quick greeting, coffee without you, the idea of lowering a coffin in the cemetery gives me the shivers to this day, the curiosity of the rest of the dead, pulling at our sleeves with anxious questions, have you seen my cousin, do you know if the vicar got better from his gall bladder attack, did my wife remarry and my grandfather, with the blade in his vest, don't tell me that you don't notice the rats, all of you, don't feel them in the corn, one afternoon in July, when I thought my husband was in Spain with the other woman and in fact my husband was in Spain with the other woman doesn't stop hurting me, I didn't want it to hurt and it doesn't stop hurting, it's not my fault, there are sensations that grab on to me, when I met you in the doorway did I hurt you by any chance and you were arranging the books in your arms, no, not arranging, you blushed, recoiled, lying I'm in a hurry, stopping by the café near the fence we'll serve you in five minutes and they served me, it wasn't five minutes, forty at the same table with the napkin holder between us not separating us, my hands were far away, yours little by little came closer, not ready to touch mine, just to talk, a deaf Sheee saaills seeea sheells and I was intrigued with the deaf boy, the breast surgery, in passing, in a casual remark and I loved you even more, what effort it took not to embrace you then and there, put you on my lap, cradle you, your husband was also away, a hippopotamus named Ernesto whose role I didn't get at the beginning and made me interrupt you, a hippopotamus, until I realized it was small and made of cloth, I said I loved being little and made of cloth and I regretted it right away in the embarrassed pause and the sugar packet twisted in my fingers, immediately correcting myself, I loved to be a rag doll because I never met a sad one, you, weighing my words, I don't know, and me to myself, maybe you've saved me, I, nattering on, I have a monkey named Jorge and we were happy, Jorge was my father's name, in the prison fort under the birds, hallways, chains, the lunch bucket, the stabbed meat pastry, one of the uniformed guards if I were in charge there wouldn't be any queers or communists, one of the uniformed guards to me, slapping his holster with pistol grip sticking out, when you grow up I'll be waiting for you here, I remember asking my mother, or my stepmother, am I a communist, me, and my mother or stepmother scolding me in front of the guards and a wave, shut up, that took a while to break, when it broke a gull was on a post letting out a screech that was not human but animal that on certain nights, in a deep sleep, still wakes me up, I sitting on my bed with a multitude of rats around me, their canines exposed I didn't think they were so sharp, bigger than those of a hippopotamus, bigger than a monkey's, I should buy a monkey and call it Jorge, I'll sleep with him, take him to work, I don't know if I can lend him to you, maybe, I'll lend him to you for a little while as long as he likes me more, look at the rats snorting in my direction, grandmother, you, more confident since Jorge disappeared, if I am still behave nicely with Ernesto and you can't imagine the effort I made to hold my hand so I wouldn't reach for yours in a handcuff made of flowers, I accompanied you to the metro where I got two friend kisses and a see you tomorrow as you walked away, tomorrow we are friends, tomorrow we are together, the roots of your hair are gray showing under the blond, as stupid as that is it pleased me, what doesn't please me about you, gentlemen, the princess earrings, the petals on my nails, your fifty years where death begins to lurk, not all of death, a piece of shoulder, a piece of torso, the promise I'll wait a few years, take advantage of it, and therefore you have time to spend with me, sitting on the same couch, looking at you, I asked my father do you think I'm a communist, father, and he was distracted, there's no prison fort any more, there are no uniformed guards, why so much silence, sir, he didn't tell me anything, he didn't ask for anything, he didn't complain about anything, the cat ate his tongue, don't worry about us and when you said don't worry about us he bent his head in the direction of the window and it was certain that not even his body was there, he returned to the bulls, the waves, and to a plainclothes cop demanding names, he couldn't lie down, he couldn't sleep, if his legs folded they beat him, the plainclothes man said gives us the names and you can sleep, mornings with you in the teacher's room between classes, afternoons with you in the café before the metro, the place called Alto da Vigia, and your older brother up there, after leaving the bicycle on the beach wall, the appearance, which made me jealous, of Tininha, the diary in the wall that a stone hid, your mother and a syphon that had to be changed agitating your father's bottles in the pantry, they didn't even need him there, they shook, calling him, tempting, fearful, because why don't we have tea at my house one of these days, it's quieter than the café, more comfortable, you I'm married, me, my grandfather smacked the calf and the calf jumped sideways, I won't be able to sell the animal and a contraction in his mustache that he erased with his finger, they worry about a calf, they don't worry about us, I felt like telling him if I were an animal you'd worry about me, he didn't worry, sir, and he almost embraced me with an embrace of the face, not the hands, and after the embrace left his face, get out of my sight, cretin, I was grateful he called me cretin, call me a cretin again, sir, and he picked up a clod of dirt and threw it at me, I need to kick you to get you out of my sight, so I went down to the orchard where there were dozens of yellow butterflies on the cabbage and the water sobbing along the irrigation pipe made of pieces of zinc, I said to you, risking it, there are three free hours on Wednesday afternoons, how about Wednesday afternoon, you mulling over the reply and I understood I had won, you with your chin on your chest, it could be, I don't know if it could be and me not breathing, you, piling papers on the desk, it could be, me with unveiled eyelids about what could be grew inside me dressing me inside, the doctor, who warned me to pay attention to cholesterol, so distant, the gas bill that was overdue was so distant, the twinge in my hip, at night, forcing me to limp through the house to reach the pills in the medicine cabinet that was so far away, my sixty-four years so distant, buying cinnamon tea, buying biscuits, buying Jorge in a toy store and installing him on the couch between us, at the first store we don't have monkeys, we have a piglet, at the second a gorilla, and a gorilla is a monkey, with interminable arms almost my size, that I forgot to pull the price tag off of, tied with a nylon thread to its foot, the feet and hands were the same or rather four horrible paws and glass eyes that weren't friendly, but furious, the sales clerk said we can't sell him because it scares the kids the way it scared me, if it squeezed my ribs it would break them, fortunately it didn't hang from the chandelier and beat its chest, it stayed still, its limbs by its side, examining the room with a quizzical lip, I tried Jorge and it didn't lift a finger, in fact just the thumbs moved independently the rest were glued together and the eyebrows were just like those of the guys at the prison ready to inspect lunch pails and poke holes into meat pies, through a half-open door a man in a torn shirt was on his knees, a guy with a machine gun, outside, asking will I hit it or not, shooting at a yellow dog that fell, got up, buckled, yelping, you can't imagine how many yellow dogs there've been in my life and on Wednesday I say to you as we leave school, you don't have to take a bus, it's ten minutes away if that, and not ten minutes, fifteen or twenty because, once in a while, there's a window display with mannequins in dresses, with rouged cheeks looking at the world from a place above us, exactly how many yellow dogs have I come across, the entrance to the building that seemed ugly to me because you were with me, the junk mail from the post office littering the floor, one of the mailboxes was warped with smeared paint, on the stairs potted plants with names I don't know, the leaves half green half gray, green near the stem and gray on the tips, you, because we are co-workers, aren't we, and we have gotten to know each other better, how long has it been since they were watered, poor things, so that tomorrow, a man who was on his knees at the prison, I'll come with a big watering can to sprinkle them, the man on his knees leaned forward and a policeman straightened him up by pulling at his neck, if we don't control you, you'll control us, you arranged your hair in the elevator mirror, numbers lighting up, one following the other, except number two was out, on the landing the door to the left with the remains of a Christmas wreath, the key turned three times to release the bolt, on the coat rack in the hall an old jacket made of rabbit fur that I took a while to acknowledge that it belonged to me, the parakeet cage in the kitchen, the living room, the Chinese furniture and Jorge in the position I had left him, come on, you didn't eat a single cookie or almond from the plate, you on the edge of your chair, prim, nervous, looking at the dragons, I pulled Jorge to my side, he's better over here, and the stupid thing was in between us, askew, I picked it up by its back, threw it across the room, you were startled and I said it's not a hippopotamus, it's a gorilla, they like violence, have you noticed, in the documentaries, the brutality with which they break everything, if I were nice to him, he'd be offended, the man on his knees appeared in my head and I added you need to pull them by the throat hard for them to sit upright, me to Jorge, if we don't finish you, you'll finish us, I ask myself if the seagulls at the prison pull out the eyes of the communists, break their skin, eat their viscera instead of this I show you the cushion to my right, the sofa is more comfortable, you are sitting the same way as you did in the chair, at the edge, with your satchel on your knees as if you were about to leave, a cookie forgotten in your hand, I asked myself and what now, Jorge's head screwed on to its body, one elbow backwards, the other sticking straight out, the price tag that I tried in vain to tear off without you noticing, the violence that exists in me, Our Lady of Mercy, in whom I don't believe, if I had been born earlier I'd torture bad guys at the prison and then immediately afterwards I'm fragile again, at your mercy and you didn't notice it, I was afraid of you and you were afraid of me, if you had met me on the beach you'd be irritated,

I bet, you and Tininha would avoid me not understanding that I'm not that girl, I'm the one who serves you tea, melts your sugar, likes you, I swear, from the first moment only I didn't know what to do, I've lost my touch, how to do it, teach me, don't leave me, and without my noticing, I said out loud, don't leave me, not in a woman's voice in a child's voice don't leave me, sixty-four years old and I don't have the strength, I swear, I've stopped fighting, I didn't return to the village, they don't remember me, an old lady in the deserted alleys, and if I were there, I'd be an old lady too, mixing with the cold, the gate must still be there in the ruins of the houses, a few stone vegetables, a few sparrows without a destination, little twigs floating in the stream, a desolation of absences, don't leave me in the October of this house and your body gave me the idea that it was closer to mine, your satchel wasn't on your knees, it was on the rug, alone, don't pick up your purse, don't leave here, and suddenly, who would believe it, your palm was on my shoulder, and mine on your waist, your thigh on my thigh, at first afraid and then heavier, it is heavier still, don't worry about hurting me, my father was still when I asked are you a communist, father, and my mother or my stepmother battling with metal in the kitchen, making more noise than usual to keep me from hearing him but hear what, suggestions, orders, throw a bucket of water at him to see if he'll wake up, look how he's waking up, stand him up and let's restart the conversation, friend, if I returned to the village there wouldn't even be a shadow on the beams, if I am still not even mine as I walk through them, bushes, steps, hurt me, the perfume on your neck is hardly a perfume, flesh, the perfume of your flesh and I am transformed by the perfume of your flesh, I'm not alone, my God, thank you for not being alone, your forehead against my forehead, my nose in your cheek, my nose in your ear, my mouth in your thieves' cave, I almost confessed that there was a boy in the village who and I didn't confess because it wasn't important, your face in front of me with Tininha next to you, no, just the two of us, Tininha and her cousin on the other side of the wall and you, without being annoyed at her, I don't miss you anymore, your eyebrows, your eyelids, your mouth, I didn't remember what a mouth tasted like, your open eyes getting ever closer, chestnuts with green flecks, with black flecks, your thumb and your index finger holding my chin or my thumb and my index finger holding your chin, which of us held the chin of the other, which of us made a kind of sound, not words, a kind of sound in our throat, in our chest, I had the idea that Jorge was spying on us and me and your hippopotamus never spied on you, my breasts against your belly, the springs of the sofa less elastic where my husband used to sit, if he called me saying I want to come back to you, I made a mistake, what would I answer, two or three of his medicine bottles in the bathroom to this day, a toothbrush that he didn't use anymore, in the glass, a jacket, the kind that detectives wear in movies, hanging in the closet, my stepmother he's a gentleman, see, accepting the flowers, freeing them from the twine, changing the water in the vase and the tulips breathing heavily or my stepmother breathing heavily, proud, a gentleman with the idea of what a lady is, your mouth on mind again tasting like cookies and little grains of sugar, you and I don't have any sense, do we, a kind of remorse, if my family dreamed and at that if you jumped rope with your feet together on the patio, it seems I'm watching you jump rope with your feet together on a patio and the melancholic answer I don't know how to jump rope, I didn't have sisters, just brothers on their knees with cars made out of leaves or throwing stones at animals, shooting at one without caring about the others Sheee saaills seeea sheells the whole time, the only thing he could say, they paid a maid to take care of him, we married them so she wouldn't leave, we promised them things even though there's not much to inherit, the apartment is old, the beach house and speaking of the house an idiot showed up, with ridiculous hair, dyed blond, admiring me leaning against a newspaper stand, you must have been some woman, as idiotic as that sounds you must have been some woman it made me feel proud, I who never found myself, Sheee saaills seeea sheells where did he find that, I never thought of myself as a woman, I remember my son, when he was little, entertained with blocks on the rug, raising his head you're so ugly, I standing in front of him almost crying, tears come to me from everywhere, my stomach, my kidneys, my eyes are the only things that stay dry, I don't need Kleenex, if I wanted to say goodbye to a train I'd have to wave my hand, the ones that pass by down below, in the village, after the corn and the elms, trains from France, according to my grandfather, where everyone lived except us, my son in Switzerland but foreign countries were just one place, they don't know us, you never happened to me what is happening now and nevertheless in holding my hand, I lying it's something new for us and now and nevertheless you're holding my hand and I lying it's something new for us, shutting Jorge's mouth so that he couldn't express his opinions since gorillas are full of themselves, the ridiculous idiot evaporated with the newspapers and October was back, I playing with your hand why don't you use "tu" with me, it started to play too, one finger, another finger, I don't think I'm comfortable and the fingers went slower, I don't know if with you, my stepmother, indignant, if your father were here, but luckily starting with him, because a bad knee that's turned to mush isn't living, is it, at the funeral men with chains from the prison and the humidity of the walls in their minds, erased, modest, their knees also ruined and what did they gain from that, there are no tomorrows that sing, there are yesterdays that have fled and narrow todays, rented rooms, a lukewarm soup to help you sleep, fifteen days on your feet until you lie down the names, out with them, my lovely, a dozen names and addresses and then, we're not bad little ones, you, what more do you want, a little angel in a crib, if necessary we'll package you up and shake a rattle in your ears so you'll sleep better, one day you'll discover you didn't have partners like us, we'll put more light in your snout, we'll help you with a few punches and until the doctor comes to examine you, how's this fool doing, doctor, he might last another hour or two, where's the syringe, your fingers climb from my hand up my arm, on the inside where it's more sensitive, I touch my breast, on the left there's a breast, on the other nothing or a prosthesis, your deaf brother in a house that I don't know where it is, on a beach, in a village, this side of the Tagus, the impression that you talked about pines, about blackbirds, your father drinking to punish I can't remember whom and to punish himself, repeating how can I be so weak and the father of your father, wearing a hat, lifting his son in the air, that kid will go far, you don't give a toss for him and nevertheless he'll go far, the idiot diminishing us, snapping his suspenders, two fine looking women, let's see, one of them swearing she's met me before but where, the beach back then was so full of people that you forget those you met and fat women were invisible, you forget that you lost your memory, I said to you weren't we better in bed and the answer, after the wristwatch, Jorge took my hand from his mouth but he stayed, the answer was, as he circumvented my ear with the fleshy part of his middle finger, it doesn't seem to me that we have time, or rather we might have time, or rather we have time, just a moment then, to beyond the bed, the spread had to be ironed, I should have remembered the bedspread this morning, woodcuts of seraphim on the wall, one of them was crippled, each one holding a candelabra, a bottle of water on the night table, trains from France with a cattle car between the others, not calves, bulls, cows, with their snouts resting in the cracks between the wooden slats with those expressions that bother me whenever I think about them, men gathered at a grave without greeting anyone, no, they greet my stepmother and me, I was going to ask them about the mornings that sing but I held back feeling sorry for their worn jackets, scuffed shoes, everyday clothes, one of them, adjusting their mourning tie, eighteen years of eating rotten fish for this, a bottle of water on the night table with an glass upside down on the bottleneck, the closet was hard to close because the door was warped, you have to push it on top until the latch catches, he brought out a pillow from the storage chest that was hidden under a diving suit with a harpoon that left me baffled because neither my husband or my son dove in their life except into shit, one day, as the train car went by, bottles of oxygen in the pantry, the pillow, without a pillowcase, with a stain of I don't know what on the fabric and smelling of, smelling not very good, where are the pillowcases, I bent over the drawers and straightening up with difficulty, adjusting sixteen vertebrae, at a minimum, with the same shove at the closet door, you unbuttoning your blouse and instead of feeling amazed I, with the diving suit in my head in search of an explanation that wouldn't come, someone walked into the wrong building and left it there, terrified that I would find live fish in the drawers, with the hole from the harpoon in their gills, writhing, or flopping in steel basins in the corner, you with your clothes at your feet in a puddle of cotton in little squares, with one ankle lifting itself out of the puddle and the other ankle following it, I peered at your shoes to see if they were wet or not, I swear, I should feel happy and I didn't know why, the communist, adjusting his mourning tie, eighteen years of eating rotten food and losing your family for this, I who lost my family in exchange for nothing, my husband with his assistant, my son reproducing himself in Switzerland, not that I miss him, I don't, that is, maybe on some nights, that is, the phone never rings, that is, I say I don't feel it and I do, the buttons of my blouse, easy until today, become a fierce battle and my bra isn't black or red, sorry, it's flesh colored, how awful, I sitting on the bed with my back to you, pulling at the clasp with my fingers and I bet there are marks in my skin from the clasp, I by your side in the sheets fearing that my cold body will displease you, the softness of my belly, the age spots, the loose skin of my arms, Jorge silent at the door showing the price tag and nodding his head, sixty-four years old, what a wreck, you wearing princess earrings and petals on your nails waiting for me on the pillow without a pillowcase, after beating it on the mattress to get rid of the dust but not getting rid of the smell, the impression that a ghost in a diving suit padded toward us slapping fins in the hall, wearing a rubber diving mask and a snorkel in his teeth, dripping the entire ocean, including drowned people and neptunes, along the carpet, in turning toward you the ridiculous idiot admitting, discouraged, they're not good-looking women, I was wrong, near a beach that I didn't know, with rocks on the other side and the remains of a boardwalk above, where it seemed that donkeys and a goat were trembling at a corner of the rocks, while the waves carved a kind of sack between them that would hold your entire family, your parents, your brothers, a bicycle, a swing, your friend, with a felt animal stuck to yours, introducing us formally, Ernesto, Rogério, a lady in a lounge chair lowering her dark glasses with her index finger asking with your eyelids who is that now, ready to call your friend in a rapid whisper that will reach me, come here, since it's my bad luck that there's no misery that doesn't reach me, my husband says I can't right now, I'll call later, and in a tone that he thought was casual, it was a mistake, and the vibration of the cigarette giving him away, in turning toward you I didn't find myself in the bed, with the blinds down and a merciful shade disguising the curtain on the wire and the disgraces of my body, these varicose veins, the lack of a waist, these flaccid muscles that in spite of the cellulite, the bones hold up, I was with my father on one of those occasions that they came to pick him up, or rather I was in my room when they knocked on the door minutes after the morning started, with the trucks from the market on the road, rattling crates of livestock and vegetables, the first trolley cars, a fierce drunk announcing to the indecisive façades that I haven't been happy for years, they banged on the door without interruption and my mother or my stepmother scuffing in slippers to the door, just a minute, the lock, voices, and a question over the voices your husband madame, not with respect, imperious, your husband, madame, I was barefoot at the door of my room, one voice to the others, and what if we took the girl too, reaching to grab me by the arm without doing it, my father in pajamas and the question over the voices not even a shirt and pants to greet the pals, one of the voices, from behind, with him, while the shirt and the pants, advising him don't bother with your hair we're not going to a party, you can comb your hair later, my father with his hands behind his back because of the handcuffs and his voice was worried, when they locked the handcuffs, they won't cripple you, I was trying to understand, my mother or my stepmother what is it this time and the question over the voices routine madame, a conversation between people who respect each other, if we go too long without your husband we get nervous, the voices and my father on the landing, on the stairs, in a car in the second row with the drunk informing them it's been years, word of honor, that I haven't been happy, the first car was empty, nobody at the stop, my mother or my stepmother go to your room in a low voice, a dog barking somewhere in the neighborhood, I back to the bed and you're in the bed, your cheek on the pillow without the pillowcase, moving slowly toward me, caressing my breast, my flank, my legs, and saying, satisfied, I thought you weren't coming.

SATURDAY, AUGUST 27, 2011

I.

On Saturdays the beach is full despite the fog, people sitting on the sand early in the morning, transported by cars that drove by the kiosk, wrapped in beach towels waiting for the sun, that is at nine o'clock, nine thirty and the fog is also in the pines, you almost couldn't see the road, you couldn't see the chapel, I was cold, I noticed, from the expression on my older brother's face, that the lounge chair was empty, he went to the window and looked out, when they abandoned the house next door he walked along the wall for a long time, disillusioned with the overgrown grass, the climbing vine loose from its metal support and a cat, owner of it all, occupying a windowsill they had forgotten to close, he threw a pinecone at the cat that jumped into the room, offended, Tininha didn't say goodbye to me, Tininha's mother didn't say goodbye to him lowering her dark glasses with her index finger, we arrived and they weren't there, a chain on the gate, the sign on the façade, for sale, in blue capital letters, one of them, with too much ink, dripping to the border of the sign, that is a year before my older brother on the Alto da Vigia, my mother to me, after a sidelong glance at the sign

—You've lost your friend

In removing the stone from the wall there was no goodbye in the diary, the meaning of sentences from remote summers that time was erasing, the memory of Tininha also being erased, what exactly did her face look like, what was her voice like and nevertheless after a long time and Tininha's face was so different, I recognized her right away in the hospital, how astonishing memory is, what we think is lost is suddenly recovered with frightening clarity, details that align in one jump, precise, complete, like the cat at the window, closing its eyes it closed itself up completely, hiding from itself inside its skin, how does my deaf brother, for example, remember things, if they are silent in his head, noises that I'm not familiar with, conversations, minimal sounds, he turned rigidly to look at us with disdain, my mother out of the corner of her mouth

—Doesn't this one scare you?

and I was scared that he'd kill us one day, always trying to say without being able to say it and walking in the hall in a frenzy of anger, suspicious of us, he looked for my older brother pulling at his shirt toward the bike and pointing at the ocean, my older brother put him on the bike and he was calm, trying the pedals without reaching them, behind the seat a metal rack and my deaf brother was holding on to my older brother, his chin on his back, riding around in circles in the yard, the way he held on to my father's pants and my mother was so pale, at the edge of a

—I'm sorry

without

—I'm sorry

seeing him, my older brother

—What is it?

And nonsense, brother, don't get angry, people are complicated, that's all, I almost have breasts, two, not one and unhappy with them, I didn't want to grow up, heat up soup, always be right and besides this if I grew up, become another person, and how would I get along with that other person, would they understand me, if I became a very big adult I'd hide in a place of adulthood so they wouldn't notice me and I'd live inside myself doing the same things I do now in spite of the fact of being a prisoner in the dark because inside people is darkness, I've seen X-rays and it's dark, only the bones are lighter and I, in the light of the bones, trying to discover the seven differences, if I stood up and became the person I turned into at the doctor's office

—I swear I can't explain doctor the sensation that they are walking in my spleen

The doctor opened it and found me in there

—What are you doing in here, girl?

My older brother with my deaf brother on the bicycle, my not deaf brother chasing the blackbirds with a butterfly net, even if he brought it down on them suddenly they'd escape, on Saturdays people you could barely see were sitting on the beach early in the morning, wrapped in towels, the ocean was invisible, just its heart, full of water, emptying and filling itself, the Alto da Vigia was also invisible, if you took advantage of the moment but if you are still it will be low tide and if you are still, when you get to the beach, the sun, or even, close to the grocery store, before you get to the beach, the sun, Senhor Manelinho's wife opening the kiosk

—Until she finally looked up

Probing the labyrinths in her head

—I'd swear I know you, but I can't remember your name

Disappointed in herself

—Am I that old?

the colitis, the glands, the tension, all I need is for my brain to go too, why the hell did I allow myself to get into the conversation about time, you get that way, very slowly at first, without our noticing, and then so fast, following the blackbirds my not deaf brother tried the lizards but there are no lizards without a hole nearby, they don't move for centuries, we imagine that they are not living creatures and you hardly expect it's theirs, the same is true about age, in fact, you're doing fine, wearing princess earrings, and in a second, unexpected disgraces and the femur that doesn't turn, what's happened that I didn't notice, you reconsider and your marriage is over, the dishwasher with a loose gasket flooding the kitchen, call Senhor Nivaldo, where's the number in my address book and the page with N and O, just that one would be missing, the dentist studying our mouth with the little mirror and Senhor Nivaldo and the dentist, in a chorus, they must be linking arms

—Even the dishwasher gasket and the molars go bad it's not just us

A few funerals went by too, wreaths of tragic flowers and unknown cousins who examine us like Senhor Manelinho's wife

—Your mother's name is on the tip of my tongue

Just what's preserved underneath, it doesn't go to the other side, what emptiness, memory with no lizards, if we are able to unstitch it a faraway voice

—You keep getting fatter

with a woman behind it

—Leave the cookies alone

and the blackbird in the hand escaping from the can before its butterfly net said

—What did I tell you, girl?

The suspicion that my father liked my deaf brother more than me, once I saw him on his shoulders, in the olive grove behind the chapel, not feeling the need to drink, and the suspicion, as long as we are on the subject, that they talked with each other, the fog started to lift at that point, a section of sand visible and you could make out the rocks, my deaf brother asked, my father answered, and then my father asked and my deaf brother answered, they got home very late, my mother

—Where have you been?

and my father already in the pantry not remembering to put him on the ground, the jam jars clinked three shelves above the clinking of the bottles, my father drinking and my deaf brother sticking his fingers in the jars so that when they entered the living room my father wiped his throat with his left sleeve and his forehead with the right where he was convinced that there were drops of sweat instead of jam, both continuing to talk until my father

—We better shut up

my brother let out a

—Sheee saaills seeea sheells

which sounded fake to me, who can prove he hasn't spent his life deceiving us, Dona Alice's relative

—He says things when you least expect it

my mother, in the clouds

—Really?

and then trembling

—Excuse me?

and my deaf brother pretending to be innocent, the night my father died there were voices in his room, one of them hoarse like his, the other, more discreet, coughing, when he realized they were opening the door the hoarse voice

—Leave, fast

and we found her sitting on the bed in front of the open window, that is in Lisbon, not on the beach, there were footsteps on the street below we don't know whose because the awning of the Thebes Bakery hid it and it disappeared around the corner where the trolleys were, my mother looking for a string on the windowsill and there was no string, calculating

—How many meters?

my father turning toward the wall in the hospital, so weak, a stomach from which tubes emerged and didn't fit in his pajamas, I to the lamps

—Father

and silence like my deaf brother's silence and at the end of the silence the gravity with which one ends a speech

—Sheee saaills seeea sheells

stretching out on the bed distanced from us, which is why Dona Alice's relative said

—He sometimes says things

and my mother emerging from her mourning, quicker than a doll from a box

—To whom?

from time to time my co-worker talks to me about a fort, the relative of Dona Alice takes a step back because the doll in the box enervated her, where it accompanied the mother or the stepmother

—Ask him

my deaf brother not noticing her and us, I look at our building from the street wondering how you climb up there, if my deaf brother could refer to my father I'm certain he would say, just as I do

—My father
even knowing it wasn't his father, he'd say my father and I used to take walks in the olive grove, on certain occasions, in his muteness, we heard perfectly my father and I used to take walks in the olive grove, it was with me, telling me stories about his life that nobody knows, besides visiting me in my room almost every week
—Son
still today visiting me in my room
—Son
my wife, already in bed
—You went in there
telling my mother
—Sometimes he says things
I who most of the time don't say things, I listen, a fort next to the ocean with a crown of gulls where my co-worker accompanied her mother or her stepmother I can't recall which because my co-worker can't remember which, visiting a prisoner without mentioning which prisoner, adding up the gulls and the waves, more waves than those on the beaches, she insisted, many more waves than on the beaches, stubborn, heavy, how did the walls hold up, when I asked which prisoner her features piled up into the center of her face
—Just some prisoner
I don't believe it was just some prisoner, my co-worker, in answering this, not to me, alone, I hear echoes, chains, drafts of air, birds, I feel foam against the chest of drawers, and if in the olive grove nobody walks with me today, tomorrow at twenty to seven my older brother
—Girl

and in my mind the olive grove is fields, a herd of goats lifting their heads to chew and they trot two or three meters on their slender hooves, no fog, the beach completely visible, and as I expected, the ebb tide, a fishing boat, its engine doing somersaults, parallel to the horizon, on Saturdays we stayed home since according to my mother with so many cars there was no space for us down there, olive grove, fields, the herd but not my father, I would have liked to hug his pants too, my nose against the cloth, some prisoner in a fort near the ocean and my co-worker looking at him through me, me in the Thebes Bakery

—Did my father come through here on a night a week or so ago?

and Dona Helena looking at me as if I were drunk, everyone knows children inherit their parents' vices, it's in the blood, if blood is the same the vices are the same, my tubercular uncle put the sickness into his kids or maybe he didn't, they were born with it, the owner of the guest house on the floor below ours scandalized by me

—Are you already twenty-three?

I, equally scandalized

—Sorry

and he didn't forgive me, angry for pushing him to

—You're pushing me to

death, I'm not afraid of dying, I'm only afraid of suffering, of pain, what a lie, I'm afraid of the Alto da Vigia, and my body, my body falling and not of suffering or pain, it's death that terrifies me, no older brother waiting for me in the water, I helpless and nevertheless I have to do it not for my older brother, for me, I don't expect they'll find me one day, I don't expect to see you with me, we are a family again because, in spite of each of us being a rat standing on its hind legs, ready to fight, bite, between us, without noticing the wounds, we were a family or I like to think so, not believing in what I think, that we were a family, the same way that I never believed that the princess earrings were real or that the flower petals were nail polish

—Just some prisoner

helping me notice, in affirming that my father, my mother, or my not deaf brother, what does it mean what the owner of the boarding house said if he met me today and he doesn't, he lives in a hospital bed in a home with a device in his throat, he listened

—Fifty-two years Senhor Tavares

and the bed balancing him with difficulty

—You want to kill me, girl?

in a home or in the shadows full of ghosts on the stairs because the tenuous ampoule, specters of guests here and there

—Do you rent rooms to dead people, Senhor Tavares?

his cane didn't end in the cane, it continued to his wrist, on his forearm, his arm, turning into wood as well, his teeth were imperfections in the wood, his eyes nodules of wood, sorry, Senhor Tavares, your hospital bed and the tube in your throat, I'm sorry I made you older with my old age, the number of creatures that our destruction destroys one by one, with luck I won't end up on the beach like my older brother, the cartilage will stay at the bottom of the ocean not shining, sunk in the mud, maybe the princess earrings and the nail polish petals will end up on the sand, what remains of me a girl leaning against a wall looking at you or if I'm still not looking at you, waiting for Tininha who doesn't come, doctor Clementina comes without smiling in the direction of the past

—That was so long ago

not surprised, at the paint, or not at the paint, detesting her mother

—Did you like my mother?

who didn't talk with her, she talked with her friends, in the lounge chair, near my older brother, how many men have you had, madam, Dr. Clementina looking at an X-ray

—Nobody liked her

without emotion or longing, the mother, now a widow, climbing into a car with the help of a driver

—Take me to the movies, my peach

restoring the eyebrows she had lost with a little mirror and an eye pencil, when the fog disappears completely and the people on the beach unwrap their towels I see her, a hat hiding the lack of locks of hair, long sleeves because her arms are so thin, the ankles, without firmness, sharp under the skin, the driver making fun of her

—Which movie, auntie?

Dr. Clementina's mother inventing eyebrows with the pencil

—It doesn't matter

no fingers, rings that jangled on her purse, the freckles on her Adam's apple, the freckles on her clavicles, Dr. Clementina's mother not to the driver, to her hope of never dying

—It doesn't matter

recriminating the crucifix in her room where the nights transformed into voyages through archipelagos of insomnia in which nobody kept her company

—Don't worry about me

the glass of water that didn't come, the lamp she couldn't reach, footsteps without origin in the hallway

—Don't dare get up

as if she were capable of getting up to whisper to her toys or eat the sweets in the cupboard, the porcelain teapot, full of scratches, that had belonged to her grandmother, always advising, solemnly
—I belonged to your grandmother, respect me
the doll she gave her for Christmas with the hanging arm, as much as she tried to push it into its shoulder, her father trying and it didn't go in, he wouldn't rest until the plastic was broken, men are such cretins
—I'll see if I can buy you another one, daughter
and he forgot, the vital affairs of adults always forget us, ask the doll
—How do you feel, Aurora?
and she, although she didn't exaggerate, the dolls, as a rule, even make our difficulties easier and encourage us
—It hurts
the way it hurts me so that any movie will do, I don't even see what's happening on the screen, I show the porcelain teapot to my grandmother
—Do you remember this, ma'am?
the grandmother, with unexpectedly light hands caress the shards
—My God
I who refuse to caress mine, I don't even glance at them, I despise them the way I despise myself, how did I fall into the stupidity of using myself up so fast, I don't remember any beach, any lounge chair, any boy, if I call Tininha
—I can't talk now, I'll call you later
so that I don't remember Tininha either, not just the clear sky, the pines are back and the circles of the gulls I don't know why, that seem bigger, made of wood and larger, with an electrical

mechanism that somebody, at some place in the olive grove or the rocks, controls, circles to the yard and their shadows on the garage roof, on the ground, the neighbor's cat jumps over one of the shadows trying to grab it and lost it, a disillusioned cat makes you feel as sorry as a person, my husband, who didn't meet Tininha's mother

—There are times I think you are crazy

that was before we got married, afterwards

—There were times I thought you were crazy and now I know you are

at the head of the table without any smile to decorate it, it was only in the dark that you didn't grumble that I was mad, when I was with you trying to be with me or when you were with me trying to be with someone else, I don't understand the reason you didn't leave, Sundays of boredom and the newspaper until you opened the door to the street

—It's suffocating in here

without you noticing my parents in the room with us, they came in through the walls, only after the door slammed you noticed them, when you paid attention to me, they disappeared

—Don't wait for me for dinner I'll be late

and they came in right away, sitting on the sofa, the armchair, the chair that they brought from the desk with a defect on the back, my father looking at the liquor cart not daring to serve himself, a sideways glance, palms on his knees, on his lapels, on his knees again, my mother raising her index finger

—It seems you didn't die for once and for all

my co-worker, with a sigh

—Just to say that I love you if your husband comes home say it's the wrong address and I, even alone, answered that it was a mistake, you got the number wrong, sir, while Tininha's mother dozed in the movie affirming

—I hate people who sleep in the movies

her forehead on the driver's shoulder rubbing a place between the buttons on his shirt before losing her fingers in there

—My peach

and the hat fell on to her nose, when I was little Senhor Tavares had a foreign wife who was always washing the stairs, if a neighbor

—Hello

she hid behind the mop head, I still don't know how she fit in there

—I don't speak preteguês

the sun frightened her so much that it dissolved the spots of light until it created

midnights, she was the one who sent the sun away although she followed it up the stairs, running after it on the walls, Senhor Tavares lamenting

—So much darkness tires me out

but the foreign wife brought the ordeals of the mornings when the clarity touches things lightly, now the bench, now the stove, the woman crouching in a corner of the kitchen protecting herself with her arms

—I don't speak preteguês

almost Sunday now, look at the clouds over the mountains, the Moorish castle with one of them on the battlements bent over with the weight, curved walls that stood up straight as soon as the cloud left my deaf brother

—Father

no
—Sheee saaills seeea sheells
my deaf brother
—Father
we don't believe it
—Repeat that
he nervous with so much attention starts to shout and shout, louder than the gulls and the dogs in the pine grove when a neighbor got sick, long howls that weaken our guts and we tried to hold them in until my mother pushed them back inside and stitched us up
—Don't move
protesting
—Those dogs
my stomach full of white thread, on the breast that I'm missing the stitches are brown, that is at first they were brown and now there are none, a scar that continues to evolve well we'll take it off and then your breast will be good as new, how abnormal to have a new breast at fifty two years of age, my deaf brother, nervous with so much attention, running away, stopping in the middle of the hall, turning around with his eyes covered because that way we wouldn't see him, peeping through his fingers until he flattened himself against Father's pants while my father's hands, like the bottles, with his knees on his lapels, on his knees again, my deaf brother raising his head, we waiting for him to say
—Father
and he, in the same tone as
—Father
rounding each syllable, enlarging the letters, applied, serious, one of his palms on his throat and the other on another throat

that nobody could see, approximating the sounds, my deaf brother, radiant
  —Sheee saaills seeea sheells
  while the gulls distanced themselves from us and Tininha called me, not Tininha, a shutter that banged with the wind in spite of the fact that the cactus flowers were still, along road to the Moorish castle there were immense trees, ageless, if we wanted to ask them something I don't know what to the trunk, a drowned lung or a secret larynx
  —I don't know
  beyond the trees a fountain was dripping, a broken hose, in a shell of silt where a little white flower was being born, my older brother and I looking at the minuscule petals under the surface of the water, she had lost one of her eyebrows, in the car again
  —Take me home, my peach, I need a massage on my kidneys
even so, I guarantee you
  —Take me home, my peach, I need a massage on my kidneys
  besides the trees and the fountain dozens of frogs were in the branches, I didn't dream that there could be frogs in branches, I thought they just lived in lakes and bogs, on the tip of each phalange a little sac and its throat pulsed, pale, I brought a bottle to my father whose hands didn't stay still, trying to perfect the knot in his tie twisting it more, he took out his handkerchief because of the sweat on his brow and dabbed his eye with it, he lifted it again and not to his forehead, his lips, he didn't seem to recognize us, he looked at us strangely, I screwed the bottleneck into his throat and I'll remember to the last minute the sound of the glass against his false teeth, my mother to me
  —If he dies again, it's your fault
  my husband frightened that I had spilled alcohol on the floor

—Now I know you're crazy

he had a cousin who made it rain in Spain, she walked on tiptoes on the verandah giving commands to the clouds

—To the left to the right again to the right now straight ahead

Until his uncles committed her to a house where she couldn't make it rain anywhere, she made paper windmills with the others, if they asked her about the rain, she continued to cut out the paper

—There's enough there

and she applied the sails to the windmills sticking them on toothpicks, my husband to me, suspicious, the room with the windmills has a shutter on the ceiling, the cousin and her companions wear identical smocks, one of them has a daisy in her hair, a mulatta laughing to the shadows

—You don't say

when nobody spoke, a lady suspended a string of nonsensical sentences informing my husband, then a child

—I'm praying in Latin

so that a child, not he

—Do you also make it rain in Spain?

surrounded by dozens of windmills the size of a palm that, blowing hard, moved their sails or rather in a quarter of a circle by pushing it and it was a drag, an attendant

—We'll continue tomorrow, my dears

and they filed out past my husband and his parents, there went the daisy, the prayers, the laughter, the last one, white haired, told them a secret

—I'm pregnant by a judge

the attendant removing sieves

—She's been pregnant for at least twenty years

and on the way out we went by them in the cafeteria, that

had no forks or knives, just spoons, to eat with, napkins at their throats, aluminum bowls, each napkin had an embroidered windmill and the sails of the windmills were embroidered, those did turn, my father after the bottle, putting the napkin in his pocket
—I even feel younger
declaring to my deaf brother
—When we go back to the beach, we'll go by the olive grove
the mother of Dr. Clementina to the driver
—My peach
who with an open blouse squeezed her ribs, pink curtains, pink covers, pink napkins, an engraving with a couple kissing, she wearing high boots, he in a cap and a legend in French Mademoiselle Et Son Chauffeur, a woman inclined on a pillow, lace around her waist, the man with a moustache and shiny hair, that is in black and white, not in color, with a yellow stain on the bed canopy from which little balls fell down
—Lower, my peach
while Dr. Clementina, busy with an inert patient, took blood from his arm, the needle missed the vein, she found it again and impatient with the inert figure
—You don't stop lie still
with princess earrings and petals on her nails, thinking, without wanting to, about Rogério which she had forgotten, and getting angry at him
—That's all I needed
and with Rogério she came from the house next door whose name had been lost and occupied bed eighteen, the turns that the world makes and shouldn't, she didn't have the right to bother me here, force memories on me that don't interest me, I don't want to think about. my childhood, my father washing the car,

the idiot with the enormous toes in his sandals that kept me from feeling sorry for him, married to a creature like my mother, what stupidity, always undeserving of my father if he really was my father

—You're a dope

because of the life she had, the brother-in-law of my father, all attention and fawning, with him she played backgammon and whom she called

—My peach

the Australian partner who suddenly stood up straight, a little disheveled and with orphan hands, when I entered the room, with what seemed like lipstick on his neck, which seemed like tooth marks on his cheek and the one in bed eighteen throwing me, in the name of what, the brother who didn't talk spying on us or smiling from the flowerbeds, the grandfather praising her father lifting him like a trophy

—He'll go farther than anyone, this one here

and he went to the pantry where he collected bottles, a great feat, inside the embarrassment of her father an excuse

—I did what I could, sir

like my father did what he could and couldn't except collect the money from the family business and shake the car mats that my peach drove in Lisbon, my mother in the back seat wiping the corner of her mouth with her little finger

—Take me wherever you like, my peach

not my actual peach, my peach from before, several of my peaches one after the other, my mother lowering her dark glasses to my older brother in bed eighteen

—What a strange boy Tininha you've got to bring him over to meet me

and I didn't bring him over, I pretended not to hear her and forced Rogério to pretend he hadn't heard her as well, I to Clementina because it was Clementina's mother
—A lady
whose caliber I can guess taking her daughter into account, how I detest the name badge on my smock, for a while I wore it on my pocket and the nurses didn't call me any name until the hospital director said
—It's regulation, doctor
so that I was always
—Doctor Clementina
a revulsion, nausea, feeling like barking at them, not speaking, barking at them
—Don't call me that
and what could I do about it, accepting, I hate bed eighteen mutilated from, what fear of the words, cancer, to the point of forgetting her name, it's not a ribbon, I forgot it, when she came to me with the past, the stone in the wall, the diary we wrote together, I could only answer
—That was a long time ago
wanting to step on her until the past died, my peach, die so that it never existed, there's my life today and that's enough, no husband washing the car, two children for whom, thank God, I don't have time, after a long dinner that begins to take effect, waves and waves, Senhor Manelinho from the kiosk
—You'll be a good-looking woman when you grow up
and good looking my ass because I pull the sheets up and before the voice of my mother answers in me, I repeat
—My peach
fortunately, I fall asleep.

2.

When it rains at night there's a different smell in the house, the vacant lot in front of the well, which is strewn with stones, loose tiles, and garbage, you approach and it seems to encroach on the yard, the blackbirds hide and I don't know where they are substituted by dragonflies and beetles, the director to my co-worker and me

—You two don't set a good example for the school

the director is sitting at his desk, the two of us are standing next to the chairs where he didn't ask us to sit down, on the wall is the Cape of St. Vincent in Sagres and the Infante, Prince Henry the Navigator, with crossed arms saying farewell to the fleet, when it rains at night there's a different smell in the house, not of clothing, not of people, not of food, getting smaller in the distance, sailing in the picture, not of wet earth, the smell, which is no longer in the pantry, is with me, it's got what I brought to eat during these days, and that I haven't touched, on a loose shelf, not warped, loose, the nails are missing on the left, the director, holding a pencil in his two ands

—I appeal to your maturity and your decency

and a spot on his lip that he would best show to a doctor, a smell of abandonment and mold, nodules on the ceiling, a floorboard has gotten loose, the money it would take to fix this place up and if I am still it's impossible to fix this place up, all of them have gone forever, this house was sold, even the cactus along the wall they will certainly pull up and they will replace the wall itself with a fence the way it should be, maybe iron bars, trimmed hedges, plaster decorations, maybe they'll buy the house next door and put a rich people's house there, with two floors, a terrace and a patio, taking up all the space, an umbrella on the terrace and a man in a bathing suit serving himself from a pitcher and smoking, tricycles in the garden, butterflies, the director, assessing us with half-closed eyelids, exploring with his tongue what was on his cheek, a gap in his teeth, anxious to use his little finger without using it so as to maintain his authority, we had barely abandoned the store the little finger, leaving the pencil, digging, digging, maybe a mirror was guiding his nail, maybe the gum sucked vigorously, I regret not spying on him at recess, a new house next year, a dog, near the remains of the swing, that noticing my presence takes off at a trot afraid a piece of wood or a can tossed at it forcefully, I never hit them, my aim was always off, I stomped my foot on the ground and that was enough, poverty taught us to fear people, I met several that walked on just three legs, the fourth folded into the air, withering, the director without abandoning his tooth

—What happens outside of school is none of my business but the rumors going around here disturb me

since his staring eyes were trying to decipher the state of soul of a molar, if he wanted to frighten me, he frightened me with the spot on his lip, I was about to say

—That spot there
  but I gave up on trying to warn him, it was a question of time, somebody, one day sooner or later
  —It wouldn't be a bad idea to show that spot to a doctor and then, yes, the apprehension, the fright
  —What spot?
measured in the bathroom, on tiptoe, stretching his chin toward the fogged mirror that prevented him from seeing clearly with a towel, when it rains at night there's not just a different smell, the house is different losing sounds and echoes, the rain enters your sleep changing the plot of our dreams, we return to the surface and come up against the shutters, the certainty that they're calling us with a harp of raindrops and we sink again taking a trace of music with us, or rather not exactly with us, disappearing and nevertheless the member of the harp touches the silence, in the building almost in front a person I can't identify played in the afternoon on one of the floors, but which one, my God, making mistakes and starting over, the same cadence interrupting itself against the wall of the same note incapable of passing it, you heard a metronome to the left and the right in a cardiac anxiety
  —A second fainting spell is coming on
  an invisible eraser wiped away the sounds and wrote over it making spelling mistakes in the usual chord, approaching the errors in a slower rhythm, swelling its chest for the leap, missing and falling again, the director examined the spot every ten minutes hoping that in the intervals it had disappeared by itself, a blemish, a scab, not a serious spot, he tried to deceive it by focusing on his nose or his eyebrows, convinced that his lack of interest would make it give up and find another victim who

would get more upset, the director starting, the rain stops and the blackbirds come back, two in front of the house, three near here, one of them with a white spot on its breast, the first blackbird with a white spot that I've seen so that maybe it's not a blackbird, a bird that sang like them and if it's another bird what is it called, the director poising the pencil aligning it with the blotter on the desk with the points of his index fingers, the fleet is so far away that you don't see it anymore, you saw the Cape of St. Vincent at Sagres and the Infante with a kind of ribbon on the brim of his hat

—I don't want to hear any more rumors

me thinking what do the blackbirds eat, seeds, grain, lizards, occasionally my not deaf brother at the door without leaving the doormat

—I don't want to see anyone

almost the director

—I don't want to hear any more rumors

only that in secret, without a spot or a tooth, a shadow on the threshold, fearful that the huts would start to burn, my mother brought the change purse that opened and closed with a snap that accompanied me from the time I was born, if I pay attention I can still hear it, five blackbirds in all, no, six, I hadn't seen one of them, between two pines, on the ground, tail feathers in the air indicating they were happy, she rummaged around in the change, started to pick it out, my not deaf brother

—Hurry

before the gunshots in the hallway, at the entrance, and the sobs of the chickens that the soldiers ran after, my not deaf brother going down the stairs to meet the army truck that waited for him on the street, according to my mother there was no truck on the street

—What can I do?

    the cars of the neighbors along the avenue waiting for Saturday, I didn't know what the blackbirds ate just as I didn't know where they made their nests, they don't seem mysterious and they are, they hide everything, my mother

    —If your father were here

    how deluded you are, ma'am, if my father were here nothing, did he ever help you, he hasn't worked for centuries, he'd sit on the sofa twiddling his thumbs and thinking of the pantry, pressing his palm against his liver, the swollen ankles keeping him from putting on his shoes, and he not moaning, without protests, he limited himself to crumbling bread at dinner, my deaf brother with Dona Alice's relative, I alone with my parents, they sold a silver cup, they sold the tureen, the spaces between bigger things, my husband, who was still not my husband, visited us on Sundays, a perfume for my mother

    —This will turn you into a young woman

    a check for my father, sticking it in his vest, in a casual movement that he didn't notice, you could see my mother looking at the check during the entire lunch

    —You never know with your father

    fearing that he, when he found a piece of paper, would tear it up or throw it away, I think a dozen blackbirds this Saturday morning but where did they come from or maybe they came out of nowhere, born in the flower beds, they came to say goodbye

    —Goodbye girl

    the way I took my leave from longing for Ernesto

    —See you tomorrow

    although you might think they don't know about my older brother, on the Alto da Vigia, the director

—Don't force me to

and interrupting himself, dignified, not even the Infante was in the picture now, just the cape, he waved us out of the room, when she took the check out of my father's vest pocket my mother said to my husband, even though he wasn't my husband yet

—Thanks, dearie

with the diminutive endearment making me even more ashamed, I accompanied him to a room in a guest house out of gratitude and the owner looked at me reprehensively

—Do you think this is a place for a serious girl?

next to an old woman who turned the knobs of a prehistoric radio

—I can't hear shit

furious with her own deafness without noticing us

—All I need now is to go blind

with a plate of beans on her knees, everything was so dark, so shabby, I was almost wearing princess earrings, confused, certainly the owner said to the director

—Do you think this is a place for a serious girl?

with the picture of the fleet on the wall and a pencil in his hands

an almost vertical stairway where the radio followed us hissing loudly, a woman plucking chickens on the porch under a provincial Venus de Milo whose eyes criticized me

—Are you going to stop being a serious girl, you?

a second woman to an older man, at the entrance of an alcove with a pillow and a mattress

—Are you sure you can take it?

and between her legs, running fast, a cat, my husband, still not my husband, as nervous as I was

—I don't have a lot of experience

in a childish voice
—I don't have a lot of experience
me feeling sorry for him and for me, more alcoves with pillows and mattresses
—Wait a minute
and they changed them, we were very upset
—It won't take long, will it?
it's for those things that tears come but they didn't for me, what locked up inside me that keeps me from crying, if I found my mother
—Don't you have any pride?
and she kept cleaning what was already clean, in her eyes, without my expecting it, my name, with such intensity I was forced to shut up, or rather with such intensity that I
—I'm sorry
and what was locked inside me became unlocked, not sitting on her lap, sitting her on mine, telling her stories, making her laugh, guaranteeing her that we, as if it were possible to guarantee that we, my grandfather to my mother, smacking father's behind
—You're holding a gentleman
and so many bottles in the pantry
—It wasn't my fault
it wasn't anyone's fault, forget about it, we're alive aren't we, I consented out of gratitude to my husband, still not my husband, undressing me tugging at my clothes, maiming me, so tense, don't be afraid I'll handle it and I'll handle you, don't despair, it's fast, a few moments and it's over, the window didn't exist, there was a crack without a window frame and behind the crack there was siding, my husband, not yet my husband, took off his jacket and shirt

—Where do I put this stuff?
   not even a hanger, a hook, a nail, a helpful doorknob, a second woman to an older man, patience there are good people in the world
   —Calm down a little and try again
   the older man remnants of clothing, a rasp of the throat, more remnants, an object that fell, a nervous pause, the second woman
   —It was my shoe, don't pay any attention
   my husband, still not my husband, didn't take his off as he struggled with his belt buckle, my husband, still not my husband, in an attitude that Ernesto would understand
   —You don't have to pay me for the money I gave your father
   and I was ready to like him, I swear, ready to embrace him, I spoke to Tininha and we could have been friends or three as children, we said to you
   —Bring this bring that
   and you brought it, the buckle got loose by a miracle, I to him
   —Come here
   even wearing shoes and with his belt around his knees come here, it might hurt, it might not hurt but that doesn't matter if it hurts a little, come here, when it rains in the night there's a different smell in the house, the empty lot behind, in front of the well, my co-worker
   —We won't stop seeing each other, will we?
   made of stones, tiles strewn around, most of them broken, garbage, we seem to enter the yard and I say to my co-worker
   —No
   how is it there were no drops of blood and no pain, a sensation of being torn open that got better little by little, the second woman to the older man

—Wait, I'll help you

I said to my husband, still not my husband

—Let's get dressed fast

and he, prone on the mattress, hiding his face from me, his shoulders trembled, his back trembled, one of his shoes tapping the floor

—I wasn't any good

while my cousin made paper windmills sticking the sails on toothpicks, each year they were more crooked, more hollow, an absent smile and on the other side of the smile a vacuum, how do you empty people out, the director in the bathroom, next to the office that said Private, fussing with the molar that the cloud of his respiration took away from him, when he got home he went to the kitchen to find a spoon, he gave his wife the spoon

—Look inside my mouth

the Cape of St. Vincent in Sagres was like the Alto da Vigia but without donkeys or goats, a black majesty where the Infante received the world from a few exhausted bearded men with mussels in their drawers

—Take Madeira and the Azores

the director on his knees in front of the couch where his wife with an open magazine under the lamp peered at his gums

—That's all I needed

an inspection that took seconds

—You're fine put the spoon in the drawer

the director doubting it, placing the spoon on a table and the wife not turning away from the magazine

—I said put it in the drawer

the drawer was open, a compartment for the knives, a

compartment for the spoons, a compartment for the forks, the wife guessing

—In the drawer not the dishwasher it's not dirty

—Please don't watch me

me thinking that we had missed being happy by a thread, what did we do wrong, my co-worker and I in the teacher's room where, when they saw us, first in low voices and then louder, pretending they didn't see us, we heard the children at recess, calls, running, one of the blackbirds half a meter away from me on Tininha's wall, not the one with the white spot, one that was all black, authentic, that had no eyelids, diaphragms of a camera that closed in a circle, they don't eat seeds or grain or lizards, they eat the frogs from the trees that even if they are speared by their beaks, keep wriggling, my husband, not yet my husband, assessing me out of the corner of his eye

—You're not mad at me

at the same time uneasy and proud, thinking of his friends, telling them don't tease me, finally without envy

—Just that?

so that he was less sure of himself, contemptuous, when it rains at night there's a different smell in the house, my husband, who was not yet my husband, reeking of lotion

—We'll come back to the guest house next week

dragonflies, beetles, insects with six wings on the edge of the puddles, they lay eggs in the mud and after a few days they break the gelatin sac and fly to the lizards waiting for them with outstretched necks, a frog in the flower bed dilating its pouch, I walked down from the kiosk where Senhor Manelinho was interrogating a crony

—And did the broad stay?

the crony taking a moment to emphasize his answer
—What choice did she have
the impression of having seen him, when I was little, curved under the weight of a carton selling wafer rolls on the beach, umbrellas, wearing white shirt and pants that guarantee hygiene, in the afternoon he delivered cannisters of gas with a handcart I still remember the sounds of metal hitting metal, the quantity of memories that will accompany me to the end, the way he carried the cannisters and the burlap he wore to protect his neck, from today to Sunday at twenty to seven how many hours are left to me, I will count them as if time were measured in hours, I won't count them, I give up, my deaf brother is eating a wafer roll that's full of sand and my mother to the next-door neighbor, cleaning it off with her towel, tearing it into pieces
—Do you see the cross I bear?
handing the wafer back to my deaf brother
—We bought this for you so you could eat sand and you don't even notice the difference
I with sand molds and a bucket of water, lining up sand cakes on a board
—Are you served, ma'am?
a blue bathing suit, a white nose, the hat, my mother refusing
—No thank you, bon appétit
a scrape on my knee forming a scab that I picked at, the pleasure of picking at scabs will also follow me, the hard surface coming loose and the red flesh underneath, my mother giving me a smack
—Do you want to get an infection and have them cut off your leg?
me jumping on one leg, not upset, happy, I tried to climb

stairs that way and also tried to go back home jumping on one leg and I got tired, when I put it back on the ground my leg was like new, it seemed they had just given it to me, fresh from the store, at this point you can't imagine the happiness of an unexpected leg, when it rains at night the smell in the house is different and you felt the wind, waiting for I don't know what to exist in the pines, not down here, without ruffling anyone's hair, I'm afraid of dying, just in the treetops, rustling the pine needles, searching, like fingers that rummage through papers and coins in a pocket looking for keys, the wind, what does it look for in me, talking endlessly, I

—Excuse me?

taking care of myself and on the way back I am accompanied, I lack not even the pine trees, very thin insects, remembrances, memories, the used gas tanks waiting in the storeroom, you turned the spigot and there was a dull whistle

—We're empty

when we returned to the guest house, the proprietor, resigned,

—You acquired a taste for it

the old woman with the radio knobs was holding an ice pack to her cheek, no compassionate voice helping an older man

—We almost did it, what a shame

the stairways, the alcoves, the mattresses, the Venus de Milo not looking at us, what part of Greece is Milo and what does it matter if I've never been to Greece, the pharmacist's wife, in Lisbon, Greek, always with a poodle on her lap, majestic, immense, a fine-looking woman, Senhor Manelinho, you can't even dream of what you lost, if she walked along the beach, a cigarette in her mouth, the whole world in ecstasy, the waffle cone seller dropping his box

—I don't believe it

a necklace of gigantic pearls that I thought was very expensive and my mother

—Knock-offs

my older brother almost kneeling as if he were in front of the litters of a religious procession, my husband, who was still not my husband, looking at me, looking at the mattress, looking at me again imitating the courage he didn't have, there was the lotion, there were the friends who would stop teasing him

—Let's get to it?

and we went to it, clumsily, soullessly, no sensation of tearing, no pain inside me, I

—Calm down

my husband, still not my husband, face down on the mattress, the shaking shoulders, the shaking back, one of his shoe tips tapping the floor

—I'm no good

my left arm was asleep because his elbow was digging into me

—You're digging into my arm with your elbow

and out of politeness I didn't say, your face on mine is full of creases, lose them, something humble slipping out of me, my husband, still not my husband, on his knees over me, as I lay supine, it gave the impression that he was victorious

—What about that?

not a kiss, why kisses, I'm a man, kisses are for the movies or quickly on a corner, looking from side to side

—I don't see anyone

on the way home I suspected there was lotion on my skin too, my co-worker

—How long have you been married?

and suddenly I don't know, I have to do the calculations, I don't remember if my father went to the wedding, I remember my mother and my deaf brother with one of his collars sticking up and Dona Alice's relative to the side, renting our first apartment, so small, a drafty box, the one we live in was bought with a mortgage that I don't see an end to, the Greek wife of the owner of the pharmacy is lost, when she walked it wasn't her buttocks that rose and fell, it was the walkway, her buttocks were fixed, she combed her hair at the window not letting go of the poodle, when her husband came out, in his lab coat on the stairs, proud, I've never seen such thick lenses, such a big chin, his nonexistent eyes in the thickness of the lens, my co-worker kissing my neck where my curls end

—Doesn't that make you shiver?

and I didn't shiver, it was a wet discomfort, increasingly less important when they touched me, so not to disappoint her I agreed as I agree with my husband, with all of you, thinking about whatever or not thinking, I don't think, the owner of the pharmacy went back inside, entrenching himself behind the counter surrounding himself with cabinets with curative odors, a scale where a customer weighed himself, we get fat, we get fat, the era of elegant figures is over, a frosted plaque, Laboratory, in which he stored our health in capsules filling them with a little spatula, tongue out, to help him get it right, the powder that was left over was swept into an aluminum shell

—Doesn't that make you shiver?

to be honest it doesn't make me shiver, when I wake up at midnight and the Greek wife comes to mind I have the impulse to ruffle her hair, pick up the poodle, watch her walk around the room, poking the bread, and sweetening her coffee, in a month or two another woman in my house in my place, I hope, without

my clothes, an object, a vestige, my belongings at the entrance of Catholic charities, waiting to be given away to the poor, the other woman who will take my place
—Don't they take these anymore?
until the parish van frees me of it and then starts to move the curtains, the furniture, the trunk I liked, the other woman to my husband, not my husband anymore
—Don't you prefer my taste?
not tenderly, defiantly
—Don't you prefer my taste?
the one he visits when he arrives late
—A terrible accident
or
—You wouldn't believe the traffic
or the company that gives continuing education courses on weekends in a hotel outside of Lisbon, he doesn't tell me where it is, my co-worker
—When does he go?
radiant, a new nightgown, cleavage, liquor, if it rains at night there's a different smell in the house, the empty lot behind the house, in front of the well, when I go inside the room and I guarantee, word of honor, I'll miss the smell, my husband, not my husband anymore
—Of course, I prefer your taste
forgetting the guest house, the nervousness, the
—I'm no good
week in Modelo running on the beach throwing seaweed at each other, you took my hand, we sang, nights of unknown sounds around us, not threatening, accomplices, you kissed my neck without asking

—Doesn't it make you shiver?

and unlike my co-worker, you made me shiver, you know, no uncomfortable wetness, a jolt in the spine, I pulled your neck to mine

—Do it again

your shoulders pressing on my chest, your hands finding me, a gull on the verandah with unhappy feet, while my heels spur your buttocks

—Deeper

and why two pillows, one is enough, the other one is on the floor, drinking water at five in the morning, while you slept, feeling tender toward you, so defenseless, so, it makes me pause to confess it, so small, turn to me, let me wrap you up with all of this, which seems immense, my belongings in the hallway that the Catholic charities van takes away, the other woman throwing your wedding ring into the garbage

—This finger is mine now

with the name I had engraved, his skin annulled the letters and the imprecise date, before school, the son we lost, my breast surgery, I told you about my diagnosis after dinner and your eyes were on the ceiling, I've never encountered eyes that looked at the ceiling for so long, and your hands opening and closing, wrinkling the napkin, how strange faces are when the features stop belonging to them, changing places before they go back to their place, and if in this moment if deaf brother offered me the cone wafer full of sand I'd eat it all, my husband's mouth, not my whole husband, or my whole husband except for the mouth that didn't make a sound

—Are you sure?

astonished that the house was the same, the trees were the way they always were, the same buildings, what seemed like his voice or became his voice because of the traces, the teeth, the tongue accompanying it

—What now?

and when it rains at night you hear the ocean better, the water in the syphon sounds like the waves swelling and receding, the foam that boils, disappears, returns, fisherman wearing rubber boots with two or three fishing rods anchored in the sand, little bait boxes where the worms wriggle, the blackbird with the white breast, and therefore not a blackbird, the branch within my reach, first the left profile, then the right, then the tree canopy swallowed him up, I was about to say it swallowed me up but I corrected myself in time, and now they will check me into the hospital on Thursday and I'll be fine, don't worry, one of the bulbs in the lamp blinking in agreement

—Don't worry about me

so bring the ladder from the pantry and fix it, that's what they'll do in the hospital, you'll see, open the ladder, climb five steps and fix me, the check in my father's jacket, my mother removing the stopper from the perfume bottle and shaking her forearm to bring it to her nose, the ease with which women do this in a store, extending their forearms to each other

—Too weak?

and out of gratitude for you I should confess that when you asked me

—What now?

I wanted to say I'm sorry for my rudeness, I'm not joking, for getting cancer, my co-worker pressing me against her

—That was centuries ago

the way my older brother passed, right, like my father, without answering me in the nursing home, he passed, he didn't spend the week in Modelo running with me on the beach throwing seaweed at each other, broken whelk, pebbles of the whitest porcelain, shells, I don't know what that I can't remember, little pieces of bone, you gave me your hand, we sang sometimes, I hadn't learned all the verses, just the refrain, so that I waited for the refrain dancing around you, I wasn't such a great dancer, really, I can't harmonize my body like the reeds when the wind searches for them, nights of unknown sounds, I found them unthreatening, accomplice, and finally when they insisted

—The day after tomorrow

terrible, when the gurney went by your expression was the way you looked in the guest house, I with an IV in my arm waving to you with my fingertips and your fingertips waving back, didn't you find the transparent surgical cap ridiculous, didn't you think I was ugly, Senhor Manelinho saying about me, disdainfully

—That one, a good-looking woman?

lights, people, don't move, friend, I wanted to ask

—My husband

as strange as it seems I wanted to ask for you, not that you were in the hall, I don't know where, that you'd be with me, kiss me on the neck and I'd shiver, seriously, shivering, a jolt in the spine, holding your neck

—Again

not out of kindness, desiring you once more, your hands lowering to find me, my heels spurring your buttocks

—Deeper

my heels wanting to hurt you

—Harder, deeper

the owner of the guest house

—They've taken to it, those two
and we took to it, ma'am, the people in masks around me but wearing caps that were less ridiculous than mine, one of the masks
—Count to ten slowly
and I remember counting one, counting two, counting half of three, you can't even imagine how much we took to it, after half of three an abyss, like starting Sunday, or rather the high tide at twenty to seven, an abyss, I arrive at the Ponto da Vigia and I don't even feel myself fall, Ernesto
—Is this necessary?
it was really necessary, Ernesto, as much as you search, you'll not find a better solution, my deaf brother on my father's shoulders, not me in spite of the princess earrings, in spite of you saying to me
—Girl
and incapable of touching me, you answer, with sincerity, you were never able to touch me, of course, what you put into the world in sandals was never able to touch me, only my older brother picked me up to sit me on the bicycle frame and ride with him to the beach ramp, so fast despite my mother
—Careful
his chin rubbing against my hair, one of my hands on the steering wheel, the other grabbing his shirt, my older brother, if it weren't for the waves, locked in a fortress, on his knees in some room, my older brother, my
—Bro
and I bet that on Sunday, at seven o'clock, if you tell me
—Count slowly to ten
I will count one, count two, I'll count half of three, starting at half of three I'm in Moledo running on the beach, throwing

seaweed, and finally, it's not that I didn't want to, it's that I couldn't make myself say to you, my love.

3.

There is another bird here besides the sparrows and the blackbirds that's been calling to me forever, now on a branch at the corner of the house, now in a well inside the walls, sometimes in the bottles in the pantry, sometimes on the gate, how many times did I say
—Don't you hear it?
and everyone would stop to listen, their foreheads wrinkled with attention, the bird calling louder and they
—I don't hear it
looking at me as if I were crazy and I'm not, there he is, look, he flew from a pine tree to my mother's sewing box, you open the sewing box, and there's nothing in it, and nevertheless, even though you don't see it, it's there calling me, there and on the wall, on the swing, in the apple tree, smaller than the blackbirds and bigger than the sparrows, when I arrived yesterday and I thought it was lost I heard it in the hickory tree that didn't grow, a few strands of moss and that's it, it was afraid of the waves, I asked it
—Are you afraid of the waves?
and the answer didn't come, you know it's very rare for hickory

trees to talk, if at all, or in the eventuality that they feel bad
—I don't know what's going on with me
the acacias are so talkative, the elms laugh a lot, but the hickories are still, this one has almost no nuts at the top, a kind of trunk, half a dozen branches that don't give up and aren't alive, one doesn't understand why they don't fall to the ground, you think with the wind they'd break, and they still hang on, not even
—I'm supposed to be a hickory tree
they affirm, satisfied with staying two meters from the kitchen, a little leaf in August, not even green, that the next day the hickory was sorry that it had, and got rid of it quickly
—Where's your leaf?
and it ate it, if I could I'd eat my nose that wrinkles without my consent when I'm not happy
—Are you happy?
I answer
—I am
and that's a lie, all my features affirm
—I am
and my nose betrays me
—You're not
they don't notice the nose
—It's obvious you are
I get angry at it
—One of these days I'll give you to a starving child
the pines telling my mother and my mother
—What's wrong with you?
in the house next to Thebes Bakery, over the boarding house, with our beds intact, everything identical except for more footsteps, those that don't live there, my mother

—The first floor is deserted

and the floor is deserted, my ass, shoes without rest on the floor, the pantry door opening and closing because of the bottles, the hollow in the sofa bigger because they don't stop sitting in it, the open window

—It's better to air out the room because there are so many people around

my mother insisting

—The first floor is deserted

which gives the idea of sadness and why sadness, ma'am, instead of four or five or a dozen people at a minimum, tons of clothes to iron, tons of silverware on the table, my mother shocked at me

—You're not right, you

certain that there was no plate, she eats standing in front of the dishwasher or in the armchair, a plate on her knees

—If I threw a fit it would take a week for anybody to notice

the bird is in this apartment too, I sense it's in the awning, in the chest, on the electric meter, not mocking me, not irritated, just calling me, I walk to the beach, and it doesn't leave me, I'm in Lisbon and it accompanies me, even in the hole of my school friend, I find it, in the middle of the chinoiseries, it's stubborn, she asks

—Are you all right?

how do explain to her about the bird, the certainty that if I mention it, I'll lose it, tomorrow on the Alto da Vigia, and despite the waves, I will feel it under the wind, as alive as the minuscule rattles of the toys of my childhood, hidden in the grass or perched on the goats' rocks, any place will do for it, I

—Even here?

he, not understanding me well
—Even here, how?
the gulls don't drive it away, they swoop around me, not it, they just find me annoying, they leave, return, snoop around
—How old are you?
and I'm ashamed that I'm fifty-two, if I look back I see very few years, scattered in my memory like tricycles and illnesses, if I search slowly I discover more, a napkin appears and my twenty three years are under lace, you pull a drawer open and forty nine is in the middle of pliers and twine, I distributed my life at random, without paying attention, if I am still they'll take away my seventeen when they took the furniture from the beach, if I am still my eight years old will be in the orifice of the wall, magnified, mixed up with the diary and a wire bracelet, my fifty-two years are just with me because the rest of the time got lost, I remember my mother at thirty and what they did to you, ma'am, since they escaped from you, if they asked me
—How old was your father when he died?
I'd answer that he wasn't any age, he abandoned all of them, some keep them in albums, put them in frames in a room, convoke them
—On my seventeenth birthday
surrounding themselves with them, my older brother pedaled by his birthdays and if any one of them resisted they'd be turned into sand or the water dragged them away, pieces of fabric without an owner, boots that no man ever wore, they walked without legs in them wearing them down to the bone, they must have been legs like ours, on streets that don't exist
—How many kilometers did you walk?
and they, reflecting

—We have no idea

my mother's sandals walked meters upon meters on the floor, as soon as she found them empty, she pushed them with her foot, my mother on her knees looking under the mattress scolding them

   —Don't you have any sense?

and they didn't protest out of fear, something of my father in the way they accepted it, the way he weighed like lead when he was little, I suppose that a piece of him remained to the end of his days, when he got on the scale, at the doctor's office, what percentage is you and what percentage is lead, my grandfather immediately said, proud of his son

   —By my calculation, eleven percent lead

   so that my father

   —We need to discount eleven percent lead

the doctor discounted ten percent, eleven percent is a complicated operation, interminable calculations, restarted and abandoned, on the prescription pad until there's a definitive cross over it

   —As for me, that's enough we're not going to rack our brains all afternoon with square roots

   not mentioning the sigh that everyone noticed

   —In any case, you're fucked

and he was fucked, the poor man, a few pebbles, some beams, those lizards, changing color whenever they feel like it, that love the garbage, that is inside their skin, outside their skin

   —I'm tired

at home for now and I bring him the bottle, he lingered looking at the label, not drinking

   —I'm tired

   his throat retracting and swelling very quickly, my mother

—Are you still bringing him that?

and what difference did it make if I brought it to him if he could hardly move, the bird said my name without applause or censure, I presume from the curtain or the copper pot that had a coin at the bottom that nobody had used, my mother put it in her hand, returned it to the pot where it clinked minutes before sleeping

—For better or worse, best not to spend it

and it really was better not to spend it, I don't know anyone who can control the intention of things, malevolent nails, pillows with pits, a pin, discrete until then, suddenly fierce, look at this little line on my hand, at first it was red and then turned black, it's rusting, it didn't make the lock on the gate bleed, when it got scraped, if you touched it, it would fall apart, the ring where it lived was twisted, at night the boards made pitiful sounds, my older brother worried

—Isn't there anyone who can help them?

but at one in the morning who dares approach, in daylight they would calm down, like the fever of the sick, the screws gave a sigh, the boards turning, my older brother with the tools and the gate dismissing him

—Thank God I'm feeling fine

a pinecone hid in the flower bed with the begonias in a soft fall

—Leave her in peace

and my older brother was indecisive, it's simple on the Alto da Vigia, you jump and that's it, and at home, hesitations, remorse, a leather bag hanging from the bike seat with essential tools, glasses with no lenses, a broken wrench, crumbled crackers for the Gobi desert, the begonia or hyacinth bed for the pinecone, except for roses the names of flowers are unfathomable or rather

I learned the names but I don't know what they are, tulips and daisies I can remember but peonies, orchids, camelias I have no idea, my co-worker
—Would you like some tea?
she solved everything with teas, stomach aches, birthdays, colds, celebrations
—We met each other eight months ago, shall we have some tea?
and there came the trembling solution, decorated with cookies, on a tray with a tea towel where some places smoked and others threatened to fall off, the variety of the universe a richness that exalts and messes with me and at the same time confounds me, fortunately it's just a fistful of hours until Sunday, from minute to minute I check if the waves continue, if the Alto da Vigia is still there, the rock in its place, I look at my father reconsidering the articulation in his knees, not drinking
—I'm tired
and my grandfather swearing to us
—He's from the same stuff as I am, he'll perk up in a minute
and he didn't perk up, sir, he faded, you grab him by the waist and lift him up, even toothless with diapers it could be he smiled, speaking of teeth, lion's tooth, it just came to me, that flower is called, although I don't remember where I saw it, certainly eternities ago still lion's tooth you don't forget that, a snippet of dialogue
—What flower is that, Dona Igualdade?
—Lion's tooth, dear
heard I don't know where, the impression that my mother asked the question, but Dona Igualdade disappeared from my memory
—Who was Dona Igualdade, mother?

my mother, interrupting dinner
—That name says something to me
giving up, restarting dinner, interrupting again
—Wait
with the past growing in her head
—The daughter of a sergeant who was a friend of one of my uncles
a man in a uniform accompanied by an albino girl, my mother's head grew smaller, and the sergeant and the albino girl evaporated
—He visited her with my uncle
in a neighborhood in another corner of the city, a basement apartment under sidewalk level, in which the albino girl
—If my father were here
while a melancholic dog lay depressed in a basket
—That one is always lethargic and sheds hair everywhere
and the uncle really did spend days cleaning himself up from the dog, his sleeves, his waist, his back, where the animal rubbed against him, not just the hair, the drool, he wet a brush because the drool had dried, my uncle's wife
—Wait there
discovering stubborn stains on his vest, his pants
—If I find him one day, I'll wring that animal's neck
my mother cleaning herself off
—I get a rash just thinking about it
—Lion's tooth, dear
in a muffled echo of trains, me to my mother
—Were there trains there?
that went through the middle of the block knocking down walls, the sheets in the windows dripped ashes and smoke, there's

another bird, besides the sparrows and the blackbirds, that's called me forever, now from a branch, now from the roof, now from the well, now inside the house and what is the house today, now from the bottles in the pantry, I would like it to show itself to me when it says goodbye to me, I've got to find a way of saying goodbye to myself, if the bike worked I'd take it with me but the steering wheel, but the tires, the handle of the bike pump didn't let out any air, the chapel bell gave a solitary ring, I who never saw a bell, just the place the doves perched cooing tenderly, made of glazed tile, I'd give I don't know what for my co-worker to shut up for a minute

—Is it so disagreeable to ask you for a little kiss?

not offended, hurt, full of secreted diminutives, I shrink back

—I'd like some peace

precisely what I haven't had for years, peace, precisely what I will have tomorrow after seven in the evening, peace, and a ceiling of ocean in which the waves move without hurting, not even the other bird calling me, I just hope that my older brother

—Girl

not in the cemetery where they think he is and I don't think he is, my older brother with me

—Girl

the beach house waiting for those who will arrive for the weekend to demolish or construct a house expelling the blackbirds and the sparrows and tearing down the well, I feel sorry for the hickory tree, poor thing, not able to reassure it

—I'll take care of you

in the hope that one day, who knows, it will grow a little leaf, the hickory was grateful

—I didn't think you'd be concerned about me

in the hospital they weren't concerned about me, they just treated me, whoever was in my place in bed eighteen, brutalized at five in the morning by the violence of the lights

—Two little pills, friend

copying the numbers on the screen to a pad, taking my temperature, changing the IV drip and the catheter bag, flipping the switch, I didn't care if I died because it wasn't about me, I was on the beach with my mother whose index finger was dipped in the jar of suncream

—Turn your nose here

four white noses and the boats sailing by us, stray dogs and why aren't there cats on the sand

—Why aren't there any cats on the sand, Mother?

my mother, who was giving a recipe for baked fish to the next-door neighbor

—So many questions, I don't know

pausing with the recipe to meditate on the absence of cats

—It hadn't occurred to me what would the motive be, in fact?

combing through her Augusts in search of it, a dog would be there, not a cat, accept our present and that's all, my not deaf brother not climbing into an army truck, in a hut with the rest of the Blacks, burning, chickens, also not on the beach, occupied with running away from the soldiers, one of them crashed into a tree trunk and fell, my father stayed at home between the pantry and his thumbs

—I think they just gave me two

suspecting a third on his ring finger, in the place of the pinkie, he studied his pinkie

—It's a pinky, what a relief

inattentive to the pines, from afar walking down to the kiosk where Senhor Manelinho, all flattery and friendship
—Take a look at this flower of a man
forget-me-nots, snapdragons, birds of paradise, at school with an atlas with all of that in pictures, the names in Portuguese and Latin below them, the Biology teacher
—An endless collection
Senhor Manelinho's wife pointing out my father to a customer browsing magazines
—He was a perfect man
now deformed and red, with difficulty speaking, sentences that took time to unravel, he liberated his tongue a little in the café with the foosball table, thanks to the drink
—I feel better already
ready to go far if his liver gave him permission but it didn't, the rascal, the body turns against us if we trust it, Senhor Manelinho, whose heart was betraying him
—You have to train them like the animals
and even training it like the animals, which was his case, God knows, Senhor Manelinho stabbing his chest
—I have two plastic veins
not in bed eighteen, in a nursing home in Coimbra, looking at lines on a display
—I spent twelve days after the operation looking at that movie
and stitches in his thorax patching up disasters, lunches through a straw, dinners through a straw, an Indian squeezing his sides forcing him to cough
—Cough up the mucous from your lungs, partner
and my father going up the street with us holding on to the sides of the buildings

—I'm coming

we waited for him, and he felt like staying for hours on end next to a tile plaque. Come in friend, the house is yours, in which a maid beat rungs on a verandah, the Italian's home, the bridge engineer's, the house of the widow sergeant major with the fat goddaughter, both harvesting secrets, once the fat girl placed her forehead on the widow's shoulder and the widow stroked her cheek

—My little princess

while my father unstuck himself from the plaque, leaning on my older brother, my mother with a canvas bagful of towels

—Holy God

and I felt sorry for him, I guarantee it, what I wouldn't give for the plumber not to have showed up and the other one, ma'am, what you wouldn't give for my father to be perfect again, the customer looking at the magazines to Senhor Manelinho's wife

—On that we agree

and even the fat girl forgot about the plants, her hair disheveled and her fish mouth opening for air, my father a lovely figure, strong gestures, laughing, my father to Senhor Manelinho's wife and to the customer browsing magazines

—Hello little ones

or going into the café with the foosball table, imperiously

—Hi guys

the next-door neighbor to my mother, covering her mouth with her palm

—Lucky for you he turned into a hunk of a husband

the hunk of husband going out to conquer what was missing on the street, a heap of rubble and the little bathroom stalls in the back, too far away to anchor his tiredness, his eyes said

—Help

maintaining the body, not the eyes, blind slices of water, my older brother

—Just a little further, Father

and the infinite little further, a curve to the left, the minimarket, the gate, everything distancing itself instead of staying still, my deaf brother around us

—Sheee

there's another bird here, besides the sparrows and the blackbirds, that has been calling me forever, stains of clouds on the ocean that I will not see down there, maybe I'll see the reflection of the sun in a thousand fragments, I don't write any letter like my older brother, why, my mother reading it

—I don't believe this

turning the page hoping for more sentences and there are none, it's over, my father took longer to discover words that were there without being there, lifting his head his face was serene, he thanked the fire rescue people, he thanked the police, he put my deaf brother on his shoulders and disappeared into the olive grove, how many kilometers did you walk around there without noticing a genet trotting along the path, who knows if the genets on the Alto da Vigia make their nest in the coves, during the vacation after the last year of high school, the fat girl said to me, waving with her hoe, while the widow of the sergeant waited

—Do you want to have lunch with us?

me

—No thanks

very fast and I didn't run away out of timidity, from then on I changed the route of my walk pretending to look for whatever in my blouse, my father put away my older brother's bicycle pushing the steering wheel and the seat with an unexpected delicacy, why not put it on your shoulders, sir, why don't you take a ride on it and my father's face was serene, he didn't search through drawers like my mother or kiss a forgotten shirt on the bed, he sat on the steps with an empty bottle, without the cork, that he picked in the pantry and we observed his proud straight shoulders from the kitchen, my grandfather was right to be proud of you, you went far, Father, this is not the praise of a daughter, it's the praise of a woman for a perfect man, not a drunk with a liver turned to mush moping around the house, a perfect man, my mother to the next-door-neighbor agreeing with her

—So lucky, it's true

I didn't visit you in the cemetery because you weren't there, when my mother

—We must move your father

I didn't hear and if I heard

—Move him where?

as if my father were in a cave, if I have the chance this afternoon, I'll take a walk in the olive grove and find him, I don't need to look for him, I just need to wait until I hear

—Girl

and as usual his hand almost touching my head not touching my head and his mouth at the edge of a smile without becoming a smile, he'd be his age today and I'd be a child, with princess earrings and petal nail polish and he'd pretend he didn't see although I was his girl, it hurts me that he didn't say

—My girl

just

—Girl

only I bet that he meant

—My girl

when he said

—Girl

only and therefore don't get mad, sir, I understand the way I understood the way you looked at me in the hospital, the way I understood that you turned to the wall so that I wouldn't see you that way, so that I wouldn't see you and that's all, you wanted to sleep, don't take that from my head, you wanted to rest before sitting on the sofa and what happened after was falsehood, a lie, my father isn't that way he didn't have to push me on the swing to push me on the swing, he didn't have to give me a bath to give me a bath, my mother

—They're crazy about each other

and what did she know about that, neither one of us told, it's something you don't talk about, the next-door neighbor when I took off my sandals on the beach, the right sandal with the toe of the left, the left sandal with my toes

—You're like your father, kiddo

and who gave her permission to talk like that, first I'm a girl, not a man, secondly my father is my father and I'm me, the cone waffle salesman in the line of the tents closest to the ocean, the kiosk in the shade of a bus loading people, the wife of Senhor Manelinho, with a big suitcase, going to visit family, while she visiting family Senhor Manelinho, forgetting the good-looking women, installed himself on the patio of the foosball café letting the dog sell the newspapers

—Keep the change if you like, I don't give a damn

I don't know if they had children, I think there was a son in Germany, I'm not sure, there are things that for reasons that escape me dissolve in my memory, a son or a daughter, wait, a daughter, almost as blonde as her father, very thin, I remember that they grumbled about the cost of tonics they bought for her to gain weight and she didn't, perched on a chair, with a doll on her lap, I who was always was suspicious of dolls, they had to prove many things to me, and they didn't, so that I would accept them, I saw them in store windows looking at me with fake innocence, the little mouths, the little fingers, the nylon eyelashes, an unexpected memory of Tininha's mother to her driver

—My peach

distracted my thoughts alerting me that the other bird is here, besides the blackbirds and the sparrows, that has been calling me forever, now on a branch, now on the roof that is starting to fail, now in the living room, now in my parents' bedroom with the moisture stain on the ceiling spilling over to the wall, how many times did I say

—Don't you hear it?

people in the middle of a gesture, their ears tuned, waiting, the bird calling louder and they

—I don't hear it

the way they don't hear my father and me in the olive grove, he

—Girl

without

—Girl

me

—Father

without

—Father

and still, we were together, in a distant village, on the road to Lisbon where military trucks and my not deaf brother in one of them, returning from Africa

—Don't talk to me

the suitcase like the one carried by Senhor Manelinho's wife and we didn't talk, during the entire trajectory of the taxi ride weighing his soldier's beret in his hand, my father to my mother

—Leave him alone

the way I would say

—Leave me alone

if they saw me climb the rocks, when I got to the top, I was certain he'd be sitting on the steps, with an empty bottle, without a cork, that he got from the pantry, his straight, proud shoulders, his face serene although you noticed his hands clasped together with such force that nobody except my voice

—Sir

because I know, understand, because happen what may, I know, understand, he could let go.

4.

After dinner I'd walk down to the wall to listen to the waves in the dark, I thought of designating one of them
   —That one there is my life
   and then another life followed, and another, and another, in a little while nobody will remember me, the certainty of being forgotten frightened me because, in not being, I never was, and if I never was, who existed in my place, who exists to this day in my place, eats my food, sleeps in my bed, uses my name and will disappear the same time I do, the lifeguard building is just walls and the table on which they laid out the drowned people is empty, not just my house, everything disappears in this place, things become pieces and the pieces become weeds or thorny bushes whose names I can't remember, growing where nothing grows, who remembers my older brother, my father, the father of my father inviting him to stroke his cheek
   —Baby's bottom, baby's bottom
   and believing my father a sober baby's bottom, where is all of this, a hollow silence around me that the waves batter and leave, if I asked Dr. Clementina

—What happened to Tininha, ma'am?
  a sigh around the hope that they hadn't heard and a sharp voice growing distant
   —Shut up
  Dr. Clementina at the door
   —I lost her
  not just
   —I lost her
  the rest of the sentence strangled inside her
   —I lost her for good
  just like her mother with the dark glasses and her father washing the car were lost for good, a fig tree was left at the lifeguard building
   —My peach
  but who pays attention to fig trees, you can talk as long as you want and nobody will pay any attention to you, the windows of the building don't have frames and the marble table for the drowned is in a deserted room, a homeless guy lives there, his rags, crumbs, pieces of cardboard against the cold strewn around, how many drowned people have lain on that table over the years, purple, naked, observing me, the enormous feet, the tiny head resting on a wooden block, I hope they didn't put my older brother there, I hope they don't put me there, naked, my feet also enormous, the toes one after another that is a feat that always amazed me, stuck together, in a row, I don't know why I'm amazed but I am, if one part of me is still, it thinks there should be a toe for each part, and when you speak of a part of me what part are you speaking of, leave me in peace in the water, don't take me out of the ocean, I want to be like a leaf from a tree on the street decomposing, in February, in the puddles, just tendons,

just filaments, if we step on them they come apart, don't make me come apart by stepping on me, if my not deaf brother were here he'd set fire to the lifeguard building and from the first flame chickens would be born, my toes stuck together too, all in order to the little toe, the nail of the little toe, I find myself at a loss to trim it and even with glasses on it's always twisted, poor thing, the number of socks I've ruined with it, if I found a pillow I'd drag it behind me, the pedicurist

—You need to use soap more often

to the rocks on which my mother wanted to climb to the light

—Go back to your room before I lose patience with you

convinced that I'm her daughter and not her daughter, a wave that disappeared a long time ago

—I'm not your daughter I was a wave that disappeared a long time ago

a wave that is fifty-two years old walking around in the yard, it's a good thing there are no mirrors where I appear, if I appeared I wouldn't greet her, I'd wrinkle my brow

—Another fig tree

and I'd abandoned her without remorse disillusioned with myself, what does she want, what is she demanding of me and not demanding, accept it, what can you do, the pedicurist back with a file

—There are some nails that are more difficult than others each one is different

but the nails of the drowned are enormous, with sand under them, with files, I say to the pedicurist

—Have you ever trimmed the nails of a drowned person, Lili?

the file and the basin of lukewarm water tipping over on the floor, my mother turned off the light on the Alto da Vigia while the wind rumpled the sheets

—You don't leave me in peace for a minute

she and my father sleeping with the donkeys and the goat and nevertheless there's a chest of drawers, and nevertheless there's a curtain, the clothing strewn between tiles and thistles, where is the hall to go back to my room, my mother calling me

—What did you want

the yellow nightgown, my father turning on the pillow without noticing me, talking with his dream in their language, he had breakfast not with us, with the night, morning everywhere except in his gestures, he asked, despite the cup between the placemat and his mouth

—Just a drop more, Madrinha

with his hand without the cup looking for the cover he didn't say

—Madrinha

he said

—Iáiá

he said

—Just a drop more Iáiá

—That's all I needed

giving her a sidelong glance, jealous, her hand on my father's shoulder

—My boy isn't like the others

wanting my mother to leave so she could come back, even as an adult, to her own

—Iáiás

as a child, so intelligent, so sensitive, so handsome, my mother wanting to complete the list

—So drunk

It's a good thing there's no longer a marble table at the lifeguard building, with a hole in the middle to drain out the tides since we bring so many waves with us, those we went towards and those that followed us and in a certain way were us as well, we didn't reach the beach and leave it again like the anemones, perhaps the innocent little souls of children, we didn't stop existing, staring at you with eyes that the water cleaned and in which the past is more real than the present, the foosball ball hitting the goal, the afternoon that a scorpion

—I'm going to sting you

picking up a pebble, near the well, putting the bait on the fishhook for me, Senhor Leonel pointing to the horizon

—It's a big world, young lady

and what do I do with such a big world, sir, what good is it to me, to Senhor Leonel, now, all the world fit between the couch and the bed, the walls narrowing blocking the gestures that I was no longer capable of, what a mist on my eyelids thinking of this, times I decide

—I'm taking the pillow with me and leaving

but the displeasure of my father binds me to you, the suspicion that there are wasps on the Alto da Vigia and my fear of them, I remember the godmother of my father, very old

—For you I'm not Iáiá, I'm Dona Deolinda

jealous of me

—Just a drop more Iáiá

and she, intractable with us, without the courage to send him to school, the bottles multiplied when Dona Deolinda died, I don't have any recollection of seeing a tear from my father or hear him say he missed her, I remember his hand in hers and I was undecided about which of the two belonged to him, my mother didn't go with him to the wake

—That nitwit

I followed him because he pulled my sleeve and just the two old women, candles around the bier, a presence in the coffin that you couldn't see even if you stood on tiptoe, my father's hand inside that thing and I was terrified that he'd pull out the wrong hand, if he touched me with a hand that wasn't his I'd faint for sure, my grandfather was already dead, the rest of my father's family was dead, I

—Only you are missing sir

two old women in a corner of the deserted chapel, with a dark crucifix, and outside the barred windows a tree waved its branches, only you were missing, father, you're waiting to join the dead, maybe the two old ladies will stand in the same corner for you, with the same crucifix, the same window and the same tree waving its branches, everything ready and waiting for you, see, my father's hand, not Dona Deolinda's, on my sleeve again, me without dragging my feet on the cement, suspended in your mute pain, at the entrance to the cemetery my father

—Wait there

I was alone at the gate in the midst of the vendors of flowers and packets of candles, the terror of death is with me to this day, for me, a pair of older people, I thought they were squatting but they were sitting on benches in a silence without mouths, just chins and noses, beyond the panic of death the panic they would bury my father by mistake and I would pull him out of the earth shouting his name, in the parking lot a well-dressed man adjusted his toupee, depending on whether his forehead were bigger or smaller he'd have a different face, I remained behind the vendors so they wouldn't rob me, a flock of pigeons flew incessantly above, one sensed the river, vertices of cranes, of hoists, a beggar opened his violin case and started to play a waltz, Dr. Clementina, who had lost Tininha forever, stepping on herself, not on bed eighteen, in the cemetery women in black and gentlemen with a black ribbon on their lapel giving condolences, it was my father who held my hand, not Dona Deolinda, in the car home the man with the toupee, using the windows as a mirror, adjusted his hair, my father's hand held mine with such force that during months I checked for marks on my skin, I was relieved there were none, and even this Saturday, thinking back

—Baby's bottom, baby's bottom

I would prefer it so, something of his that would calm me down now, I don't feel alone, that is, I am, to be honest, I don't know if I feel alone, I think that I do, my father is dead, my older brother is dead, my mother's heart will give out any day now, fed with fifteen drops in a glass of water at lunch and dinner, each drop an orange spiral that expands, my mother

—It tastes like shit

and the throat engaged in slow work, full of folds and valves, swallowing that for how many years has it been since I heard my husband singing, one Sunday he whistled as he shaved and when he noticed me, he stopped, if I asked

—why don't you whistle, what's wrong?

he didn't listen, there was always leftover shaving cream on his ears and if I said

—there's shaving cream on your ears

he'd wait until I left to wipe himself off with the towel, on occasion I

—Do you remember Moledo?

and silence, I search for what I did wrong, and I don't find it, an attitude without intending it, an absent answer, my co-worker

—Why does that bother you?

annoyed with me, not accepting that it did matter to me, after dinner, when I was fourteen or fifteen, I walked down to the wall to watch the waves in the dark, there are times when the ocean seems unhappy to me, the same words as always

—I'm the ocean, I'm the ocean

taking shells from the beach, during the high tides of September when there was almost no beach, the strip of thick sand that only the rain wet and seaweed strewn about, my deaf brother affirming, by the temperature of his eyes

—I know everything about you

and I think he does, hundreds of unformulated secrets between us, I bet he guessed that I am here, and he is pacing back and forth in his room, Dona Alice's relative

—Why are you so agitated?

before lunch on the terrace and my brother looking for me with a spoon, pushing away the turnip greens where I'm sorry there are none, bro, there would be, convince yourself, if it weren't for an appointment tomorrow, at twenty to seven in the evening, that I can't miss, I waited for you for years and years not just in the soup, in the salad, in the sauce, inside the little packets of butter, the same way you always found me with the spoon or the fork, and you kept eating with the look of someone who didn't notice, I found the two flecks of shaving cream from my husband's beard and I felt like, I won't tell you this, it's ridiculous sentimental nonsense, I'd pick them up with my finger, I'll finally tell you, and spread them on my face until the flecks became me, on the day I was released from the hospital Dr. Clementina did not say goodbye to me, she remained, very busy, writing on a clipboard, I turned halfway down the hall and Dr. Clementina was wearing the princess earrings, the conviction that instead of a clipboard Rogério was with her the same way that Ernesto was with me, the conviction that

—Don't forget to read what I wrote in the diary

without needing a voice and I didn't have the chance, I might read it later, the wind breaker swallowed me, the street swallowed me, and she, still with Rogério

—Won't you show Ernesto to me

wanting Rogério to turn into a rag, as a nurse handed her the test results

—I'll look at them in a minute

looking from the entrance at the taxis that were lined up at the hospital door until my mother

—And why aren't you at the table?

while from the other side of the wall my mother

—And why aren't you at the table?

our gestures symmetrical as if we were still together and we never were again, at the time it happened, right, goodbye Tininha, good luck, when we had already lost each other I walked down to the wall, the last lines don't count, they start over here, my life is a wave that has broken, they were the lives of others that I stayed to listen to, my mother's for example

—And don't you put your napkin up to your throat when you start to eat?

and my mother's voice

—How many times do I have to repeat sit up straight?

and my mother's voice

—Those aren't manners of a person they're the manners of a ditch digger

while my father crumbled the bread, my father disappearing into the sheets

—Just a drop more, Iáiá

and Dona Deolinda, instead of picking him up, tucking in his clothes and explaining to my grandfather

—He has plenty of years left to make mistakes, leave him alone, Cristósomo

my father not on the beach, at the wake with the two old women, holding my by a sleeve when it was his sleeve that needed help, my father

—And now?

what a question, sir

—And now?

with a dozen bottles just for him in the pantry, what else could he want, what else appeals to him, not a dozen, ten since he's already drunk two and his nose getting rounder and his features dilated, his stomach poking out of his shirt, my mother

—Do you like the image you give your children?

me feeling the pines and the insects of the night, there was always one of them insisting against the lamp, gigantic, hairy, probably wild rabbits on the Alto da Vigia, identical to the ones that crossed the road in the hills and disappeared into the hedges, my co-worker

—Bunny

stroking my ears in her perpetual October while I, little in her lap, thought about my husband's flecks of shaving cream hearing a whistle that finally wasn't interrupted, continued forever, perhaps it would be possible for the two of us to be happy, don't

you think, we might pull it off, if you invited me to go back to the guest house, I'd agree, assuring the proprietress
—We're married, ma'am
and I'd show my wedding ring to the proprietress
—There are stories that end well, thank goodness
and there are stories that end well, it's true, one of these days, if I accept the invitation, we'll take her to Modelo with us, dance on the beach, run, visit Galicia, my co-worker insisting on a caress in a voice that made me sleepy as she rocked me
—What are you thinking, bunny?
I'm not thinking, big rabbit, I left for Moledo and I promise I won't be long, I feel comfortable in this October and in these severe pieces of furniture that close over me like an egg, they round out my skin, take care of me, don't order me to have manners at the table, don't make me leave the room, even the gilded brass balls on the iron bed, badly fastened on, please me, thinking
—they're going to fall off
and they lean, start to loosen, hang on, my co-worker not noticing them
—Such pretty ears
me feeling nothing, or almost nothing, or rather feeling a little, staring at the balls, if one of them rolled to the other side of the room, hit the baseboard and stayed there wobbling I'd put it in the hole in the wall to show Tininha, but Tininha died, Dr. Clementina between two patients
—Where did you find that, what a bother
sticking it in the pocket of her lab coat
—I'll return it to you tomorrow I promise
and it's obvious she'll never return it, never return it come what may, it happened with the shell, it happened with the

sparrow's nest. what she took from me, swearing to give it back, would fill a drawer, I must get a ball for myself and by the way, Dr. Clementina, where is what belongs to me that didn't stay in the hiding place, you must have it at home in a box, with the enamel Andalusian dancer and the ring that was missing a stone and what does the stone matter

—That was a long time ago

and the time that was long ago is still with us, see, one afternoon my father emerged from the newspaper with a childish expression

—Iáiá

he burrowed into sheets of newspaper to ask the news

—Take me to the circus

and immediately an Indian in a turban started blowing fire, he put a burning spit in his mouth and returned the flames to us, Dona Deolinda, shocked

—See it to believe it

my father tried with the kitchen matches and burned the tip of his tongue, the newspaper, not him

—I was spitting out borate for a week

the newspaper, not him

—If you look, you'll see the scar

my older brother arriving on his bike

—Do you want a push on the swing?

because when he noticed the blister he took care of us, my big rabbit with the ears that I didn't stroke, I'll have time tomorrow, sit on my lap and I'll

—What pretty ears

thinking of Moledo and my husband singing, Dr. Clementina

—Are you married?

I'm married, doctor, it should be in the file along with the fifty-two years of age and other miseries, look what they did to me, my older brother
—First the girl
at the time when I was first, when I was a girl, I'm just anybody today, change the dressing and go away, don't visit me here, no swing in the living room so I can touch the treetops with my feet, losing a princess earring, reaching the pines, that my not deaf brother climbed on purpose, I saw his shoe sole get crushed, my mother from the window to my older brother
—A rope will break in a minute be careful with them
and Tininha's mother lowering her sunglasses to watch him, if I had her eyelashes and used lipstick my older brother would spend the whole afternoon with me, after dinner I'd walk down to the wall to listen to the waves in the dark, trying to synchronize my breathing with the rhythm of the water that I could almost not see, instant scales always in unexpected places, if I am still the ocean will look at me
—Are you there
rising with more force so that I would not leave it, what we'll do to make people notice us, take giant steps, take baby steps, pinch your nose with a clothespin, twirl around my mother until I felt dizzy, the furniture turning and the floor at an oblique angle, the minutes that things take to be still, the nausea, the dizziness, my mother not letting go of her sewing
—Are you happy after all that nonsense?
not clear, opaque, also twirling, if they gave me a candy, I'd vomit it up, the next-door neighbor
—Kids are so stupid
my mother, experienced in these matters

—It's the tendency to stupidity that they inherited from their father

and tomorrow I'll be on the Alto da Vigia, throwing myself from the rocks because of my older brother, have you seen the cross that I bear, a husband that treats her well, school, a good apartment, what I would give for her life and her age, she had a few knocks, who doesn't, the story about her son, the operations, episodes that mark us and nevertheless we recover, what more do you want, my father, without Iáiá, folding the newspaper, with a strong desire for folded sheets and unhurried fingers

   —Bunny

mussing her bangs, not between chinoiserie and Octobers, in a cubicle in the station where they store the electric trolleys with hammers under them to fix their axles and a guy giving orders, women typing with maps on the walls, if it depended on us we'd be bunnies every day and the brass balls and flattery, we'd be grateful

   —Maybe it's true

even Dr. Clementina softening, watching the taxis from the window, moved by Rogério

   —Why was I so stupid?

you weren't stupid, Doctor, it was the tendency to stupidity, let's be happy with the shadows that isolate us and hurt, my not deaf brother I don't know where, your old man with a pipe and his wife stretched out, my deaf brother running in the room

   —Sheee saaills seeea sheells

before he ran in the yard forcing himself to talk without being able to, an inarticulate sound, a kick to a tree trunk, hanging on my mother's blouse

   —Bring the pills so he'll calm down

forcing him to take them and in a quarter of an hour he was calmer, if my mother approached him, he'd shove her

—What did you do to him, mother?

and my mother, incapable of speaking, locking herself in the kitchen, one afternoon I found her amid the dishes, the pots and pans

—For how many lives will I have to pay for what I did?

not out loud, in a whisper

—For how many lives will I have to pay for what I did?

and there you are, Dr. Clementina, what I was saying, shadows that isolate us and hurt us, who is the father of my deaf brother, tell me, born after my older brother and my not deaf brother, you are lying in bed feeling your belly and thinking

—What stupidity

with my father next to you pretending to sleep, not the one who fixed the dishwasher syphon, another one before him, who read the gas meter, the one who cleaned the chimney, the mailman, a stranger from the street, it wasn't just your mother, Dr. Clementina, it was both our mothers

—My peach

a man I never knew about, my father knew about him because of me and you were aware that my father knew, every time he walked with my deaf brother on his shoulders in the olive grove you

—My God

without God getting annoyed, dealing with it the way I'll deal with it tomorrow on the Alto da Vigia looking at the beach that will be empty, I hope, the pines more numerous as you climb the slope and the sound of the needles without getting to the top, no sparrow, no blackbird, gulls ready to peck at my body, not just my father, my deaf brother also must know, my older brother I'm not sure, he talked with us without ever referring to us, he went out, returned home, piled pamphlets on top of the closet, my mother

—What are you doing?

and no answer, my grandfather, if I had known him

—This one will also go far, he inherited my blood

and everybody went far thanks to your blood except you, grandfather, a laborer in a suburb, I wasn't born into wealth, Dr. Clementina, I'm sorry, in the event you don't have bed eighteen, I'll take a room just for me, attention, flowers, visitors, the bunny of my co-worker waiting for the morning that didn't free her from the disease, didn't cross the road in front of us in the hills, stayed there curled up, if you looked for it an embarrassed silence, your house doesn't exist anymore, the wall doesn't exist anymore, how funny the princess earrings were and the petal nail polish, we were incapable of playing, what does my existence matter, what does the street matter to me, we're too old to believe in each other, we don't even believe in people and we expect so little, a few months, a few years and then a pair of old women in a corner of the chapel not praying for us, just there under a single shawl, not in slippers or sandals or shoes, with the army boots of our sons, a cooked onion, a tangerine, a piece of bread, my deaf brother pressed to my father's pants and my mother

—I can't stand it

and my mother

—For how many lives will I pay for what I did?

and the mortgage is almost paid up, after eighty-five years the payments in the end are like drops in a glass and still a guy whose face I can't see comes into the house in the morning

—Are your children asleep?

not in the bedroom, in the kitchen since the back stairs don't have steps, there are always missing steps on the back stairs, the guy
 —Hurry
while the refrigerator hummed and vibrated, I don't understand the exhalations of machines, the rocks and plants I can comprehend, and then murmurs, footsteps in the hall, the door, he must be waiting in the threshold of a building or behind a van that my father left in, my mother watched over the sleep of my brothers fearing my older brother would wake up, she rubbed his back, and he
 —Leave me alone
in a voice that rolled out the letters, my mother, not daring to ask him questions, weighing the morning, walking down to the wall down to the wall, my co-worker going from my ears to my neck in a long caress
 —Whose little bunny are you?
her nose against my shoulders, teeth or nails, I wasn't sure, light bones, one of my hands on her ankle slowing making its way up, my face turning toward hers
 —You are
as if it were true and at that moment it was true, but I wasn't thinking of my co-worker, I was thinking of Tininha's mother and the Greek wife of the pharmacist, the poodle not in her lap but in mine, while I unbuttoned myself smiling, my deaf brother jealous of me because of my father, my mother with her palms on her face
 —I can't take it anymore
lifting the features distorted by her fingers, ordering me in my ear

—Deal with it, lady

    Dona Deolinda calling my father

       —Let's get out of here

    and my father obeying her, still, following a blackbird outside as if he loved blackbirds, promise me you won't put me on the table for drowned people in the lifeguard building, purple, naked, staring at you, with enormous feet, a tiny head, toes in a row, in order, abandon the bunny in peace in the water, I want to be a leaf on the trees of the street dissolving in the puddles in February, just ribs, just filaments, don't take me apart when you touch me, leaving the hospital, after losing my son, I walked randomly for the whole afternoon, I leapt over potholes, I sat down on benches to rest, I remember a lady that a girl covered with a jacket

       —I'll go do the shopping I'll be back soon

    I remember the park where they played dominoes wearing caps on their heads and the onlookers watching the game, I remember the hospital

       —He got away with it

    I don't remember my son, I remember a clock in a church, I don't remember what I felt, I remember the river and the boat dock, even today, with the receding of time, I don't remember what I felt like I can't explain what I feel, I never thought as much about the name of a day, Saturday, Saturday, when my steps the steps of many people who walk with me, that is all the girls of my diverse ages, high school, university, the steps of my husband, not yet my husband, approached at the exit to the classroom

       —Would you allow me to invite you to a coffee?

    fearing my answer and I accepted, and I drank it, the sugar in the packet fell into the saucer, not in the cup, my husband, not yet my husband

—Weeks ago

in the sharp voice that didn't find the tone of an upset boy and we didn't look at each other until my husband, not yet my husband, groping for coins in his pocket

—I must go

and he escaped, leaving me alone in the café counting the coins, grouping them until they formed a triangle, until they formed a square, two or three were left over that I put in my wallet thinking

—I'll never see him again

and he was waiting for me on the street, his umbrella open, saying

—I'm sorry

in a voice that was not as sharp, covering me with the umbrella, and getting wet himself, that dripped from the rods and ran down his neck and my husband, not yet my husband, stepping in the puddles without noticing, I informed him

—If you keep that up, you'll have a cold tomorrow

and my husband's smile, not yet my husband, puzzled, humble, with raindrops on his eyebrows, on his cheeks, on his lips, while I followed under the umbrella, also stepping in puddles, distant as if they had stretched me out purple, naked, on a marble table.

5.

Around this time my mother would walk with us to the beach the way I now walk alone, with nobody telling me not to stray from the path

—Do you want a car to kill you?

when there were no cars only a few that were parked, without people around, near the grocery store, when we got to the crates of fruit, my not deaf brother jumped into the street opening his arms to a car that didn't come

—I'm not afraid of anything

and my mother running to him in her flip-flops, pulling him by the ear

—Well, I guarantee you'll be afraid of me

and I checking to see if my mother yanked his ear out of place and dropped it in the beach bag, in case she had dropped it in the beach bag, I'd steal it back as soon as she got distracted by her conversation with the next-door neighbor and I'd give the ear back to my not deaf brother

—Take it

ready to correct him if he put it on backwards, we on one

path and my mother on another, where it was easier to police what we were doing, also wearing flip-flops, my not deaf brother referring to my mother

—You cow

not softly

—You little bunny

a large animal

—You cow

face to the wall to diminish the sound, the flip-flops in a pile against the umbrella stand, mine were pink, his were blue, my older brother's were enormous, different from my mother's that had a space for each toe and sparkles on the straps, if I put my toes in they didn't reach the spaces, now my feet would be too big, it was so surprising for me, at thirteen or fourteen, to grow bigger than she was and still obey her, realize that my mother was small is an incredulity that stays with me to this day, what would she look like pregnant with me, I looking at her belly, suspiciously

—Was I really in there?

she turning the reply into a sigh

—Unfortunately, you were

when I was pregnant with my son, I didn't show yet, I had big breasts and hips, pains, the doctor

—There's trouble in there

and before three months they took him, I say my son and I don't know why I say my son and I don't say my daughter even though it was no child yet, compresses, bedrest for a week at home, not a week, five days, looking at the window without noticing it even, I heard the doctor

—Get accustomed to the idea

and I didn't get used to the idea, if my husband took my hand, I'd withdraw it quickly
—I want to rest
it's not that I hated him, I didn't hate him, my husband
—I didn't realize it was tiring to have your hand held
and his hand really did tire me, the way his presence tired me, my co-worker
—I don't tire you, do I?
not precisely tiredness, words don't express what I wanted to say, malaise, agony, it's not that either, repugnance won't do, I give up, if by chance I laid my head on my husband's pillow he'd abandon it immediately, I didn't fold his towels, I dropped his clothes into the washing machine with the tips of my fingers, it was the smell but it wasn't just the smell, my husband turning on the light in our room
—What's the matter with you?
propped up on his elbow staring at me, his features so strange when we looked each other in the face, I incredulous at his lips, his nose, his eyebrows, we didn't imagine they were like that and the person, not my husband, my husband was someone else, propped on an elbow
—Have you gotten yourself another man?
and I was trying to find him in the intruder, there's nobody else, calm down, it's not your fault, sorry, and when the light went off, I noticed he was suffering, I decided to caress him but his arm rejected it, I tried to reassure him
—This can happen
and my mouth stayed shut, sure it didn't happen, the suffering that in general makes me feel pity didn't provoke any pity, how do I explain it, in a voice almost like a child's

—May I take you for a coffee?

I felt sad for Moledo, sad for us, I don't understand what happened to me, I don't understand what I became, before I took the flecks of shaving cream and painted myself with them, when you got home the, my co-worker, kissing one of my hands

—I'll never get tired of you, doll

when you came home my silence, my co-worker reaching out her hand

—It's your turn, sweetie

my husband restless in the dark guessing from the movements of the mattress, not just the mattress, the night tables, the curtain, maybe the floor, just I was calm, my not-deaf brother pointing to my mother with a reed

—When I get home, I get the scissors and cut off your entire ear

and he didn't cut it off, he forgot because a gull with a broken foot was dragging itself in the yard, next to the swing it was much more fragile than on the wall or on the ocean, my not deaf brother brought a spade, my older brother took it away, my not deaf brother

—I'll cut your ear off too

my older brother

—I'll cut both of yours off

and my not deaf brother not listening since the gull stopped dragging itself and bristled at him, the next morning my husband avoiding me, I was sure his footsteps had the intention of harassing me and they didn't, he didn't drink coffee, he didn't come into the kitchen, he left without saying goodbye and I was turned toward the wall like my father in the hospital, I heard him on the stairs although the words of his footsteps stayed with me

—Confess, who is he

and I was afraid to run into them in the hall, going around them the way you go around the potholes in the street lifting a cautious foot, measuring them, praying you're right, the size and the depth, my older brother tried to catch a gull and the gull bit him, he brought a blanket from the garage to throw over it and my not deaf brother and I shouting because a dog grabbed it in a single jump and went off with it, we saw them near the well, we saw them go by a tree trunk and we lost sight of them

—What's all the noise about?

agreeing with my not-deaf brother

—As far as I'm concerned, you can cut off her ear

while my older brother ran after the animals, jumping over bushes and wild flowers, with the tire jack, the ocean is so peaceful today, so slow, my bones would float to the transparent bottom, I ask myself if the pivots, with those screws, would last longer than teeth in the salt and the seaweed, my older brother came back alone with the jack, scraping it against the wall, my husband didn't scrape anything, he came home later, sat at the table, took the napkin out of the ring and spread it on his knees, he waited fifteen minutes for dinner, his fingers folded as he contemplated his nails, he waited for me to, gull beaks have a kind of hook on the end, serve him, I wished him a

—Bom apetite

he ran an index finger along a crack on the rim of the plate and his index finger announced

—There's a crack on the rim of the plate

he served himself stew with gestures of a watchmaker, he peeled an orange over what was left over of rice and sauce, got up from the table, installed himself in the armchair, got up from the armchair and his beak was not just curved, when it opened it was immense, my older brother

—I'll crush that dog

or rather a severed ear and a crushed dog, so much violence in our family, my husband sat down again in the armchair after opening the window, with the open window you could hear the wail of the ambulance sirens, along with their turning lights, passing between us so that he closed the window, announcing

—See you tomorrow

and disappeared into the bedroom with muffled footsteps, when I went to bed he had propped the cushion on the headboard and continued, with the concentration of someone looking through a microscope, the intense inspection of his nails, I pulled my nightgown from under the pillow, dragging it behind me like the pillow of my childhood, I undressed holding on to, my older brother spent days swinging the wrench looking for the dog in the streets, in the empty lot, on the beach, he cornered him at last near the lifeguard station among a dozen strays that were chasing it, biting each other, a bitch in heat, I undressed holding on to the bathroom sink and then stretched out next to him, not a vertical cushion, horizontal and with closed eyes, the lamp didn't turn the world white, it turned it blue like the lampshade, all that was missing were leaves inside my eyelids, then a hiatus when he breathed quickly, a pause, a question

—Don't you have an explanation to give me?

I wouldn't be capable of grabbing a gull or any bird, in fact, feathers frighten me, my father told us about a friend of his who had the same reaction to peaches, his wife, and

—Be patient

would give them to her peeled, the bitch meditated for a

moment, between canvas and buoys, with the males salivating around her, a Minorca chicken tried to fly and failed, my co-worker coming close to me, sticking a triangle of toast into my mouth

—The stuff that happened between you and your husband will not happen to us

a large dog bared its teeth to the chicken, growling, I had never seen so many teeth at one time, which ones would be pivots, it doesn't hurt but you can notice the nail piercing our gums, canvas, buoys, lifeboats, that needed ink, the peel in the air, my older brother hit the mark with the iron wrench, my co-worker

—Well?

the dog that twisted and yelped, a bather grabbed my brother's arms

—What are you doing, kid?

the sea is so soft, so slow, hopefully starting tomorrow my bones will be at peace, lying next to each other without even scraping together, hopefully my blouse will oscillate slowly, my older brother unable to free himself from the bather

—He tore apart my gull, let go of me

while the bitch went away, offering its eager hind quarters next to the wall, they crossed a deserted terrace and a mound of rubble, the wife of my grandfather's friend to my grandmother

—A big man like that afraid of peaches

and my grandmother was shocked, that was the only time that my father told a story in detail, holding a piece of imaginary fruit in front of us, and when the story was over he continued to hold it, turning his fingers to one side and another exhibiting the peach, the wrench fell to the ground noiselessly and how can an iron wrench fall to the ground without making any noise, if anyone knows please enlighten me, the animals crossed the deserted terrace and a mound of rubble, they turned the corner that led to the empty lot to the old road that led nowhere except to itself and after itself to the foothills, the bather let go of my older brother

—Nobody owns the gulls, kid

my older brother was capable of cutting his ear off, the mestizo bather discovered a half smoked cigarette in his pocket and jammed it in his mouth, I'm beginning to get sick of teeth, energetically patting his chest and thighs looking for matches

—We have to own something, don't we?

like my co-worker thinks she owns me pinching my chin

—Kiss your owner, my pet

and I, without paying attention to her, kissed her, a wet sigh in my ear, something between a command and a supplication

—Confess I own you, tell me

I'm able to talk about the peaches, my problem isn't the birds, even a canary, even a sparrow, their rapid heartbeat makes me nervous, their feathers make me nervous, I say to my husband, in a sentence that constructed itself and for which I wasn't responsible

—I need time

the ability to turn its head three hundred sixty degrees makes me nervous, the talons make me nervous, who asked you to harm me, the mestizo bather

—Do you happen to have any matches, kid?

bending over a crate, barefoot, I remember seeing him in the café with the foosball table, the sentence this time with me inside it

—I need time

and what do you need time for, maybe Moledo will reappear,

maybe we'll dance the two of us, maybe I'll I hear singing, waiting for the refrain to sing with you, we pretend that we don't know what the future holds, the bather who grabbed my older brother returned the iron wrench that he picked up from the ground, there are still gentlemen in this world, let's keep our hope alive

—I didn't hurt you, did I, kid?

and except for humiliating me you didn't hurt me, sir, if it weren't for the dog I'd like you, the bather brought a bottle of beer, took off the cap, with his, there we are, go figure, took off the cap with his teeth, I don't feel like insisting, I'm already here, but he took off the cap with his teeth, offered the bottle to my older brother

—A drink among friends

and my older brother, who hated beer, accepting, the mestizo bather approved

—Beer makes a man grow two palms you see it right away in the muscles

my older brother flexing his muscles, feeling more grown for real, he picked up a buoy effortlessly, he picked up a bundle of driftwood and couldn't lift it a centimeter, the mestizo consoling him

—It doesn't happen with the first one, it's a slow process

tomorrow I'll be with you, bro, and we'll pick up the world, my husband, still concentrating on his nails

—Time for what?

the automobile headlights on the ceiling of the bedroom, more ambulances, the garbage truck, making its pickup, explosions, booms, conversations, echoes that mix, cover each other, insist endlessly, a fall somewhere, a protest on the floor, a pipe inside the wall affirming

—I'm here

and it was here, the sorry creature, stuck in the plaster without seeing anything of the house, trying to guess, trying to exist, the bather threw the beer bottle into a trash can

—We killed this one

and me to my husband

—I just need to get used to what happened

me to my co-worker, my nose in her cleavage

—You own me, Sweet Mama

not in the bedroom, in the living room with the chinoiserie, if Tininha's mother said to my grandfather's friend

—My peach

what would happen, my husband making a noise deep in his chest, warding off tears by studying his nails, when will you turn off the light, when will I have peace, your left leg almost grazing mine so that I could feel the hairs, fortunately you didn't rub your leg on mine because your nails required absolute attention, my co-worker buzzing me

—Another little kiss for your Mama

I didn't kiss my mother, I didn't kiss my father, I didn't kiss my brothers, my husband yes, I kissed him or rather he kissed me, he still kisses me but he's distracted, quick, on the occasions when I accept it, resigned

—Everything will be all right

the next-door neighbor about my deaf brother who had found a piece of stale bread in the sand and immediately started chewing it

—Everything will be all right, I guarantee you

while my mother

—Do you see the cross I have to bear?

ordering my deaf brother

—Spit out that garbage

putting her little finger into his mouth
—Spit out that garbage right now
cleaning your little finger on the towel
—He'll do anything to irritate me
my older brother visited the lifeguards in the afternoon, he helped them arrange the tents, carry them up, pile them into a dismantled warehouse, he sat on the wall with them to watch the sunset looking out for the dog that didn't come back, it must be wandering in the hills smelling the blackbirds or the wrench was doing him in slowly, either he'll die fast or he'll die slowly, everybody knows this, my father died slowly, Senhor Leonel died fast, when they brought him lunch that he a minute before had said
—I'm hungry
his mouth open, eyes staring, without the courtesy to say goodbye to his family, as for me, with the water, I don't know, it could happen in an instant, or it could be an hour until my older brother finally discovers me and then my body will give up, the bather who held on to him entertained with the way the gulls disappear into the rocks
—You have a strange brother kid
passing him a slug of beer to celebrate the night, they lived in shacks, in the middle of bricks, in the middle of planks of wood, not very far from us, with clothes hanging on lines, children naked from the waist down getting dirty without my mother saying
—Do you see the cross I have to bear?
commenting from a distance
—They must be sick all the time they must eat worms
and tiny vegetable gardens in a hard life with the wind of the waves, the vegetables insisting on being green and the wind

yellowing them despite sheets of plastic tied to stakes, out came the beer bottle, and my older brother grew, if he continued that way he wouldn't fit inside doors, in the foosball café they allowed him to drink a glass

—Next year, kid

the same refusal of all Augusts

—Next year, kid

until the Augusts ended precisely in the year that maybe, who knows, it could be he'll hang on

—You're already eighteen, right?

he was already eighteen, he'd hang on, but the Alto da Vigia happened first, they took him off the beach, they came to this house to greet my father, they gathered behind the chickens, ceremonious, counterfeit, their caps held to their chests, they didn't dare come close to my mother or to me, their skin was dark, their thumbs askew, the rest of the fingers even more clumsy smoothing their hair or tightening their collars out of respect, out of esteem, although the button resisted too small for the size of the phalanges, the mestizo to my father

—Your son was my friend

I was seeing that my father wasn't handling it well, almost hugging them, but fortunately he did handle it and I admired him for this, congratulations, a kind of smile without room for the eyelids because the nails got in the way, but congratulations anyway, it could be that tomorrow I'll take a glass to my older brother for him to drink there in, my co-worker

—That one was very little, give a big kiss to your Mama

rubbing my ass pretending to spank me

—Bad girl, bad girl

for him to drink it down there, one of the pines, distracted with the blackbirds, making less noise than the others, the impression that new blackbirds came every year, question number one how long do blackbirds live, question number two and how long to they take to brood on their eggs, a week, two, a month if you're still, I don't think it's a month, we tried hard to find the nests, but couldn't, my mother, when she forgot about being sad, the thieving blackbird that made a nest on a bald guy's head where a hair was sticking up, but what do blackbirds matter, the big man with the peach won't leave my head, avoiding the fruit bowl, give a big kiss to your Mama and I gave a big kiss to Mama asking myself why do people like kisses so much, asking myself if I like kisses, in my house not even for that, in the October of this house, whether or not, leaves falling, swaying, inside us, something inside my co-worker that, the thieving blackbird, my mother chanted, and I clapping my hands

—Continue

Senhor Tavares praising her

—You could have been an artist if you wanted

and my mother pointing to us one by one

—With this husband and these kids?

the husband just like the lifeguards, the same vocabulary, the same race, he must live in a shack, and we, naked from the waist down, chewing worms, diseased and covered with scabs, with scrawny chickens around, dirty thumbs in our mouths, not answering greetings from people, Senhor Tavares putting water to boil in the kettle

—There's not that bad

me to my co-worker, settling me on her knees

—Am I really that bad?

the leaves fell, in the middle of the chinoiserie, in a mild autumn, the sun wasn't yellow, lilac, sweetening the curtains, there was almost no noise outside, a kind of eternity guaranteeing me life for a few more years, a big kiss, another big kiss, I don't know if I believe the story of the peaches, my co-worker

—You're my sweetheart, you're my happiness

taking off my shoes so I don't dirty the sofa

—You're not going to dirty Mama's sofa

her palm on my stomach

—I love your skin can I touch your belly button?

the lifeguards came to Lisbon to ruin my older brother's funeral, they didn't even wear ties, we didn't see them because they wouldn't let us go out, fortunately, in the cemetery, not in the middle of the people, in a corner, they arrived in an old van, loose metal parts making a racket, they left in that thing that by some miracle drove away belching and smoking, on the beach they gain importance, far from the ocean they are just poor and your father, imagine, saying goodbye to them one by one, acknowledging them, embracing them, now yes, the one who took the wrench from my older brother

—Thank you

grateful because he was being acknowledged, because, if I am still, I'll belong to their class, not knowing how to talk, not having manners at the table, your father with a bottle in his vest that everybody scolded, it's natural, the priest made no comments at all but you could notice it in his blessings

—Aren't you ashamed of yourself?

two months later my mother was in the kitchen training to be a singer, the thieving blackbird went who knows where to make its nest, convinced that at least Senhor Tavares appreciated her talent, she should have been a singer, what I gave up because of you, when the lifeguards' van disappeared my father had a forlorn look, more crumbs at the dining table, more lost eyes that he could pick up with his fork and my mother would throw out to the street when she shook out the tablecloth, examining it to see if there were stains, in spite of our plates making a protective rectangle we found a way to stain it, my older brother seeded pieces of fish in the yard hoping that the gulls, Tininha's mother

—My peach

my peach doesn't remind me of shit and as far as the bits of fish it was the sparrows that ate them, now that we're talking about the sparrows I didn't see any walking around, they dart away on impulse like coiled springs, swallow what's in their beaks in the sky the way I should so I don't choke so much, I suppose I'm missing a valve in my throat, after that night my husband was suspicious of me until he slowly stopped being suspicious, the phone rang the whole time, if I answered it was nobody, if he answered it was work which wasn't called work, it was called exploitation

—I have to stop by the office tonight don't wait up for me

and a washed shirt, the brush from the dresser, not the one with the handle, the other one, my grandmother's, that my mother said was made of silver

—When I die you'll get my silver brush

working his shoulders, first this one, then that one, then this one again because of something on the lapel and I don't think it's silver since you could see, if you scratched it with a pin, the dark metal underneath, I wanted so much to be rich, you, like Tininha's parents, all the lights on at night, a sprinkler revolving in jerks, it didn't just wet the grass, it wet the wall too and the plants on our side, the maid carried the lounge chair inside, folding it into three parts that resisted her efforts, she had to use her foot to help her, a sigh of disdain at us, before disappearing in the terrace, a flowering camelia, a ceramic dwarf, with a lantern and a pick, they turned on the lantern switch, on a column on the terrace and even in the morning it attracted insects, the maid rubbed dozens of corpses with wings off the windows, some returned their souls to the lord crackling, toasted, the maid rubbing with more soul

—Damn the dwarf

with a white beard, red tunic, and miner boots, I saw one, a beautiful one, wearing eyeglasses, almost looking serious, in a store, begging my mother with a sidelong glance and my mother

—Not in your dreams

my not deaf brother wanting to climb the wall and bring it here, not even the dwarf has been spared, the camelia is chopped down at the base although there's a thinner stalk, I'm not sure of what, I hope a camelia, growing on it, I don't have the chance to confirm it and I don't know much about trees, the word camelia, not to go further, Tininha taught me, or rather she didn't teach me, she called it a camelia in the middle of the conversation and I, who until then had not even noticed it, contemplated it with respect, almost envy, the thieving blackbird, etc. doesn't leave me alone, I arrive at the gate and the verses are in me, on the little hair on top of the head and going back to the beginning, when I suppose that I am free, ready for reason, it hits me again, my co-worker interrupting the dinner grouper since my husband was an exploiter, that business about computers making you work all night and things only get resolved in the morning

—Where is that little head of yours?

it's on the beach, Mama, on the Alto da Vigia Shellfish &

Drinks, which insists even though I'm not going down to the beach without straying from the path
   —Do you want a car to pick you up?
when there are no cars and the few around are parked, with no people, with sunscreens over the steering wheel because of the sun or with covers on them, the foosball café is smaller than I remembered, darker too, with two tables outside, before they were red and now there's no color, a few pink parts here and there, lupini bean shells, and mussel skeletons, glass stains, rust on the tabletops, Senhor Manelinho alone, smoking his own fingers and stepping on them with his heel, no blond snail, a cap hiding his baldness calling attention to itself, Senhor Manelinho's wife in the kiosk and the dog dead for centuries, probably it was dead from the beginning, so distant, so still, clothespins holding down the newspapers, getting old intrigues me, as if everything bends over, unbuttons, gives up, my co-worker, forgetting the kisses, the gallbladder, a hot water bottle, a blanket, age spots on your hands that you didn't think you'd find, you phalanges thicker, closing your eyes like my mother, without an image inside, the bones of the temples so prominent, who sinister, little veins throbbing, an exhausted murmur
   —Sit next to your Mama
an arm on my knee and I wanted to remove it, I want my body without anyone bothering it, I want to reflect, I want to understand what I feel, I feel there's so little left and there's nobody to accompany me, the thieving blackbird, insisting, my God, where can I find peace except down there tomorrow, my older brother at peace, my not deaf brother is a hut that doesn't stop burning and he runs from the hut taking her with him, we never talked, we never said whatever it was, the gull with the

broken wing tried to escape him hissing, sometimes he fell asleep in the middle of the soup and my mother shaking him

—What is this?

my father wanting to protect him and remaining silent at the head of the table, as if occupying the place at the head of the table meant something, what happened to your authority, father, who didn't hit anyone with a sandal, make the universe be still with a gesture, not even words, a gesture and the house, obedient, in silence, not a gesture, a sigh is enough, where did it make its nest on the head of so and so, hopefully tomorrow I'll be free of this, it will dry up, I didn't feel like eating fruit and my mother cut up a pear for me, without checking if it was ripe

—If you don't eat vitamins, you won't grow

as if I wanted to grow, I didn't, ten was perfect, not fifty-two because of pears, Senhor Manelinho lit up another finger with his lighter and forgot it in his hand, he probably falls asleep in his soup too, his wife, without pity

—So many years of filthy habits and one of these days you'll have a stroke

not just without pity, with a secret happiness, the triumph of widowhood, the joy of mourning

—You spent your time on stupidity and what could you expect?

the house just for her, no abuser to insult her, to demand pressed shirts for excursions to Lisbon with the motor scooter mechanic, as chic as he was, they came back hung over bragging about their prowess

—What a good looking woman

the wife not uttering a peep because Senhor Manelinho would slug her, at the slightest protest, raising his arm

—Bad
and she was taking care of customers, all day, in the kiosk,
while the old man slept, demanding when he woke up, hunger
biting him
—Serve me the conger eel now
not finding the cruet
—You're not even good as a maid
and the cruet in front of his eyes, with the porcelain duck
with the oil and the porcelain duck with the vinegar, broken,
substituted by a flask of syrup with half of its label, it stuck to
the glass, the rascal, not even the steel wool removed it, don't
hold my leg, don't say anything, adjusting the hot water bottle
on my stomach
—This will pass
don't ask me in a pitiful whisper
—Who's your Mama, tell me?
settling yourself in the blanket, close your eyes like my mother's with no image inside, don't open them, please, because they're empty, empty and you won't see me get up, pick up my purse, step on the doormat, the bones of my temples prominent and the veins throbbing, you won't notice me going down the stairs, reaching the street, walking to the beach house, finding a gull with a broken wing in the yard, so like me, and a dog sniffing me suddenly taking me with him.

6.

Sometimes we feel forsaken without knowing that we are always forsaken, the other person in the room is also forsaken, we smile at them, they smile back and even though we think they do, the smiles don't cross, the words don't meet each other, they disperse before they arrive, what words would they be, the hand that takes ours isn't touching us, the furniture turns its back, the pitchers, although they are there, are absent, the objects we think we know ask

—Who are you?

searching for us in their memory which we are not part of, they lost us without finding us, the beach house surprised with me

—What are you doing here?

I looked for Dr. Clementina's number on the list and as soon as her voice answered

—Yes?

I hung up, what is the past worth, if we're not certain it existed or it gave us images that pile up in the hopes of finding what they call life, I encounter the pines and I decide

—I've had them since I was a kid

I peer at the ocean through the window and decide

—Tomorrow at seven o'clock I'll be a shadow in there

my mother on the floor next to the Thebes Bakery doing whatever, visited me one afternoon in the hospital, wearing her Sunday best out of respect for the doctors, looking at me offended as if I'd gotten sick to spite her, and who gave you the right to keep bothering me after having left one by one, no next-door neighbor to talk to

—Do you see the cross that I bear?

because they forced the next-door neighbor to stay in Lisbon after her lungs got weak, an oxygen bottle and she breathes a hiss through a tube, not a loud hiss, a bubbling that you hardly notice

—Camphor injections all day, friend

that the nurse from the polyclinic gave her protesting

—You don't stop, stay still

the next-door neighbor to my mother

—With so much camphor don't I smell like a wooden chest?

and she didn't smell like a wooden chest, she smelled like the memory of a fever when the fever breaks, my deaf brother appeared between them to put a chicken bone he'd dug up on the beach in his mouth and my mother didn't get mad, later she didn't care less

—Put whatever you want into your mouth

not having anything to do with that kid she'd lost centuries ago

—I don't have anything to do with them now that they're grown

nobody to knock over glasses or twist the fringes of the rug, it was no longer necessary to spread newspapers on the floor after waxing it, no danger of stepping on a tin car, with a sound of a crushed lobster shell, looking at the wheels, going off in different directions, spinning on the floor boards, one showed up in the bedroom, another in the kitchen, there was a third, we don't understand why, in between the cushions of the sofa, mixed with bottle tops, coins, peanut shells, not chicken bones, that my deaf brother, before they were able to hide them, picked up on the beach, my father came and went according to the caprices of his memory, outside the pantry remember it, inside the pantry when he forgot in spite of not having bottles on the shelves not even the rubbing alcohol that he drank sometimes and gave him bad breath, the syphon man, and the other one before him, whirlwinds not memories, colorless prints

—Did that happen to me?

and it happened to you, it's not important, forget about it, dead stories that your head has swept away, finding the blackbirds was such a surprise, an idea of blackbirds that I wasn't certain of the way I wasn't certain of the idea of the waves although I couldn't explain it because they don't stay still instead of moving, the geography teacher blamed the moon, a stray beach pebble that gets stuck in the trees and on which the clouds trip, it seems the wind frees it, the next-door neighbor to my mother

—If I've turned into a wooden chest, you can put sweaters in me since the camphor will preserve them

my father's and my brother's starting to collect mold in the closet, a smell of mushrooms in which no voice speak to us, like my older brother's

—Girl

or the bicycle bell that lay mute in the garage, an old house, old waves

—We're limping along here

other lifeguards, what has become of the mestizo, if I ran into him

—Do you remember my older brother who hit the dog

he sitting on a crate trying to remember, giving up, hitting a mosquito on his thigh and flicking it away

—There were so many people

wanting to help me, you could see it in his expression, the same shirt, the same pants, the same cap, time, despite going by, stays still, Tininha's voice turned into a woman's

—Yes?

on the phone, not happy, dragging, how voices become worn, not just the face, the stomach, the skin, if I talked with her about princess earrings, she wouldn't believe me

—Are you serious?

the lifeguard appeared with a cigarette stub

—Do you have matches, ma'am?

not girl, ma'am, don't say that I've changed, and I hid her again, my older brother's dog, what other dog could it be, we go through life finding the same creatures and the same things, nothing changes, at the end, he turned over the buoy and disappeared, what am I doing here, there was a time when men followed me, they don't follow me anymore, my husband running into me in the living room

—I didn't even notice

my co-worker talking with an intern in a long secret conversation, the same tender attention that she gave me, the same fingers that almost touch, don't touch, embroider designs in the air, authoritarian expressions, comprehensive, needy

—Give Mama a kiss, precious

and the intern listened to her, lining up circles and pentagons

on a pad, probably she had an older brother who threw himself off the rocks too, probably a lost child, my co-worker to me in a casual tone
—Friendly and small
without giving me her arm on the pretext of a step, look she can go down, she doesn't get dizzy spells, she lied, Tininha on the phone
—Wait
not for "tu", for the formal you, você
—Wait
a long silence inspecting what was left of childhood, only her father washing the car and the name Rogério
—Rogério, how ugly
in a corner, who would this Rogério be, what's he doing here, he didn't do anything but he bothered her without understanding why, she abandoned that Rogério when she came back to the surface
—I have no idea, I'm sorry
of bed eighteen yes, from Rogério no, if all her patients assaulted her with idiotic stories her Sundays would be hell
—I'd appreciate it if you didn't call me anymore
and a bang without a goodbye that prolongs itself to this day, although from time to time, in the middle of a consultation, Rogério disturbs her
—What does this one want with me now?
a gardener or someone like that who worked for her mother or a peach that showed up and left at the same instant, her mother on a red sofa
—Say hello to Rogério
a gentleman running his hands up her leg and stroking her cheek

—You have such a big daughter?
not for her, so that the mother would be happy
—You had her when you were twelve, right?
the mother giving a jovial elbow nudge to the gentleman
—I'm starting to like you
and Tininha, as she left, her back to them
—She had me when she was thirty you dope
slowly before
—She had me when she was thirty you dope
and then quickly, taking refuge with the cook who let her lick the dessert pots and snuck cookies to her bed, if it hadn't been for Consuelo my childhood would have been a nightmare, whether she hurt a knee or got frightened by an animal the cook would hug her
—Conceição is here
she left for her part of the country when her parents got sick and Tininha spent weeks dripping her unhappiness on the pillow, after years went by her mother
—Go see who's in the kitchen
and in the kitchen was a provincial woman with white hair, without an apron or sandals, dressed as if for a baptism, wearing a cheap necklace, one of those who give away the traitors
—They bought me in the fair
and the dentures, emotional, slipping on her gums, extracting a handkerchief from her bag, and with the handkerchief a train ticket that immediately escaped to the floor, liquid eyelids on the handkerchief
—Don't you recognize me, girl?
it was Conceição's voice but the rest was an old country woman with a gift of a little basket of eggs on the table and an

idiot ring in a cardboard box that Tininha buried in the bottom of her draw, if I wore that ring with its ridiculous filigree and its pink stone everybody would make fun of me

—Did you find an address for a day maid?

Tininha, annoyed, because she let herself be squeezed by those immense emotions, contained in a cheap blouse, it was enough to feel the rough cloth, clumsy hands that held her head, pushed her away to better observe her, then hold her close again without worrying about her dentures, moving them back in place with her tongue, Conceição in a sticky love that irritated her

—My girl has grown up

I stopped licking pots and being afraid of animals, I don't need you, don't suffocate me with your manure breath, your smell of the provinces, your smell of silent misery, the egg basket with its embroidered cloth, and its crude gift tag with her misspelled name, Fer yuse frum Conceissão, the box in the corner, it's been centuries since I thought about you, it came out of her, unbidden

—It's been centuries since I've thought of you

and the emotional immensities quivered, the clumsy hands separated from her, how many hours were you in the train, crushed between emigrants and soldiers on leave, to visit me, how much did you spend on the ring, pulling coin by coin from your purse and putting a down payment on it to the owner of the store who agreed to hold it for a month, you were my only mother, the other one, when I came near her, was occupied with the peaches

—Do you want to mess up my hair?

her hair, her makeup, her dress, the nails that hadn't dried yet, Tininha's mother shaking them and blowing on them now applying a drop of nail polish remover that you couldn't see with a magnifying glance and discovering it in a flash, Conceição

—Don't treat me that way, girl

seven hours in the train, more emigrants, more soldiers, crates of livestock, boxes, wooden benches that ground up the kidneys, I won't tell you that the ticket fell down, when the conductor asked

—Ticket please

if you don't find it, it's your own fault, who told you to show up here to bother me, the conductor

—If you don't pay for another ticket plus the fine, I'll turn you in to the police in Santarém

as soon as I go into my room, I tear it up maybe the police will have pity on you

—Conceição is here

deception, so many skinned knees, so many terrifying insects and I was alone, an excuse to my mother who could not excuse whatever her reason was

—My father and my mother are in a bad way

my mother, who any driver would deceive, believing you, Fer yuse frum Conceissão, what a hoax, what's more, tiny chicken eggs fed on pebbles and this ring, frankly, who do you think I am, I'm a doctor, not a little kid, respect me, Conceição spreading herself in the emotional immensities

—I didn't mean to disrespect you, forgive me, girl

and she didn't see her again, at certain moments when anxiety gripped her, she

—Sit on my bed Conceição, until I fall asleep

and realizing she had asked

—Sit on my bed Conceição, until I fall asleep

only after having said this, she was furious with the cook

—Are you going to follow me forever?

face down on the mattress, buried in the pillow

—Who gave you the right to abandon me, tell me that?
　　she
　　—I hope the Santarém police put you in jail for a thousand years
　　the secretary handing her an envelope
　　—The X-rays you asked for, Doctor
　　and Tininha in front of the window
　　—Can't you see I'm busy, put them in my office
　　losing herself in taxis the way I lose myself in the gulls and the blackbirds, I lose myself in my co-worker descending the stairs without help, far in front of me
　　—She's nice, the little one could be your daughter
　　doing the numbers in her head
　　—Fifty-two, right?
　　comparing me with the intern, repulsed by my body, my arms, my face, I'm not your pearl, I'm not your doll or I stopped being it this morning, look at the tide rising, look at the fans of foam, the fishermen reeling in their catch with slime on the hooks, not fish, what fish are there in these waves, there are the bones of drowned people, tattered clothing, farewells that the water dissolved, fifty-two years old, how awful, and my mother, always thinking of herself
　　—Imagine then I was
　　as if it were possible to compare my age to yours, you are old and I'm aging which is worse, once it takes hold of you what a difference it makes in us, we endure and that's all, you resign yourself to enduring and if I continue after Sunday I'd give up on living to endure just the same, there are already parts of me that endure, in fact, this cellulitis, these stretch marks, getting out of breath on the stairs, once in a while my left arm

—Do you think I'm what I used to be?

tapping my shoulder, I put cream on it, and it softens warning

—If you wait a little the cream won't make any difference

we don't resort to creams, we don't resort to massages, we don't resort to pills, we just go on with a prosthesis, ma'am, substituting the humerus because our organism is like a car, after driving I don't know how many kilometers you have to change the parts, this explained with your hands, one in the shape of a shell and the other a fist circling the shell, one finger coming out of the wrist impeding the rotation, in a little while two fingers impeding it even more

—Do you see?

I see, Doctor, how much does the surgery cost, instead of

—How much does the surgery cost?

I fascinated with the hands imagining myself made of cylinders, screws, and connecting rods

—Does it work?

and my co-worker with the intern on her mind

—What if we don't have tea today?

since the first moment that I feel blocked, not hearing her, occupied with my interior mechanisms that are increasingly more audible, bellows, fan belts, oil, the heart is a salient aspirant pump, at least that's what I remember from school, Dona Isaurinha, my ignorance about what aspirant and salient meant didn't bother me, it was the fact that the heart was a pump that intrigued me, at eight years of age, a number inconceivable to me, I'm just fine in my chair and suddenly boom, Dona Alice abandoning her cleaning

—Exploding at eighty isn't bad, congratulations

Dona Isaurinha, imperturbable

—No matter how many emotions you stuff into you you're nothing more than a pump

and I was apprehensive that if I could kill an archduke with mine, a guy with a beard taking my heart out of his trench coat and throwing it at a carriage, his hand in the shape of a shell and his wrist

—I can't guarantee that it will work but most of my patients improve

and because he called me a patient, what a lack of tact, I refused the operation, let my little bellows come to an understanding among themselves and on the next day my co-worker was with the intern again, without any blockage, her attention growing and this time not the fingers, the knee almost on the knee of the other, moving away, moving closer, brushing against her with a casual movement and remaining there, the intern moved with the pretext of looking behind her and in resuming the position of her knee on the opposite side of the chair, inaccessible, what kind of Saturday is this, in a little while it will rain because the earth seems to rise up to meet the clouds, an exaltation of plants like before a kiss, Tininha looking for Conceição's ring in the drawer

—Don't tell me I lost it

taking things out quickly, nightgowns, stockings, scarfs

—What happened to you Conceição?

the blackbirds flying heavily, my grandfather lifting my father

—He keeps getting heavy as lead, the rascal

in the direction of the chapel, no, going beyond the chapel in the direction of the olive grove or what was behind the olive grove, mimosas and weeds, a kind of swamp where larvae grew and unicorns came to drink, with a tractor in ruins, half sunk, inside, if I woke up before dawn I was almost sure I heard it working. God willing it won't rain on Sunday and I won't slip on the rocks, my grandfather proud of the lead I don't understand why, the obsessions people have, Tininha found the box but the ring was too small, on one of her pinkie fingers it fit on the first phalange, on the others it went passed the first but the second blocked it, there must be a train to the provinces, full of emigrants and soldiers, next week, thinking

—There must be a train to the provinces next week

certain she wouldn't take it, in the first place I don't know which village and in the second place, even if I did, Conceição would be dead the

—Don't treat me this way, girl

feeling pain in her salient aspirant pump, it's not just a pump, Dona Isaurinha, take care that it doesn't hurt and it hurts, cars suffer the same way people do, treat them with more consideration

—Do you feel ok?

and of course they don't answer, they're proud, my mother saying to us as she closes the windows

—Are you going out with this rain, are you crazy?

and the waves, gray, rolling down the beach, Senhor Manelinho's wife unfolded plastic sheets over the newspapers, held down by clothespins that were born out of her hands, teach me that trick, ma'am, to show my co-worker, disappointed in the intern

—An irritating little bitch

consoling herself with me

—How about tea with your Mama at home, what about it?

her mouth seen up close had too many gums, my not deaf brother to my mother

—We have nothing to play with here

my not deaf brother with his nose on the glass, I sitting on

the floor trying to make a braid, my older brother in the garage
fixing a pedal, with Tininha's mother observing him inside a
transparent robe, abundant with gauze roses and petals, until she
gave up on my older brother
—I've never liked this place
Conceição in a pauper's cemetery, at the base of a hill, toppled
crosses and stones turned on their sides, a skeleton sticking out
of the ground that they buried again
—I wanted to come back
and the tendency of the dead to communicate with us,
Conceição didn't pay the owner of the store for the merchandise,
if I enlarged the ring it would fit but who enlarges fake jewelry in
Lisbon, the goldsmith choosing his words carefully
—This isn't worth stealing, Madam Doctor
and Tininha standing tall at the counter
—Enlarge it anyway
because I don't care if they make fun of me and I don't care
if I'm a day maid, who knows how many knee injuries are waiting,
how many insects, how many pots to lick not mentioning the
compotes, the almonds, the sugar on the cakes, Conceição's room
in the back of the house, not a window, a crack that the vine
covered, the doll on the bed
—One day when I leave the doll will stay, girl
and my mother wanted to put it in the garbage but I didn't
let her, I stuck it into the laundry room where the sewing
machine without a needle was stored, the refrigerator without,
my co-worker
—Since you're here sit closer
not asking, ordering
—Sit closer

and I sat because this October makes me lazy, no deaf brother trying to talk, no not deaf brother throwing gasoline on huts in the middle of threats and gunshots, a creamy October, rose colored, leaves that fall, trembling, on the roof, a long melancholy in which my zones turned to liquids and others slowly fall asleep, my father not almost with a hand on my head, his hand on my hair, and staying with me, look at the sewing machine without a needle in the laundry room and the refrigerator without a door, the doll stayed in her parents' home and it was the doll she visited, not her mother, she lingered in the threshold, promising

—I'll come back

her mother

—I thought I heard your voice

and Tininha left without saying goodbye, it wasn't that she detested her, she had grown up too much for hate, she just irritated her

—That's normal with old people

my deaf brother screeching like the gulls at the equinox, the

—Sheee saaills seeea sheells

of an albatross that got the wind wrong, it searched for the updraft that would take it far and it caught a current that threw it to the rocks tearing open its breast, my co-worker with her nose close to the teapot

—Are you happy that your Mama is with you

mother, at the iron

—What's that smile about?

and she wasn't smiling, she was looking at Conceição's ring in a real velvet box, with a silver clasp, she looked at Dona Clementina with it on her finger

—How much

turning the hand in the goldsmith's mirror, proud of the ring
—Make fun of me, I don't care
going down to the beach on the bike and my older brother
—Hold on
going up and down the path, swerving around the fruit crates, avoiding a shadow without substance, able to go through walls with a subtle whistle and that people call a cat, in which there are suddenly eyes, suddenly claws, and in between the claws a velvet that refuses caresses disappearing into the air, my mother to my older brother
—Don't be late sooner or later you'll kill yourselves
and it sooner or later we'll kill ourselves, imagine your aim, you hit the target, the mestizo lifeguard
—Your brother was cool
the rain slows down, just horizontal drops, a blackbird returning, two blackbirds, don't recall an August like this one when there is so much joy at my return, it's enough to notice the pines, there they are talking about happy things, the water dripping down the needles in a slow jubilation, my co-worker
—There are times that I act silly forgive me
and I don't have to forgive you. I don't care the way I don't care that you guarantee that you're my Mama because you're not, see, if my husband called me, and he doesn't call, I'd not come back here, I'd be in my living room with him, the albatross flying from rock to rock until reaching the water, poor thing, one of the donkeys trotting along on the pebble beach, my mother, in a time that continues after all, the thieving blackbird where did he make its nest, if you were an artist you wouldn't have married my father and we wouldn't exist, my deaf brother would be in a home making paper windmills, my co-worker

—We won't talk about it my pearl, give your Mama some love

I gave Mama some love, Mama gave me some love, the police to Conceição in Santarem

—If you weren't so ridiculous you'd be in a mess Auntie be thankful to God that your feet are in the grave

and she waited on a bench under the timetable for the next train, one was a freight train that carried cattle, with two cars for country hicks as still as she was except for children that stilled down with a piece of bread, a woman was breastfeeding in the middle of the groaning boards and rusty sacks, I've never breastfed, I never felt one, Dr. Clementina leaving the goldsmith's shop, doubting

—Will I have the courage to wear this?

I've never felt a child breastfeeding from me, Dr. Clementina thought she would, thought she wouldn't, put the ring in the box

—After all, she was just a maid, I'm out of my senses

a maid like the rest, calculating, sly, capable of stealing because they all steal, lying because they all lie, if an ashtray breaks they don't take responsibility

—I broke it

they answer

—It broke

convinced that they are smart and stupid, if they weren't stupid they weren't maids, they'd be ladies of the house like my mother and give orders, humiliate, I'll discount the ashtray from your salary so you'll learn to be honest, how did it break, you learned to walk on her legs, didn't you, to the corner of the furniture and you decided to fall on the ground

—I'm coming

show me the little legs of the ash tray, go on, point your feet

straight ahead, see your leg here and they were stubborn, with not response, repeating
　—It broke
　swearing
　—I didn't even brush against it, ma'am
　and I with the ring of one of them on my finger, when I learn not to be stupid, if we give in a little they twist their answers, with those people you can't dream of trusting them my uncle used to say, keep them on a short rein with high stirrups, they won't let you ride them, Tininha opened the car window, threw the box and the ring out the window
　—Bye bye Conceição
　and she felt better, Fer yuse frum Conceissáo, imagine, my mother pushing the egg basket
　—Who knows what those chickens ate, throw it in the garbage
　and I threw it in the garbage including the basket and the cloth so that now yes, my friend, you're dead once and for all I need to deal with the doll in the laundry room, my co-worker
　—We were made for one another
　made for one another in your autumn of chinoiserie, embroideries, pagodas, the chest with carvings of trees dwarfs and dragons, there must be a hammer around here and a doll in pieces that you sweep with a broom underneath the closet, the woman breastfeeding covered herself and the child with her blouse and the child, my son, sleeping the way I sleep at night, without scrapes or insects, after putting down the twins who didn't want to go to sleep, they wanted to make me crazy, my mother to them
　—My peaches
　the idiot, the kind that don't learn, how come I was born from

her, the result was I started to do stupid things from the moment I was born, my co-worker

—Agreed

and here I am with the blackbirds, if my father threw them a piece of bread they'd call him names, Saturday afternoon now, a suspicion of sun, Senhor Manelinho's wife folding the plastic sheets and therefore everything was all right, everything as I had anticipated, the mestizo lifeguard

—Your brother was cool, ma'am

and you'll see how his girl is also cool, climbing up the rocks to the very highest little hair.

7.

I thought of going to the hairdresser, so that my older brother will think I look good tomorrow, but then the thought came to me of Tininha's mother on the last afternoon I saw her, there were almost no blackbirds or sparrows in the garden, other birds in the flower beds, after a few minutes they disappeared and everything was naked suddenly, an invisible turtledove and my father on the steps listening to it

—They cry all the time, why?

not knowing how to answer him although he wasn't asking me, he was addressing a woman you couldn't see and he was little like I was, looking like the pictures in the envelope in Lisbon, from the time he weighed like lead, when he stayed still he grew and my deaf brother, squatting in front of a turned-over bucket, seemed to hear the turtledove too, I thought

—That can't be

and it didn't seem to me, the certainty that he too heard the turtledove, the certainty that the turtledove heard us too, even though we were still, just like dogs hear noises that aren't there and they smell odors that don't exist, death before it arrives, for example, walk around us, get agitated, my mother used to tell us that on the day my grandmother died the Rafeiro dog disappeared without tasting its food, not obeying when they called him, Tininha's mother's birds I think were thrushes, they say they live abroad, I don't know, they say they eat the birch bark, the intern looked for me in the teacher's room

—I'd like to talk with you, I don't know anyone here

I thought of going to the hairdresser but I didn't want my older brother to confuse me with Tininha's mother, and even if he didn't confuse me with her I ask myself if he'd recognize me and if I'd recognize him with so many people around, after forty years which of us has changed more, if the thrushes come from abroad where do they sleep at night, on the telephone wires, on a roof, in the woods, not on just one roof, on hundreds and hundreds, I must have asked Dona Isaurinha and Dona Isaurinha explained, even with her back turned, writing on the blackboard, if anyone burst a paper bag she'd suspend the intransitive verbs without changing her tone

—Arsénio leave the room

she turned back to the verbs and never made a mistake, Arsénio was alone in the recess yard, his hands in his pockets, kicking the dirt with the toe of his shoe, we saw him through the window and noticed his fear

—What if Dona Isaurinha tells my father?

beyond the recess yard was a textile factory, this was on the extreme other side of the city, far from the river, the factory was on an avenue of sycamore trees, I went by there months ago and just the building was left, if I were inclined to feel a longing for the past I'd spill liters of tears but the broken windows and the oblique railings didn't upset me a bit, because of the factory the school desks wobbled messing up my calligraphy, periods that went up and down without aligning with the lines on the paper, the noon day whistle had barely sounded when the locomotive of a weaving machine crossed the room and after its passage, in the direction of the playing field, you could count the corpses of students lining them up on a ramp, and I not satisfied that it had not crushed me, astonished, Dona Isaurinha, not concerned with Arsénio, sent one of us to the podium

—Repeat what I just taught you

scratching her face with the eraser leaving chalk powder on her cheeks, her forehead, the intern to me

—I talked yesterday with a co-worker of ours who invited me for tea but I thought she was unfriendly

and nevertheless, I think my older brother will know right away who I am, who else would look for him on the rocks, who else would come and go, rolling in the waves with him, now deposited on the sand or swept off the sand in the company of the pebbles, driftwood, the jellyfish, my mother, in the building next to the Thebes Bakery, to the next-door neighbor who wasn't with her

—Do you see the cross that I bear?

and an absence agreeing under the camphor mist, she managed a sentence or two, she didn't manage dialogues, holding on to her sheet since the bed was balancing on the edge of a black pit toward which it was sliding, Arsénio to Dona Isaurinha

—Are you going to complain to my father?

and Dona Isaurinha wiping off the blackboard

—I haven't decided yet

inside a dust cloud of chalk, oscillating to the right and to the left to the rhythm of the weaving machines, when the waves receded, I shook the drowned people

—Have you seen my brother?

one of them with a shoe missing, a girl checking to see if her bracelet was on her wrist

—I hope I haven't lost it

a child wearing shoes with clip-on bows and a dress trapped in a boulder, I wanted to free her but they didn't let me

—It's not worth the trouble, girl

people who could be in the room with me instead of me being alone, there is Dona Isaurinha teaching intransitive verbs to nobody, if we showed her the turtledoves she'd

—The turtledoves

and a cousin returning home to my aunt and uncle's house with a dozen tied to his waist, I remembered they ate them with bread, finding the tiny bones in the meat

—The bones of small birds to be able to fly

threatening to escape from the plate and to land on the porch, the bones, coming back together, turning into a new bird that grew feathers, the intern about my co-worker

—Her behavior is so strange

not my hand on her arm, her hand on mine

—Her behavior is so

gnawed nails, almost childlike, her heel on my foot stepping on me slowly

—So strange

stepping on me harder

—As strange as mine

don't you find this strange, you, it doesn't usually happen to me, I live with a friend who until the end of the month is working in the north and I was afraid my friend would come in, Dona Isaurinha inside the chalk

—I might complain to your father I might not it depends my older brother
—I didn't expect you, girl
not near the garage, coming in the gate pushing his bike
—I rode over a nail and the tire went flat
on the avenue where the school was there were new buildings, stores, a bridal shop, another with Indian rugs, a man who sold books at a stall lifting his pants to massage his ankle, my older brother with white hair and something of my father in his smile, the way the corners of his mouth, the way his nose wrinkled, the intern changing the subject when she noticed my wedding ring
—Are you married?
and recovering from my being married, with a silver ring on her thumb and an alert dove's throat, I have class in five minutes, what's your schedule tomorrow, a vest like Dona Isaurinha's uncle coming back with the turtle doves, the rifle barrel over his arm, I was impressed by the bird heads hanging upside-down from his belt, when they tore off the feathers my skin accompanied them until they came off making me more naked, don't undress me in school, don't take notice of the scar on my chest, give me a new breast if everything goes well and there's no time for everything to go well
—There wasn't time for things to go well brother and for them to give me a breast
I who thought of going to the hairdresser so my older brother would think I looked good, I don't put on princess earrings because they fall off when I climb up the rocks, I don't do my nails because they'll be ruined on the hillside, the intern wasn't just wearing a man's vest, she said with disdain
—Do you see how she prepares

Tininha's mother deep inside her gauze roses

—What is that?

and while Dona Isaurinha walked away, Arsénio, his hands in his pockets, still kicking the dirt with the toe of his shoe, Arsénio's mother, timid, under the shadow of her enraged husband

—Take your hands out of your pockets, stupid, and don't drag your feet

Arsénio who ended up stuffing ads into mailboxes because the intransitive verbs forbade him from flying, if one happened to run into him we'd fold a banknote that Arsénio's palm received as if he didn't understand, but what money did she give me, gentlemen, greeting us alone, on Saturdays the mass in the chapel that the sea didn't reach, one or two sheep and an empty cart came, Christ was a turtledove over the altar, the beak sideways and the wings bleeding, during the prayers hammering without ceasing on the roof, a beggar outside exposing the stump of his leg

—I'm diabetic

and hesitant pigeons between the olive grove and the empty lot, the intern

—Am I late?

with the same vest and the same blouse, my co-worker, alarmed

—What does she want from you?

suddenly exhausted, threadbare, starting Sunday she'll drink tea without company, and then the change, entire afternoons contemplating the wall, one of her knees with the needles inside it burning her, torments in her liver because of a bitter weight that isn't exactly pain, the diffuse impression that is the antecedent to pain, the pain receding, distant, one of these days it will install itself in her stomach and stay, a spigot in the bathroom that won't close and it's a good thing it doesn't close, with luck it will flood everything, how many sleeping pills does it take to, she took out a dozen, not a dozen, fifteen counted with her index finger, the second count sixteen, the third fourteen, she looked at them for a moment, it seemed there were eleven, and before so many caprices, she returned them to the bottle, the pain in her liver doesn't continue, throbbing, in the medicine cabinet expired prescriptions, the validity date always on the back of the box, stamped on the cardboard and very difficult to read, lights behind the lowered shades that went out one by one, men arguing on the street, kicking over a crate, arguing again as they walked, my co-worker sitting in the dark noticing the noise that lives in the shadows, not of the furniture, not of the wooden floor, not of creatures being born, a tenuous sound, the same, without jolts, neutral, at first she thought it was coming from her lungs and it wasn't, from a motor running in the basement and that wasn't it either, the panic of death in her guts, a hand's length away from death, the sensation that she was sleeping and walking up, the uncle with whom she spent vacations, dead for centuries

—What's wrong with you?

with the magnifying glass for the stamps transforming his eye into a glassy monster, enormous, and I'm fine, dear uncle, why dear uncle if they didn't like each other, the noise he made when he chewed bothered her, the half dozen hairs that he combed over his head to disguise his baldness bothered her, his way of saying

—Your aunt

in a gesture that, signifying nothing, signified everything, that she had exchanged him for a merchant in Estremoz bothered her, maybe she wasn't the niece of her uncle, she was perhaps the niece of the merchant who waited for her aunt below to carry her bags, looking at the porch while her aunt pulled her clothes off the hangers, his uncle with a gun in his hand

—Watch out I'll shoot myself in the mouth

the aunt feeling no remorse, bent over her blouses and skirts, folding them in order

—So shoot yourself

and he didn't, the gun is still there, in the desk or the pantry, the intern

—I'm glad you waited for me

with eyebrow pencil on her eyebrows like Tininha's mother, I

—Hello

and not just the eyebrow pencil, the earrings, not princess earrings of course, small amethysts that I felt like playing with but I didn't, the adolescent nose that I wanted to play with too, the little chin, my co-worker's aunt gathered her suitcases at the door of her room, opened the window and the curtain started to breathe right away, she called the merchant

—Antero

leaning over the windowsill on the tips of her toes, so simple to push her, my co-worker's uncle pushing the barrel of the gun near his mouth

—You want to watch?

everything was so ridiculous, the curtains swelled and shrunk in a rhythm of sleep, a dead mosquito in one of them, who flattened it there, the stairs started to be born one by one, ever closer, with intervals of soles on the landings, it's not us going up, it's the steps that are coming, playing with her earrings, her chin, the intern

—You won't be offended if I tell you I think you're sweet?

perfecting a curl with her chewed nails, after mass, in the trees

around the chapel, also turtledoves, Arsénio put away the money in a magic sleight of hand, transferring the bags to the other arm
—What does it matter we're still here
and we're still here, you're right, drink what I gave you to my health in the first café, a threadbare jacket, shoes torturing your feet, the mother, always in the shadow of the father, both in a drawer in the cemetery that she didn't visit, without a flower to lay there, even if it's dry, even if it loses petals, even if it's reduced to a stalk with a gray leaf younger than I am, less than fifty two years old, when I was little I thought thirty was really old, how unexpected to have wrinkles, not to walk doing pirouettes, not sitting on the floor because on chairs my legs didn't reach the floor, the table coming up to my throat when we ate and later, little by little, going down, when the chest got smaller in turn my mother put the curios in the bottom
—They won't reach you
the china fairy, the glass gazelle, my parents with locked arms in a photo, dressed like in the magazines I found in the pantry that were missing pages, a car with a spare wheel attached to the back, men with straw hats on the beach, the steps brought the merchant from Estremoz to the doormat, the aunt of my co-worker pushed away the gun with her sleeve to talk with him, a kind of redneck, wearing lots of rings, for whom the gun didn't exist equally
—Get the bags, Antero
and Antero, not making a peep, with a suitcase in each hand, the stairs started to go down imitating the sound of footsteps, they were still, the gun detached itself from my uncle and fell to the ground like fruit, not a metallic sound, a rotten sound, I wouldn't be surprised of the ants didn't walk over it, in a

little while they'll eat it, the intern occupied with a corner of her thumb

—This is my first teaching job

I could feel her apprehension and her breath, an almost transparent down on her neck, the certainty that she had an almost transparent down on her back, my peach, my co-worker didn't have any down, nails, bones, moles, he watched the aunt's departure from the porch, I never visited Estremoz, what would it be like, as far as I knew he didn't receive letters, the uncle pointing to the gun

—Put that away for me, please

she picking it up with two fingers as if it were a rat, her uncle worked at a bank branch counting packets of money with a rapidity that threw her into ecstasy, so agile with things, an unexpected agility, he picked up an elastic band with three fingers and made a perfect knot, instantly, to hold the packet together, the number of times my co-worker tried it in her room and the elastic, dead until then, now full of life, escaping her, my deaf brother hearing us, don't tell me he didn't, he hears not just our conversations inside his head, he hears my silent father on the sofa, he hears me waiting for my last night and the pines

—Girl

not a reproach, happy, I don't believe they know, they're so innocent, poor things, when you talk to plants, my mother guaranteed, they grow better, they don't wilt, I didn't say goodbye to her, why, I arrived at the Thebes Bakery and gave up, so much time in this neighborhood where, there on the heights, you can see the Tagus, the same gulls as on the beach, the market, the little plaza, old women with their knees exposed to the sun hoping they can dance when they get home, almost a sigh when I see the

building across the park, however I am too busy for emotions, if I had the time I'd feel emotion but I don't and my co-worker
    —What did that little hussy want from you?
    just eyebrows and fury
    —Didn't you explain to her that you have an owner?
    like her uncle, the poor thing, owned her aunt, one afternoon he showed her the dry grip of the gun and put it away in the drawer again
    —Does Estremoz tell you anything?
    where they met Antero but didn't meet the aunt
    —He went to Spain right away, that one
    a house with locked windows and a chain on the door, in the windowsill a cat surrounded by kittens stretching and yawning, she walked along a street or two, on the sunny side, calling her aunt in a low voice, if she taught her the song the thieving blackbird where he went to make his nest could be of help, to me, you might not believe me, help me, the building next to the Thebes Bakery on the street in front, look at the blue tiles, look at the spaces where they're missing, every year there are more empty spaces, the trolleys on the right, a ramp of tiny stores to the left, workers crowded into a garage, blowtorches, banging, two women nodding off, nobody, not even vases of flowers, my older brother always came back late, I would wake up as he tried not to make noise in the hall, when people try to be still there's always some kind of sudden noise, my husband in the middle of the night, talking secretly on the phone and I hearing her shouts on the other end of the line
        —I swear my wife isn't a threat we haven't slept together in months
        and his place in the bed warm next to me, I didn't even have

to stretch out my arm to feel it, he came back probing his way in the dark, hitting the corner of the China cabinet where the teapot handles were hanging from hooks, and the plates and cups tinkled endlessly, so many little chimes from the dishes, so many clinking glasses, my last sunset in a few hours and I to myself, did you ever think, you, your last night and what are you going to do on your last night, the crow on Tininha's chimney looking at you, looking at you, when a person dies they start to moan for the deceased, my co-worker

—Didn't you explain to her that you have an owner?

you do, like in the theater, didn't I explain you have an owner and the lines in your cheeks are deeper, the intern, who was correcting tests with a pencil, half black and half blue, winked at me from afar, not a vest or a man's shirt, a dress, I swear, ugly, it was badly made but it was a dress, woman's sandals and nails painted red, go figure, if there were one of my father's bottles left in the pantry I'd celebrate my last night, my husband in a murmur

—if she weren't sick, I'd have been there a long time ago, the doctor guaranteed in a few weeks she won't get up

a light under my older brother's door, he's not lying down, he's writing, and I still haven't found a single piece of paper since the Alto da Vigia, he delivered them to a stranger who left immediately, diagrams, reports, how do I answer a wink with my co-worker

—Did you explain it to her or not?

ready to twist my wrist, my uncle, absorbed in the wall, a sudden order

—Bring me the gun

checking if it was loaded, clicking the magazine into place,

releasing the safety, pointing the muzzle into his ear, my co-worker thinking that first he was going to shoot himself in the mouth, then he shot himself in the ear, at least he'll vary the place, the first onions blooming outside between the garage and the well, in the day they hibernate in the weeds, my co-worker preparing herself for the bang
    —The mess I'll have to clean up
    blood, brains, cartilage, the brains and cartilage I might be able to clean up but not even bleach will clean up the blood, fortunately her uncle handed her the gun
    —I won't give that sow the satisfaction
    he who on Tuesdays counted money with such speed that you couldn't even see his fingers, if he were a pianist he'd carry off a concert in two or three minutes with the orchestra lagging behind in the pit after the first measures, the cricket are still not singing in the dark, those who arrive too early the others devour, me to my co-worker
    —The director is looking
    and my wrist in peace
    —Is Estremoz a city or a village, Dona Isaurinha
    and a scandalized scolding in the cloud of chalk
    —Dunce
    not complaining to my mother, in my case not my father, my mother
    —It's not worth the trouble to call him, her father is a filler verb intransitive verbs, transitive verbs, and filler verbs, not my grandfather
    —You should give them all the sandal
    my grandfather disappointed
    —One can see that he's a filler verb

pines, crickets, the last blackbirds, the last sparrows, tomorrow I'm leaving with you just not to the olive grove, to the rocks, I'm tired of walking in the sand with my sandals in my hand, my legs heavy, with no strength, do you remember your flip-flops, mother, with the sequins, and the little grooves for your toes, there is the flag pole without the flag and the cork life ring feeling sorry, if I remember correctly it never saved anyone, why, leave the bones in peace in the mud of the bottom, many years from now, when they lose their calcium, they'll come back to us just like my older brother and I will come back to the building next to the Thebes Bakery with almost no tiles on the façade or the boarding house underneath, we'll arrive at my mother's door and my father in the pantry, children's voices inside, my brothers, mine, Dona Alice's vacuum cleaner over which the gulls cry with desperation

—Sheee saaills seeea sheells

while my deaf brother guides a locomotive made of cork along the floor, there's no space for the dead, there's no space for the two of us, the kitchen clock rocked from side to side brushing us away, guarantee me that bones don't lose calcium and stay on the bottom, that we dissolve into the sand and don't come back, my co-worker

—I'm just afraid of losing you, I'm sorry

and the fear of losing me as if you ever had me, sooner or later I'll be here for the last night before, I thought of going to the hairdresser so my older brother would think I look good and then I thought of Tininha's mother on the last afternoon I saw her in the lounge chair, the hairdo, the earrings, the sunglasses, the way her cheek rested on her hand and how can I compete with her, I said to the intern

—I'll be fifty-two in March, did you know?

over the fifty-two years what haven't I lost, my older brother, my father, my child, saying this at her house where the friend wasn't, a room with two beds

—We are just friends

a little living room without a sofa, colored pillows on the floor, posters of bands, drums, that you bring from Morocco, in a corner, along with clothes to wash

—a piece that you must order from Germany was damaged in the washing machine

a tiny kitchen in need of cleaning, everything needed cleaning, in fact, the thieving blackbird came and went and my mother went with it, if at least my mother would hug me or I could ride on my father's shoulders in the olive grove, rest my face on one of the pillows, sleep until Monday and wake up far away from the pines, the crickets, the night that begins inside of me and stretches in the direction of the waves, if the father of my father hadn't died he'd pick me up by the waist

—This one's heavy as lead

the intern on my shoulder

—Can I stay like this for a little while?

and you can stay here for a little while, why not, next weekend I won't be here, I have something to do somewhere else, no lampshade, a light bulb in the ceiling, the lamp base was a cookie tin with an image of two crossed Japanese fans, the intern didn't weigh on my shoulder, I didn't feel her, I felt a leg over mine and a hand, with gnawed fingernails, still on my stomach, a little stick of incense burned somewhere hidden and I could smell it, an open book turned its pages without help, reading itself, the lightbulb on the ceiling was inside me, illuminating my veins, so that the first waves after the Alto da Vigia were pink, then less pink, then the color of sand and then the color of sand forever, rest

—Did you ever wear princess earrings?

and a smile against my neck, made of memories as if there were memories in it and there weren't, there was a little elf toy that if you pressed its bellybutton started to laugh and she was afraid, you pushed it and the elf, for minutes that didn't end, they still haven't ended, shaking, mute, the intern took her hand off my stomach to rub her nose with the toy in her mind, at the same time that I noticed her looking at me

—Your age makes no difference to me

so it made no difference what the age was of the Greek wife of the pharmacist who combed her hair at the window, with a poodle in her lap, if they asked her if she'd seen me she'd answer

—Who?

continuing to comb her hair, keep combing your hair, I think, her tongue or the intern's tongue, her tongue slowly exploring my mouth, the poodle's heart faster than mine, the little nose wetter, the vibration of its paws on my breast

—Girl

while the night crickets, the ones that chase me, entered the room one by one, my deaf brother pulling my skirt

—Sheee

wanting to save me, I to him without understanding, I'm lying, I to him understanding

What is it?

and with the arrival of night the presence of the earth is stronger even though it wasn't going to rain anymore, I heard the blackbirds on the roof and my surprise

—Finally they're living here

not on the rooftop, inside the crawlspace in which I imagined rats and not rats, the birds, wriggling through a tiny crack in the tiles that allowed them to make themselves comfortable, little feet, wings, beaks, if I'm still eggs too, what will happen when in a month they tear down the house, how will they knock down the walls, the roof, the wall that separated me from Tininha, what will they build here and none of us will see it or they won't build anything, an empty lot of agave plants in which a bicycle bell doesn't ring, my co-worker

—When are you coming back from that house?

I

—I'm leaving the house on Sunday

it's true, I'm leaving the house tomorrow at six o'clock, I'll walk down to the beach, pass the last bus to Lisbon next to the kiosk and the driver talking with Senhor Manelinho's wife who is starting to pile up the newspapers, I look to see if a toy elf is moving around on the shelves and there is no toy elf, fortunately, I to the intern

—There are no more toy elves, and you don't need me

while the Greek wife of the pharmacist lifts her skirt at me

—Why is age important, girl?

it's not important, the proof is that my mother at the table

—Fifty-two years old and you still don't know how to lift your fork

my mother

—I want to know if the Alto da Vigia will at least straighten you out tomorrow

my mother to the next-door neighbor

—What bothers me is that they think I didn't know how to raise them and her voice, that has forgotten us, where did the thieving blackbird make its nest, thinking of Senhor Tavares's admiration too far away to hear her, a man who sang in the amateur choir when he was young, that is before he was fifty-two, and he knew how to appreciate talent, my older brother taking the bike out of the garage

—You don't have to walk to the Alto da Vigia, I'll give you a lift

the intern kissing me again

—There's something about you that makes me feel safe

something in you that makes me feel safe, imagine, something in you that makes me face the toy elves without hiding in anyone's lap or behind my father

—Father

my father almost your age, forty-six or forty-seven, I think, my mother forty-four, they had me early and if they had me early what about my sister two years before me, I didn't tell you I have a nephew, I have to show you the picture if I find it in the drawer, when we get up I'll look for it, the proof that age doesn't matter is what I was capable of, believe me, don't believe me, of, let me change position because my arm fell asleep, I need to open and close my fingers to feel them again, what was I saying, I know, I'd be capable, if you were good to me, if, and if you feel like being good to me, of falling in love with you, I like your way of speaking, your skin, the petals instead of nail polish, the taste of, do you mind if you move over there a little on the pillow because I'm starting to feel a twinge in my neck, they say my bones have been weak since I was a child, I took more than a thousand spoons of syrup and the doctor told me to be careful because of fractures and complications, in gym, for example, they didn't let me do almost any of the exercises, if I moved around too much my father would say

—Watch out

and I in a cast like a mannequin, one of these days I'll imitate a mannequin for you, don't consider me rude if I kiss you again, play with you this way, just with my little finger so I don't hurt you, my little finger doesn't bother you, of course, if you allow me I'll experiment with two fingers, my mother leaning over the laundry basket

—Deeds are like seeds, they grow to flowers or weeds

while my father leaves the pantry, he notices his shirt is out of his pants and he straightens his shirt without straightening it, one part of the shirttail inside his pants the other hanging out, my father who put the whole world inside a slipper

—Girl

looking at me, even though I wasn't sure he saw me

—Girl

sitting on the sofa almost missing it and now it's night and an enormous cricket is coming toward me determined to eat me.

8.

I didn't remember there were so few lights in this place except for the occasional street lamp between the trees, one or another lantern on a porch and the halo of the sea, the dark house, the dark street, behind the well a dark mass of bushes that shudder in the wind and then grow still again, I don't see them, I just know they exist, a walk in this house because the moon, when the clouds forget to hide it, invents walls that are larger than the day walls that allow me to displace myself among them, who knows if it's in this house that I lived or in another one that the moon created, a shine in the window frames, a piece of walkway, a box that they forgot with dishes and clothing, where I am, in fact, it seems there are voices and not voices, presences and not presences and nevertheless the suspicion, in a corner of my soul, that we live here, a cousin of my mother's, with a candy in one of her hands and the other one empty, hiding it behind her back like the clouds did with the moon and showing me each one in turn, with closed fists
—Which hand has the candy, girl?
my mother smiling, suddenly so young

—Do you hear your cousin Fernando?

cousin Fernando was very tall, everyone was very tall at that time

—Which hand has the candy, girl?

my mother was my age at the time, funny, wanting to pick one of the hands, she can't boss me around now, she can't scold me, Cousin Fernando to her, his hands outstretched

—Do you remember you loved this game?

my mother pointing right, pointing left, hesitating

—Wait

afraid to pick, my grandmother, who was also smiling, stopped smiling and suddenly became old, what would she have been like thirty years ago

—I never met a child who was so indecisive, she'll be that way her whole life

my grandmother, in the course of time, looking at her with displeasure

—Even as a young woman you couldn't decide on Cousin Fernando's candies

and Cousin Fernando, who had meanwhile gained the authority of his cane and his twisted mouth conferring him with the monopoly of reason

—Leave the girl alone, Filomena

through the less oblique vertex of his lips, in a vague sequence of syllables that increased on the ascendant, what's going on with your larynx, Cousin Fernando, who has to construct words using his tongue like a finger that chooses the pieces of a puzzle while contemplating the solution

—Leave the girl alone, Filomena

and my grandmother

—The one who speaks doesn't live here

Cousin Fernando, installed in the armchair, to me, with his cane between his knees and with one hand weaker than the other, and fewer wrinkles, the inert thumb between the remaining fingers

—Where's the candy, girl?

a much more serious candy than regular candies and which my life depended on, I pointed at the normal hand

—Here

my heart in shreds, what will happen to me if I guess wrong, Cousin Fernando prolonging the agony, with his hands side by side

—Are you absolutely certain?

with an impassive expression, conscious of my agony, my mother agonizing with me, and I, surprised,

—If you stay silent, you like me

given that I assumed she didn't like us, I only heard prophecies and censure from her

—You won't rest until you kill me, isn't that so?

a question that my grandmother agreed with in a sigh in which coffins and solemn people floated paying respects to my father

—You all are killing your mother

and it's possible that this was true, I don't know, sometimes she cried trying to hide it from us and I didn't understand why, the thieving blackbird forgotten, if my deaf brother approached, she shook him with brimming eyes

—If it weren't for you

and my deaf brother astonished, Cousin Fernando didn't open his hands and the universe waited, if one tried to help him get up he said haughtily

—That's not necessary

with my father supporting him with difficulty since the

bottles in the pantry didn't help either, the two in a disjointed dance that ended with Cousin Fernando in the chair again, not upright, twisted, looking around in surprise, I didn't remember there were so few lights in this place except for an occasional street lamp between the trees, one or another lantern on a porch and the halo of the sea, I heard the owl in the direction of the chapel in which there were possibly lizards and rats in the little saint's cloak because the chapel had been abandoned, there were even daisies on the altar climbing up from the floor slabs, this house is dark, the street is dark, after the well a dark mass of bushes that shudder in the wind and then grow still again, with so many changes what has become of me, my co-worker

—Will you call me when you get there?

and if a phone booth appears on the Alto da Vigia I'll call you so you can hear the waves, I'll turn the receiver toward the ocean and you'll be able to hear them growing, what will they say about us, me to Cousin Fernando

—Why don't you open your hand?

and he stared at me with a severity that didn't have to do with me, my mother tapping me on the clavicle

—He went away for an instant he'll be back soon

a sentence coagulating, independent of him

—Is it Friday today?

and it's Saturday, Cousin Fernando, not even twenty hours are left to me, if I unwrapped the candy there was a second paper that no nail could peel off, if I put it in my mouth it stuck to my gums and the second paper would shred in my teeth, one of which hurt me, make an appointment at the dental clinic because you don't mess around with cavities, Cousin Fernando stuck for a while in his Friday, there are days like wells that you can't get out of even with a rope, you're in the muck and mud and a branch of a lemon tree is imprinted on the sky in the company of its own shadow, getting to the phone, the foam speaks for me and my co-worker insisting on my name that the gulls can't decipher, sheltered in a crevice of the rocks, how do they hear if they don't have ears and how do they smell if they don't have a nose, they just discover fish, they are happy to squawk, a fragment of paper gets stuck on my tongue, I spit it on the rug and my mother

—What do you think you're doing?

since, just as I thought, she doesn't like me, a little piece of paper that you hardly notice what harm does that do, ma'am, Cousin Fernando, tangled up in Friday

—I swear I didn't touch the sponge cake

my mother to the past of the albums where she continues to live in a faded way, hidden by buns and mustaches

—If I let you, you'd eat a whole sponge cake

this in a kitchen similar to the interior of an old locomotive, vapor, tubes, furnaces, workers in caps pumping bellows, we must have been rich back them, satisfied ladies on a square of grass, colonels playing tennis in caps, I don't remember I didn't remember there were so few lights in this place at night, my father was left leaning over my deaf brother in his crib, my mother lying in the bed

—Do whatever you want, I'll accept it

and he didn't do whatever he wanted, he kept sharing the mattress with her in silence, out of cowardice, shame, pain, the intern

—Are you with me out of pity?

I'm not with you because I pity you, I'm with you to remember who I was, the same credulity, the same enthusiasm, the same search for something you didn't know how to name and that, you'll see later, doesn't exist, there's the halo of the sea, Cousin Fernando emerging from Friday

—You guessed right

and I guess what, Cousin Fernando, a candy that gets stuck in my mouth, with more paper, after taking it out, that I can't get rid of the way you can't get rid of your cane, it's not you I pity, it's what you will become one day, when you lose a child and they remove your breast, my deaf brother in a cradle next to my mother, where my brothers before him and I lay afterwards, my father awake night after night listening to him, full of questions that transformed into new questions and answers that transformed into cliffs, how were you capable of making me sir, my older brother remembered that for months he slept on the sofa, not lying down, with a blanket on his knees, and not dreaming, detesting her, one day he returned to the bedroom, undressed and ordered

—Come here

and he detested her more, he warned

—Don't kiss me

his head far from hers, not allowing caresses, without taking off her shirt or her socks

—Be still and shut up

the dark house, the dark street, beyond the well a dark mass of bushes that shudder in the wind and then grow still again, I don't see them, I just know they exist, the way my mother existed, my father

—Don't open your trap

the only time in his life when he hit the world with his slipper, the next week there were bottles in the pantry, shoving the jars, the packages, the bottles, and the pieces of bread crumbled at the table distant from my brothers, distant from her, if my mother asks my father

—What do I matter to you?

without concerning himself with anyone, my older brother remembered that one day he brought a woman to the house, he ordered my mother

—Clear the bedroom for me

he paid the woman at the door and sat down at the table waiting for dinner, my older brother remembered my father saying

—Don't change the sheets

and for a month the sheets stayed on the bed until my father said

—You can change them, they don't smell anymore

my older brother remembered the woman saying to my mother

—I didn't know you were his wife, I'm sorry

and my father, mocking her

—You call her that, do you?

I walk here because the moon, when the clouds forget to hide it, and in which hand did Cousin Fernando, invents bigger walls than the walls during the day, that allow me to displace myself in them, Cousin Fernando to my mother

—Five réis that kid isn't stupid

he went down the stairs with a solemn gait, arranged his complicated parts in a taxi, jacket, knees, trunk, a cough that undid him, what happened to the nose, what happened to his right sleeve, they paid the driver

—Give him the change

because Cousin Fernando was embarrassed about his deformities, there he goes rattling to the first floor where his stepdaughter waits for him, my God the quantity of things, atrocious to manage, that compose a man, how do you keep that all together without losing a tibia or a kidney, my older brother remembered that there were other women until I was born and my father to my mother

—Do you want to watch?

I didn't remember there were so few lights in this place, the step where my father sat was visible in the dark, after I was born nobody, he, checked me in my crib, to the bed where my mother locked her face in her hands

—It seems that with me you are lucky

and from then on, with the help of the bottles, he slowly gave up, the intern showing me her nails

—I've stopped biting them since I met you

I don't know if it's this house I lived in or another that the moon created, if I paid attention I'd notice the waves, I still dream of ghosts that chase me, trying to grab me, at a certain point I can't escape and the instant a claw grabs my neck I wake up, my husband from inside the pillow

—Can't you sleep?

in a voice that reminds me of Moledo, without smelling of a man, smelling of a boy, speaking of boys why did they steal mine in the hospital, I didn't do any harm to anyone, I didn't offend anyone, if I embraced my husband, he'd pull away from me

—What is this?

the water glass on the night table, with a saucer on top of it, tinkled by itself, I saw the closet and our clothes on the bench, shadows of fleeting birds in the lowered shade, my last night and the intern interrupted it, distracting me from myself

—Aren't you pleased I don't bite my nails?

the sweet-smelling incense, the cookie tin lamp base with little ducks in a water tank, her parents in a café in the south with the motorcycles of the customers at the door

—When I'm on vacation I'll help you at the lunch hour

that was in Messines and what is Messines like, who lives there, do they live like us, if my husband drowns slowly he won't notice, his beard starts to itch in the morning, men are so strange, I had silkworms in a shoe box and Ernesto was jealous

—What do you want that for?

slipping from the shelf and falling on top of them, me to the intern freeing myself from an arm that was strangling me

—Did you ever have silkworms?

gnawing at mulberry leaves that you had to keep in a bowl with water and dry them with a cloth, I liked the silkworms, the butterflies they transformed into were horrible, my mother

—For how many years am I going to have to put up with those lizards?

I, closing my eyes

—I'm blind

groping at the air, because of the furniture, taking cautious little steps, I opened my eyes a slit and avoided the closet, my deaf brother, imitating me, hurt himself on the door, recoiling from the door he stepped on my mother's sewing box, made of little compartments with partitions, one of the partitions burst confusing the buttons with the spools of thread and my mother trying to fix it

—Stop monkeying around

I didn't remember there were so few lights in this place, the dark house, the dark street, beyond the well a dark mass of bushes, my older brother coming from I don't know where, from the waves, I think, covering my face with his palms

—Guess who?

my older brother with me on the colored pillows, not the intern, the long stick of incense that didn't break off, I was twelve when you left and I felt like killing Tininha's mother for looking at you, wanting to kill you both, and the post office clerk, if you went down the beach road with her on the bicycle fender, I'd find the fish knife, the big one, in the drawer, and stab her, when you're twelve you don't think you aren't capable, I was capable, even today I'm capable, the intern

—You look like you're about to hit me

taking my older brother's place on the pillows and who gave you permission to take his place, he was the one here with me, he let me come in his room, he let me rummage around in his drawers, he gave me paper to draw on while he studied, once I broke the clip of his pen, it wasn't fake gold, it was almost gold, it didn't have the ambition to be gold and it didn't get mad, I hid the clip in the cap and my older brother

—Don't worry about it

fixing it with his penknife and straightening it out with little taps on the edge of the table, gold resists everything, when he changed one his bike tires he made me a rubber bracelet with a tin clasp that I keep in my jewelry box, that and the ring my husband gave me, a few necklaces, a few earrings, a four-leaf clover made of enamel, that was supposed to give me luck and didn't, if it were lucky I'd still have my breast and my son and we'd all be together, my father almost touching my head, my not deaf brother with no huts burning, my deaf brother saying

—Sheee saaills seeea sheells

not even a bottle in the pantry, I leaned my forehead on the intern's and she began to calm down little by little

—You scared me for a minute, you know?

the Messines café, the father at the counter, the mother waiting tables, an African cook handing the plates to the mother through a square opening rimmed with tiles, remains of magazines and newspapers on the freezer chest, men in caps all day under the altar candle of a glass of Medronho liqueur that was missing the saint's prayer card, in church just one knee on the ground, a handkerchief underneath it to protect their pants, the intern, grateful, rubbing my back

—Tell me you believe what I feel for you

and I stayed far away so I wouldn't have to hear sincere lies, a turning in the pines and silence again after a pinecone or a nest freed itself from the branches, my older brother made me tiny pots and pans, with handles and everything, tearing off a page from the spiral notebook full of written sheets of paper, copied from a book, not the *Manual for the Perfect Carpenter*, another one, without drawings, that he hid in his T-shirts, titled *Power to The Working Class*, I

—What is the working class, bro?

the intern's fingers in a place that tickled, and I laughed despite myself, my older brother not realizing he was imitating my mother

—You'll understand when you grow up

placing a notebook over the book

—Forget it

and I thought I'd forgotten it, it came back without my wanting it to, the amount of junk, buried inside us, that resuscitates saying

—Here we are

bringing more ruins along with it, for example Tininha's

father holding the hose, to Tininha's mother, looking at my older brother and then looking at her

—At least show me some respect

not indignant, asking, I don't remember there being so few lights in this place and the enormous toes in the sandals getting bigger and bigger, Tininha's mother brushed him aside with a gesture and the hose wilted in a single drop, if my co-worker would read what I write she'd invite me to sit on her lap

—Sit here, little one

on her blouse a brooch that pricked me, just my luck, the younger one tickles me and the older one pricks me, my husband doesn't tickle or prick, he doesn't come near me, he asked

—What are you going to do at the beach house, can I at least ask?

without curiosity, inattentive, if I saw him in the armchair, I wouldn't even see him, I would find him in bed pointing his nose at the ceiling

—There's a stain there

followed by a lecture about crumbling plaster, speaking slower and slower until he fell asleep, lulled by his own voice on his mattress of words, he jolted awake for a moment

—Tomorrow I'll talk with the upstairs neighbor

and I lost him, the upstairs neighbor who played, fewer beetles than I thought, violin in the opera orchestra, she read letters in the vestibule and put her junk mail on our mail slot in spite of the sign on the door No Soliciting, she never greeted me when we met, she lowered her hat a centimeter and the mark of her instrument was imprinted on her skin, in the intern's apartment was a viola now, to keep the Moroccan drums and the Japanese fans company, my husband spent hours talking about the stain with the neighbor and when he came downstairs he had French perfume on his right lapel, the same that permanently floated around the mailboxes, different from Tininha's mother's and what my mother wore from the perfume spray bottle or at Christmas, darkening her eyelids with a kind of coal that turned her eyes into two long anxious kisses for someone to receive them, from which my deaf brother escaped moaning and forced my father to linger in the pantry between bottles, my co-worker pinching my nose like a bulb horn

—Poop

and arranging me on her knees because the leg I was sitting on was exhausted

—Won't you give Mama a little love?

and why not give Mama a little love, you give Mama love, a peck on the cheek that transformed her face, my finger pinching her nose

—Poop

and we are two cars, imagine, a race from here to the bedroom, the latter obeying what the first one commands, look at the tin knobs on the bed and the curtain screening the autumn, jade horses lined up on the dresser, asking

—Knock us on the floor with your elbow

and I wanting to satisfy their demand, when winter dies here, the lace bedspread, the pillow of the husband that she took out from the chest, the siren from a fire station unrolling its announcement of pain, Lisbon so melancholic inside this floor, I to my co-worker

—Have you ever thought of killing yourself?

she, busy unbuttoning her blouse, first serious, almost thinking but keeping herself from thinking, deciding I was joking, and although she decided I was joking, she doubted that I was, the blouse on one of the bedpost knobs, her aging skin reaching against me

—If you let me, I'll die, I don't have to kill myself

as lost as I was

—Poop

in her nose again, that I, out of pity

—I like to fool around with Mama

on the night table an alarm clock with three legs, and a key like the wind-up objects from when I was little, advancing the hands in a confusing whirl, a second key for the bell, that she never turned, pointing to the top of her head

—I have a clock inside here

she kissed the mole on my cheek pretending to chew it

—Yum that mole is so good

a kid on some floor crossed the planet with hammers instead of shoes, my co-worker pretending to swallow

—I'll take another bite

and I was missing my husband even though he didn't care about me, eating as if he were alone, without passing me the salt or the serving dish, raising his eyebrows looking for more stains, if I changed the color of my hair he didn't notice, if I put on a new dress he didn't see it, the neighbor with the viola was ever more present on the ceiling or I became more aware of her, a chair being dragged along the floor, domestic sounds in the kitchen, even the mattress springs I started to feel the way I feel the pines and the cane field beyond the well, a wave not calling me, why would it have to call me, distanced from me, my older brother placing the draft notice on the hall table and informing my parents

—I'm not going to the war

not desperate, calm, my father crumbling bread at random, I to my older brother

—What war, bro?

and nobody answered, giving my not deaf brother a plastic machine gun that shot ping-pong balls at my older brother

—don't play with that

breaking it on the step, my not deaf brother grabbed a stone to throw at him, but he didn't dare throw it because my older brother

—You'll get the bike in August

the bike in August and an outing to the circus, my mother remained mute

—What war, Mother?

my father got up from the table without touching his lunch or going to the pantry, he returned at dinner with a wrinkle on his forehead that meant

—Be still

he closeted himself in the bedroom with my older brother and even with my ear to the door I didn't catch a word, my mother in the hall waiting for them to come out and they weren't going to come out, my not deaf brother to me, with the bike on his mind

—If you're nice I'll lend it to you on your birthday

my older brother came out first and sat down in the living room, my father appeared afterwards and squatted on the steps, I didn't remember there were so few lights in that place except one or another lamp between the trees and the halo of the sea, the house was dark, the street was dark, beyond the well was the shadow of bushes that shivers in the wind and then stills again, I look for them but I don't see them, I just know that they exist while I don't know if it's this house I lived in or another that the moon created, a shine in the windows, a piece of roof, a box that they forgot with silverware and clothing, it seems there are voices and there are no voices, presences and not-presences and nevertheless the suspicion, in a little corner of my soul, that we lived here, my co-worker

—If I could, I wouldn't just chew your mole I'd eat you all up

and it's not the sea that fills my head, it's the neighbor, my husband handing her the soup tureen without bothering about me

—Are you served?

my husband offering her the salt

—A pinch?

and her perfume poisoning our table, my living room, my whole apartment from the front door to the back, the neighbor as if I didn't exist or rather, because I am not, I am for my co-worker, I am for the intern who was excited that I noticed her viola

—I'm learning how to play

not with a teacher, with a sheet of drawings of fingers on chords, music decided to take over my last days, the intern and the upstairs neighbor together and my husband accompanying the rhythm with his shoe, look at the viola sticking its tongue out at me mocking me, my co-worker

—Make more doodoo for Mama

she was just missing the princess earrings and how ridiculous to see an old woman with princess earrings, put the petal nail polish on now, hug a felt doll, not me, complain about the way your mother punished you

—No sweets for a week

because you slathered yourself with her makeup looking at yourself in the mirror wearing her high heels that made you wobble, not

—Make doodoo for Mama
　　rather ask
　　—Make doodoo for the little girl
　pick up the eyebrow pencil and make yourself pretty with two lines across your forehead, enlarge your mouth with lipstick to your ears and I'll
　　—Make doodoo
　I promise, until the metal bulbs on the bedframe come off rolling toward the hall, make doodoo for Mama what idiocy, how is it that at sixty-four, sixty-four or sixty-five, it's sixty-four right, how is it that you're sixty-four and you haven't grown up, a decrepit girl under the light of October, with a comical pout growing
　　—You don't like me anymore
　her blouse shaking
　　—You don't like me anymore
　her hands tearing themselves apart
　　—You don't like me anymore
　the intern twisting the chain I wore around my neck
　　—There are times when you're so distant
　pulling at the pendant and letting it go, my mother took it one day from the little box that was an imitation of a pirate's chest and placed it over my head
　　—It was my grandmother's, take it
　observing how it looked on me
　　—I hope that Our Lady will give you more luck than she gave her
　I don't know what happened to my grandmother but it really did give me luck, I'm happy, I know how to serve myself to the soup, they don't give me the salt and I don't spill the potatoes,

my husband can confirm if he paid attention to me, my gestures with the silverware are as perfect as those of the upstairs neighbor, I don't lift the fork with my teeth, I don't pick up the knife by the blade, I don't put my elbows on the table

—Tuck in your wings, girl

they don't have to put books under my arms, the *Manual of the Perfect Carpenter* in this one and the *Working Class to Power* in the other one to force me to have manners, I take up very little space, I wipe myself with the napkin before drinking water and I don't tie it around my neck, I sit with my knees together, I only speak when spoken to because you can see if a person has manners when they're at the table, the game table and the communion table, the intern picking up the viola

—Do you want to hear me play?

I'd love to hear you play but there's no time, one day when I come earlier I'll sit on the pillows and listen to you, I'll ask for more, applaud, only now there's no way, you see, there's a nose waiting for me in the hope that I'll take it to the point

—Poop

that I'll take it back to the point

—Poop

that I won't take it to the point

—Poop

and the nose so happy

—You came back

without noticing that I was in the pines, waiting for a cloud to extend its fists to me so that I can guess which one holds the moon.

9.

Saturdays didn't used to be this way, we got up later, my mother stayed in her robe longer, the sun stopped in front of the shutters without coming in, my father went down the hall dragging on his ankles the shackles of sleep and passing his hand over his face to free himself from the night, the bed and I slowly detached ourselves from each other, it kept the mattress and I kept my arms and legs, my body, still belonging to both of us, deciding which one of us to choose, coming back to me even if with tangled sheets and with folds that it supposed belonged to me and the blanket stole from me, a dog barked inside my ears or outside, I don't know, even if it were outside I felt its paws in my bones, my father opened the kitchen door and you could hear the ocean, my older brother's room from which nobody came out, with the key not inside as when he was alive, on this side, you'd open it and the bedspread was smooth, the desk tidy, not even a sock on the floor, he left everything in order, in fact, his pen, his pencils, his notebooks, his creased pants on the hangars he who was never concerned with creases, I remember saying to my mother

—I'm going down to the beach soon

   and Senhor Manelinho informing us at the wake

   —He leaned his bike on the wall and came over to the kiosk to shake my hand

   I thinking to myself that my older brother never needed to shake anyone's hand, not to say goodbye because he didn't say goodbye, to confirm that he was alive, I asked him

   —Take me on the fender, bro

   and he walked by me without paying any attention to me, I who kept hitting a beetle with a stick until my not deaf brother, who didn't like me, stepped on it, stole my silkworms, hid Ernesto, my mother

   —Where's your sister's hippopotamus?

   he

   —I don't know

   and we found him on top of the closet or twisted up in a pot, my mother grabbed a wooden spoon

   —Give me your arm, you liar

   and my not deaf brother backing up to the wall

   —It wasn't me, ma'am

   Senhor Manelinho showed his palm as if something from my older brother was still in it and I wanting to shake it in turn to be able to find him, don't wash it, Senhor Manelinho, so that my older brother won't die again and Senhor Manelinho considering it with respect for his own hand

   —I was the last person he spoke with

   the room empty today, just like the others, there's an extra lamp in the living room, a second one at the end of the hall, the last one in the kitchen, my not deaf brother

   —I'm sorry

immediately escaping in the direction of the well, the kitchen lamp was far away, how many kilometers is it to get there, how solitude increases distances, if at least one person, it doesn't matter who, accompanied me, they don't have to talk, it's enough for them just to be there, whenever I had a fever or felt afraid or when objects were mean to me, I'd say

—I want my father

not out loud, silently, and even so he'd come, look at my life and tell me who gave you permission to die, I hate the Alto da Vigia, I hate hospitals, how many afternoons, in bed eighteen, I didn't hear the waves, they asked me whatever it was, and I was thinking about the goat on the rocks, legs failing me

—I'm going to fall

the nurse

—How are you going to fall if you're lying down, woman?

without noticing that I wasn't lying down, I was standing, scraping through the shells for a little recess to hide in, a support, everything came out of my eyes, and I didn't see, my father could see and nevertheless

—I'm alone too daughter

spending more and more time on the steps, not on the sofa, counting swallows, his bed wasn't number eighteen, twenty-three, twenty-four to your left, twenty-one and twenty-two ahead, visitors talking in low voices like in church, sweets, pictures of grandchildren, my mother touched my father and my father, father, father, to her

—Now?

not in the voice he had before, with the sound of an air chamber emptying, my deaf brother on the extreme opposite of the mattress and my father

—Hello

disappointed he couldn't manage a smile, not even his face obeyed, his fingers crumpling the sheet talking for him without our being able to understand what they are saying, and they give up, they called at dinner time, I returning to the table

—He's gone

and my mother's fork falling on her plate, mine hovered between the salad and my mouth while my chin continued to chew and my throat swallowed, contrary to what I expected, the empty chair didn't change size, it looked the same as ever, it was my deaf brother who crumbled the bread, I remember the sun on the plants on the porch and my mother with the watering can

—If I don't water them, they'll dry up

not even a drop spilled from the glasses, I noticed them, from the corner, over the sign of the boarding house, what does this matter, I

—They took him down to the morgue and they'll wait until we take care of the rest

and we took care of the rest, or rather my mother took care of the rest and my husband, not yet my husband, paid for it with borrowed money, you might not believe it but there are times when, how do I explain, there are times I miss you, I don't understand why we started to become distant when my son, not even why I blamed you, the way I don't understand my father in church, I understand him here, cousin Fernando to my older brother

—Aren't you going to say hi?

and my older brother said hi like many years later to Senhor Manelinho, cousin Fernando

—You're a man now, no more kisses

and my older brother showing me the candy that Mr. Hi had,

as mushy as the paper that stuck to it and the two of us wiping our sticky fingers on the sofa, Cousin Fernando to my older brother

—I can't eat them because they stick to my dentures

taking out his dentures, when they came out of his mouth Fernando's face was thin, when they went back in, it looked rounder

—Do it again Cousin Fernando

and I wasn't just envious of him, I was astonished, white teeth, even, with plastic gums, my older brother

—Do you brush them when they're out or in?

my mother to my older brother

—You don't ask those kinds of questions

while Cousin Fernando came over to us

—Do you want to see how they bite?

and my mother going to the bathroom hoping she wouldn't throw up until she got there, just three lights, the pines were invisible, the world was invisible, my husband, still not my husband

—May I offer you a coffee?

I ready to accept until I realized he wasn't a husband, I'd accept whatever from whomever now, even dogs, who bark in the yards once in a while, I wanted them close, even the flies, until my co-worker in a voice filled with suspicion

—Is there someone else?

so old, so tense, suddenly looking like Dona Isaurinha, I visited my mother the evening before I arrived at the beach and I swear that my father's absence surprised me, I thought if I'm still he'll be in the pantry, if I'm still he be on the park bench nearby, the same way that I was surprised by the absence of my brothers and my own, with princess earrings, my mother

—So you remembered I'm still alive?

not scolding me, accepting, our rooms, my God, the picture of my father on the sideboard that didn't look like I remembered him, thinner, younger, looking at me steadily wherever I was in the room, I almost became irritated

—What do you want?

my father, in the frame, not smiling, condemning me, he never scolded me or got mad at me and waited fifty-two years to blame me, my mother

—You look thinner

thinking of the breast operation

—Have you at least gone to the doctor?

complicated tests, X-rays, lab work, serious people waiting, those diseases don't forget about us and the deeper you probe the deeper it goes, don't make your life complicated and don't complicate mine, doctor, I just needed strong lights in this house that could protect me from the dark, my not deaf brother pulled a plant out of a planter, roots and all, and came over to the wall where I was waiting for Tininha, to hand it to me

—Now that I'm not messing with Ernesto, we're friends, aren't we?

we're friends, say hi, the dirt in his hand and mine, Tininha's mother to a friend I'd never seen, with the sharp gestures of a river bird pecking at crabs and tadpoles in the stones

—After forty we have to choose between our face and our ass

I was afraid she'd see me at the wall and peck at me, my not deaf brother with reservations about our friendship

—For real?

so that I accepted the plant hoping to convince him we were

—What am I supposed to do with this?

holding it in my hand all afternoon, Tininha's mother to the bird, who was giving her advice about my older brother, puckering her lips in a kiss

—What about the kid?

and afterwards they laughed and spoke French so we wouldn't understand, my older brother to the east of her hammering a little doll house with the *Manual for the Perfect Carpenter* helping him, the roof that he put on and took off, a door, windows, a kitchen with a balcony

—Only the furniture is missing

the bird to Tininha's mother, sculpting the air with its wings

—and what about that tender neck?

before going back to speaking French, with more little sighs, more laughter, I had the impulse to ask my not deaf brother to throw a stone at them, the more you hit bottom the deeper he goes, and hopefully I'll be at the bottom tomorrow, my mother arranged curtains, mattresses, the tablecloth, the way you change with age, ma'am, being in good spirits, without needing to choose between your face and your ass, he raced me from the garage to the gate and won, one afternoon she did a handstand until she propped her feet on the wall, her skirt falling over her, backwards, she had no head or shoulders, just knees, thighs, a belly, tired with happiness when she got up looking for her sandals

—Years ago I could walk on my hands down the entire hall

and today pushing up her glasses to look at me

—You look like you've lost weight

I felt badly that we hadn't been accomplices like Tininha's mother and the bird, my mother, looking at the teapot without a cover

—If your brother makes me a sideboard, I'll put a cloth runner on it my father, squatting down with us, almost smiling, smiling, becoming aware of his smile without being able to hide it, putting his hand in front of his mouth so we wouldn't see, there were moments when we were a family, I swear, moments when we, who made me remember this, my eyes are stinging, I feel like, strike that, I don't feel like anything, Father, Mother, brothers, I, it's not emotion, it's one of those irritating specks under my eyelids that won't come out, they burrow under my lids and the eyes defend themselves, it's gone, if my mother were here I'd challenge her

—A little race to the gate, ma'am?

she trembling on the couch

—It's so late

if I could convince my father's picture the three of us would race, I saw him run when my deaf brother ran chased a cat, waving a cane, not just running, calling him

—Son

and my mother, it's family, with specks under her eyelids, the word

—Sorry

not said, etched on her mouth, another word like that one that I forbid myself to write, I don't write it, you can rest easy, from minute to minute the lighthouse brings the waves and my older brother with them, the sand, the beginning of the rocks, now scarlet, now lilac, never blue, never green, and takes them with it, what is left of me, my co-worker

—I'm here for you, sweetie

taking care that I need her, and I don't, I needed, I don't need but since you're here stay or rather repeat

—I'm here for you, sweetie

although, if I try, father, mother, brothers, co-worker, I, the co-worker unrelated to us although she says

—I'm here for you, sweetie

no relation to me and nevertheless I don't protest, I am so nervous, my husband if I touch his hand when I serve him dinner

—What is this?

the neighbor's perfume not just on his lapel, on his collar, on the, I'm not exaggerating, pants, white hair already, his jaw getting bigger, the napkin expanding with his belly, you paid for my father's funeral, and you didn't have any money, I remember you doing accounts on a bank envelope calculating the payments and interest, my mother

—He still hasn't married you the shame I feel depending on strangers

rain on the windows, I'm here for you sweetie, half a dozen umbrellas in the cemetery so you couldn't see the people, the handles were specks under my eyelids because they dripped, dripped, a little jar on top of a grave had toppled over, so many names on the headstones, lines of prayers, verses, country of poets and navigators I salute you, mud on the pathways blackening the gravel, the dollhouse that my older brother built for me and I still get emotional about it in spite of the unglued chimney, my not deaf brother

—It's not straight

I was offended with the remark

—Real houses aren't either

the lighthouse again and my older brother

—Girl

from down under, forty years later he still calls me

—Girl

they must be about to close the café with the foosball table and the café that the intern's parents run because, except for my older brother's voice, no voice reaches me, my mother to my husband, still not my husband

—You can't imagine how I hate to bother you

without paying him back later, the remodeling was so minor, the pawnbroker returned the package of silverware, pitying her worthless collection

—What do you think this is worth, ma'am?

and the silver disappeared in a package, they returned to the sideboard with the marks of our fingers embedded in the metal, my grandmother said when she gave it to my mother

—For a rainy day, girl

and in the end, it was the silver that became the rainy day, the man's face

—What do you think this is worth, ma'am?

half a dozen umbrellas if that, a second funeral, for or five graves beyond ours, many more people than at ours, I thought I saw my not deaf brother leaning on a vault not even wearing a jacket, when he realized I was looking at him he evaporated, the handle of my mother's umbrella was made of ivory, she said to the pawnbroker

—It's ivory, isn't it?

and the pawnbroker

—No

so you should try to register for a race, ma'am, maybe they have a category for your age, and if you win, they might give you some prize money to pay your expenses, my mother

—People with no money have no soul

and that could be but it's not worth anything, a cheap soul

that not even God is interested in, He at Heaven's gate, refusing her
 —What do you think this is worth, ma'am?

the earth falling on the coffin made a hollow sound and therefore why spend money on a coffin with nobody in it, my father, father, mother, brothers, I, on the step, on the bench in the little park in Lisbon or at the Thebes Bakery trying to buy bottles putting it on the account
 —Do you realize how much you owe me?

looking at my husband, now almost my husband, who searched in his wallet
 —Next week I'll come by to pay you the rest

and I noticed he stayed late at work to earn what we still owed, my mother
 —How can I even face the guy?

with my husband already in the hospital after drinking the universe because of you, ma'am, and my deaf brother understanding, we could see that from his gestures, his throat swelling with the desire to talk, tendons, muscles, veins, his hand squeezing our arms and letting go of our arms, his feet planted on the floor, the relative of Dona Alice trying to restrain him
 —Calm down

and he didn't calm down, running back and forth in the hall
 —Sheee

at my father's funeral there were no specks under his eyelids and nevertheless, I think I'm sure, I am sure, better than being sure, I can swear, he was suffering more than we were, no flowers except those my husband gave or rather a modest wreath and a bouquet that was already next to the grave, tied with a ribbon, it was enough for me to see my not deaf brother from a distance
 —Are we friends or not?

to understand where it came from and, in my head, father, mother, brothers, me, without ceasing, a bouquet of flowers that he didn't buy, obviously, how would he buy them, he must have stolen it from the vendors at the entrance or pulled the flowers from some nearby garden, he pulled a string from his pocket, there are no beggars without string, tied the stems and after a while, waiting for us, in the rain, while the huts burned around him, in the midst of shouting and gunfire, chickens, people running between the garage and the gate

—I won

people running in the village chased by machine guns and grenades, an old man with a pipe, a woman lying supine, my co-worker

—What I'd give to know what's going on with you

and nothing important is going on with me, Mama, nothing important in your sweetie, only people running, only explosions, only gunshots, my not deaf brother wandering in the streets, looking for the military truck that was calling him

—Hurry

While the helicopter with the gun circled overhead, you could see the pilot, you could see the mechanic, you could see what it was shooting as it aimed at its targets, the sky wasn't transparent, it was yellow, the earth wasn't brown, it was yellow, my not deaf brother was whipping ghosts with the open palms and it was useless because the ghosts were inside him, I wanted to whip the sickness in my chest, the more you hit it the deeper it goes, Mama, to goes so deep the depth we can't see the way we can't see ourselves, I'm with you and I'm not, I stay in the cemetery not in the vaults of the rich people, in the section where there are graves with no headstones and not in October like in your

house, in February, my husband, not yet my husband, almost my husband, taking my fingers that were as wet as my coat, my husband, almost my husband
  —Girl
  and I couldn't hear him because people were running, because of the explosions, the gunshots, the helicopters aiming at me, me a woman lying supine and my not deaf brother, smoking a pipe
  —We're friends forever, I promise
  don't let the truck leave without you and the lighthouse bringing me back to the waves again, who will assure me that there are no bones in her not even my older brother building me furniture under water, a bed in this room, a bed in that one, a little stove, chairs, my husband, almost my husband, taking my fingers, so much hair plastered to my forehead, to my cheeks, my neck, growing, growing, me in the sand, under the rocks, without a blouse or a skirt, dressed in hair, my co-worker hugging me
  —It's ok, it's ok
  softly, my husband, almost my husband
  —It's ok, it's ok
  and still, if my husband, almost my husband had said
  —It's ok, it's ok
  we'd be happy to this day, we'd talk at dinner, at night he'd say
  —Come here
  and I'd come, I
  —Don't make me wait
  I'd say
  —I want you inside me
  I'd say
  —My love
  not

—Mama

I'd say

—My love

not your body, the body of a man, the strength of a man, the violence of a man, the despair of a man

—I don't know what's going on with me

and it won't go away no matter what, you can do it, I'll help, you can do it, my not deaf brother didn't go back to the grave, the intern, puzzled

—Your not deaf brother

and I said

—Sometimes I say things that don't make sense, don't pay any attention

and after helping him I rocked my husband, almost my husband

—It's ok, it's ok

without remembering my son because

—You're my son now

and my co-worker to me, not understanding that I wasn't with her

—You've never been so caring, what's happened?

as if something had happened to me, what an idea, nothing at all happens to me, you've got me here, you don't, my legs are on yours, they're not, don't plague me with questions, caresses, attention, don't bring me your toast, your jam, your tea, don't iron my dress before I leave, leave the dress alone, don't embrace me, looking at the grave again my not deaf brother was gone, the rain loosened his flowers from the string and dissolved them in a puddle, my not deaf brother in the truck and I, supine in the village, waving goodbye to him, what's left for me are the pines, the beetles, the reeds by the well, a big fly that threatened me and flew away, fuck off, Mother, don't put on mascara when you're an old woman, stand on your head, go on, my husband, almost my husband

—Let's go

since it was almost only us left in the cemetery, umbrellas on a path behind another grave, another priest, another coffin that had nothing to do with us and therefore didn't exist, February what a month, fortunately it's August, fortunately it's Saturday, tomorrow when I go down to the beach, I'll find Senhor Manelinho in the kiosk, if I say goodbye he won't recognize me

—Excuse me?

Senhor Manelinho's wife, suspicious of me and who I can hear saying

—Who's that?

—I have no idea

that at six in the afternoon, that, despite not having done it yet, it's been so long, something lights up in Senhor Manelinho

—I'd bet that was the sister of the other one but I'm not sure

Senhor Manelinho's wife standing up from the newspapers

—I believe you as far as I can throw you, what will you come up with next?

and Senhor Manelinho, who had lost his strength due to a blood disorder, stayed silent, it was the wife who was in charge these days, he sat in a chair taking his pulse

—I can't even stand up

before the Saturdays weren't like this, we got up later, my mother stayed in her robe longer, the sun and the pines stayed behind the closed shutters, they didn't come in here, my father crossed the hall dragging the chains of sleep from his ankles, you could hear them clanking on the floor, rubbing his fingers on his face to clean himself from the night, the bed and I separated from each other slowly, my co-worker

—Are you leaving without even giving me a kiss?

the bed kept the mattress, and I kept my arms and legs, our two bodies hesitating which one to choose, I returned to myself even with rumpled sheets, confused, the folds that thought they belonged to me the bedspread said

—They don't belong to you, they're mine

taking them from me, a dog barked inside the spiral of my ears or outside, I don't know, even if it were outside I felt its paws on my skin, Senhor Manelinho's wife to Senhor Manelinho

—Jerk

my father opened the kitchen door and you could hear the sea, throwing the waves with eternal patience, if I am still they are still the same, not I and those who will live after me, on the beach, my older brother's room from which nobody emerged, with the key not inside, on this side of the door, the bedspread covering the pillow, the pants hanging by their creases on the hangar he who never bothered about the creases, everything in order the way it is today, the funerals are over, the rain and the distress of my husband, almost my husband

—I don't know what's going on with you

assessing his failures in the dark

—Don't turn on the light

in a panic that his was visible, my co-worker

—Not even a kiss for Mama?

and a kiss for Mama, two kisses for Mama, my arms around her neck

—Mama

because I'm afraid, understand, so afraid, not of the Alto da

Vigia, the rocks or the waves since it's always just a single wave, it's always me, it's me who arrives at the beach and I abandon the beach dropping in the sand, not pebbles, algae, garbage, dropping in the sand the princess earrings, the petal nail polish, Cousin Fernando's candies
—The little one is so smart
Ernesto, who my mother sewed, comforting me
—I'm here
with the pinpoint of light of the lighthouse, finding him and forgetting him, I
—Hi Ernesto
and I suppose he heard me because something in his eyes changed, I'm afraid not of thieves, flies and being alone, I'm afraid that my husband
—I was always normal, I don't understand
with the upstairs neighbor to whom he said, not to me
—Come here
and she went, the neighbor
—Don't make me wait
the neighbor, intrigued
—Why are you making me wait
the neighbor who won't be able to help him, lying on her back
—I don't believe it
and my husband asking her to wait a moment before she leaves
—Just a moment, all right
lying supine on the pillows without anyone to rock him
—It's ok, it's ok
until the pillow cradled him to sleep.

10.

Since the sneaky blacks can put their ears to the ground and hear a vehicle more than thirty kilometers away, we left the barbed wire enclosure on foot. The Berliet and the Mercedes would come later to pick us up. If anyone was left. If nobody was alive, they'd come to collect us anyway, piling us up in the trunk. The lieutenant talked about a helicopter gunship but after six months we were on to his deceptions. It was always the same story, a simple mission, yada yada, if it wasn't simple there'd be coffins for everyone. The joke was to relax the troops. I don't know if the others laughed. I also don't know if I laughed. I probably thought it was funny, because when we started to walk close together, dick to butt, in single file, the guides in the lead, my stomach hurt from laughing. It was the moment before the end, ahead of the quartermaster and a guy in new camos, who were transferred from the peace of the command center to our company for having pulled a fast one with the chaplain. It seems they put rubbing alcohol in the chalice instead of wine, or some such crap. The chaplain complained to the major, and the major said, since you're already a clown go entertain the troops down there, they like circuses. The clown can't shoot, he's a clerk. He arrived at the supply column, pissing his pants. I was always unlucky with the guys who don't put their skin in the game and then, in their airmail letters home, swear they pulverized the enemy. Since I didn't know how to pick up a gun it was natural to hole up at the first mortar blast. I think the quartermaster had the same idea, he looked over his shoulder every ten meters, ordering the guy in front of him, your gun, asshole, before I bust your chops, so that's how we kept going, avoiding the trails since you never know when an IED or a trip wire will get you, stepping on the footprints of the guys in front of us, even though the grass was higher than we were, every so often we'd see an abandoned colonist's house, destroyed by the red ants and the vines, the columned porch with no columns, a bird on the roof, following us with its gaze without moving its head, me thinking I hope the guide is trustworthy, although I knew that none of them are, the blacks are in cahoots with each other, all herds are the same, sheep, horses, the fuck, and I knew more than one that led the dumb shits right to their machine guns. As a rule, we took two guides, since, if the first one pulled anything, we'd give him his ticket to Luanda and the second one suddenly turned into a nice guy, don't shoot, don't shoot. We could see the natives on the other shore and nevertheless, if we were inside the barbed wire, they put on their sunglasses on Sundays danced around, groping their way, running into the corners of the huts, but they were happy since they didn't feel things the way we do, they don't yell, they don't complain, they smile the whole time with their sunglasses on crooked and their women, if you can call them women, don't kiss their kids, they carry them on their backs, I remember one of them, her son had died a week ago, and that monkey still had him on her back in spite of the fact that the corpse smelled worse than rotten manioc, pulling him down once in a while to nurse, we tore him away from her by force, and the stupid woman, without letting go of us, yelled soldier, soldier, we buried the kid in a hole, covered the hole, and damned if she didn't fall on to the grave, it didn't occur to me that she'd start to dig him up to put him on her back again, until the kid, who happened to be a male, I was going to write that who happened to be boy, started falling apart on her. If my mother were here, she'd start on her rant about maternal love, my mother who as far as maternal love was concerned, at least in my case, just ran off her mouth and that's it, show me a sincere girl, and I, although I won't believe it, will tip my hat to her. They just give you a hard time, when I was little we had a beach house, next door, across the wall, lived a friend of my sister's, the two of them fooled around the way kids do, toys made of flowers, etc., and the mother of my sister's friend, a married woman, flirted with my older brother, under her daughter's nose, so that I, who was just a runt about nine or ten, was ashamed of her, I guarantee if she were my wife I'd think hard before letting that whore take advantage of me, and I'd give her plenty of time to think, lying in bed with her legs spread. We left before sunrise for the enemy camp, who were crossing the frontier with Zambia with the goal of surrounding the Huambo, and they pitched their tents there, before continuing, to scratch their armpits, that's what they like to do best, scratch themselves, give little squeals, and eat crickets, they spear a few on a stick and roast them, I'd rather eat manure than put my teeth on one of those, before dawn, drugged with sleep, there I went into the bush, snarling at the clown in front of me, put the safety on that gun, asshole, understanding my older brother, the smartest one in the family, who threw himself into the waves so he wouldn't have to put up with this shit, by the way I inherited the bike, a useless wreck that wasn't even good for scrap, when I return to Portugal, if I return to Portugal, I'll give it to a hungry kid and he'll eat aluminum for lunch. After an hour or two we fall out of line because the lieutenant ordered a rest, or rather we huddle together and six or eight of the blacks stay on guard, we're holed up fifty meters into the grass, the lieutenant, poring over the map, doesn't eat or drink, it's just to give his body a rest, according to his calculations we'll reach our target in three hours, but, by the way he looks at the map, comparing it to an instruction manual, I had the impression he was uncertain of the route, he asked to talk to the captain on the radio but there was just static with an unintelligible voice in the middle, the radio antenna was hanging from a branch, the lieutenant talked into the radio, the radio transmitted his voice to the company radio, where the captain spoke back in turn, and with transmissions back and forth they adjusted the azimuth bearing, while the two guides gnawed on a manioc root they had pulled out of their pockets, their camouflage uniforms were torn at the elbows, the one who wore sunglasses on Sundays spoke a sentence in Bunda and the other one replied in Yoruba, since he had been jailed by the PIDE, his face was pocked with the caresses with which the agents counseled him on the high and rocky road to virtue but in the end it was soft and sweet, the evangelical fervor of the secret police is moving. One afternoon when I demonstrated friendship to an informer who lied to us the sergeant showed up right away, back off, my bear, and the love ended, every month they delivered letters from home, from my mother and my sister, my father had lost his ability to write because of the bottles, the same letters, the same questions, and what a horror it had been to live with them, there's also a deaf brother but he doesn't talk much less write, he forces himself, he says, Sheee saaills seeea sheells and disappears into the yard. Consequently I didn't even read the letters, what was the point, I called my parents mother and father because that's what they taught me to do, the same way they trained me to say Lieutenant, Sir to the Lieutenant, but what father, what mother, I was alone as a child, I'm alone as an adult, when I get out of here, if I get out, I'll be alone, my sister is married to an idiot, my mother and my father, we assumed they were married to each other but we never saw a marriage certificate, they existed to forbid, scold and that's the end of it, when I grew up I left my mother and father and exchanged them for you all, the person who thinks she's my mother anyone who listens to her should know we are strangers, we have no connection, going back to her room to spill tears, women are convinced that tears solve everything, that if they let out a sob we'll go soft and the hell that works on me, I announced as soon as I can I'm out of here and I stayed without knowing why, the lieutenant put away the maps, got up, declared it's time to go, we got up too and the single file was formed again, on the way I came upon a boat and don't tell me I won't leave this place in a coffin, we visited the store and each one chose something, the officers got the best stuff, a tin crucifix and a yellow doll, the two sergeants so-so, those of us who went to the park sat in the bodegas, I remember my deaf brother chewing sand at the beach and I searched for sand fleas, they built mounds and jumped from inside and I smashed them with my palms, from what I imagined their life was like I was doing them a favor, I like to be helpful, the breathing of the clown was calmer, gaining confidence, I disabused him of that soon you'll see what confidence is and the quartermaster to me that trombone is still, he wrote every day to his fiancée in Porto until she stopped answering him, when they opened the mail bag his hands shook, he leaned against the barbed wire to stare at the swamp and in looking at the swamp it wasn't just his hands that shook, it was his shoulders, his back, that's what happens to you when you trust women, in March an envelope from my cousin who's getting married I don't know when and he was asking the doctor for pills, put me to sleep, doc, give me a shot like you do to the cats, the captain rounded up the lefties because of the way things were, the remaining soldiers were guys, they found a young black girl, a virgin, gave her a bath, covered her with talcum powder, a captain invented a perfume with sugar and alcohol, they put her in a new hut, with photos of naked girls on the bare boards, sending kisses to us, one of them, straddling a motorcycle, her privates on display, and the quartermaster, without touching the young girl, she doesn't appeal to me, a few days later, in his cups, started to want her, and he said she's starting to appeal to me and they followed him to the hut, fragrant with talcum powder, where a goat shared the mat with the girl, one of the soldiers kicked the goat, that took a while to leave, persuaded by a cane it trotted off, each hoof in its rhythm and chewing a liamba stalk, goats and blankets are the coin of the Angolans, who buy a girl, who doesn't even have breasts yet, from the uncle who owns her, for five blankets and two goats and she's ours for the time we are there, whether it's a month or a year, it's a way of arranging for company, the quartermaster came back from the hut dejected, complaining that she wouldn't move, the other soldiers asked what's the problem, do it for her, the doctor gave him vitamin shots and the man's health returned somewhat, when the mail plane came he wilted and returned to the barbed wire but not shaking so much, the captain knocked him around with a rifle butt there's no case of cuckolding that doesn't heal, he lowered his head, remembering his fiancée, you're not going to butt your head against the wall, and in that state of mind, the injections and the black girl who still wouldn't move he started to forget the girl in Porto who in the end married his brother, there are still families in which people are meant for each other, it's the blood talking, we weren't born English or Swedish, people who don't give a fuck about honor, in Portugal, thank God, we defend our name, at the beach house the pines talked, I don't remember the sea, I remember my father's back on the step, curving to the night and Seca Adegas, in Africa, drinking and ordering right on the first day, two pints of beer and he lying at the entrance to the store his stomach in the air sleeping, he woke up asking what day is today, mama, and they answered it's Sunday, even if it were Tuesday and he asked for his Sunday suit, my Sunday suit, he prayed for an hour, shouting, in the barracks, he came out of there fierce, waving his arms, his prayers forgotten, where's the enemy, the lieutenant your mama said to tell you to behave yourself, Seca Adegas, emotional, didn't bring me coffee, poor thing, if he's still he's sick, the lieutenant told the cook to bring the coffee to him and Seca Adegas tried to kiss him, you're thinner, ma'am, with the help of the coffee his head started to clear, I drank two pints, didn't I, and from that moment he returned to his old self, only happier, moving his hand carefully down his camouflage uniform, I like this little uniform, and tying a kerchief around his throat because he didn't have a tie, he asked around when are we going to get the blacks, on one of the last sorties a machine gun ripped out his guts, when they put him in the Heli to Portugal he said if my mama asks for me tell her I'm coming and he didn't come, he had worked in the country, a neighbor came and cut his father's throat with a spade, in front of Seca Adegas when he was six years old, because of a dispute about irrigation, I never met a guy with so much hair on his body, my mother, on the beach, you're getting body hair, and I in front of the bathroom mirror, proud, counting them, I discovered thirty-eight, no thirty-nine, no forty, after a few weeks I asked the Lieutenant what happened to Seca Adegas, my Lieutenant, he said don't worry and I stopped worrying about him, he could be in the country with his mama, cutting the neighbor's throat, I'm certain, where could he be if not there and the Lieutenant, agreeing with me, I hadn't thought about that but you made me see the truth, he's with his mama in the country, how could we doubt it, the line of soldiers got longer, mountains to our left, fewer trees, we crossed a path, a pit, a burned village, farms of poor colonists, deserted, little plots that the animals had eaten, Dona Alice, to me, I'll tell your parents that you stole that pastry, me to Dona Alice, sticking out my chest, tell them whatever you want, Dona Alice, I'm not afraid of them, and I wasn't, I wasn't, I wasn't, the Thebes Bakery popped into my head, my room, my mother, locking the door, you'll stay in your room for stealing the pastry, give me that toy car, me, holding the toy car against my bellybutton, no, I won't, until she gave me a shove and there was the sound of footsteps moving away in the hall, my sister said you deserved it and me when I leave here you'll see, a noise diluted all of that, it was a wild boar escaping, the order came, from man to man, to me, the smell of dirty feet, although, if we are still, they'd already seen us from I don't know where, a black here and there following us sending signals, finding out how many of us there were, where the flamethrowers were, where the bazooka was, who was in charge and I, noticing the water in the canteen next to my leg, felt thirsty, the combat rations and the tent were starting to feel heavy, and if I paid attention I could count my bones one by one, the captain who was the medic, bigger than the others, was about ten guys ahead of me, with the tourniquets, the bandages, and the rest of the medical supplies, at the second rest stop, the last one before our target, they might let us have a smoke, at my house nobody smokes, I don't smoke, if cousin Fernando took his smokes out of his pocket as soon as he left they'd fling open the windows, my mother would say that poison kills, on the beach she wore flip-flops with sequins and I, so stupid, asking, are you rich, ma'am, I was scared of the robbers at night, in bed, from time to time, I still feel them circling around me, we're taking you to Spain, you know, my older brother telling me to calm down don't worry they won't take you but he threw himself off the Alto da Vigia and therefore he's there, he visited me for months whispering I miss you and don't disappoint me, brother, not really my older brother, a skeleton with his voice, even without a voice I knew it was him, even here, in the asshole of the world, he's found me, the world came down the line to me, the target's in front of that hill, and we were sure we heard sentinels crawling in the bushes, they have a commissioner and a commander with them, if I am still the Chinese that the PIDE security police talked about and the captain to the PIDE guys, you're imagining thieves, but he stopped talking to think, he delivered a message in code and the return message calmed him, fuck the Chinese, he was like my father and his love of the bottles, all he needed was the steps, and since he didn't have steps, he put his chair outside and sang, not the thieving blackbird where it did it go to make its nest, that belonged to my mother, but a French hymn, when the supply column brought the chaplain he got nervous, are you certain there is a God, Father, distracted, I'm certain that there is, my mother went to Mass, my father closed himself in the living room to study the wall, more word came, passed along from column to column, attention, the quartermaster didn't play the clown and took it quietly, my mother forced me to go to Mass and I was as bored as an orangutang in a cage, I counted the candles on the altar, I counted the number of little angels, I counted the old women in the pews, the Captain that asked if there's a God, Father, are you certain God exists, the chaplain, busy with the pocket of his camouflage uniform that wouldn't open or wouldn't close, choose the hypothesis that suits you, it doesn't matter, go ahead and lose, you always lose, those who win whatever it is in life only get complications and trouble, the chaplain if God didn't make all of this can you imagine the mess that we'd be in, only a couple of hours or less to the target, an hour or so keeping up this pace, some shooters left the line to walk parallel to us, on either side, in case there were enemy troops in the grass, with luck, the way you hunt crabs, you'll catch one with your hands, distracted by the whistle, weapon by their side, and later either you give him a ticket to Luanda or leave him to the PIDE which is the same as giving them a ticket to Luanda only that they take longer to pay him, I remember one, on his knees in the garrison, to him the wife of the chief of the brigade, a shriveled up Spanish woman, applied electric shocks to his genitals, the fat husband, amateur radio operator, approving, keep it up Pilar, babbling, into an enormous machine that belched and whistled with truncated syllables, even with Belgium, he bragged, even with Uruguay I can communicate, full of numbers and codes, the chief of the brigade to the captain, proud of the whistles, the one from Belgium is an engineer, the one from Uruguay is a mathematician and the captain, impressed, in this case if I am still there is a God, look, the target was a village where the black monkeys rest from the trip from Zambia, swimming up to their necks in palm liquor, and dropping along the way, little mines in the ditches, not simple ones, the first vehicle, a dented wheel for the third or fourth, the first vehicle, throwing the driver, sand bags so they wouldn't fly like the sparrows, it flew for a few meters and when it hit the ground there were no wheels or hood, before it landed in the grass and the dirt, everything was black, everything was gray and therefore everything was normal, the explosion from the depot and flames of gasoline in the air, on the beach the gulls and the blackbirds didn't burn up anybody, today I'm not sure, don't send me back there to get hit again, a new message was passed from head to head, continue the assault but increase your distance, not a platoon, two, two lieutenants, six soldiers, seventy shitting and coughing like me, the second lieutenant was a blur and in a few minutes it will be day, a breeze in the vegetation calling us, not loudly, in secret, my deaf brother would understand it, not me, the chaplain was distracted from God in sighting the clown who came into the sergeant mess with a coffin, he's still alive, the rascal, and he was alive the rascal, trying to get off the hook from the sorties, I have malaria, I can't doctor, without squeezing the thermometer under his arm, you have malaria my ass, relieving his fever with a hard kick, you come back and I'll stick you with an injection of distilled water that will twist your knickers in a knot, my mother, on the beach road, don't leave the path, rascals, me, my arms crossed in the middle of the asphalt, I'm not afraid and my mother twisting my ear, coming back from the grocery store, stay here and see if you won't be afraid of me, my sister, consoling me, your ear is still there, I swearing that I'd cut off my mother's ears with the fish knife but when I got home I'd forgotten about it, if it were now I'd cut them off and keep them in a bottle, after eight months in Africa you don't think, you do, first shoot then rationalize, counseled the Lieutenant, if you rationalize first you'll get a present of a bugle and a salvo and you'll keep rationalizing to the worms, so I left my mother and siblings while the target grew, waiting for the single column to transform into a fan, with the useless guys in the platoon with the howitzers posed, almost as incompetent as the clown, not just the breeze in the underbrush, the first wings in the canopy, the first murmurs, a small animal looking at us and disappearing immediately, like a squirrel but not a squirrel, I've never seen any here, the dark continued to be dark but with sparks that rose one by one and stayed, leaves clearly outlined now, little drops of dew, the suspicion of a pallid sun before the real sun, we started to have shade, long stains that gained thickness, joined to us by the feet and advancing with us, the captain to the priest, still with the notion of God plaguing him, I just see confusion, what did He put in the trough, the impression that someone lifted the sun with a hand crank or a rope, one of my boots hurt, not on my heel or toes, it was the boot itself that hurt, the target a kilometer away if that, not huts, not people, my sister and her friend sitting next to each other with their stuffed toys in front of the wall, they invented cartoon voices and insisted we greet them with their floppy limbs instead of chasing snakes near the well like I did, my older brother's bicycle pump served as a cudgel, my older brother showing it to me

—Did you dent this?

since the plunger only went halfway and got stuck, my older brother fixed it with a rod and a hammer, without getting mad at me or snitching on me to my mother, a sigh and I felt bad, because of the sigh

—I'm sorry

He thought I was too big to ride on the fender and I wasn't, my feet didn't drag on the ground, my cap didn't block his vision, I shrank a little

—I'm little, brother, look

he was convinced that I was an adult

—You're huge

as if I were huge on purpose and that was a lie, the proof is that the mother of my sister's friend didn't even throw me a smile, just to make sure I checked myself out in the mirror

—Am I ugly?

without noticing if I was ugly, I had the same things that the others did on their faces, eyebrows, mouth, eyelashes, I discovered a tooth that was crowding the one next to it, I stood in front of my mother disposed to forgive her for twisting my ear and not to touch the fish knife

—Do you think I'm ugly?

she without raising her eyes from a hem

—What nonsense, young man

and that's what my mother thought, not boy, young man, being a man I'm not a son anymore, nobody puts a man on their lap or turns off their light at night, they make him turn it off by himself, they don't debone the fish for him, I have to do it

—You're old enough to do that

and what is it work to be old enough for whatever still intrigues me, I am, possibly, old enough to be here, I am, possibly, old enough to die from a bullet, aren't I, and above all she thinks I'm ugly, answer, Mother

—Ugly, ugly, maybe not

the knife jumping from the drawer, without needing my help, and an ear on the ground, the column of soldiers disbanded, the Lieutenant, almost in a whisper, not even the little pores of your skin do I want to hear, we surrounded the huts of the lepers guessing they would not burst out and surround us, white man, white man, extending their horrible stumps toward us, those gigantic cavities, the absence of eyes, they observed us from behind caves without eyelids in which nothing sparkles, instead of lips a canine and the jaw bone visible, children, without arms or legs, leaning against pieces of wood, a skeletal goat, her milk dried up, a muddy stream of water and they give that to them to drink, they bathe in the mud of a stream, the mud tears off their skin not in drops, in sheaths, bringing flesh with it, they drag themselves along dislocating their body in chunks, my mother said ugly, ugly, maybe not, my sister said I'm already used to you, I don't know, I didn't ask my father because he was a man and it would be uncomfortable for both of us, the shadows quickly dissipated, ever more dense, darker and my boot throbbed, there were times when my shirt hurt, not my chest, at my father's funeral it was my tie that decided to choke me, my throat was fine, the tie gave a sob that had nothing to do with me, it can be sad but don't count on me, standing straight and calm, and the tie, without warning, gave a little jerk, fortunately I wasn't with my family, what family, in fact, leaning against a headstone engulfed with the moldy stench of the flowers and the old age of the dead, feeling the jerks of my tie communicating with my eyes, before they forced me to wipe them with my sleeve, and that wasn't my fault, it was the fault of a piece of rag around my neck, I chilled out along the paths of the cemetery followed by the dead who whispered in my ear don't abandon us here, round photos, boys carved in stone, even the statue of a dog guarding its owner with the melancholy of its snout, the owner to me how is the animal, I, without softening, full of longing, rest now, the clouds raining inside my gut, if I'm still it won't be inside my gut, in my belt, in my shirt, in my boots, fortunately the clown is far away from me now cursing the prank with the chalice, if the lefty escaped it wasn't my belly that would get the prunes, the radio, to the Lieutenant, the Heli gunship will be here in twenty minutes, my Lieutenant, the other Lieutenant, whispering to each other, their twenty minutes I know them, we took four sharpshooters for a tussle in the grass and a black with his head in the grass, no blood except on his throat, resting, sleeping, the Lieutenant gave his weapon to a corporal, take it, it's a good Israeli gun, I didn't trust it, it hits the ground and shoots, if you get into an exchange of fire it lets out a blast, you want it to fire it gets stuck, if you put on the safety it blows a hole in the roof, the bitch, I turned back, out of politeness, to the sculpture of the dog, what's your name buddy, but the owner, who had already forgotten me, was haranguing the poplars because a root was bothering his ankle, my brother was right to throw himself from the Alto da Vigia, since, from what I could see, there are no poplars in the ocean, I don't swear there aren't, I swear I haven't seen them, my family didn't pay attention to me in the cemetery, the dead as well because they're convinced they're still alive, my mother, my deaf brother, my sister and her husband around the grave, imprecise in the rain, everything imprecise in the rain except us four hundred meters from the target, what four hundred, two hundred, us and two hundred meters from the target, I'm not good at guessing distances, I put flowers on my father's grave that the rain stole from him, there is nothing more desperate than February in Lisbon, it's not just my opinion, it's the month, we have the story of the boot, the tie, etc., repeating itself, the afflictions of winter are not my fault, February is fucked up because of its own problems, don't blame me because I'm serene, ever since I returned from Africa I calm down when the huts consent, the sun is now up in the sky, not yellow, white, it's always white in the morning, it matures later on, my memory conjured up the Greek wife of the pharmacist brushing her hair at the window, moving the poodle from hand to hand depending on the side of her hair she was brushing, if it weren't for the damned target I'd lie down on the cot and entertain myself for a few minutes, alone with her, she wouldn't have to put down the poodle or the brush, the four of us would be in a dance, I wiped myself on the sheet and for five minutes my life was pleasant before the tie, out of spite, started to choke me again, why can't you see it's not me, it's things that don't let go of my hand, at least the Uzi is behaving, still, the sharp shooters are with us as we leap to a slope and my friend with the bazooka on his shoulder, we could hear a woman, not my mother, singing the thieving blackbird and so on, we heard the chickens, you always hear chickens, the hawks were flying overhead, targeting the chicks, they swooped down and destroyed them in their claws, rowing, rowing, as much as I tried I never got any of them, even stationary in the air, with open arms, there must be a God my Captain, soothe your soul because the crucified persist, I understand everything in life, I just don't understand what the tie is up to because I didn't care about my father, I want to say, the hell I didn't, because I didn't care about my father, don't pester me with this, the Mercedes have been on the way for a while to pick us up later, with so many hostiles coming into Zambia it's not healthy to grow roots here, especially with the new weapons the PIDE swears they have and the Communists train them, what did my father give me, tell me, if I talked to him he didn't answer, he didn't walk with me in the olive grove the way he did with my deaf brother, he didn't give me a bicycle the way he did to my older brother, there are times when the certainty hits me, and what I say applies to my mother as well, that he treated me like a beggar, if I tried to talk with him my father would suck on his tongue hoping to prolong the taste of the liquor, I saw in the newspaper, by coincidence, the announcement of his death and I went to the cemetery out of curiosity, that's why I don't understand the business with the tie and much less my eyes, what does the burial of a stranger do to move us, when I saw the death notice with a picture of my father as a young man, not my father at the end, the tie choked me and I was pissed at it, it wouldn't let me swallow, it's not just the behavior of people that astonishes me, it's that of objects without souls, their manias, their whims, beyond that of the hostiles, at the target, the people in the fields and now I'm being sympathetic, what's wrong with me today, calling them people, sometimes I'm generous, calling the blacks people, for example, calling my father a father, my siblings siblings, and as far as my mother is concerned, it's best not to say anything, alone in the building with the tiles waiting for I don't know what, what do you wait for when you're eighty some years old, what do I wait for at sixty, what did I wait for at twenty, almost entering the village, under a roof of hawks, with the sky the color of straw in my face, the Lieutenant let's go up because it's a kind of small hill and already there are voices, noises, a goat snout nudging us, the smell of manioc, their smell nauseates me, especially that of the women, and I include the Europeans, a stink that frightens me, I'm incapable of sleeping with one of those creatures and then there's their way of talking, the diminutives, the nonsense, the senseless flashes of anger, to hell with all of them, we sensed something going on with the target because there was a sudden silence, one of the cretins in the mortar platoon tripped and got up, the guys with the machine guns on tripods moved back to exchange fire, if I had had a son I would have killed him at birth, what do I care about that, made of mucus and stubbornness, kicking, demanding, diapers, vaccines, screaming, I remember my father rubbing my sister's gums when she cut teeth, my deaf brother barking when he had ear infections, the Lieutenant raised his arm and I began to run, as much as the suffering of the boot allowed, the pack on my back and the mud consented, a circle of huts, monkeys of all sizes, a bunch of them with weapons, old men with sticks, kids who weren't mine, chickens, goats, misery, the machine gun from the left started to sing, you might not believe it, I think it's unbelievable, that the picture of my father in the paper, open on the bench, pretending I was going to buy it, and I do, and my blood froze, substituting it with a pathetic song, on the head of a bald guy, and wanting to, wanting to close the newspaper with my childhood inside, suddenly intact, the morning that, without wanting to, I opened the bathroom door and found my mother naked drying herself on the towel, the fear and shock were so big I couldn't run away, me thinking who are you, until, when she had her clothes on, she was herself again, although the other one was still there underneath, if the other one embraced me, I'd die, I felt like not just cutting off her ears, cutting everything into little pieces and saving ourselves that way, my father, my siblings, myself, the machine guns sang in a chorus, the first mortar blast, the second, one of the hostiles taking up a weapon and kneeling, eyes wide with surprise, letting it fall before falling in turn without protecting his face with his arms, the bazooka pierced the different walls of the dwelling leaving it in ruins so that you could see the bush behind it, there was no hawk up there, the goats ran from one side to the other, in a gallop or a trot, same thing, running over the sleeping mats, the Heli gunship appeared over the canopy, the Lieutenant, who had lost his cap, shooting at random, the medic in a kind of shelter waiting for the wounded, many more blacks than I had calculated, dozens, hundreds, thousands, the certainty that my father didn't know what my mother was under her dress, if I could dream of taking us from there I'd solve the problem with the fish knife, the way the legs met the stomach and what existed there, I preferred to turn off the light before I went into the bedroom and I, covering myself with sheets, saying don't touch me, for the love of your ancestors don't touch me, one afternoon I saw two dogs humping, I ran after them throwing stones and they didn't uncouple, they jumped in circles, moaned, I, lacking the courage to explain to my father, watch out if my mother gets you, you won't be able to get loose, the shame of my mother and him stuck together in the street, in front of the Thebes Bakery and the neighbors watching from their windows, and Dona Alice going away without demanding we pay her, the trucks waiting for us, at the other end of the target, the Lieutenant saying when this is over we'll torch the huts, nobody leaves without torching the huts, besides the rifles they had muskets, machetes, the old women wore skirts layered over skirts, dirty rags, poverty, I didn't see my older brother on the Alto da Vigia, I didn't see him throw himself over the cliff, I saw Senhor Manelinho with his arm outstretched, he squeezed this hand and people, respectfully, looked at his hand, everything so close to the dust, the noise, the shouts, the manioc mats jumping with life, the clown hiding in his sleeve, I can't take it, can't take it, Senhor Manelinho wanting to unscrew his hand to display it in the kiosk, it was the last thing my brother greeted before dying, Senhor Manelinho's wife, in agreement for once, it's true, in the middle of the burning huts an old man with a pipe in front of a woman lying on the ground, legs and stomach exposed, that at first I thought was my mother, that I wished was my mother and wasn't, it was a black woman missing her face and the old man observed her as he smoked one of our pipes, not one of their gourds, you're alive, lady, in spite of nobody paying attention to you, when you deserved to be in the village in Angola, swinging your hips around there until you ceased to exist, don't get near me, don't serve me lunch, if I go into the kitchen I want you in the verandah, if you cross the hall close the door to the living room so I don't run in to you, not because of the clown, the children, the goats, the girl who was burning between two huts the way everything around me was burning and more gunshots, more gasoline that a match ignited, more flamethrowers evaporating whoever came down the hill, the sun not white or yellow, colorless, returning from the barbed wire I go into the beach house and stand on a brick looking at the lizards not cutting off their tails, looking at the beetles not cutting off their wings, listening to the pines, the ocean, the gulls, when it rains they swoop around the chapel or disappear in the rocks that the waves don't reach, the fellow soldiers in the trucks dragging the clown and I like an imbecile surrounded with huts in flames, the captain insisting with the priest do you seriously believe that God exists, don't come to me with stories, don't come to me with proofs that don't prove shit, don't come to me with talk about church for dumb pious old women, talk to me man to man, believe at night, when there's nobody around but us, the dark and the dark that awaits us is darker still, answer me, eye to eye, where is He at this point, and the chaplain stuck in the swamp where our trucks were coming from, seven or eight of them full of soldiers with their foreheads leaning on their weapons, grimy with ash, dust, the monkey blood, the roots that stuck out of the ground after the Heli gunship and the pieces of bodies, the chaplain

—I don't know

while the driver called me on the other village in front of the old man with the pipe and the dead woman, me taking from my belt the last grenade, pulling the pin, throwing it at the old man thinking it would take five seconds, the only thing I thought about was that it takes five seconds, and in the enormous amount of time that is five seconds, the driver saying hurry and I not in a hurry because there's still awhile before five seconds is up, how long did it take my older brother to fall from the cliff, how long will it take for all these people to die, how much time did my father take between the sofa and the pantry, if at least the old man with the pipe would look at me and he doesn't, the grenade lands at his feet and my boot hurts, not my toes, my boot, my boot hurts, my tie didn't have to hurt, the Lieutenant saying to me you idiot, the Lieutenant can go to hell and he coughs into the box bring me the son of a bitch, and it wasn't necessary to bring me, the boot took me to them, the Lieutenant said if we need a stretcher on the road I'll put a plug in your throat, so low that his voice covered the explosion of the grenade, the way it covered the fall of my older brother into the water, the way it covered my mother's voice when she called me to dinner

—Do you want a slap?

and, since I didn't want a slap, I ate quicker than the others, I chewed the pear they made me chew, I held the utensils the way they told me to, I folded the napkin the way they told me to fold it and I left to go out to the yard where the old man with the pipe kept smoking, on top of the grenade that still hadn't exploded, and the two of us stayed there, without counting to five, helping the bats.

SUNDAY, AUGUST 28, 2011

I.

I had never said goodbye to a house, and I didn't even know if it was listening to me, when I was a child I was certain that it did, the gurgling of the pipes, the sighs of the furniture, and the creaking floor were its ways of talking to me, after I grew up I don't know, perhaps a door that turns on its hinges and if I were interested
—What's the matter?
it turns a little more
—You stopped caring about us.
and I didn't, that's a lie, I do care, I look at the cracks in the walls, the ceiling tiles that are missing, you may not believe it but I feel bad about having sold you, I showed the bedrooms, the yard, the living room, I almost showed the wall where Tininha and I played and the hole where we kept the diary, I didn't show the step where my father sat, my mother insisted, a place where nobody goes and more than that it just reminds me of sad things and it's an extra expense, you think I'm rich, and what could I do, my mother looking at me without looking at me, or looking through me to the other one who I'm not and she imagines that I am, perhaps the one I was when she was young

—Are you still there?

how long has it been since we lost each other, my co-worker

　　—If you're going to spend the weekend alone why the hell can't I come along?

and who says my mother says this house, how long has it been since I lost this house, father, mother, brothers, me, the pines, and the blackbirds familiar no longer, me, to my co-worker

　　—I'm not going to spend the weekend alone I will spend it with them

as if they existed and they don't, do I have to bring them back in spite of the cracks in the walls and the missing ceiling tiles, no more flower bed, those little flowers on the steps that peep out of the stone the same way the gulls come out of the rocks, you think they brood eggs but they don't, the Alto da Vigia opens its hands and a bird, my co-worker, not believing me

　　—Who are they?

because my brothers and Tininha are beyond her, on my mother's face is a smile that has no relationship to her lips, separated from her skin, when my father got sick, he smiled that way to us and there was so much hidden fear in it, we asked him

　　—Is it the bottle that you want?

and he did want the bottle, we didn't concern ourselves with it, who are all of you, or who is she, and what do I have to do with you, perhaps a man in a hat accompanied him pretending he couldn't lift him

　　—The old man weighs like lead

and then, memories at random, a belly almost leaning against his shoulder, with a cough

　　—Now, recite the names of the planets in order

and the stubborn silence of the other creatures, weighing like lead, the old men, who were suspended around him, one of them with a box of matches, full of ladybugs, in his pocket, another with a penknife, with just half a blade, stuck in his shoe, it was many years before death would visit us, and if there were many years, it wouldn't come, many years, anybody knows that, mean nothing, my mother

—I didn't imagine time that way do you remember me running from the gate to the garage?

and not the gate to the garage, the garage to the gate, you've even forgotten that, ma'am, you confused things, you see, if you're still, many years doesn't mean never, it means in an instant, it means it's here, the ladybugs and the pocket knives are transformed into bread crusts for the doves in the garden that a guy, wearing a neck scarf in July, didn't offer them, he let them fall, who would guess that time passes so quickly, nobody can take the idea out of my head that it's our fault, what did we do wrong, the cough over his head left in disgust

—Neptune and Pluto are missing, stupid

the cough over the stomach to the man in the hat

—It doesn't look like there's much here

and the man in the hat is suddenly tiny, much smaller than my father, wearing shorts, collecting knives and ladybugs, without baby bottom cheeks, not bald, mixing up the rivers on the school map

—Where the hell did the Guadiana River go, that sneak?

recovering his size and his certainties as they got near the house, extending my father's plate to his wife

—Put more potatoes on his plate, caramba

declaring with disdain

—Planets

letting Mercury, Saturn, and Uranus tumble on the floor in a pile of asteroid dust, explaining to my grandmother

—Even without constellations because of the potatoes, go on

I had never said goodbye to a house, and I didn't even know if it was listening to me, I assume it did although no pipes are gurgling, there is no sighing in the furniture that isn't there, the floor, which is missing boards, is still, if I could answer the professor instead of my father, asking

—Excuse me?

explaining

—He died, did you know?

and listing the planets one by one, correctly, my co-worker

—At least promise me you'll call

and I think I promised, be sincere, what use are false promises now, and I promised, look at the gate falling apart, poor thing, if my deaf brother were here there would be dozens of lizards just for him, what luck, I wanted to hear my mother's slippers in the hall or Tininha calling me but I'm not sad, there's the ocean that follows its destiny to come and go, in the afternoon, when we're together, you'll say my name, I hope you don't get confused with your habitual excuse

—There are so many of you

when, as far as I know, just my older brother, me and the priest who exchanged the Church for Senhor Leonel's niece, and before throwing himself in, blessed the rocks, insignificant at a distance but gigantic up close, the intern

—I'm ashamed to say it but the idea of your roughing me up excites me

the viola not leaning on the wall, on the rug, I pushed it with my heel and there was an endless vibration, the priest, in the café with the foosball table, was discussing religion with an intact chalice, Senhor Leonel's niece, at the door, not daring to come in

—Come on home, Germano

and the chalice, like Senhor Manelinho's dog, stayed to wait for him until the next day, obedient, faithful, the priest, who nobody had seen without his hassock, continued to bless us as he descended, just three people and the ocean

—There are so many of you

with the hope we would respect him, they say that Senhor Leonel's niece was the only presence at the funeral, they say her take the bus from Lisbon and Senhor Leonel responded with displeasure by cutting bones with a single chop, angrily

—You should be in Vouzela

in spite the fact that the newspapers mentioned a girl under a train in a town that I can't remember the name of, if it were Vouzela I wouldn't forget it, the trains, they have the privilege of confirming

—There are so many of you

trains by the dozens on all sides while the ocean is just one and doesn't change places, monotonous as grazing horses, my deaf brother had one, the difference was that the ocean gives and takes the algae, gives a board, takes a board and the grazing horse didn't give or take, it advanced little by little, just its head, saddle and a hemp tail that became less and less abundant until it was no tail at all, one afternoon it was in the yard in the rain and it stuck half of its muzzle into the gate, we threw it into the reeds behind the well, I searched for it and didn't find it in the thickets, the newspapers of Senhor Manelinho's wife didn't mention any grazing horse, without hair on its tail, under a train there was a

beggar, who is certainly walking around rattling the wine bottle, the horse is galloping around a tumbled down shack, my mother
—It's possible
and I was surprised at her knowledge of beggars, where did you learn that, and full of respect for her, I asked Tininha
—Do you think my mother was a beggar?
Tininha pondered the question
—Does she pick up garbage?
and, since she didn't pick up garbage or panhandle at traffic lights, she was probably not a beggar, I say probably because months ago, a well-dressed woman approached me on the street
—I'm hungry
hands moving aimlessly and her unbearable eyes scavenging me, I feel them inside me, the doctors, when they auscultated me in bed eighteen, certainly found them, Dr. Clementina raised her stethoscope in disbelief
—You
like before on the beach, I said to her
—Take off the princess earrings, Dr. Clementina, what good do they do us now?
the same way that Ernesto doesn't do me any good now, not an animal, a rag, if I ran in to her on the street I'd say
—Goodbye
I ran away from you as fast as I had run to you at the wall in the old days, my mother from the kitchen
—I bet you want a slap, everybody's at the table
I had never said goodbye to a house and I'm not saying goodbye today, I pretend that I'm staying with the hope that I don't get bored, or I declare, in the most natural tone of voice in the world,
—I'm going to walk down to the sand for a bit

the house, that likes to know what it's dealing with, believing me, calming the pines
—She won't be long
my father and my brothers waiting, my mother, at the gate
—I don't see her
and even though I am tranquil in what was my room, a floorboard says
—What's wrong with you?
the way things observe us intrigues me, they pretend they don't notice, and they see every detail, gentlemen
—Oh, girl
my co-worker
—If you forbid me from going with you, you'll have to be twice as tender with me
so that I, tenderly
—What's going on with my Mama?
me, with my nose in her neck, thinking, you're old, did you realize, old skin, old lady clothes, even old lady furniture, me, caressing her shoulders
—I'll keep your smell on my hands, I will
and how awful, I like my husband, what an obsession, his nervousness in the boarding house, his relief after he did it
—I did it
seeing him sleep with closed fists like my son would sleep if he were with us, his child's hair when he wakes up, asking me when he sees me
—Is that you?
and it's so good when you say
—Is that you?
pressing your face against my chest, telling you

—I want you inside me
    and you
    —I must go to work
    you
    —Just for a little bit
    you
    —Yes
    you
    —Yes, yes, yes
    you
    —It's a relief that I can do it
    while the wave that will receive me this afternoon doesn't stop growing
    me
    —Hold me, love
    me
    —Hold me with everything you've got
    and gulls, the foam, Senhor Leonel, about me
    —She must be in Vouzela
    chopping the bones with a single blow, angrily, all my bones are severed when you look at the clock, get up, leave me, you invisible in the bathroom but your hair brush cuts me, your electric shaver cuts me, your shower cuts me, each piece of clothing you put on cuts me and cuts me, each shoe you put on crushes my toes, your goodbye kiss is half on me and half on the pillow, a shroud that hides me from the world, don't hide me from the world, don't stop me from breathing, my distress if I find in the kitchen a sugar pill at the bottom of the teapot, not in the dishwasher, on the balcony, and me wanting to kiss the teapot that continues to declare

—It's a relief that I can do it
it continues to ask
—Faster
demand
—Come my God come
a letter that you forgot on the table, the imprint of your body on the couch, Senhor Manelinho who doesn't remember me, a diffuse image in his memory but he doesn't remember me
—Where have I seen her before?
Senhor Manelinho's wife stacking newspapers on the counter
—All you think about is whores, you dirty old man
while the ocean takes algae gives algae, takes boards gives boards, the ocean, about my older brother
—There are so many of you
while the priest who doesn't stop blessing us falls, if you don't find me at home, I'll be in Vouzela, my co-worker
—Be twice as tender with me
and I, as tenderly as possible
—What's up with my mama?
not
—Hold me, love
me
—What's up with my mama?
sitting on her lap, my nose in her neck, thinking you're old, did you realize, old skin, old lady clothes, even old lady furniture, me, what am I doing here, even in August it feels like rain, I suspect there's mildew in the chest of drawers, my caresses are gestures of a mechanical doll about to wind down, my co-worker, grateful
—What will happen to Mama without her baby?
our features separated from each other in a happy ecstasy, the

little ring, that she couldn't get off, stuck on her finger, I don't know what will happen to Mama without her baby but I know what will happen to baby without her Mama, she'll be happier, the pines, listen, where is Vouzela, the pines say my name, how funny, they remember, father, mother, me, a blackbird on the wall, maybe the princess earrings, that no longer serve Dr. Clementina, they are worth something to me, who stole them from the flower bed, I am fifty-two years old, help, a wisp of mist in the yard and a braid of reeds, my co-worker confusing the mechanical toy with me

—You taste like honey

without noticing that the smile painted on her face twisted in the window of a dress shop, the amount of junk that they put in the display windows, little dogs wagging their tails, their snouts balancing a ball on their nose, even a toy soldier marching in place, when my not deaf brother appeared at home for the first time, in his uniform, my mother tried to embrace him, the way mothers do, and my not deaf brother said

—Get off me

standing like a stranger, observing things with the formality of one who doesn't know them, he didn't sit down, he didn't talk with us, he locked himself in his room, this wasn't at the beach, it was in Lisbon, in the building with the tiles next to the Thebes Bakery, we heard him rummaging around, breaking what I thought was picture frames, sticking a bag in the waste bin at the entrance, coming back up by the stairs, not in the elevator, as was customary, lingering in the living room with the porcelain fairy in his hand, turning it and examining it in a way that the fairy seemed not to have been there forever, one of its feet badly glued on and without the star on its wand, my mother

—It almost seems like you don't live with us

my not deaf brother putting the fairy on the lid of the sideboard, away from the napkins, fifty-two years old, how unfair, save me, my not deaf brother

—And you think I do live here?

he didn't take his place at the table, he chose the other end, where the tablecloth didn't reach, where my mother had exiled the copper flower base, that she called bronze

—Are you coming to dinner, or do you want me to go there, girl?

looking at us like a visitor, distracted, or losing himself, through the curtain, in the building facing our house, he didn't drink a glass of water, refused the fruit, didn't touch the quince dessert that my mother put in front on him, with a spoon and everything, I remember that he used to steal a spoonful from each jar in the pantry, hoping they wouldn't notice and my mother

—Bad boy

she who wouldn't notice now, what's happened to the years, there were moments when I thought he was going to say something and he didn't, moments when he gave the impression he thought he was part of us and then he retreated, moments he seemed to be moved by something because of an expression impossible to describe in his unaltered features, how do you write this, my co-worker searching for me with her nose, eyes closed, with little kisses from my forehead down the rest of my face

—Your body makes me crazy, darling

we didn't get along too well, did we brother, despite our pact

—We're friends, aren't we?

you didn't like me, I think the fact that I was a girl frightened you, and as I became a woman, it wasn't fear, it was panic, you squeezed yourself against the wall of the hall so you wouldn't touch me, if you were at the door of my room you turned your head afraid to see a naked shoulder or a glimpse of a breast, I who hardly had breasts, two little buds starting to grow that gave me a fright

—What's happening to me?

and what happened was the operation, bed eighteen, waiting for the mornings looking at the blackness beyond the window wanting the light to bring me the redemption that didn't come or maybe doesn't exist, didn't exist, I'm not in the hospital, I'm at home with my husband, and only if it's for a little bit, and you enter me, and now he, incredulous

—Was it really good, seriously?

propping himself on his elbow, trying to read my feelings

—Swear it was good then

and I swore

—It was good

although his insistence forced me to think

—Was it really that good?

thinking

—Is there more that I don't know about?

without discovering the other things, my co-worker

—That little honey mouth

and some honey, maybe a cold sore, the inside of my cheek that I bit and that bothers me, I bet I cut it, the fear that I'd have bad breath at the end of the day and besides the pines said what honey, teeth, tongue, spit, I in the dentist's chair with a kind of bib around my neck and a tube with a hook in my gums

—A little cavity, madam

so that I gripped the arms of the chair, anticipating the pain,

how is it that such a small molar, makes you suffer so much, while a cruel instrument buzzes and drills, drills
—Let's see if it hasn't reached the pulp
bringing the memory of workers with jackhammers in the street and the foreman watching in silence, not just the men were vibrating, the entire neighborhood vibrated with them, not forgetting the blackbirds, the dishes were always shy, not understanding the modesty of the porcelain clinking in the sideboard, no affirmative sugar bowl, no authoritarian soup tureen, they raise their finger to ask permission
—May I say something?
the reticent opinions doubting themselves, the porcelain was so insecure, so afraid of deciding their own destiny
—Do you think so?
or
—You won't think badly of us?
and I don't, we finished dinner and my not deaf brother said goodbye to us in a silence that you could hear down on the street where the trolleys are, merchants hawking their wares, offices, my husband
—I didn't hurt you, did I?
and you didn't hurt me, don't worry, you gave me a hickey that isn't important, I like it, a little bruise that will take a while to heal, from purple to green, from green to yellow, from yellow to normal, and when it goes from yellow to normal, I'm being sincere, I'll miss the hickey, imagine what I've turned into, I even miss hickeys because they were part of us, understand, here's a stronger wave and when it disappears I lose you, if it were possible, and I hope it's possible, don't leave me, how strange love is and it will be love, answer me, is it really love

or do I feel alone and if I feel alone bed eighteen comes back, Dr. Clementina

—Good morning

and her shoulders slumped, I know her shoulders better than her face, I almost only know her shoulders and the legs that carry her, ignoring me, not exactly ignoring, forcing themselves to ignore me, writing in the diary that we left in the wall

—Don't ignore me

in a twisted, childlike handwriting

—don't ignore me

and they did, you didn't read it, your mother

—My peach

mine

—Where are you, daughter?

and therefore goodbye Tininha, we grew up, they fell off the tricycle and we are fifty-two years old without tricycles nearby, in a few minutes we'll take the petals off our nails and it's our turn to fall, my not deaf brother got up from the table, looked at each one of us, adjusted the fairy on the napkin, at least he adjusted the fairy on the napkin and I still hear his footsteps on the stairs, the door to the street that he closed without a bang but that still echoes inside me, it will always echo inside me, father, mother, brothers, me, when we go into your room not a picture is left, the drawers are open, one of them on the floor, hangers on the bed, the poster of the English singer is torn, we discover a bag with everything in it and my mother, as if inside the bag and all its contents is a snake about to bite

—Don't touch it

incapable of doing a handstand, incapable of running a race but still alert, alive, my father consoling himself

—Baby's bottom, baby's bottom
    I know that no man in a hat would be of any use to you, so heavy on the sofa, rubbing your own cheek where there's no baby's bottom, stiff bristles poorly shaved and dried blood on your lips, at six thirty I walk up to the Alto da Vigia, I thought my last Sunday would be different from the others and in fact it's the same, I don't feel tense, I don't feel that good, I presume that I don't feel that good and it doesn't matter to the others, to my co-worker maybe
   —My peach
   she who doesn't say
   —My peach
   she who says
   —My baby
   when she undresses me, lies me down, treating me the way I treated Ernesto, put your right foot on his shoulder and the left foot on that one, press yourself against my body, show Mama a little action, be patient, that's it, how lovely, the phone rang somewhere far away, we didn't answer, what's a breath, not a normal breath, a rapid breathing and then the sound of hanging up, my not deaf brother, I bet, one afternoon with one word
   —I wanted
   interrupted, immediately, by the receiver at rest, my mother called the Kaserne and
   —He can't come to the phone
   until, the last time
   —He doesn't want to come to the phone
    pines, pines, the yard, the well, my conscience is clear, I don't know what this means but I think the expression is nice and besides people spend lifetimes saying it, my conscience is clear,

how curious, isn't it, everyone has a clear conscience, the whole world is serene and without sin, why did you run away from us, brother, father, mother, brothers, me, where did we fail you, what did you think we were guilty of, my mother went to the Kaserne and came back looking so old
—They wouldn't let me go in
She saw jeeps and cannons at the gate, she didn't see him, hidden in a Kaserne or behind an armored vehicle, the suspicion that he was peering at him from a post, or a tree
—Mother
almost clinging to us, he father, mother, brothers, me, he pointing to the Kaserne
—What now?
to cling to us again, fortunately it will be high tide soon, it's hard to keep going much longer, me to the intern
—You want me to hit you, is that it?
kicking the viola and when I kicked the viola, a hollow, deep sound came out, she with closed eyes
—That's it
and me, to myself, how old are you, twenty-one, twenty-two, an incomplete nakedness, gestures that aren't round yet, doubt about which button to push for life to start, child-sized feet that fit in my hand, wanting to hit you, not hit you, to get out of these pillows, these fans, this apartment, with a spider web between two walls, that hangs a meter from the floor, phrases written on the walls, naïve verses, drawings, we knew when my not deaf brother shipped out, January, January sixth, I'm no good with dates but this one belongs to me, we went to the docks my father, my mother, my deaf brother and I who always come last, we encountered soldiers marching in formation, the boat, the

handkerchiefs, gulls pecking at straw and oil, what does the Tagus offer besides this, we saw the boat pull away from the marches, we didn't see you, my deaf brother
—Shhheee
pointing at a someone waving between hundreds of people waving, tugging at my mother's clothes
—Shhheee
and waving in turn, my mother
—Where?
pushing ahead, shoving people out of the way, coming back to us, discouraged
—I didn't see him, did you?
while my deaf brother kept pointing, even when the ship was a tiny dot he kept pointing, even when the ship disappeared, he kept pointing, even when we got home, he opened the back window that didn't even face the river
—Shhheee
he continued to point, for days and days he kept pointing, my mother
—For the love of God stop that
and he continued pointing, and if he wasn't pointing, he was twisting his wrists
—Shhheee saaaills
wandering around the house looking for him, opening the chest, the suitcases, my mother, grabbing him by the shirt
—Are you trying to drive me crazy?
without the courage to look at my father, with the past rising in her throat, like vomit in her mouth, and a man laughing as he said goodbye to her
—I might come back to see you

and I figure he didn't come back to see her, I figure my mother looked for him at work and he said in a low voice, so his pals wouldn't notice and it's obvious they did

—I don't feel like it

so it's obvious that my mother said

—What do you mean, you don't feel like it?

Thinking she could wipe out with a whisper

—What do you mean, you don't feel like it?

the front office, dozens of desks, file cabinets, a calendar with a Swiss landscape, cows, snow, that kind, the man to her not in a whisper, in a whistle

—Don't even think of coming back here

evaporating between the desks, my mother followed out the door by laughter that tore her up inside, it subsided later, but insisted on tearing her up every time my deaf brother

—Shhheee

and I think that it didn't stop tearing her up even when she got old, even when she's dead it will tear her up including when they forget her, it will last longer than her bones, the cemetery, the ocean, another big wave, the morning high tide, not mine, that's starting, the red flag up on the beach and a bather whistling, it could be that while resting on the way up to the Alto da Vigia, I squeeze Senhor Manelinho's hand

—I was the last one to

for him to be the last person who also took my hand, can you see the importance of that my friend, there's no body on the beach to say goodbye to, except the priest of Senhor Leonel's niece

—Come on home, Germano

blessing the rocks below, I think not to bless us, to absolve us and therefore I am without sin, I am pure, Senhor Leonel's niece in Vouzela or under a train, what does it matter, even the strongest bones cut with a single chop, me circling the neck of my co-worker with what they haven't cut off me yet, an old woman's skin, an old woman's clothing, even an old woman's furniture, sixty four years old and no son at the Lifeguard station like my mother, no son in the war, no son pointing without ceasing God knows where

—Shhheee

tugging at her blouse, desperate, stubborn

—Shhheee

father, mother, brothers, me, blackbirds, pines. the step with little flowers peeping out of the stone, me stepping on them with my heel

—This is my father's step not yours get lost

and they, with no excuse, disappeared, obediently

—Sorry

me, firm

—I'll decide if I forgive you

the mist abandoned the reeds dissolving its worn fabric that shredded between our fingers, Senhor Manelinho

—Thank you for saying goodbye, girl

Manelinho's wife remembering

—I thought you were the girl, but I wasn't sure

her voice when I reach the wall

—You'll see that it won't hurt it's just a jump and it's over

it doesn't hurt the way the train doesn't hurt, waiting at the docks, around a curve, first just the plants and trees, then the locomotive, the carriages and the smoke that approaches swaying, you feel the knocking of the rods, the cylinders that empty and fill, the coal, the oil, Senhor Manelinho's wife, you know, you'll

see it doesn't hurt, it just hurts that father, mother, brothers, me, the only thing that hurts is father, mother, brothers, me the rest is simple, I guarantee it, my co-worker
    —Do you like me to play with you baby, do you like to laugh with me
    me laughing with her, me not saying
    —You're old
    bending back on the sofa pillow
    —I love it
    not mocking her, sincerely
    —I love it
    my father happy for me, my mother happy for me, the pines, the floorboards and the roof tiles that are missing are happy for me, my whole family is happy for me since I
    —I love it
    cousin Fernando
    —Five réis that she's very smart
    five réis and she loves it, from the Alto da Vigia she will see Senhor Manelinho and his wife, his wife to him
    —Didn't I tell you it was her?
    and she hadn't but so what, who cares about a fifty-two year old woman telling her husband
    —I want you inside me
    asking her husband
    —Hold me love
    and staying in bed for a while, not knowing if they were awake or asleep, while a coffee pot, almost empty, was waiting on the kitchen counter with a little sugar tablet at the bottom.

2.

In the mornings it's not just the shadows of the pines that enter the house, it's the branches too, we walked through the living room avoiding the tree trunks, we stepped on pine needles, moss, pieces of bark and there was a blackbird on the sofa, a cricket singing in the fruit bowl, I thought it was a voice and it's their wings that vibrate, if I spoke with my arms, instead of my throat, what a noise it would make, I move them, and at most, there's just a rustling of cloth that you can hardly hear and a pinecone falling to the floor just like the knob on my co-workers bedpost that for weeks wasn't there, just the aluminum post, the headboard was like a person with a missing eye, we discovered it in the laundry basket, we lifted the wicker lid and there it was, disappointed at us.

—You took long enough to find me, caramba

and we did take a long time, I'm sorry, how much time did it take for you to go from the bedroom to the laundry room, how did you get in there, the knob, looking away

—It's a secret

the obsession things have with obscuring their answers, they don't clarify, they clam up or answer in riddles, I know their wiles and I can't get used to them, the second drawer of the desk, for example, full of photographs, got stuck one day, for no reason, the wood hadn't warped, it hadn't jammed, there was no picture frame blocking its way, it wouldn't move and that was it, my co-worker brought the knob from the laundry basket and stuck it on the window sash bracket, it looked out of place, in the mornings it's not just the shadows of the pines that enter the house, it's the branches too, we walked through the living room avoiding the tree trunks, we stepped on pine needles, moss, pieces of bark and there was a blackbird on the sofa, a cricket singing in the fruit bowl, my husband removed the bottom drawer hoping to fix the one holding the pictures, he hit it with his palm, shook it from right to left, lying on the floor, his features twisted to one half of his face and his legs bent with the effort, me wishing

—I hope you can't fix it

because I don't like to see the dead who criticize us, blame us, me to my mother

—They detest us, don't they, ma'am?

my mother correcting the way I held my fork

—So many questions, eat

that I hold the way she wanted, at the tip, it was hard to manage, and it didn't even hold the peas, my husband's mouth clenched as if his mouth were holding the lever with which he twisted the drawer with a crack of the wood

—I don't understand this

and later, as the morning went on, the shadows of the pines abandoned the house, everything was finally in the place that it should be, the mountains, the clouds, the ocean, the intern to me

—Do it again

on the Japanese fans were Japanese ladies with fans, wearing sandals like our flip-flops, how would they manage on the walkways carrying their boxes of fruits, my mother, twisting their ears

—Do you want to get run over?

and the Japanese ladies, who must not have understood her, responded in their language, sounding like parakeets, my husband emerged from under the desk with the slowness of someone being brought back to life

—We must call a cabinetmaker

and we never did call, the dead are still inside the drawer, occasionally there's a murmur of protest or a request that I ignore, what do they want of me now, your time is passed and mine is almost over, just a few more hours, eight or nine, Tininha to me

—Look at the watch they gave me

the hands weren't real, they were drawn on the face, five and twelve, and the band was elastic, in my parents' room was an alarm clock with illuminated dials, at night, in the dark, it gave off a bluish glow, some numbers were less clear, the three, the nine, while the seven was enormous, Tininha didn't come here, her mother wouldn't allow it, she thought we were poor

—You can play in the garden, that's enough

each one on her side of the wall the same way, when I was in bed eighteen, she was on the side of health and I on the side of sickness, me to her, Doctor, she to me, you, a wall between us, my co-worker, checking the resistance of the knob

—Maybe it will stay

and, God willing, it will stay on, it will rest, with age things, like people, give up on poetic fancies, they stay still, their eyelids lowered, not even answering, decrepitude is concentrated in the hands that rest on the knees, the fingers much more worn than the rest of the body, veins, spots, the wrinkled skin, how many years is sixty-four, I don't know, I know we lean in the direction of something, I don't know what, my brother is always eighteen, I'll always be fifty-two starting this afternoon, my father and no photographs, the way the pictures look at us makes me feel guilty and I don't understand of what, one of the blackbirds is a lost note and I am certain that if I understood the note I would understand the secret of the world, if I am still there will be no donkeys on the Alto da Vigia, just brush, it's cold on top of the rocks even in August, flecks of foam, in the open palm of the world, that graze my skin or don't touch me, I'm just imagining it, the building next to the Thebes Bakery is losing its tiles, on the back porch you could see the divorced woman in the house second to the left eating dinner with a book, and speaking of books, I ask myself if we got help from the *Manual of the Perfect Carpenter* the problem of the drawer would be solved, there must be a chapter on drawers that get stuck, with diagrams, instructions, drawings, the divorced woman turned her head in our direction still chewing, more inexpressive than the sheep seen from a train stopped between two farms, the intern, her neck resting on a blue pillow

—Don't you think I'm crazy?

the divorced woman returned to her plate and the book, it wasn't just the façade of the building, there were missing tiles in the kitchen as well, the only lamp hung from a chain, it had an enamel shade, it concerned me that I didn't see the woman on the street, just in that black, the book leaning on a water jug, my co-worker

—When you leave, I feel like

finishing the sentence with a vague gesture, it bothered me that the chinoiserie hardly paid attention to her, is there anybody that has a moment for us and gives us attention like Senhor Leonel's niece paid attention to the priest

—Come on home, Germano

and the priest giving a long blessing that lasts me to this day, after dinner the wife of the second on the left closed the book and remained for centuries with her elbows on the table and her cheeks in her hand, they sent me to bed and the woman was still there but when I checked in the morning her kitchen was deserted, once I knocked on her door, she had hardly opened it when I said

—Sorry, wrong address

and I ran away, a woman younger than I am now who seemed to look at me not with her eyes, but with mine, eyes change faces, I learned then, and observe each other even if they're over a strange mouth, behind her was an umbrella stand and a mirror reflecting the umbrella stand, for lack of anything better, to not lose the habit, in locking our door my eyes, in the sockets of the neighbor in the second on the left, stopped looking at me as if they were about to scream and therefore I was in the hall crashing into the furniture, my mother

—What happened to you, girl?

what happened is that I can't stand hearing my eyes shouting in the doorway, I can't sit down at the kitchen table, elbows on the table and cheeks in my palms, thinking

—What now?

in the mornings it's not just the shadows of the pines that enter the house, it's the branches too, we walked through the living room avoiding the tree trunks the way I avoid the drawer with the dead people in it, my father who doesn't touch me, strangers who don't know who I am, asking each other

—Whose daughter is she?

and when they got the answer

—She doesn't look like us

old clothes in a closet, hats with veils, overcoats, I even found half of a spur between bills for kid gloves and a cough syrup with a bearded gentleman and celluloid collar on the label, Jesus Christ, how people lived back then, if I don't look like you it's not my fault, my mother always swore she'd found me in a box at the front door and she took me in out of pity, or a little basket, if I'm still in it's made of wicker, with my co-worker's laundry, and I was in there, in the middle of pillowcases and knobs, with Ernesto next to me, the blackbird's not explained all of this, I was anxious to understand

—Repeat please

but a wave wiped out the words, after a while there was no divorced woman in the second to the left, the book stayed there until the owner took it with the hangar and the mirror, I was sure that my eyes had stayed at the door on the verge of a scream that's going to come out at twenty to seven contradicting Tininha's watch, eternally stuck at five and twelve

—That time doesn't exist

when they took my pulse, in bed eighteen, it was with that watch, not a real one, that counted my heartbeats and about the screaming eyes, when they scream what image remains in the mirror, teeth and tongue under the eyelids, an enormous throat, pieces of ourselves that knock us to the ground, my co-worker for once doesn't have kisses or features, sharp bones that I don't recognize

—I have a pain here

trying to smile

—It should pass, I hope so
   and under the
   —It should pass, I hope so
   her father, on his knees in the fort, crawling between the legs of the police, he found a T-shirt and held it to him, he found a shoe and embraced the shoe until one shoulder went to the floor, the other shoulder, his head, the doctor peering at his pupils with a flashlight
   —He can't take any more today
   people with bags and towels arriving at the beach, fishermen not on the Alto da Vigia, on the smaller rocks, my co-worker felt better with tea and the noise she made when drinking annoyed me, the sound of the cup on the saucer annoyed me, the fingers with which she caressed me annoyed me, however the
   —Come here to Mama
   even though it annoyed me I forced myself to feel grateful, in the morning it was not just the shadow of the pines that came into the house, it was the memory of my co-worker as well, Cousin Fernando took his arms from his sides, advancing toward her
   —Guess where the candy is, ma'am
   while a crow, swooping into the trees, flies in the direction of the olive grove, at first, I didn't believe it and it was really a crow, if I told Senhor Manelinho he'd argue with me
   —We don't have crows here
   the same way that we almost don't have crows in Lisbon, they're in the wheat, the corn, in Vouzela maybe, if I kept still, and I don't, I'd look up Vouzela on the map, on the beach there are sour figs, magueys, and waves, my deaf brother has a float with a little dolphin figure, I have a float with a blonde mermaid, my not deaf brother pierced them with a nail and my mother

—Do you know what you deserve?

my father fixed them with adhesive patches and blew them up, his veins bulging in his neck, the number of body parts that hide under our skin, cysts, glands, muscles, Senhor Manelinho's wife has a hernia in her navel that she spoke of publicly while insulting her husband

—This thing will pop one day, and you go around with whores, you idiot

every three breaths my father squeezed the nozzle, resting his veins without being able to focus on us, my mother

—At least when you're blowing these up you aren't drinking

but the adhesive patch covered half of the mermaid and I refused to take the float, my deaf brother brought the ice pick, turned to my not deaf brother

—Shhheee saaaills

and my older brother separated them, my not deaf brother

—I didn't mean it

ever since he was a child he's had so much anger in him, what harm did we do to you, tell us, his pockets were always full of stones to throw at the dogs, thinking back, it probably wasn't a crow that flew into the trees, a blackbird that was bigger than the others, there it is, me to Senhor Leonel

—Where is Vouzela, Senhor Leonel?

Senhor Leonel, butchering a baby goat, turning to the terrace

—Far from the ocean, up there

or rather it went beyond the terrace and you continue walking but beyond the terrace were the houses, beyond the houses was a street, beyond the street were more houses, after the more houses were little farms, fences with loose stones, a tractor with nobody on it, I remember storks on a chimney and a eucalyptus stand that smelled like convalescing from a cold, menthol compresses on your chest and a vaporizer, my mother

—Breathe this in

me moist with the steam and my father worried in the hall, of course it's a blackbird, Senhor Manelinho, I was mistaken, asking fearfully

—Has the fever gone down?

back and forth two visits to the pantry, when my deaf brother broke his arm, he brought a chair and watched him sleep wiping off the daubs of plaster from his fingers with a damp cloth, my mother observed him with an expression that if it weren't my fault we would have been happy and we were happy, I swear, even without the mermaid float we were happy, don't worry about us, Tininha

—Do you poor people feel like us?

her house had grass, ours had weeds, beyond the wall was a pool, on our side was a well, you had a camellia, we had pines, Dr. Clementina had new cushions, bed eighteen folded into a sofa and nevertheless I didn't think I was badly off, if I did I'd lean a book on the water jug during dinner, *Power to The Working Class*, if I rummage around I might find it, you never threw anything out, there's no trace of the *Manual of the Perfect Carpenter*, straight and curved arrows explaining the movements, numbers indicating the order and part of the cover was torn, my co-worker

—It seems I won't die after all

you won't die, nobody dies, there are already enough dead people, almost all of them are in my desk drawer, in fact, those who wander around are the niece of Senhor Leonel and the priest who blessed everyone, the others are piled up at home fighting over cupboards, figurines, a pewter pitcher

—They don't shut up, see?

so that we went to bed with them and woke up with them, whispers of lovers, speeches, in the morning it's not just the shadow of the pines that enter the house, it's the branches too, my husband

one of these days the pictures will stop reproducing among each other

the way to the living room leading me away from the trunks, I step on needles, moss, pieces of bark, if I were to look at Tininha's watch I wouldn't go to the beach today and the wave, almost breaking as it waited, the people like stone statues, Senhor Leonel's knife poised over a bone, he looking at the terrace pointing at Vouzela, my co-worker

—Mama

without finishing the sentence, her hand about to touch me but never reaching me, my father weighing like lead on the stairs before putting the whole world in a slipper, me hoping for a party that never came, if the dead let loose and start reproducing among themselves the drawer won't be able to carry their weight, the neighbor in the second left went away, everything escapes me, what's left over, tell me, without a soul to keep me company, Tininha doesn't exist, there's Dr. Clementina who knows where, if I had the number I'd call from the grocery store and wouldn't say a word, maybe she'd realize it was me and

—Where are you

and

—I'll be right there

and

—Don't do anything before I get there

addressing me as "tu" like before, not "você" the way she did when I was in bed eighteen, I wouldn't be doing tests, procedures, exams, I'd be a person again imagining you with me, they forced us to grow up because the years are mean, forgive me for taking up a few minutes of your time, don't be impatient, I'm confused, you know, it's not true that father, mother, brothers, me, I'm alone, it's not the Alto da Vigia, it's being alone that's hard, if you put me in front of the mirror that reflects the umbrella stand you wouldn't see anyone, if you lost interest in the mermaid float you wouldn't mind the adhesive patch and you'd put it on, not the princess earrings or the petals on your nails, it was the float that I put on and I didn't think I looked ridiculous, my not deaf brother, surrounded with burning huts, with a pipe in his mouth stretched out before me

—We're still the same, girl

not paying attention to the machine guns, the grenades, the voices calling him

—We're still the same, girl

and it's not true, the huts, the old man and the woman lying on the ground belong to you not to me, I'm not in Africa but in the beach house with a blackbird on the sofa and a cricket singing in the fruit bowl, I thought it was a voice and it's their wings that vibrate, if I spoke with my arms, instead of my throat, what noise would it make, I move them, and at most, there's just a rustling of cloth that you can hardly hear, if at least my co-worker would tell me to sit on her lap and let me hide my face in her shoulder, me with the memory of my father and my older brother's bike that, if necessary, gives me a ride down to the beach or through the neighborhood, my not deaf brother is nobody, he looks at the building next to the Thebes Bakery fighting the desire to go in and instead of going in, leaving with the fairy in his mind, I luckily have my husband, the intern almost asleep on the blue pillow

   —I'm so happy you don't think I'm crazy

   and the viola, if I touched it, would make an infinite echo, that's what I say about things, they intrude in our lives, approve, disapprove, criticize, I had more friends besides Tininha, in Lisbon, in high school, Ermelinda, Dora, but the princess earrings were missing, the diary was missing, Ernesto was missing, I wanted him to be pals with Rogério and he wasn't, he was jealous, Ermelinda worked in her stepfather's restaurant, Dora disappeared and therefore she's in Vouzela, everybody learned, it's no secret, that there are no more places to go, my co-worker

   —I've been sick, I need some affection

   and how is it that my beach lips are there, sometimes a traveling movie, a circus, you heard, outside, the circus manager at the microphone, addressed the girl on the tightrope

   —Be careful, Ândrea, your mother died that way

   and you noticed a shaking inside the tent, in the mornings the shadow of the pines enters the house, how many times have I insisted on this, there's a nervousness in me that doesn't stop, doesn't stop, the movie shows Mexican films with bad sound, the man running the projector went to the street to smoke with the filter in his teeth, the lady at the ticket booth talked with Senhor Manelinho's wife, disinterested in the ocean, the man at the café with the foosball table tossing coins with the bathers, my mother to him, after looking at the billboard

   —Are there lots of kisses?

   and if there were lots of kisses she'd watch with us, Tininha, it's the branches too, we walked in the living room avoiding the

   —They don't let me go they say you can get fleas

trunks, it doesn't stop, we stepped on pine needles, moss, pieces of bark, a blackbird on, a blackbird not on the sofa, in the garage, if I could sleep for a moment it would come, my father in the pantry fumbling with the bottles, my mother blew her nose with emotion when she watched the films, while I left walking just like the actress, swinging my hips like she did, if I ran my hand through my hair I'd certainly find a flower but I didn't run my hand through my hair so I wouldn't mess it up, it was the actor who put it there before he galloped away, I waved at him from the verandah and then hid my face in my hands, my pleated blouse, my long skirt, I warned my deaf brother

—Be careful, Ândrea, your mother died that way

I warned my deaf brother

—Don't step on my skirt

my not deaf brother, alarmed

—What skirt?

my mother also had a flower in her hair, eyebrows substituted by very fine semicircles, huge daubs of cream on her cheeks and infinite eyelashes, tortured figs, cacti, an Indian girl in braids behind me

—Be careful, Ândrea

and Ândrea, with open arms, advancing cautiously, an Indian girl in braids following me with a tray of drinks that I didn't even see, a second one behind my mother and my mother refusing the drinks with a sad little gesture

—I miss him

how incomprehensible not having a verandah with columns at the beach house and my full-length picture in a carved frame, what happened to our crystal, our emeralds, the canopy bed, even a little truck, with the man behind the projector at the wheel and the ticket lady next to him, he'd leave with the screen and the benches, looking up, during the film, the stars of the beach insignificant at the feet of the stars of Mexico and looking to the left boat lights between the fenders that protected them from the docks, the owner of the foosball café, disappointed

—Hardy any violence, just the foolishness of love

Ândrea, without a tightrope or ballerina shoes, missing a ribbon on her blouse, ate from a pan with the other performers, it was the magician, instead of doves, took potatoes from his hat and roasted them, if he were at our table, I'd ask him for

—swordfish

and swordfish, cream, shellfish, my deaf brother hearing, my father forgetting the pantry, not an old bicycle, four bicycles with headlights, a horn instead of a bell, and a wicker basket for the peaches

—My peach

carrots make your eyes pretty, Tininha

—Aren't my eyes blue?

and even though they were brown, I said

—Very blue

when not even the waves are blue, at most, they're sometimes green, sometimes gray, Ermelinda came to greet me at the entrance of the restaurant and for days the garlic didn't come off my skin, my husband

—Did you change your cologne?

and I hadn't changed my cologne, it was the same just that the garlic ate it, the stoves had aged Ermelinda, the strands of hair that came out of her cap were gray, the second degree equations, always so necessary, guaranteed the teacher, I don't remember what for, lost, when she smiled a silver tooth showed where one is missing now, she realizing what she didn't want to show me

—I've aged, haven't I?

varicose veins, the holes in her ears without earrings, her stepfather

—Aren't you working today?

and Ermelinda, what happened to your waist?

—I have to go inside

her shoulders curved, one of the clavicles was higher than the other, she wanted to be an educator when she was a child and now she educates fillets of bacalao in the freezer, scars from burning oil on her hands, the flower in my hair should stay here, I hope, if we are careful the Mexican films won't end, Restaurante Central das Avenidas a whisper on a neighborhood corner, the menu in pencil on a piece of paper taped in the window, the Restaurante Central das Avenidas instead of a kindergarten, that's it, at least Dora is safe in the drawer, I hope, with the second degree equations that are so necessary, on the tip of my tongue, me to my co-worker

—Do you remember second degree equations, by any chance?

and she, who had not heard the questions, stretching, and curling her index finger, a cricket in the fruit bowl, you thought it was a voice and not wings that vibrated

—Stop talking about grammar and console your Mama

my co-worker lounging like a lady instead of falling off the tightrope, how many tiles are missing from the building, when I was little it was eight or nine, now two dozen at least, the stepfather with the plate over his head, spilling sauce on his collar

—Who asked for the cuttlefish?

I didn't have the courage to go back, I'm a coward, don't think badly of me, understand, I've got to go to the desk and tell Dora in secret, so that the rest of the dead don't hear me, we had signals to call each other with, remember, three knocks, one know, two knocks, so that you said to them

—Just a minute

I speak in a murmur that only we could hear, and you put your ear to the wood, if anyone approaches you give a quick knock, I wait a minute until they leave and then we continue, see, Tininha's eyes are brown, I lied to her, yours are blue, your dead father, your mother to me

—You're a good girl

she worked full-time at an insurance agency, never took off her mourning clothes, when Ândrea wasn't on the tightrope she was crouched in a box without a sidelong glance to the ocean, she didn't pay attention to the Alto da Vigia, she didn't pay attention to the waves, I should bless you this afternoon, I would have liked you to meet my older brother, I prefer you to Tininha's mother, I prefer you to my mother's friend, even without dark glasses or money, look how magical it is to urinate on a bush, look at him folding and stretching his legs when he's done and shake himself because the seat of his pants move, not in a tuxedo, colorless pants, instead of a belt a rope, instead of a shirt a torn pullover, even dressed like that make Dora appear, friend, take Ermelinda out of the restaurant and put her in a living room, with dolls on the walls, playing with the children of others because none of us has children, I don't have children but I have my co-worker

—Console Mama

and it's she who consoles me

—My pearl

or

—My doll

or some such nonsense that nevertheless helps, don't ask me how and I don't know how to answer but it helps, the same way that the second-degree equations would help if I hadn't forgotten them, the prefixes, the suffixes, the capital of Thailand

—What are the principal products of Canada you there

and I clueless, Ândrea clueless, the magician clueless, and nevertheless he made little doves appear in a single gesture, pull out Ermelinda's cod so she doesn't get burned by the oil, Dora's mother didn't call her Dora she called her Dorita

—Good girl, my little Dorita

a room for both, the narrow kitchen, the hall that served as a living room, the Sacred Heart of Jesus, full of color, on the wall, that lifts the soul, in addition to giving one courage to face the hellish days, the dead father in a frame

—He was a railroad worker

lifting their soul as well

—I know he's taking care of us

and you can believe he is, ma'am, pull those little strings in the sky, pay a debt here, a debt there, and walk on, right, the way I'll walk to the ocean later this afternoon, like my brother did, before me

—I'll only be five minutes

in the middle of the donkeys, the weeds, the goat on the rocks

—Be careful, goat, remember your mother died that way

Ândrea, in the box, rubbing calluses off her feet with a piece of sugar cane and her circus bustier drying on a line, little buttons of mother-of-pearl, a few torn off but with some skill and, you'll get fatter, like the lady with the pins who will notice, her hair in rollers, cotton in her mouth to fill out her cheeks

—You need to look plumper

and with time and potatoes, you'll get plumper, like the lady with the parakeets, that fly through paper gunnels, balance, advancing and retreating, on little nylon trapezes and they peck her nose at the end, lined up on your decolletage, the lady, in a robe and rollers in her hair, just a few because age strips us, look at how white her skin is, Senhor Manelinho sends her smiles and she responds batting her eyelashes, Senhor Manelinho's wife, vigilant

—Even with old ladies, you creep?

Senhor Manelinho, with theatrical indignation

—Me?

summoning the newspapers in the kiosk as his witnesses

—You're crazy, you old bag

and turning on the smiles when a customer distracted his wife, my Dorita, my Ermelinda, not my Tininha

—You don't have any money, do you?

not my Tininha, Dr. Clementina stepping on me with her heels, even in the hall she continues to step on me, I know it's her because my body hurts, the nurse

—Bed eighteen, Doctor

Dr. Clementina walking away

—I'm busy, I'll get to bed eighteen tomorrow

It's not just the shadow of the pines that enters the house, it's the branches too, I walk in the living room, I can't escape this, avoiding the trunks, I step on the pine needles, moss, pieces of bark, through the night on the branches that are still sleeping, I don't make noise so that they don't say

—What's the matter?

and a startled pinecone falls to the ground, the presence of the ocean is so intense at times, the shine on the water, so many sun scales, in the sand on the bottom the sparkles of pebbles if the bones from long ago are still, my co-worker

—Even if you don't believe it, if it weren't for you, I would have killed myself already

I don't know if I believe it or not, people anxious to please not for us, to receive something in exchange, except for my older brother who really liked me and if I think about it, not even Ernesto really liked me, about my brother, there he is calling me from the bike

—Girl

in the path that flanked the house along the wall, before going down to the beach for the last time, at first, I only noticed the

—Girl

but when I looked at his face, I understood, I could have answered

—Don't go

and I didn't answer, I could have answered

—Take me with you

and I didn't answer or maybe I answered not with my voice, with my arms like the crickets, a first whirr

—Don't go

a second whirr

—Take me with you

but he was already gone, out of the gate, and Tininha was calling me because the hands of her toy watch had moved, at first, I didn't believe it and they changed, I remember our surprise

—The hands changed

so that when I looked at the street my older brother was far away, even if I ran to the beach, I wouldn't be able to catch up with him, you could see it was him climbing up the rocks, and at that moment, the divorced woman in the second to the left, her door open in front of me, started to scream.

3.

And then, I don't know why, I stopped singing when I was seven years old, "*Maria linda Maria meu raminho de alecrim toda a gente tem inveja do amor que tens por mim*" and my brothers applauded, my mother said
—Get lost
you could see my father was happy, me not missing one word, a ribbon in my hair, not a ribbon you tie but one that was already made, you put it on with a kind of clip to your hair and I don't know where it went, I must have liked it because I miss it, my mother kept it in a little box so it wouldn't get ruined and once in a while she'd put it on me, besides singing I'd dance, that is, I lifted my arms and shifted my weight from one side to the other trying to snap my fingers, I couldn't as hard as I tried, to this day I can't do it, everyone can do it but me, Dona Alice, changing the position of my fingers
—Not that way, this way
and suddenly, who knows how, I did it, it came out, a first little snap, a second, I didn't push my luck and try again, I was going to mention the pines but what for, they're there, enough

of talking about trees, after a certain point Dona Alice stopped working for us

—I'm too old for this

she moved slower and slower, she was becoming forgetful, she didn't turn off the washing machine, she ironed two creases in the blouses, instead of one, if you ran your index finger over the furniture it was dusty, besides this her heart was suffocating her

—My poor heart's out of whack

and she didn't wear shoes anymore because she couldn't fit in them, she used checkered slippers, I found her leaning on the dish washer looking at me with a plea for help, she moved with painful steps, she leaned on the vacuum cleaner instead of pushing it over the rug, my mother was incapable of firing her

—Take it easy, Dona Alice, we don't have a train to catch

and she felt like stretching out on the floor like the dogs that you need to take to the vet for their shots, we had one many years ago, my father held him by the scruff of the neck the whole time, the veterinary assistant

—That was centuries ago

and my father, *Maria linda Maria*, not listening, rubbing the dog's back, his name was Lord, he didn't bite anyone, my not deaf brother pulled his tail and he let him do it, I envied the way he could drink water with his tongue, I tried to do it and my mother

—Are you crazy?

at the beach house he rolled around, *meu raminho de alecrim*, in the shade in front of the garage, putting his nose in his paws to take care of us, I thought, only the lizards excited him and he didn't catch any, he returned to the shade, defeated, in Lisbon he slept in the kitchen alcove, here he slept in the flower bed, everyone envied our bird of paradise flowers until they are

crushed, we scolded him, he seemed to agree, and nevertheless he snuck back to the flowers, the next day more stems were broken, and he lounged innocently in the shade of the garage
 —It wasn't me
 except for that, he didn't do any harm, everybody envied us, he didn't get mixed up with the stray dogs, he didn't pay attention to the cats, and as far as the blackbirds were concerned, I think he killed one near the well, in the middle of the bushes, since I found a little bundle of feathers that I hit with a stone without telling anyone, I scolded him
 —You're not supposed to do that
 I warned him
 —Don't let that happen again
 a warning I copied from my mother, it didn't work with us, and it worked with him, the veterinary assistant took Lord from my father and cremated him in the oven in the patio, for the love you have of me, they asked my father
 —Do you want the ashes?
 my mother, when she saw the cardboard box that wasn't even that big, a little box, I'd like to know how a whole dog could fit in that little box, before my father could accept
 —No
 and something vibrated in his face, the little box stayed on a board, who can tell me they didn't throw it down the sink, there was never so much silence as on that afternoon, despite my mother's silence
 —I don't want to hear a word
 not to us, to herself since nobody was going to talk, we stayed quiet and my mother was making a racket with the dishes, a voice like hers although sharper

—Take away the damn dog

which, although she didn't admit it, was one of her ways of crying, people cry in such different ways, certain smiles for example, certain interrupted gestures, certain ways of wiping one's forehead on a sleeve or the silence of a cave, and inside, drops into the fissures of the stones, a little box, imagine, me feeling guilty for having gotten furious about the blackbird, Dona Alice, at the end, hardly able to dislodge herself from the refrigerator, struggling to gasp for air

—I'm too old for this

nevertheless, she wasn't too old to count what my mother paid her

—You've given me too much money, ma'am

my mother, then, I don't know, I stopped singing, almost embracing her and incapable of embracing her, it's always that way in our family, people stay in the almost, we want to but it doesn't come out, and then we take people on the bike fender or we give them a ride on our shoulders in the olive grove, we don't say

—I like you

or

—I missed you

there's the bike, the olive grove, and whoever wants to understand it can try, my mother

—I know very well what I put in there

she knew very well what she put in there and forgive me for not embracing you, Dona Alice, it won't come out, it's not that I think I'm better than you, it's that I'm not capable of doing it, when my older brother died on the outside we were confused, not sad, we don't show our grief, and so as not to show grief, we bang pots and pans together or a bottle falls down in the pantry, objects grieve for us, we sing *Maria linda Maria*, and that's it, our emotions aren't precise, when I had my operation nobody gave me a single word of encouragement, they came, stayed awhile, left, my mother and I visited Dona Alice months later, she wanted to get up from her chair to greet us and she wasn't able to, her ankles were enormous, her body was like a bellows, she raised her hand a few centimeters and it fell down again

—Here I am

just her eyes were the same, they fed her soup, little pieces of fish that she chewed exhausted, after two spoonfuls

—I can't anymore

if my father were with us he'd caress the scruff of her neck, I hope they don't put her in a little box too, however big people or animals are a little box is big enough, starting tomorrow I'll be in a little box of bones and sand, and I hope you refuse, sir, let the veterinary assistant throw me down the sink, Dona Alice in the little cave of her bed, without tin knobs on the bedposts or the number eighteen, next to the door, a photograph of a solemn communion with a country girl, holding a yellow lily, in front of a cruel crucifix, that would take years to turn into a grown woman waving the air with her hands, a second woman, younger, on her way to an identical metamorphosis

—Here she is, poor thing

the lamp increasing the darkness, a plastic bowl without a handle, branches of a mandarin tree on the frames, with the reflection of the sun on a leaf, the leaf

—Here I am, too

everything was there waiting for I don't know what, probably a solemn communion at the Church in Vouzela which is where everybody lives who doesn't live in Lisbon, in the middle, I calculate, of hundreds of trains

—Come on home, Germano

ask for the chalice, like the priest, in the foosball café, as you go down to the beach, and leave it intact on the table, a pair of votive candles, one outside, the other on the counter, burning endlessly while the leaf of the mandarin tree burned endlessly, the second woman to us, pointing at it with her eyes

—Fortunately, it's sunny

Dona Alice agreeing, also with her eyes, saving her voice because it's hard to breathe, her lungs are full of very heavy pebbles

—It's sunny

how difficult it is to force the body to keep going when it says

—I don't want to

and, under her skin, *Maria linda Maria*, organs piled on each other, inert, or not organs, a dozen Ernestos inside there by coincidence, my mother put an envelope on top of the counter that Dona Alice didn't even see, busy trying to stay alive, what will there be beyond the Alto da Vigia, more beaches, fields, Vouzela, if I asked Senhor Leonel, he'd say

—Nobody knows

with a light like that on the leaf of the mandarin tree on his butcher knife, the hooks where the meat hung a light was suspended as well, my *raminho de alecrim*, sprig of rosemary, a pretty verse, maybe my father, if he were alive, would be capable one day, I distracted with something, it doesn't matter, he suddenly

—My little sprig of rosemary

and me, pretending I didn't hear him, shivering with emotion, the other verses don't matter, my sprig of rosemary exactly what I need, when, in a little while, when I get to the Alto da Vigia, what happens next, I think of houses like this one, blackbirds, a yard with a swing, and in the yard, I am looking at you, my co-worker

—Are you worried about something?

and she was wrong, my little sprig of rosemary pleases me, worried about what, I can even get myself to kiss you, see, my mother and I didn't go back to visit Dona Alice again in the two-story building, one of them with an awning and a man on a scooter shouting to the upper windows

—Are you coming any time today, Osvaldo?

and Osvaldo, in pajamas

—I'll be right down

I bring myself to kiss you, make you happy, to have hope, after a certain age people don't ask for much, you throw them some grains of tenderness, it's easy, you take them out of your pocket

—Here, take this

and they construct a kind of future, in my case my sprig of rosemary is enough, what happened to Dona Alice's heart, Dr. Clementina, to give me a general idea, once I stole some change from the grocery shopping, which she left in the kitchen, over the receipt, to buy bubble gum at the Thebes Bakery, my mother

—There's a mistake here, Dona Alice

and Dona Alice pulled her glasses from her purse, which must have had an electric motor since it shook and it made her hands shake, not the rest of her body, now affecting her throat since her voice shook, in the timbre of, my little sprig of rosemary, dreams

—That can't be

counting and recounting the coins

—I'd swear by my dead and buried sister that I put it all there

my older brother looked at me, looked at my mother, looked

at Dona Alice, looked at me again, this time longer, everyone is envious, that's what I'm here for, brother, save my, my older brother

—Don't upset yourself Dona Alice, I took it for something I needed, and I forgot to replace it

searching in his pockets, a box of matches, a pencil stub, the bus pass, at last a worn banknote, my mother looking at me in turn, looking at Dona Alice, looking at my older brother, looking at me again, also for a longer time, Dona Alice's handbag was so nervous, her throat repeating in the timbre of dreams

—I swear by my sister

how could I foresee the little cave, the mandarin tree, the lamp that increased the darkness, how could I imagine the second formless creature, the misery, if I were capable of asking for forgiveness, and I'm not, I'd ask it I felt like asking for forgiveness and what came to me was *Maria linda Maria*, I don't know what kept me back, I wasn't aware that I was bad, it's not my fault, I was born bad, I'm bad, my co-worker

—Don't say you're bad blackbirds, blackbirds, you berate me

the blackbirds don't believe it but I'm bad, I guarantee it, Dona Alice slowly stopped shaking with her dead sister in her memory, the two had arrived in Lisbon at the same time, from Vouzela I bet, I was curious to ask what the thousand trains are like there and how many people get run over on the tracks but I didn't ask, I presume hundreds are killed if we include Senhor Leonel's niece, if we don't include them there are perhaps a few dozen, my mother looking at my older brother, looking at me, understanding, pretending that she was adding up the change but with closer attention, putting the banknote next to the match box, next to the pencil and the bus pass

—The accounts are fine put that stuff away and as for the match box I'm warning you that we don't smoke in this house
he smoked in the yard, behind the well, unafraid of the snakes, you couldn't see the cigarette, you could see a blue stain in the reeds, beyond the Alto da Vigia, it's a hypothesis, an enormous precipice with clouds, everyone envies the love you have for me, down there, the earth isn't round, it's square as a board, and therefore the South Pole is an invention, my co-worker, tracing my cheeks with a sugar spoon
—You're not bad, my lovely
mistaken about me since she's old, old people get new teeth, change their names, get lost, is this the street, or the next one, they wait, they can't decide, sucking on their index finger with their gums, my mother to Dona Alice
—Everything's ok, don't worry, have you finished the ironing by any chance?
staring at me in silence, neither she or my older brother said a word, nobody punished me or withheld the fruit, my mother whispering with my father and as soon as I appeared she stopped talking, fascinated with her little finger, if I look at mine, even with a scratch, in two seconds I saw everything, why waste time with a finger, my co-worker grabbed one of my phalanges and kissed it
—So tasty
today there are more blackbirds because animals sense death, the rain, sickness, when a storm is coming the gulls, even when the sky is still blue, fly from the beach to the lifeguard station or the abandoned wine cellar, the boarding house had fewer and fewer English people in straw hats and leather sandals, the only ones that fit their primitive feet, so white, for the love you have

for me, relatives, find a place, even in old age an unexpected youth and an innocence without shadows, you take pictures the whole time to show them in your Vouzela, my mother after many weeks, in a tone that doesn't refer to anything in particular

—The next time you pull a fast one you'll see what's coming to you

while my father without saying

—Girl

a bunch of centuries, who will guarantee that the heart problem didn't start because of me, a broken piece, a warped piston, my not deaf brother

—Thief

and I absorbed in my little finger like my mother, you find so many details when you pay closer attention, my mother told my not deaf brother to shut up, my deaf brother, who forages with the animals

—Shhheee

Maria linda Maria, that ditty bores me, moving away from me afraid fearing I'd take away his thread or his cap, leave me alone, cousin Fernando, I'm not choosing either hand, the finger, in my co-worker's mouth, slid over her dentures in the middle and right side of her mouth, on the left side she, my father, disappointed in me, spent more time in the pantry, steps of a lame elephant, returning, that buried itself in the floor boards, if Dona Alice is alone in her little cave I might be able to ask her forgiveness, who knows, I walked around her building one afternoon or two, when I had a break between classes, and I didn't even see the guy on the scooter, Osvaldo was there, in pajamas, he appeared and disappeared scratching his shoulder, after a few minutes a woman in a robe, who didn't scratch herself, watered a

plant on the balcony, I don't see a planter and I left, if I am still Dona Alice is not there anymore, in bed eighteen, or, I'm not going to stew over this, I'm bad, my co-worker
—What an obsession, doll
and I with curiosity to asks her
—Did it hurt when they pulled your teeth?
gigantic and so small on the tip of a dental extraction forceps, what lives in the gums astonishes me, it must be almost noon, I think, Tininha's watch with the painted hands is missing to tell us the right time, in what was her house there are three or four walls, a bulldozer, piles of plaster, not even a peach in sight in the rubble, or Tininha's mother lowering her dark glasses with a smile that always alarmed me, the cats ready to catch a little animal with identical smile, a slowness that becomes a frenzy, the frenzy that becomes calm, the intern
—I need to buy a whip so I can put stripes on my skin
her friend in the room, the music blasting out grievances, she didn't return with a suitcase, she returned with a backpack and when I saw the backpack I felt so old, if my son had lived, he'd be about their age, fifty-two, it won't be long before I'm sixty-four, and in a while no age at all because I will have lost the sense of numbers
—How old is she?
and an inner desert in which memories drag themselves, only the voice of my mother, so clear at first
—The next time you pull a fast one, you'll see what's coming to you
and then, lost, I, searching for her
—What did you say, ma'am?
and useless, she disappeared, where did you go, a sparrow near

me, my shoulders hunched against a wall that Dr. Clementina doesn't remember, she says, if I mention the wall
—Really?
without enthusiasm, absent, or else wandering in her memory
—A beach covered with haze where the poor people go
her clothes are expensive, she wears a complicated ring made of diverse materials, when she was a child, she wore an aluminum band, from a cake, with a glass stone, and a curtain ring on her arm, not flip-flops, like ours, shoes, occasionally a chocolate in a fancy wrapping
—It's Swiss
different from the ones my mother bought at the Thebes Bakery when we had birthdays, the sparrow flew away with hunched wings into the disintegrating in the air, the intern wielding a non-existent whip against her own buttocks
—Don't you feel like it?
and, to be frank, I don't feel like it, backpacks, whips, adolescent bras with little bear designs, laughter for no reason, tears for no reason, anguish without cause, intolerance, concession, wanting a dog, disgusted with the dog
—I've had enough
Yugoslavian films, idiotic songs, a burst of tenderness
—I love you
and suddenly, childlike
—I like you more than I don't know what
obedient, submissive, avid, happy
—Take me
in the cradle of our body full of plastic dolls, mobiles, bells
—Please take me

descending, on a ramp of caresses, towards sleep, with her thumb in her mouth because of the dark
—Don't lower the blinds because I need the light from outside
the palm, that held us, closing over her breast, returning to the wall the sparrow was complete and I
—Look, sparrow, in a little while I'm going down to the beach
the movements, like tracings, of its head, the trembling feathers, if I stretch out my arm it will fly away, if I don't it will also fly away, my older brother thinking of Dona Alice
—You must think of others, girl
not taking me on the bike, for once, firm
—You must think of others, girl
in the little cave, in the tamarind tree, on the lamp, Dona Alice hopeful that her heart would recover
—That's what I'm here for, isn't it?
so fearful of dying, as soon as the sun abandoned the leaves the shadows entered the house, father peeling a plum with a little knife that he carried in his vest to cut cheese and sausage
—Are you here to complain to us now?
mother, heating up water for tea on the stove
—The woman won't stay long
and Dona Alice unable to escape them, the desire to teach her how to sing, arrange a sofa in the living room, explaining to my husband
—When I was a girl, I did something bad to her
while the juice from father's plum dripped on the carpet, the gray mustache, the hoe leaning on the wall because of a dispute with a neighbor because of a boundary issue that a calf crossed, they changed the boundary markers on each other, put stakes in the ground, threatened each other, my husband

—Will the plum stains come out of the carpet?

cleaning his knife on his pants before putting it away in his vest, Dona Alice drank mother's infusions with the illusion of lasting a little longer in her cave, one month, two months, two months never go by and finally they do, what a drag, the same way that Friday and Saturday went by, the ocean to me

—Do you feel like it or not?

I'll come by at twenty to seven, relax, hopefully I won't slip on the wet grass, on the rocks that turn into boulders, on a rabbit or a rat running away, I think it's black, I think it's brown, it doesn't matter, it's gone, in August the days are long, it's almost cold in the afternoon or rather there's a little breeze, you don't need a jacket, the wind picks up, altering the intentions of the foam, my co-worker

—You're about to leave, my treasure

not sad, as I had thought, but accepting

—After you leave, I'll straighten up the house

if I am still, I wish this for you, with another co-worker, I hope that there'll be more space for you and not as old as I am, to take my place, satisfied with the perpetual October and the chinoiseries, satisfied with you

—Mama

so satisfied with you

—Little Mama

in the building next to the Thebes Bakery my mother is feeling her way around the room, what happened to the palm tree, the storks at the convent without nuns with a lock on the gate and an aura at night going from window to window, the nuns went out in pairs to protect each other from the temptations of the Flesh, what will become of me, barefoot in the hall, counting my steps to my parents' room, thirty-six, I had bet it was twenty-eight and thirty-six or rather twenty-five and a little, my deaf brother twenty-nine and I ashamed, trying to console myself

—I'm four years younger than he is

doorknobs of faceted glass, in the bathroom and the toilet they were loose, and the doorknob had been replaced by a hook that didn't latch inside, crochet curtains my mother had made, with a rose pattern, always covered with finger stains

—How many times do I have to tell you not to touch the curtains?

Senhor Medeiros who sat on the porch facing ours, missing as many tiles as ours did, one day I compared them and theirs had even less than ours, with a cap on his head and polished shoes, I remembered the knots in his laces, I looked at him with respect because he had been a detective, he caught crooks, he didn't catch me, because of Dona Alice's change, with a black nail, it was lucky he hadn't asked my parents if he could talk with me

—Where's the delinquent?

dragging me to the police station to book me

—This girl committed a theft

and me in a cell full of spiders, thrown in with indignant bookies and murderers

—How awful, you hurt Dona Alice

Senhor Medeiros, to my good fortune, was kind of dumb, they gave him a chicken leg that he chewed with his arm on the windowsill, if he saw me across the street, looking through the corner of the windows, if I am still, he called in to his daughter-in-law

—Get my jacket and my club inside on the bed, I've caught a girl who broke the law

suddenly not dumb, leaving the chicken leg in a flower vase
—I'll eat this later, first the law
me with my arms around my mother's stomach
—Don't let them
my mother
—What nonsense is this?
without noticing the family name being dragged in the mud of dishonor and the ignominy, the neighbors
—So young and so cruel, it's unthinkable
shunning me
—God willing, she won't touch us
the owner of the Thebes Bakery
—I thought I was missing cookies
but for the time being Senhor Medeiros was entertained with the chicken leg, when he left at the end of the day I relaxed
—I escaped this time
although I was alert for footsteps on the stairs afraid of the inexorable treads up the stairs in defense of honest citizens and guardians of the Penal Code that fortunately constitute most of the Portuguese populations and that becomes imperative to defend from antisocial elements, Senhor Medeiros's daughter-in-law
—My father was always implacable with malefactors
so that maybe, I'll hide in the garage until six in the afternoon, which my infraction prescribes, with the intention of going up to the Alto da Vigia to find my older brother.

4.

When my mother came back from shopping, we heard the bottles clinking together while she arranged things in the pantry, her voice to my father
 —You can drink until you drop, I hope you're happy now
 my father didn't answer, my mother to my deaf brother with a gesture of someone shooing away a chicken
 —Get out of here, you
 I remember to think
 —Who is she screaming at?
 because she wasn't screaming at my father or my deaf brother, it was at herself, for example she was fine taking care of the house and then suddenly she'd stop dead in her tracks, suspend her domestic chores, looking inside herself, if one of us said anything it seemed to come from far away, rising inside her with difficulty
 —What?
 there were times I was almost sure she didn't like us, she was alone in our midst, we were like strangers to her, not her children, strangers, what would she do if we didn't exist, my father afraid to touch the bottles and the world ready to punish him contrary

to what my grandfather had predicted, trying not to occupy any space, trying not to exist, my father
—You
and falling silent again if he were able to get in a word to
—You
what words would come, what kind of a family is this, who are we really, my co-worker
—What is it you don't understand?
in a fort by the sea where her father, at visiting hours
—I'm ok
and he wasn't ok, he was dragging one of his legs, his hands pressed against his back and nevertheless
—I'm ok
the guard who escorted him hitting him on the shoulder
—Repeat to your wife and your daughter that you're ok, my man
my co-worker's father, obediently
—I'm ok
and if we talked to him, my mother
—Aren't you tired of asking questions?
putting her household fairy hands into her napkin
—For what unknown reason shouldn't he be ok, what nonsense
me pretending that I believed it, pretending to be distracted, pretending I was at ease
—Everyone's ok, I was mistaken
even today, in the deserted beach house, there's suffering around, in the hall or in the living room, my father on the step at night, confused with the pines, my father is a pine tree, my father is a blackbird, my father is a bush since the dead come back, even on the Alto da Vigia I will have him at my side, in

three or four hours the two of us will be up there in the midst of the plants that bend in the wind, and my older brother will be with us, advancing to the edge of the cliff, waiting a moment, how long will it take to fall, will the foam rise to meet us, will the waves recede, what's the last image, the last memory that we will lose in the midst of the gulls, please don't peck at me, my husband turning on the bedside lamp

—Now what's your problem?

his hair rumpled, his face creased with sleep with a stubble of a beard, me, indecisive, you're my husband, you're not my husband, who are you and the sea around us separating us, joining us, separating us again, I hear you talking but I don't understand what you are saying

—Now what's your problem?

I hear, the rest the waves prevent me from understanding, I'm in the bedroom because the armoire is there, the dresser, the chair, and I'm not in the room because the gulls don't stop, my father or my older brother say

—Girl

an open drawer, with a sleeve hanging out, in a wave of greeting or farewell and who knows if I'm coming or going, my mother coming in the gate of the beach house with the grocery bags

—I'll always be a beast of burden

distributing them to us

—How about helping

and holding just one bag now her legs are straighter, there are fewer wrinkles on her forehead and the tendons of her neck don't bulge, the bent legs, the wrinkles and the tendons belong to my brothers now, my mother is younger than they are until they put down the bags on the kitchen counter and then she's older again, then she's a mother, my husband disappearing into the pillow

—When am I going to have some peace?

forgetting to turn off the light, that illuminated the room and the waves in Lisbon, a person who looked like my co-worker, coming ever closer

—What were you dreaming about?

an interrogation that stayed with me until it started to make sense

—What were you dreaming about?

that is, syllables, until finally, I started to understand, I repeated them so as not to lose them and so the gulls would leave me alone

—What were you dreaming about?

and I was dreaming about the Alto da Vigia, about my parents, the beach, about what happened to them, if tomorrow I insisted to my mother that she tell me, she'd lie

—I don't remember

and I say she'd lie since her expression went blank and one knee started to twitch, not just the two men, another cause, before the two men, or rather my dream that isn't over yet, my co-worker giving me a glass of water in which the light of the afternoon was concentrated, all the rest, including her, was in the dark

—Drink this

as if with such a flood inside myself I could drink anything, the blinds, when they were raised, brought the furniture up from the floor and life started to exist beginning with the carpet, it was my co-worker's legs, not her mouth, that said

—Drink this

and then her skirt

—Drink this
and then her blouse
—Drink this
finally, her lips
—Drink this
and now I was awake, almost seven in the evening and I had to make dinner, pick up a chicken and frozen French fries on the way home, invent an excuse that there was a meeting at school
—I thought I was going to have to spend the night there
part of the garage roof of the beach house with the beams exposed, the missing roof tiles lying broken on the ground and in the meantime my lizards, my sparrows, my wall, Tininha, upset
—I found drops of blood in my bathing suit, do you think I'm sick?
showing me the dark spots and maybe it wasn't blood, maybe it was, I don't know
—Did you tell your mother?
our lizards, our sparrows, our wall, Tininha's neck stretching to my ear, I never imagined it was so long
—I'm afraid she'll scold me
her mother, instead of scolding her
—The girl is growing up
and Tininha, not understanding her mother's words
—She didn't scold me after all, she said it would be like that every month
and it will be like that, Dr. Clementina, at fifty-two years of age, tell me, in my case it's over now, curious whether that happened to boys too, my mother, embarrassed
—What a dumb question
as far as I've seen it doesn't happen to chickens, not to doves

either, I don't know about the other animals, cousin Fernando closing his fists

—Don't you like candies anymore, girl?

and it's not that I stopped liking candies, cousin Fernando, it's that I'm a grown woman now, imagine, all the months I, you won't believe it and I can't tell you, that the time when Tininha's parents took her away from the beach and suddenly everything looked so old, colorless, the house didn't look as fancy, the grass turning brown in the back, I alone at the wall, idle, unhappy, I found Rogério on the porch, he had lost his hair, he was twisted up, more defenseless than I had thought and I couldn't help him, he looked a bit like my father in his limp orphanhood, after a time he disappeared, he must be in Vouzela waiting for the trains, and you don't go to Vouzela because you want to, I guess a cat got him on the porch, dragged him to the cane field, and chewed him up, I found him there with a tear on his back where brown stuffing was coming out of him, we don't have intestines or a liver, like the teacher insisted pointed to a flayed man on a map, we are filled with dirty stuffing and if we are how do you explain the blood underneath, much less the stuffing, which I poked at with a stick, not even a dark drop, when I open the door to the street, perfecting in my head the lie about the school meeting, my co-worker

—The glass of water costs a kiss because in this establishment we don't give away things for free

on tiptoe with lowered eyelids, so comical, poor thing, what will she do after I leave, the solitary dinner, a book propped against a water jug, like the neighbor at the second door on the left, dishes to wash, the napkin a rag, or sitting on the sofa with her stuffing coming out of her stomach, just like Rogério, waiting for a second cat to steal her and take her somewhere, if I am still on the sidewalk in front of my house looking in the window, my husband turned the latch of the porch door, cousin Fernando to my parents

—It seems the little one has lost interest in candies

to make sure they hadn't stolen his car from its parking space on the street

—There's an old woman out there standing under the streetlights

or my co-worker would write me letters that she didn't send, tearing them up fearing I'd get tired of her and not want to see her anymore, me to my husband, looking at him over my shoulder, with the fruit of his heart hanging on a bowed branch, giving in

—An old woman?

some old woman, what a stupid joke, you think you're funny and you're not, idiotic little jokes that make me sick of you, solitude can hurt, gentlemen, does anyone get used to it, me rattling around this house like my co-worker in her house full of chinoiserie, although, as for me, I didn't consider myself to be alone because there were so many people with me, a fortress of hallways and echoes

—You may not believe it, but they insist on following me

although I don't dream of people following me, my family is here and besides my family there are people who come and go, some close friends, Ermelinda and Dora, others are silhouettes without names that call me, when they call me, I recognize them, as soon as they are still I lose them, at my first confession the priest who gave off an odor of tobacco and incense asked

—Have you had any bad thoughts?

I couldn't see his face, I could make out his hands on his knees, white, fat, growing in his cassock like mollusks, those aren't veins contracting, they are gills, an adhesive on one of the nails that time turned gray, a wart that transformed into an eye, with the scab of the pupil looking at me critically, fixed, all of that was a threat disguised as something innocent, the finger with the adhesive scratched the kneecap and then stayed still like the others in a false serenity, above the finger, to the left and to the right of a line of buttons, a stone with gold embroidery, I said without wanting to

—I feel like sticking a nail in those hands before they grab me

beyond the confessional were the sad flames of candles, plaster saints floating in the emptiness, pictures in which nobody smiled behind the altars, people aren't happy in heaven, a guy with a ladder and a feather duster, wearing a smock, cleaning that vast hollow melancholy, like an abandoned basement, the mollusks jumped from the knees to the stole, frightened by the nail, my mother consoling cousin Fernando who put the sweets in his pocket

—Don't be annoyed, cousin Fernando, she has phases, tomorrow or later she'll want the candies again

without my seeing the priest's face, just his chin hovering over me in the confessional of carved wood with black curtains, almost like a coffin, sewn to a rod of little hooks and enclosing thousands of bad thoughts that were forgiven, the chin, pink in the dusk, suddenly gigantic and populated with teeth that the mollusks slid across in aquarium navigations, I had the impression that there was a fish among them, also swimming, moving its fins, and it was the tongue that was escaping

—Get out of here

cousin Fernando to my mother

—They're imported candies, look

proud of the nationality of the candies
—Legitimate imports
and noon, almost one, what a shame I couldn't embrace the house when I left it, I go through the rooms, I sit on my father's step, I say goodbye to the pines, at six there will be a few blackbirds left, at night they leave for the olive grove of the cedar forest, with the thicker crowns, at the foot of the mountains, the owls remain flying with wings like wet rags, my not deaf brother discovered one in a hole of the chapel wall, on straw and a gutted rat, bigger than a rabbit, bigger than a rooster, turning his head rapidly toward us, nobody wants the imported candies, equipped with ears and if I'm still I may have been mistaken, my not deaf brother threw a stone at it, missed, the animal puffed itself up and we took off at a run, my not deaf brother arrived well before me to the gate and locked it as if the owl were galloping behind us, assuring me
—I ran because you were afraid, but I wasn't
looking covertly up and down the street, it could have shredded us with its beak and claws, and instead of the gutted rat it would have been the two of us on the straw, already half eaten
—My maid says they even kill donkeys
donkeys, donkeys, I exaggerate, but I believe they kill sheep and children, when my mother returned with the groceries, we heard the bottles clinking against each other while she arranged things on the shelf, her voice to my father
—Are you happy now, you can drink until you drop
and my father still, he didn't get mad or answer in kind, he sat in the living room with the same newspaper, why did you get married, ma'am, what did you like about my father and, for once, my mother didn't say

—So many questions

her features knitting together with determination to prevent an answer, if I could read her eyes, and I don't know, I might understand, the foreign candies have better sugar, better milk, better eggs, and then there's the care with which they are made, the hygiene, you just have to think of their pen knives that even have little screw drivers and nail files, streets you could eat from, thousands of cuckoos in the forests, most of them real, others made of wood, bowing from inside a clock, my mother

   —A woman must find a man, doesn't she?

with my father's eyes following her over the newspaper, wooden cuckoos that a wire spring keeps from flying away, you push them and pull them, if you looked to the left you'd see the ocean waiting for me and although I don't want him to know, it will be a surprise, there are the kiosk and the back of the foosball café with the birds, garbage and dogs scavenging the leftovers, in a little while people will start to leave the beach, my mother to us, looking under the umbrella

   —You haven't forgotten anything?

combing the sand with her foot in case there was a piece of clothing underneath, I don't like the word piece, piece of clothing, piece of fruit, Dr. Clementina to the nurse

   —Starting tomorrow bed eighteen can have a piece of fruit
that is a plum, a pear, because she didn't allow bottled water
   —Tomorrow bed eighteen can have a pear or a plum
if Tininha were here I'd
   —Why do you treat me this way?
she, changing the position of the princess earrings
   —We grew up didn't we?
and it's true, we grew up, if it hadn't been for the drops of

blood in her bathing suit, we'd still be leaning against the wall, sharing secrets and fears, complicit, Tininha
—Last night I dreamt we were grown ups
me, interested
—What were we doing?
she, searching her memory
—I can't remember
I'll remember for you, you prescribed pieces of fruit, and I ate them, or told me to lift up my hospital gown so she could examine my scar
—It's not bad
you
—In a few months we can think about reconstruction
and even today, because of this and that test, since I need to gain weight, since the last exam created some doubts, since Roma and Pavia weren't built in a day, since knowing how to wait is a great virtue, understand, sooner or later we'll get there, haste is the enemy of the good, I was always waiting for Tininha to ask
—Where is Rogério?
to reveal to her that he was near the well, poor thing, his intestines spilling out, Dr. Clementina
—We're so stupid when we're young
not missing me, not missing us, remember my older brother, remember my deaf brother, Dr. Clementina, half Dr. Clementina and half Tininha
—There were so many of you
not so many, four, with my parents we were six, but my parents don't count since adults don't count, they give orders and that's it, they don't care about lizards and crickets, they take

forever to do things, after they wake up, they stagger around the house looking like sleepwalkers

—Lower the blinds because the light hurts my eyes

or

—Don't say a word to me before I drink my coffee

with the exhaustion of someone who has walked all night not knowing where, hands unsteady, the match not striking, when it did it was a large flame and my mother said to my father

—You won't be happy 'til you burn up the house

a piece of fruit, a plum, a pair, a banana to improve the potassium and what's potassium for, oh Tininha, in case you get to the beach a week later than me I'll be so lonely, my co-worker

—If you'd have dinner with me one night you can't imagine how happy that would make me

little plates of almonds, an embroidered tablecloth, even candles I bet, with saucers under the candlesticks because of the wax, the problem wasn't even the tablecloth, it was the table where the wax won't come off, you can hide it with polish but it stays there, whitish, eternal, we know where it is and notice it right away, a plum pudding trembling on the knife, if I pay attention I hear the ocean on the beach

—When are you coming, girl?

despite the chinoiserie, I didn't tell her about the Alto da Vigia because I had to warn the lifeguards, who had drunk some beers with my older brother, sitting between rolled up tarps and a lifeboat with its keel in the air that couldn't be launched

—It needs diesel, and the engine doesn't work

the kind you start by pulling a chain and the fan, that was missing blades, made a sobbing sound when it turned, me to my co-worker, turning away from her under the pretext of looking

for my keys in my bag, standing up straight, more distant
   —One day when my husband takes a business trip up north
even if my husband went north on business, I'd tell her
   —Unfortunately, he didn't go
and her face fell, the catechism teacher to my mother, horrified
   —The priest forbids your daughter to come into the church
she tried to stab him with a nail during confession
her face falling off her face made her features unequal, and the gray roots immediately became bigger, one of her ring fingers bent in a right angle because the tendon had been torn
   —A fall at ten years old
when father was in the fort and there wasn't money for the luxury of going to a doctor, mother went for food to a place that changed day by day, now a bench in the garden, now a street corner, now a blind man who delivered a package, without stopping, his nose in the air, tapping with his cane, potatoes meat beans, a bank note stating the next meeting that had to be destroyed, a phone number for urgent contacts and a code that mother forgot, just like the numbers because her memory is incapable of retaining a bunch of numbers, she remembered the cries of the gulls and the sound of the bolts, at each door she passed a bolt burst open, one afternoon two policemen appeared at our door with a folder containing photographs
   —Take a good look and don't lie
men and women in profile and face to the camera, including the blind man, without a cane or dark glasses, looking at mother, and mother
   —I've never seen them
the police flipping the pictures
   —You hesitated when you saw this one

and it wasn't just the eyes of the blind man that stared at her, it was his nose, his forehead hatless for the first time and the aureole of his hair, her mother lingering over the image, obediently

—Not him either

one of the policemen was suspicious

—Stop playing innocent

the gulls at the fort were crueler than the ones on the beach here, the evil look in their eyes, their beaks, the way they kept returning, flying in tandem with the hawks, a fish in their beaks, wings that beat against the cement walls, the red of their feet, the blood red of their beaks, the inspector to the doctor, referring to my co-worker's father

—Can we begin?

the doctor, burying the little light in his pocket with his pens

—He'll be able to take it for one or two hours

and therefore, he'll take it for four or five, he'll take whatever we want, a bucket overhead, wait a little and pour it over him, mother, returning the photographs

—I don't know them

not sitting now, standing

—I don't know them, sir

my co-worker doesn't say

—What do you feel for your Mama?

frightened in a corner, with the police pointing at her as they left, the gulls of Peniche, gigantic in her memory, even today they frighten me and if I dream of them, I awake in their beaks, squirming and dripping blood, I'm a fish, the police pointing at her as they left

—One of these days we'll take you

and if they took her hand she would accompany them so they

would free her from the gulls, there is one now, not from Peniche, here, gliding over the house, by the pines, descending in a slow circle toward the rocks, the house of my co-worker's mother was in a kind of patio, a toilet, a stove, a little bedroom, the two in the same bed, a few pots and pans, plates, when the Tagus flooded there were thick sheets of mud, her father's cap, everything they had of him, fading on a nail, what do I have of my father, a step with nobody on it, with little flowers poking out of the cracks in the stone, a hand about to touch me

—Girl

without touching me, starting tomorrow bed eighteen can have a piece of fruit, my mother coming in the gate with the grocery bags

—I'll always be a pack mule

distributing the bags between us

—Pretend you're helping

and, with just one bag, legs straighter, fewer wrinkles on her forehead and fewer tendons bulging from her neck, the wrinkles and tendons prominent on my brothers, my mother younger than them, the intern, younger than me

—Do you have time for me tomorrow?

until they put things on the counter, I've never seen a bird as big as the owl in the hole in the chapel taking a step toward us, and then older, the urge to say

—Mother

when I was a child, if I got hurt, I'd ask her, who knows why, take me on your lap, or rather, I know why but I don't talk about it, in this instant what would I give for her to hug me again, I don't ask for much time, just a few minutes on her lap and nothing bad would happen to me, to be honest I'm afraid of the Alto da Vigia, afraid of the waves, the goat and I slipping at the same time and with the same scream, a thin leg that fails, a hoof that slips, what can she do for me in the building next to the Thebes Bakery and there she might be able to, I'm not my older brother, I'm just a girl, I don't want my co-worker or my husband, I want you, I want my room, I want the hall, I want the living room, I want my family, I want the father of my father, who didn't know me

—The kid weighs like lead

and Dr. Clementina at the wall, in her hospital smock and princess earrings, pointing at a stain on the X-ray with a pen

—It's too late

maybe she remembers the blood on the bathing suit, the secret diary, us

—You'd like to be a pilot, right?

not me, a Mexican actress with an Indian girl waiting on me and I dismissing her

—Go

adjusting my hair with soft hands, the intern insisting

—Do you have time for me tomorrow?

with a sugary look and her lip swelling

—Tomorrow?

and I have all the time in the world for you, tomorrow, if we meet on the beach where the lifeguards wrap what's left of my body in a tarp, or rather on my mother's lap

—Mother

against a breast like the one they took off in bed eighteen, I haven't forgotten your smell, ma'am, the ribbon you tied in my hair, your voice calming me

—It's ok, it's ok

my father putting his hand in his pocket, and despite it being empty, announcing
 —I have something special in here for boo boos
 throwing it at me with his fingers
 —Fairy dust cures everything
 and it did, if my father had been alive when I got sick, I wouldn't have needed operations, or hospitals, or bed eighteen, or pieces of fruit, all he had to do was put his hand in his pocket remembering the little figure on the napkin
 —This is magic, girl, that a fairy gave me many years ago
 and in five minutes, almost five minutes, a half dozen seconds, I was better
 —What was the fairy like, Father?
 my father
 —Almost as pretty as you but older, of course
 so that as soon as I grow up, I won't be an actress, I'll be a fairy, I
 —Did she have a wand with a star on the tip, father?
 my father
 —Have you ever seen a fairy without a wand with a star on the tip?
 and really, I hadn't, all fairies have a wand with a star on the tip, they don't walk, they fly, they show up when you need them and my father is an intimate friend of theirs, they gave him the dust he carries in his pocket, my mother
 —Your father is good friends with the fairies
 my not deaf brother, who didn't believe fairy tales
 —Are you sure, ma'am?
 as if it were necessary to be sure, so obvious, my mother, putting me to bed

—If you fall asleep fast, a fairy will visit you

and in fact, when I woke up the next day, I found a little heap of fairy dust in a hollow in the sheet.

5.

There are times I cough just to feel that I still have myself for company, there are two of us, my family disappeared and the people I know also disappeared, sometimes butterflies, a stray dog, that trotted through the yard, stopping to look at me, the chapel bell no longer plays before the mass, God is finished, before there were dozens of dogs on the beach, in the winter, jumping away from the waves, the beach houses are shuttered, the foosball café has no customers, the owner leaning sleepily on the counter, if I call my father he doesn't answer, neither does my co-worker, she, who was always so attentive

—My little golden flower

keeping watch over me afraid that someone else would look at me and who could be interested in me, they hardly noticed me at a table, correcting tests or reading, dinners in silence with my husband, the bed, on my side, was like a board giving way, I forget to change the water in the flower vases, the maid changes it for me, the ladder for changing the burned out light bulbs with steps that shake when you climb them, and me shaking up there, the light stronger than the others and the room becomes asymmetrical, some parts are too lit up, others stay in the dark, the dog and I look at each other, he in the middle of the flower beds and I, at the entrance to the kitchen, with the impression that either one of us could be the other, either one of us could me, if I am still, the other, what stupidity, I open a spigot and a dark bubble of rust comes out, the second bubble stays there, doesn't fall, for a while, I don't know why, the plants become frightened and then calm down again, before there were snapdragons around the chapel, with a sweet, stagnant perfume, prolonging the priest's voice outside, words of salvation that don't save anybody, kiss my sheets before you leave, wish me sweet dreams, when I left my mother after a visit she accompanied me to the door

—You were here for such a short time

the floor scratched from my brothers' toy cars, kept in a closet where my things were too, coloring pencils, remains of a tiny tea set, a ribbon and a medal I never wore because if you put it on you'll lose it, girl, at least it will be safe here and what's more who wears medals these days except for the old women in Vouzela, what are you thinking keeping things from our childhood, ma'am, hopeful we will be with you and none of us will come back there are no grandchildren to take an interest in these tawdry ancient things that in addition to being useless, don't say anything to anyone, maybe you rummage in them whereas before you didn't pay any attention to them, a crack under a shoe and a tiny teacup is shattered, my mother looking askance at the shards, transforming guilt into anger

—Why do you leave things lying around for people to break without knowing it

like the train broke something without knowing it, a crack as well, Senhor Leonel's niece, her suitcase thrown far away and a sandal, keeping the frogs company, in a mud puddle, if you glued it all together, in the places that belonged to them, if she resuscitated, they would have hardly put together the last piece and she'd sit up examining her arms and legs

—How many days have I been here?

and the next morning the niece would go searching for Germano in the kiosk, in the café

—Has anyone seen him around here?

indifferent to the Alto da Vigia because however well as you fix them, there are always tiny pieces missing, a mole on a cheek, a detail of memory, Senhor Leonel's nice, incredulous

—Is Germano really a priest?

her mouth a little slanted, one of her thumbs doesn't obey her, the rest of her intact, except for memory lapses

—A train?

from time to time my mother called her to help with the house cleaning and Senhor Leonel's niece lifting the dust cloth

—Do you also dust the pine trees?

my mother, rummaging in the armoire

—A kid is going to jump out of here

wanting my not deaf brother to get off the army truck

—Do you want me back?

or my older brother in his room, reading *The Power of the Working Class*

—It's a question of time, see?

my mother to the next-door neighbor, proud of the four of us

—I bet you thought you'd never see us again

walking by the Thebes Bakery, empty in August, when we returned the carpet was dustier out of spite for us

—One of these days I'll come apart

the fairy in profile, sulking, a fly between the curtain and the window, complaining

—I haven't eaten in centuries

and to this day I don't know what flies eat, they landed on the edges of the serving dish, but you didn't hear their teeth chomping or their tongue slurping, my mother pointing at the armoire, with a trembling that came on in old age

—There are kilos of happiness in there

if you reminded her of the thieving blackbird the stone of a child's smile thrown in the direction of the past

—It's true

the mother of my mother scolding her

—What is this?

afraid that the smile would break the French ballerina or the glass cup that was missing a handle, I hadn't seen that smile since the time of the races and the pines, if we run now, from the gate to the garage, I guarantee I'll win, me to my co-worker

—Can you do a handstand?

not thinking of her sixty-four years or her hip problem, she stopped and flipped over on her hands

—I did it

walking again with a kind of hop with the gulls of Peniche in her mind, the latches came back, the echoes, father came back, five minutes before them with a fraction of her body arriving later, reaching it almost at the end of the visit, a thin cheek, a fat cheek, fingers that she had to grasp with her other hand to keep them and there was always one missing, the middle, the index finger, the guard

—Don't you get annoyed at it?

my co-worker pushed a finger in his direction

—You might miss it, Daddy

and her father going away with all those fingers in his palm, the sea climbed the walls of the fort while here it's still, my mother to the next-door neighbor, pleased with us

—Aren't they a nice-looking bunch?

in spite of the remorse of my deaf brother grinding at her, if she turned back, but one doesn't turn back if she had thought about it but she didn't, ma'am, when they freed the father of my co-worker there were fewer fingers, if I am still they had to teach him to bend them again, the building next to the Thebes Bakery was empty in August, it was hard to get used to it

—Is this where we live?

without Senhor Manelinho or the grocery store with the crates outside, nuns and trolleys instead of the garage, the nuns struggling not to sin while a voice, with mollusks on his knees, that smelled of tobacco and incense

—Have you had bad thoughts?

me to my co-worker, worried about the idea thousands of years later

—Do you think I have bad thoughts?

and she without hearing me, hearing her own steps in a stone hallway with iron bars, other women with her, other daughters, cousin Fernando with no candies, guards in the battlements following them with their rifles, the mother of my co-worker to my co-worker

—Don't say anything

my co-worker not understanding why, the building next to the Thebes Bakery waiting for winter and the mold spores in the plaster, my not deaf brother caught the fly and my mother grabbed his arm

—Don't tear its wings off

burn however many huts you want, kill as many blacks as you want, tear off as many wings as you want in Africa, one day, but not in my house, the fly, instead of leaving, buzzed around in the window frame, my older brother opened the window and shooed it out, it came back, it had gotten used to the curtain, freedom frightened it, the hallway in Lisbon was longer, and my father was perplexed with the lack of a step in the kitchen, after the kitchen not the yard, the awning, the palm tree with its pompous speeches, each branch insisting me this me that, if I still my bad thoughts, rivalries, revenge, while the pines in a harmony of murmurs

—Girl

worried about me, there are times I cough just to feel that I still have myself for company, there are two of us, the stray dog lay down in a flower bed to look at me, probably the one that left Rogério at the well, an alert ear that calmed down later, its tail fighting with a beetle, my co-worker and her mother in the bus from Peniche to Lisbon, a flat landscape, a bridge, old, maybe not as old as I am now, the intern recoiling

—Are you really fifty-two?

with bundles of wood on her head on the roadside, a bandstand in a park, a, I don't feel like describing landscapes, I don't have a lifetime, a have just a few minutes, follow the band, the intern in a thoughtful voice

—My mother will be forty-four in April I think

me thinking in turn, my neck on a purple pillow, contemplating my bare feet below, stretching them and curling them, empty, just my fifty-two years inside, Dr. Clementina, as if she didn't know, her pen suspended over the page

—Age?

writing fifty-two with a painful tone

—You're not that young

she with princess earrings and petal nail polish, showing me the drops of blood

—Do you think I'm sick?

so upset, poor thing

—I'm afraid of doctors

she must still be afraid of doctors, of herself, of me, her pauses, with all our anguish waiting

—I'll order some tests to get more clarification

as if it were necessary to clarify things further, we are going to die, aren't we, and silence or the sentence again

—We'll get more clarification and then we'll talk

as if further clarification were needed, we're going to die, right, and silence or the same sentence again

—We'll get more clarification and then we'll talk

and what can you do about it, positive thinking, please, positive thinking, how curious my feet are, they curl up and stretch, explain what's in your head, doctor, think about me and my age, fifty-two, my mother

—We must buy a new dishwasher, I'm sick of paying for repairs

and first it's the dishwasher, then the microwave, the iron, the blender, ourselves, look at that dark tooth, those recessed gums, the dry skin on your face, the cream that the pharmacy guarantees will keep you young and doesn't, the urge to stay at home, wanting nobody to talk to me, the disinterest that increases, the intern's mother will be forty-four in April, what am I supposed to do in the middle of these pillows, these Indian necklaces, this apartment that evicts me

—Her mother

and even if it didn't evict me, it didn't give me the right to stay, my deaf brother, decisively

  —Shhheee saaills

and then, the ash from the incense stick curls without falling, infinite, the way I curl up without falling and before I fell, I adjusted the pad on the right side of my bra, put on my blouse, my skirt, found one of my sandals, I can't find the other, finally I found it leaning against one of the Moroccan drums, held together by a cord that looked to me like sisal, when I left my mother after a visit she accompanied me to the door

  —You were here for such a short time

so that I went down the stairs with remorse and I felt no remorse for the intern, just the shame of being fifty-two, the certainty there was no place for me next to her, my husband

  —Did something happen to you?

and aside from the old women, with bundles of wood on their head on the roadside, nothing at all happened, even if it had I'd say to you

  —Nothing happened

the bus from Peniche arrived in Lisbon and I'm with you, aren't I, Tininha's mother would call you

  —My peach

she ordered

  —Come here my peach

bending her dismantled body over you like that of the donkeys on the Alto da Vigia that not even the thistles find, little random weeds, gull droppings, flakes of foam that the wind disperses, you

  —Did something happen?

and the proof that nothing happened is that I serve you dinner, would you like me to fix myself up, put on another dress, style my hair, at fifty-two you can style your hair, a tube of gel, a brush and there's a kind of bang, the wrinkles hidden with cream, the blush that gives color to my cheeks, and instead of younger, my age visible, the ash from the incense must have dropped a long time ago, another intern with the intern and the intern

—You won't believe this but there was a person here who was older than my mother I swear I don't know what came over me the other intern in fact not believing it, taking off her slip with an ease I had lost

—I always thought you should get work in a home and little jokes, tickles, viola chords, two pillows, three pillows, four pillows, Tininha's mother to the driver

—Two peaches

like she and her friend at the beach house where nothing was left, not even the pool

—Touch me lower down silly

my mother to us

—Don't you think they're strange?

having fun on the lounge chairs, observing my other brother

—Tender meat darling, have you seen his shoulders?

my older brother, his torso naked, fixing the swing, my mother at the window suspicious of I don't know what

—Put on your shirt, boy

hanging by the collar on a nail inside the garage, what I wouldn't give to find it there today, anything that had belonged to us and that I could touch, my husband to me, still chewing

—Why do you put on so much makeup?

his food shifting from one cheek to another as he spoke, if my mother were here

—Don't talk with your mouth full

Dr. Clementina still chewing gum, I bet the same piece as when we were little, there are habits we keep, this was before the princess earrings and twisted Rogério, she orders Rogério, in the hospital, moving one of his legs

—Say hello to Dr. Artur, say hello to nurse Manuela

and Dr. Artur and Nurse Manuela shaking the leg, embarrassed, Rogério with just one eye, moving his head to be able to see us, but since the eye was scratched, he couldn't see well and he got our names mixed up, Dr. Clementina with me at the wall, Tininha deciding on his treatments

—Give him oxygen for good measure

Tininha's mother to her friend

—He didn't inherit that from his bum of a father fortunately

there are times I cough to feel like I'm not alone and despite having myself for company I feel lonely anyway, my husband drinking water without cleaning his mouth on the napkin first

—You don't drink from your glass without cleaning your mouth on the napkin first

observing the wrinkles on my neck hidden by cream and the blush powder

—I almost confused you with a clown for the love of God take off that makeup

and he who dyed his hair and, in the mornings, applied a cream from a tube to his face, lying to me in guaranteeing that it was to soften his beard, who do we try to deceive, my peach, others who may not understand right away, ourselves too, the deceits we are unaware of, perhaps death, making its choices with a bony finger

—You are there and that creature in the back, while lighting the fire pit the one in the back is eight years old, but us, what an injustice, exchange me for my mother who nobody will miss, the intern stopped waving at me secretly in the teachers' room, when she realized I was coming in she turned away, on the other hand the other intern didn't hide from me, you could tell from the movement of her mouth

—Your old lady is here

and elbows, whispers, the intern, still turning her head away

—when she touched me, I cringed

and it wasn't true, when I touched her, she was happy

—Please don't stop

without strength in her legs like when calves are born, they get up, fall, look for us blindly, Rogério, in Tininha's office, discussing diagnoses

—Why the pituitary gland?

amidst books of medicine, framed diplomas, a deceased authority, in a surgeon's smock, in a silver frame, with a dedication in English to Dr. Clementina, I counted the blackbirds, seven, and tomorrow, without me, they'll come back, the thieving blackbird, mother, sing it to me, she, after a pause, with a transfigured expression, where did he make his nest and giving up, defeated

—I can't sing the notes anymore

and she couldn't, what a shame, my co-worker, in the bus from Peniche to Lisbon

—When is father coming, mother?

her mother squeezed her knee hard, and my co-worker felt tears in her bones

—How many times do I have to tell you not to talk about it?

because the police are certainly spying on them, disguised and stalking visitors to the fort

—If they arrest me what will happen to you?

and besides the good part of not having to brush my teeth who would wake her up or heat up her food, with luck a compassionate neighbor

—Come to our house for lunch

but the neighbors were also afraid, two strangers with the owner in the store where the compassionate neighbor worked, if that house were mine, and if I had money, I'd get it fixed up and stay there despite the humidity in March, when the compassionate neighbor worked as a house cleaner, the owner to her

—Don't take this the wrong way, Dona Odete, but I can't have you here

with the two strangers observing her from a distance, where do the blackbirds go in the winter when nobody notices them, even the swallows disappear, there are a few gulls left, more here than at the ocean, lined up, in the rain, on the roofs, you notice the discomfort of the pines and the shriveled plants, the grocery store closed with the proprietress, wearing a scarf, sitting on a little bench behind the counter looking at the rain, on the shelves and in the crates pale little vegetables, the bathers in the foosball café, the ocean making the beach tiny and I am in the house even so, drinking from a bottle of Algarve wine and a hot water bottle consoling my bunions, determined to endure the wind against the windows and the drafts without origin that make the hairs on my bones shiver, it's guaranteed that there is no hair on bones and we understand that there are when they stand up, if I run a fever who will treat me, if I croak they'll find me in June, in a corner of the floor, like a dead insect and it doesn't matter, maybe my not deaf brother will burn some huts and warm us up, there's no transportation to Lisbon because nobody arrives and nobody leaves, a single umbrella crossing the street with Senhor Manelinho under it, the waves against the wall bouncing on the stones, the Alto da Vigia a gray relief, if the father of my father were alive, he'd be proud of me

I'm strong, grandfather, despite my fifty-two years, you can't imagine my courage, I have to prepare the rooms for August when my parents and we arrive, open the grocery store, open the kiosk, throw seed for the birds in the yard, make up the beds, bring the circus and the movies, deposit Ândrea on the tightrope, stick the first crow that comes into my hand in the chapel, with a rat in its claws, change the front tire of my older brother's bike so he won't notice

—Who put on this tire?

and the gypsy carts beyond the olive grove, threatening, secret, men that look like albatrosses, women in long skirts who can tell the future, wearing knives and caps, who are still nursing, their silence not in Portuguese, in Spanish, they say that they play the guitar but I've never seen it, they walk through tree trunks, to the displeasure of my father and my father I don't cross no matter what, I stay on this side to bump against things, that instead of opening, cripple me, in three hours Senhor Manelinho's wife will say

—Look at the deaf boy's brother walk down to the beach

and they will all follow me up here with their eyes

—What's she going to do?

clustered in the kiosk, even the woman with the poodle, even the ticket booth girl, even the Mexican actress followed by the Indian with the tray

—What is she going to do?

and what I am going to do is so simple, friends, my older brother did it, the priest in the cassock did it, the goat on the cliff

will do it with me, the donkeys will remain to lick salt off a cactus, not really a cactus but it will do, that in spite of my predictions will do, Tininha's mother ordering the driver to stop the car at the lookout trying to find her glasses in her purse
 —Find your boss's glasses my peach
without paying attention to Ândrea, an unfortunate soul who circulates the earth in hopes of breaking her back on the ground, Tininha's mother observing me without lowering the window
 —I always disapproved that you played with my daughter but what was she going to do?

I always disapproved of you playing with my daughter because the poor give us terrible habits, I don't know her name nor can I imagine where she lives in Lisbon, you want to bet it's in a building with the tiles falling off it, wobbly chairs and threadbare rugs, the mother a slut, the father a drunk, the brothers unbearable, except the older brother who was more or less your type, who didn't do anything but hammer nails and blush if you called him, his body leaning in my direction fighting me, I smiled at him and he didn't answer, would there be sun in Peniche, not in the fort by any means, in the prison yard, inside, even in July, freezing, water on the walls, my peach, warping their cartilage to make them respect the people in charge, they who kill us with injections in our ears, what is he going to do, if your glasses reach the Alto da Vigia, ma'am, in a little while, a few minutes if that, you know, the circus owner at the mike, uttering advice in a slow cadence
 —Careful girl, remember your older brother died that way
while I tried to find a path, a space, a way through the openings in the rocks, asking my co-worker
 —Do you ever think about Peniche?

you never think about Peniche the way I think about my husband or about bed eighteen, how I think about my life without deciding what to do with it, my co-worker

—I think about it

vacillating

—I don't think about it

vacillating some more

—I don't know

and I think she's being sincere, she really didn't know, I suppose that she just thought about me, when there's nobody on the beach the lifeguards picked up garbage with a rake and a bucket, brushing away the dogs and one or two gulls, the others were on the roof of the lifeguard station, the gynecologist to me

—Unfortunately, you can't have any more children

I who never had children or rather I had one and they stole it from me, if my father was in Peniche there would be hallways and hallways inside of me that led to him, hallways, rooms, cells, and my father in the last one, his pants torn and a blow on his cheek that he preferred I didn't see, he didn't hit us, he didn't get mad at us, if I'm still, in his way, and what way could he have that wasn't his, he liked us, how bad of me, I'm certain he liked us even my deaf brother who wasn't, strike that sentence and not add his son, I'm certain he liked us more than I liked my son or the idea of a son, it doesn't matter, the son that was nothing more than a wad of gauze in a bucket and a scar on my stomach that was erased with time, I run my finger along it and I don't find it or I got the place wrong, the intern to the other intern

—I guarantee you that not even a mark is left

and, although in a low voice, with a dozen voices in between, hers so strong that everyone could here

—That one lost a child

to the point of asking myself if I had it, in the case of, in the middle of eating our fish, I ask my husband

—Did I get pregnant by you?

the napkin on the tablecloth and a door slamming, the eye of the fish indignant with me, Tininha's mother to her driver, while I continued to climb

—Since I pay you to be useless at least give me a kiss

thin legs, thin arms, her body in pieces, if I am fifty-two she's eighty or about that, her eyelids with the red tears of old people, her nose losing shape, stringy hair, dyed black, the same color mine was when I was little and had thick hair, the pines talked among themselves consoling me, I imagine, but consoling me of what, for half an hour they were still, the driver turned back, his hand on Tininha's mother's body, afraid to break her, and finding a tip of, the circus owner, talking over static from the mike

—We request that the audience remain perfectly still and observe complete silence so as not to disturb the concentration of the performer

and, therefore, the pines were still, sticking the tip of a limp tongue in between their false teeth, as far as I'm concerned, I don't care if they talk, where is Peniche actually, if I had the opportunity, and unfortunately I don't, they informed me, I suspect it's just beyond Lisbon Vouzela just that Peniche is the part of Vouzela closest to the ocean, the doctor's little light buried in his pen pocket

—This one is not responding

not the father of my co-worker, a red-haired guy, why do doctors use so many pens and agendas and pads if I never see them take notes, besides this, on the agendas and the pads are dozens of little pieces of paper to mark the pages, the doctor with the little light educating the police

—He didn't die in this place he died of heart failure when he was sleeping you can deliver him to his family in three days in a closed urn the way they'll deliver me to my husband in a closed urn, my co-worker

—What kind of talk is that?

she who accompanied her husband to the red haired guy's funeral, in the cemetery the wife had no tears, a mourning dress, too big for her, that didn't belong to her, they had lent it to her, two children holding the hands of a red-haired uncle, one of them a redhead the other not, that is the other one was almost a redhead, by just a little, mossy headstones with the names of the dead, the first were faded, the last legible, thank God that the names fade, I don't want to be remembered, I want to disappear completely like my older brother disappeared entirely and my father after him but less so, if I lasted another twenty years I'd be the daughter of nobody, I'd get there and ask

—Who am I?

until I conclude that I didn't exist, little bouquets of flowers that the cats tear apart, a policeman certifying that they didn't open the coffin or take photographs, more police around here and there with expressions that were too casual to believe, comparing the people with the pictures in a folder looking for communists at the funeral, they greeted the wife of the redhead who didn't shake their hands, a short little woman taller than all of us, power to the working class right, brother, and the working class is dead, Tininha's mother to the driver

—That kiss wasn't much my peach, I need something more substantial and I at the wall waiting for Tininha who will come to say goodbye to me knowing there are many years ahead of us, how old are we now, seven, eight, and if it's seven or eight years ahead of us, Tininha writing in her diary before putting it in the hole and covering it with a stone

—I'm in love with your older brother, but don't tell him

and since she asked me not to tell I showed the diary to my older brother

—Tininha is in love with you, do you want to read about it?

my older brother is in his room, not interrupting his reading of a book with a guy on the cover with a raised fist, followed by guys with raised scythes

—Oh yeah?

without giving any importance to her declaration, that was at the time when he walked with the post office clerk to the grocery story, in the store she said

—Don't come back please I don't want them to see us

my older brother was obedient, standing to look at her, even after the post office clerk disappeared he stood there looking at her, he turned and stepped on a can, distracted, and ended up throwing it under a car and he pushed open the gate forgetting to shut it, sometimes he seemed my age, imitating a limp, sometimes he cavorted, sometimes he jumped, occasionally he whistled, pulling a flower from the flowerbed and then dropping it, announcing to my father sitting on the step

—I'm happy

my father suspended the bottle with the cork in right hand and the bottle in the left

—That's good that you're happy

me insisting with my older brother, angry at his indifference

—Tininha's in love with you

my older brother, not stopping his reading of the book about the guy with the raised fist on the cover

—By Thursday she'll be over it

and it must have because when I was in bed eighteen, she didn't mention him, I felt like asking

—Do you remember my older brother, Dr. Clementina?

but I didn't ask fearing that her hands holding an X-ray would shake and the nurse would notice, or the possibility that she, in showing me the diary

—I was so dumb

suddenly full of blackbirds, she would run away

6.

The sea is calmer when it has slept alone the night before and doesn't leave its bones on the beach, ribs of boards, vertebrae of pebbles, the slipper of a ruined foot, it doesn't scale the rocks, tumble them, it approaches us with the softness of a gazelle, it laps at our heels, retreats, approaches me, it's seen us, it knows us, we don't interest it anymore, the next-door neighbor to my mother
   —What's wrong with the ocean today?
and nothing's wrong, ma'am, don't worry, that's all, there are nights when it doesn't spy on us in our rooms, it stays down there minding its own business, adjusting its clothing, behaving itself and I almost feel remorse for changing its habits in a few minutes, it will feel inconvenienced, it will look at me with astonishment, it will deposit me slowly on the sand, with a delicate open hand
   —I don't have time for you today, sorry
  if I ask it about my older brother, it can't remember
   —So much craziness has happened since then
  and it's true, so much craziness happened afterwards, I, for example, who didn't want to teach, became a teacher, imagine, all those faces in front of me and a bush against the window

—What are you teaching them?
without answering the question, my mother
—Did the cat eat your tongue, girl?
and it did, I don't have a tongue, if I look for it I can't find it, it ate my tongue and how can I teach the lesson, all those faces in front bored first and curious later, if I grow another tongue what will it say, along the street where the grocery store is there are small houses, with open doors, with ladies in canvas chairs in the doorway, fanning themselves with pieces of cardboard, pages of newspapers, fans, my co-worker, suddenly red-faced, also has a fan, with traces of Spanish dancers on the cloth between the sticks
—There's no medicine that will take away my hot flashes
I, who never learned to dance, sometimes try it out and find myself comical, I see myself in the reflection of the mirrors, and I give up right away, my mother danced with me on her hip when I was a child
—Will you give me the honor of this waltz, girl?
my fingers disappeared into hers, my trunk disappeared into hers, she placed me on the ground
—You're too big you're making me feel faint
leaning against the wall, catching her breath, my father was looking at her, with a hint of happiness in his eye sockets, my mother
—You weren't bad at this
and the hint of happiness fading immediately, his toe cap, which had accompanied the rhythm, was still now, the ladies in the canvas chairs surrounded us, some whose husbands, without fans, in shorts, carried a glass of water slowly to an oilcloth, the water wasn't still, it trembled, afraid they would drink it, a body sunk into liquid suffers a vertical impulse from bottom to top

equal to the volume of the displaced water, that stayed with me like my mother's voice to my father, plus the crack of board under the bed and the rosary jingling against the headboard
—What if the kids hear us?
my father, who still talked back then
—If they hear they won't know what it is
my mother, who sounded sleepy, yielding with a concave sigh which held all of him
—If they hear they won't know what it is
the rosary jingling louder in spite of the closed doors, we are children of God, as the priest swore, the old women in the chairs in the room with my parents in a whirlwind of fans that tousled their hair, the curtains moved like agitated chickens and the window frames vibrated, the water jar, almost falling off the oilcloth, that my father held, the rosary in repose after the last jolt, the room peaceful again, the sea is calmer when it has slept alone the night before, if I went in and they weren't there the immobile crucifix would be dying, no crucifix or bed now, dry leaves, dust, it must be in a drawer in the building next to the Thebes Bakery, with the white beads separated, ten and ten, by a black one, if I mimicked my mother on my next visit
—Do you think they'll hear
the person who didn't hear was her
—What kind of talk is that girl?
looking at me in confusion trying to understand, she doesn't remember my father the way she doesn't remember the others, she will remember dancing with me, and when she danced with me, just the two of us existed, it made me feel special, ma'am, a little dizzy from the twirling but special, I wanted my legs to reach the floor so I could move them too, so close your face was different,

a space in the right eyebrow, marks that you don't notice, would she have had a friend like I had Tininha, did she draw eyeglasses on the pictures of the people in the history books, would she have been shocked at the mysteries of her body, that became something else when she turned twelve, Tininha left before Dr. Clementina appeared, when one day when she got out of bed

—I'm a doctor

her mother suddenly a widow, her father had died centuries ago, the driver washing the car, grown-up people's clothes in the closet, twin sons, her husband in a cautious conversation that he spent weeks perfecting

—The problem isn't with you, it's with me

and the problem was the sister of a co-worker

—I need some time alone to think about us

or rather in an empty house, dry leaves, dust, an insect with its legs sticking up in the air that we didn't step on by some miracle, what was left of a peeling baseboard, what was the house next door called, I can't remember the name, with a deaf brother and another one, older, who hardly looked at us, I remember the camellia tree, I who was never interested in trees, I ran into the husband who had the problem

—What problem?

and he gave a complicated answer that didn't make sense, the afternoon of the divorce I didn't feel sorry or sad, the two of them in front of a judge listening him read something that we didn't hear, she ate dinner with the lawyer and after the dinner no rosary was jingling against the bed, the clothing of the lawyer, the ocean is stiller, so neatly folded on the sofa, socks tucked scrupulously inside the shoes that were lined up next to the dresser, when it slept alone the night before, with two fingers hooked together and the whole time Dr. Clementina putting up with a perfume she didn't like, touching him as little as possible, or rather almost not touching him, or rather touching him more or less, with the dead weight of his wedding ring on her back

—What can I do?

and the camellia tree again, the older brother of the other one oiling a tricycle, communicating in gestures to the deaf brother

—You can pedal now, bro

returning the oil can to the ping-pong table in the garage and cleaning his hands with a rag, if there was a rag around there so clean herself after sleeping with the lawyer and there wasn't, she thought

—When this is over, I'm taking a bath for hours

and, in spite of the hours-long bath, the perfume wouldn't dissipate, exclamations and words she preferred not to remember, when the lawyer asked her for a move that was different from the one she took with her friend, not her

—Get the horsies out of the rain

The guy's toenails were badly cut, his mouth was too hard, he bruised her arm, and Dr. Clementina had to wear long sleeves in June, what a drag, following the evolutions of the bruise for the next few days, while it was light brown the lawyer's bill came that she had paid for already with her skin, if you think that on top of that I'll take the horsies out of the rain, a second bill, an unpleasant phone call, the threat of a complaint, a dinner invitation

—Get the horsies out of the rain

while her friend, whose name she couldn't remember, wrote in the diary that they covered with a stone, hung up on the guy with the whiff of perfume rising again, on my next visit to my mother, I, imitating her

—Do you think they don't hear?

explaining to her, while my mother leaned over toward me, trying to understand

   —I don't forget a single episode

The ocean is stiller when it has slept alone the previous night and it doesn't leave its bones on the sand, I ask myself if I'll leave mine, I hope not, Dr. Clementina's husband didn't come up to the house on the weekend to pick up his kids, he honked from the street, promised to come get them at ten and showed up at one, if she looked out the window, and she didn't because she was sure there was a woman with him, each son had a backpack, sometimes a tennis racket, sometimes school books because there was a test on Monday, when she learned of the marriage between her husband and that the woman was pregnant, set up an armchair for me here, gave a curt response to the director and got impatient with an intern for no reason, she didn't feel like having lunch, an armchair even if the springs are broken, anything will do, she drank a container of juice that was for the patients, and wanted, what a stupid wish, for bed eighteen to be hers, something was in her breast too, preferable, if you think about it, to something in the pancreas, from time to time the lawyer sent roses, with a business card where the last name and profession were crossed out and she didn't answer, buried the flowers, head down, in the kitchen garbage can, one night with the cousin of a co-worker, much younger than she, whom she met at a dinner, she accompanied him to an apartment with no elevator, with a mountain bike in the living room and underpants forgotten on the floor, she ate sandwiches from the night before and scolded herself

   —What am I doing here?

after that the mountain bike of a journalist, a psychiatrist, an actor, also much younger than she, with an earring and film posters, a little armchair what luck, and then she gave the actor pills for a fungus that burned his stomach, while the roses came less frequently until they stopped completely, he must have done another divorce, folding his clothes on the other side with that one, putting his shoes next to another dresser, an idiotic relapse with the mountain bike guy, a weekend in London, where it rained the entire time, escorted by a pilot, boiled eggs for breakfast, shopping, a stuffed nose, sadness abroad sadder than in Portugal, she called the airline to book an earlier flight and there were no seats available, so more of the pilot, more rain, an Alka-Seltzer in an agitated spiral of bubbles, first at the bottom and then at the surface spitting gas energetically, she swallowed the swirling liquid with a sneeze, the panic that in a few years she'd be with a driver and she would say to him

—My peach

she said to the pilot

—The problem isn't you, it's me

and for a few seconds she felt like strangling her ex-husband or strangling herself even with the belt of her robe but there was no hook on the ceiling to hang the belt on, she didn't miss her kids

—Am I normal?

missing the camellia and how odd that she'd think of the camellia, she who had lost it as a child, a vague notion of blackbirds and pines and that the ocean watched her, her father, when he sat at the table with mother at his right and she at his left, in front of the grass and the dwarf

—Excellent, excellent

folding his napkin what was excellent excellent, me, to my mother

—I don't forget a single episode

not even the jingling of the rosary or the Alto da Vigia in a little while, if I had a napkin I'd fold it on my lap and say

—Excellent, excellent

and that's all, what more would there be besides this if you take away Dr. Clementina and I not whispering, without secrets, without diaries in a hole in the wall, without words, not friends anymore, strangers, and nevertheless side by side, why side by side, what joins us, in a little while I'll take myself down to the beach without waving to her from the gate, why wave if everything is excellent excellent, I don't need princess earrings, thank you, or a palm almost touching me

—Girl

they will build houses in the olive grove that will not have a view of the waves, it could be you'd see them, depending on the wind, my co-worker

—There are always waves in Peniche

and I believe in you, there are always waves in Peniche, our husbands, mine and Tininha's, maybe they will understand each other, lying to us, lying to themselves, not understanding us, side by side and separate, I'll leave you then stray dog to keep you company while I cross the beach and climb up the rocks, my co-worker

—Won't you stay with me?

and I can't, even if I wanted to, and I don't say that I want to, I can't, my mother

—What co-worker is that, young lady?

when she was irritated with me not

—Girl

her voice thicker, fuller

—Young lady
her hand almost in the air, a wrinkle in her forehead
—Are you the one who broke the fairy, young lady?

and I didn't break it, look at her in the middle of the napkin, calm down, in a day or three it will be another house instead of this one, other people, another father drinking, mine, turning to the wall

—Leave me alone

and my mother and I leaving the hospital, the much younger men making you feel like your mother, Dr. Clementina, that's it, you, not realizing it

—My peach

you don't sleep with them in your room, it's obvious, a recess in the extreme opposite of the apartment, the smell of cold food and the provinces that the maid maybe brings in

—Do you think the old woman notices?

you don't hear the rosary jingling and none is, did you give her the pill or didn't you, put on another blanket for the cold or didn't you, lower the blind or didn't you

—And what if she wants cookies and pees on the sheet?

since when we last a long time, Dr. Clementina, we want cookies and we pee on the sheets, my mother, indignant

—Do you think I'm gaga?

and don't be offended, ma'am, I asked just to ask, there are people at half our age, who pee on the sheets, it happens, if we dream, for example, of a bucket, we let go, any doctor will tell you, it's normal, Dr. Clementina

At fifty-two men don't interest me

and that's not true, don't fool yourself, they interest you, there are moments that even clearing your throat is a kind of company, they always occupy some pace preventing the rooms from getting bigger, and if the rooms get bigger, breathing is difficult, pay attention to my co-worker whom I distract from hallways and police, from power to the working class and even if the working class is in power it would never have it, understand, my co-worker, referring to herself

—Your Mama

not with me, with her father on her lap, my deaf brother riding on my shoulders, knocking over the broken door, when they ended the masses God ended too, there He is saying I know what you did and I know you're not cold or hot; I wish you were cold or hot but the way you are lukewarm I'll vomit you out of my throat and therefore what's the use of protesting, see, my older brother didn't protest, he realized, the post office clerk, without daring to approach, with her two hands over her face, I remember Senhor Manelinho's wife crossing herself raising the canvas and the reflection of my older brother in her features for an instant, if the two of us danced, mother, before I get to the doormat, a sparrow in the window, two sparrows in the window and in compensation no gull, occupied with the ebb tide, look at the little gulls skittering along the rocks and the water chasing them, my co-worker with a cloud between us and I don't know where she came in

—Are you going to give up on Mama?

me with my husband and the intern in my mind, it's not about the intern or my husband, it's that they wait for me and what would become of them if I didn't show up, Dr. Clementina to a guy I couldn't see

—We met on the King's birthday and I'm not available for more

the stray dog following me to the grocery store hoping for a handout, if I could give you one of my bones I would, the sphenoid, the clavicle, some whose names I've forgotten, I haven't forgotten them, I've lost them, the legs, a random vertebrae, it doesn't matter, choose one, and the Greek wife of the owner of the pharmacy combing her hair endlessly, raising her arms to her breast she almost touched me on the street, in the establishment on the ground floor, measure your cholesterol here, an old scale, with a pointer, the enamel broken, the owner of the pharmacy

—A year before he died my grandfather told me that the crown prince weighed himself here

handing his crown and mantle to an attendant hoping it would make him weigh less, so many sparrows, he stayed, so many sparrows how strange and nevertheless it's silent, other birds over the canopy, with long tails and feathers of many colors, he stayed staring at the scale and the crown prince didn't come back, the owner of the pharmacy, making the customers sigh

—It seems his eyes were blue

while the birds of many colors but not blue, brown, pink, black, if I had time I'd look up their names in the encyclopedia, there must be something in the school library, if not the biology teacher, who was a little worm, might know, the first cars from Lisbon are parked in front of the kiosk and there are fewer people on the beach, what I wouldn't give, I'm jealous, to learn something about those creatures, wiping the sand from their feet rubbing them on a towel, carriers, baskets, tubes of sunscreen, clothing, take your blood pressure here, test your blood sugar, save your eyes with prescription dark glasses you won't get them anywhere else, at a certain elevation, bam, those birds disappear beyond the well, where there is a stand of oak trees but their night is perpetual, who can prove to me that it's not the oaks making it in secret, the Greek wife of the pharmacist combed her hair for hours and hours, looking at men, while the little dog on her lap licked her throat, me to my co-worker, calming her with a little pat

—I won't abandon Mama, don't worry

and if it weren't for the Alto da Vigia word of honor I wouldn't abandon her, I'd visit you, I'd be with you, you'd accept that I, I'd be with you and that's enough, how is it that oaks are able to make birds, teach me, what part of the bird do they start with, are they as slow with them as they are with their leaves, observing the branches we notice or don't a little piece of bird being born, growing claws, a beak, feathers, they'll fly away in October, they'll learn to fly as they fall, Dr. Clementina ordered blood tests for cholesterol and diabetes

—Not bad for your age

and, for your age, how are you, Dr., a driver for you to call

—My peach

No driver for now but we'll get there, friend, take it easy because we'll get there, until now just younger men with mountain bikes and film posters, a divan next to the wall, an empty yogurt container on the sheet, Dr. Clementina picking it up with two fingers

—Where should I put this?

the much younger man putting it, or would it be the leaves before they fall to the ground, to avoid rotting in the water, take off in flight, the much younger man putting it in the red box that served as a night table, with yellow circles and triangles

—For example, here

and a fly rubbing its feet together on the rim of the container, my co-worker giving me a sideways glance the way she did, the much younger man wore a ring with a skull on it, didn't believe me, here teeth on her lower lips and her nostrils staring at me, lying in her place on the couch a lampshade with imitation parchment that because of carelessness the lightbulb had burned, turn the burn to the back, patience, so that I won't see it, another woman before me who I discovered from little signals, a jar of face powder with no lid, a dress my co-worker never wore, a bracelet that was too colorful in the jewelry box, the birds are leaves that don't accept death, Dr. Clementina

—Are you sure?

while the tide began, finally, to rise, it was about time, I've been waiting for this since Friday and as I finish writing the sentence I ask if I'm really waiting for this or if I didn't expect a perpetual low tide that would keep me from doing it, I always said I wasn't afraid and I am, God will vomit me out of his mouth, he won't let me get to my older brother, he'll keep my bones, what's left over from my bones will end up in some cave or grotto, my father won't say

—Girl

too far away to know I'm there or for me to hear him, my father who didn't dance or at least I never saw him dance, he walked with his swollen legs from the pantry to the sofa, in the building next to the Thebes bakery, he didn't go down to the street, I hope I have more time, I hope I go back, stay with my co-worker, the school, the intern who mocked me and it didn't hurt that she mocked me with the other intern

—If you could see her breast

the other intern

—They took one off, seriously?

and they did take one off, seriously, two or three years ago, I can't remember exactly, I must do the math, it was March twenty-second, almost four years ago, they took one off and therefore I'm a cripple, did you know, my co-worker

—Don't talk like that

and I don't talk like that because it's true, look at the way my husband avoids me, he only reaches for me in the dark and that is so rare, if I could I'd stay here, let me sit on your lap, kiss me, make me feel that is, make me feel something instead of nothing, turn the burn mark so I can't see it is enough of a favor, the birds are leaves that refuse to die, Dr. Clementina

increasing the formality between us, she met me many years ago and didn't know me, what's the different today while the tide starts to rise with a crown of gulls and albatrosses coming from the north, I remember my older brother observing the beach, the clouds along the mountains, the reeds

—Girl

especially the reeds

—Girl

alerting me about what I didn't understand and how do you understand words without syllables, I was seven years old then, the intern to the other intern

—She says she was seven

the other intern

—Bullshit how can a fifty-two year old person ever have been seven?

without any of them believing me, when I wasn't thinking and feeling guilty of thinking, when my father was invisible on the step and the guilt lifted a little my mother picked me up and we danced, her hair against my chin, my hand disappearing in hers, I looked at the end of my arm and I didn't have fingers, how strange, I had a shoulder, an elbow, a wrist, but my hand and fingers were missing, when she put me on the ground I had a hand and fingers again but don't put me on the ground for now, keep twirling, doubt about if it's us twirling or the room

—Is it us or the room, mother?

and my mother

—It doesn't make any difference

it's probably us and the room and the birds, everything at the same time, happy, my mother singing with the music, me a little dizzy but happy too, like I'm happy on my older brother's bike

—Faster bro

we going up and down and the houses going up and down too, so fast, the house of the Italian, the grocery store, the ladies on the canvas chairs, the shoemaker, I think I haven't mentioned the shoemaker in his tiny shop, his name was Senhor Café and we nodded his head instead of speaking, I retain the smell of the leather shoes and the glue, Senhor Café hammering with half a dozen little nails clenched in his mouth, he must sleep with them there, eat with them there, even on Sunday, when his shop is closed and Senhor Café is I don't know where, the nails are still there, the ocean is calm when it has slept alone the night before, more willing to forgive us, Tininha's mother to the driver

—Don't turn on the engine, my peach, I want to see how this ends

the peach turns off the engine, annoyed, what does she get out of watching waves and more waves and a person you can hardly see, a woman because she's disheveled, weak, trying to climb the rocks, slipping, holding on, climbing up again, that and the gulls making circles what's missing on this earth, when she was little her father took her here at dawn, tripping on roots, to the ducks that at least always fly to the right obeying the one in front, screeching over the lake with their ancient horns, those that who squeeze a rubber ball and they let out rusty sounds, the father squatting in a bush, with a cap with ear flaps that her mother hated

—When you wear that you look like a retard

the father taking a step toward her

—Bad

and her mother fleeing in her flip-flops going clap-clap, the father in a thick humidity from which bulrushes emerged, a kind of fog, a kind of cold, the first frogs not jumping yet, still in the leaves, swelling and deflating their sacs, a sharp little wind, the sensation that an ant was crawling on her back, if it were a scorpion, she'd faint but scorpions walk slower, it's surely an ant, crawling lightly, the mountain bike of the much younger man going where, tell me, Dr. Clementina, shocked

—What's this thing for?

an ant crawling lightly, she tried to crush it and her father's elbow brushed against her face

—Stay still

he was still, sleepy, hungry, missing his pillow, missing his mother until slowly, with a rustling in the weeds, there were dispersed movements not in the lake, in the mud, the idea that a bird was moving, two birds moving, Tininha's mother

—Give me that cheek

the driver offering his cheek and wanting to scratch it when he got it back, the old woman slobbers all over me, her mother's flip-flops going clap clap not at home, near here, an old horn still not loud yet, soft, the bullrushes to one side and the other, wanting to rub her cheek with the handkerchief and it wasn't the wind, it was blue shadows, a first eye, a first wing separating from the body, a distant rooster, a belltower, a much younger man priding himself on Dr. Clementina's shock about the bike

—It cost a shitload of money

thirty-six speeds, my older brother's had none, a special seat, a fender made of carbon alloy and what is that, embarrassed to ask, disinterest in knowing, the much younger man

—It weighs less than three kilos

the steering wheel full of buttons, levers, tabs, the ducks in the lake at sunrise, it is a clarity that didn't illuminate the trees or the plants, just outlined them slowly and the mountain bike

—You don't even have to try

scaling walls in a single jump, the father with a pair of cartridges in the muzzle, the ant settled down and returned to its work, this time on her neck, a duck disappeared into the water and stuck its head out again to shake its feathers, her father out of the corner of his mouth

—It's the female who's the boss they'll show up soon it won't be long

more ducks in the water, the sun outlined the last tree, hopefully the wind won't change, hopefully they won't see us and Senhor Café hammers away without stopping, from time to time he got more nails and stuck them in his mouth without using his fingers, just the ability of his tongue, he pulled at a thread from a spool and the glue spatula from a pot, if at least Tininha's mother didn't call him

—My peach

and would leave him alone for a second, he didn't ask for more, a minute of peace without demands

—Peach you rascal

the ducks left the lake with the female who was in the lead, the driver's father

—Pay attention because they're leaving boy

and how do you pay attention with the ant and the tiredness battling each other, not to mention the knee falling asleep and immense dangerous insects surrounding them, a frog boiled a few steps away, a tiny areola, with a lacquered iris, crossed a puddle in little jumps and suddenly there were many fans at the same time and ducks in the air, grey, white, silver, taking a long time to fly, the mother's voice near them because of the cap with the ear flaps

—When you put this on you look like a retard

the father following the flock with his rifle aimed

—They've got to come by here on the way to the river

the bike that cost a shitload of money is still in its corner, the red crate with the yellow circles and triangles, the poster of a group of electric guitars over the too narrow bed, the fly on the yogurt strolling on the packaging, Dr. Clementina thinking

—I won't fit there

—How about I leave?

and staying, not knowing why she doesn't leave, not waving

—Tchauzinho

Dr. Clementina to herself

—My peach

Dr. Clementina outside of herself

—What a drag

the much younger man checking the tattoo on his arm

—Excuse me?

the ocean is calm when it has slept alone the night before, growing, growing, her father takes a shot, two shots, dozens of echoes through the fields, multiplying, repeating, stretching, Dr. Clementina pulling down her skirt praying

—God willing you won't notice my cellulitis and my stretch marks

the tattoo of the much younger man is a purple and black condor and a complicated heart with the name Mafalda, Dr. Clementina thinking who is Mafalda, who would Mafalda have been, who is Mafalda, Dr. Clementina

—Who is Mafalda?

the much younger man looking distractedly at the tattoo

—A friend

and taking off her shoes, Dr. Clementina

—I'm leaving

unhooking her skirt and pulling down her panties, insecure in her nakedness, worried about her cellulitis, her stretch marks, the ravages of time, she didn't notice the duck fall twenty or thirty meters from the father just as she didn't notice that it was she falling and murmuring

—My peach

she just noticed, from the floor, a much younger man and Mafalda, who contrary to what she supposed, could both fit in the bed.

7.

I can see my mother from here, while they give her the news, she's twisting her hands on the sofa and I ask myself who will break it to her, the firemen, Senhor Manelinho coming all the way to Lisbon for this purpose, in a full suit and tie, everyone has a full suit even if it's from their wedding and that no longer fits them, the jacket doesn't button, the pants are a torture but you can squeeze into them by pulling in your stomach, in spite of the wife

—If I were you, I'd go as you are nobody will take it badly you move a muscle and you'll bust the seams

a policeman standing at attention, not fiercely, embarrassed, taking his hat off at the doorway and immediately ceasing to be a policeman, patting himself down, surprised

—What happened to my handcuffs and my gun?

he still had them on the stairs, there's the badge with my name on it, Mendonça, and the metal shield, could I be a peasant disguised as a policeman, could I really be a policeman, I can see my mother from here, while they give her the news, what harm did I do to God to have children like this or, then, when will I stop having to pay for my sins or, still, who condemned me to spend eternity in suffering, Dona Alice, in an apron, with a scarf on her head because you can't understand why there's so much dust, receiving the visitors without noticing that the vacuum cleaner was unplugged and I don't trip on the cord only because I will not be there, the firemen don't wear their helmets just like the policeman is without his cap and I recognize them with their helmets off, the cousin of the owner of the foosball café, and the clerk from the grocery store dirtying the carpet with sand since on the way to Lisbon the sea dried on his feet, my mother next to the fairy who participates from the chest, my mother interrupting the working of her hands

—Show me again

while the police who couldn't find his gun or the handcuffs in his pocket looked suspiciously at the drawer shut badly, and therefore suspect

—If you are still, they'll be there

and maybe they are there, maybe they're not, try to open it and you'll find candles for the times the power goes out, a roll of wire, bills, throughout our whole life bills flutter agitatedly in front of us

—Would you like to tell me how we're going to pay for this?

and we were little, penniless, thinking, my not deaf brother convinced he could help

—We can sell the girl

my mother assessing me skeptically

—Do you think anyone would buy her?

and nobody buys her, it's obvious, she doesn't know how to set the table and there's no way she's going to learn how to read, Dona Alice, in whose head under the scarf lived secretly a little shred of compassion

—Let her grow a year or two more

and in one or two years, the bills would be lapsed, there'd be no water in the sinks, the vacuum cleaner would be mute, if we wait until she grows, we'll die of hunger before that, my mother returned the floor to the policeman fixated on the drawer, approaching it reluctantly with his finger on the knob, peering inside

—What harm did I do to God to have children like this?

and in the drawer, there are no handcuffs or a gun, the candles, the roll of wire, the bills, the chief giving him a hard time when the policeman presented a candle as if the candle were capable of firing or capturing crooks

—You're screwed Mendonça

you can't imagine how badly you're screwed, a modest pension that isn't enough for soup, afternoons on a garden bench moaning with the doves or fighting over bread crumbs with the pigeons, Senhor Manelinho's suit, who out of caution moved like a float, carried on the shoulders of the floorboards, one of them lower than the others, the other wobbling under the weight, all four in white gloves, sweating, Senhor Manelinho's suit, we've got you, don't fall, it withstood the trip

—My condolences, ladies

divided between my mother and Dona Alice whose vacuum cleaner decided to work, making the carpet fringes flutter, Dona Alice shut it up by stamping on the control button with her foot transforming its task of devouring the world into a spurned muteness, my mother extended her finger to Senhor Manelinho she who never offered her fingers to Senhor Manelinho, she took his wife's side

—A jerk

my mother wanting the next-door neighbor to be with her to show her what was happening

—Do you see the cross I bear?

reading the paper using his pinky to turn the pages or it was the pinky that read and explained it to them afterwards, deciphered the paragraphs and then placed itself next to her ear to say

—This and that happened

it happened that your daughter on the Alto da Vigia, ma'am, between the wind and the gulls, so much wind, mother, you and father and all of us are in me, we were in every stone, in every thistle, in my death, the intern to the other intern

—What a pathetic old woman

trying to find our house from up there, and confusing the chimneys, in a very old building, they say that before the ocean, storks, no in the place of the oaks, in a place without trees, don't move, the float like my older brother floated in the waves, my not deaf brother floated through the villages that burned, midnight to twenty to seven that is so much light in the dark, if I could pray, if God would pay attention to me, if my co-worker

—Mama is here

me calm instead of nervous and afraid, hold my arm, don't let my bones turn into little stones that the water disregards, the storks landed with slow delicacy and your daughter waiting for a bigger wave, without a Mexican movie or a circus, why the devil don't cacti replace the pines, thick bushes blocking the blackbirds, impassive peasant women, wearing men's hats, looking, Ândrea climbing on the wire for a tightrope act, her eyelids painted, sequins sparkling, my eyelids aren't painted, sequins sparkling, wearing the only dress I brought from home, what will my husband do with my clothes, my trinkets, my little emerald ring,

another woman with him in our bed and at my place at the table, why do men never live alone, a stork brought me in its beak from Paris, and left me in the building next to the Thebes Bakery, my mother to my father, picking me up, frightened
   —Do you see this?
and my father over her shoulder
   —Pretend it's our daughter
I heard those stories when I was a child
   —You came from Paris hanging from a bird
or
   —We found you on the stairs
or
   —We bought you from the gypsies
I didn't hear
   —You were born in a maternity ward like the others
so that I never did see my mother's pregnant belly, I'm the last one, not even my belly was large with child, an imprecise discomfort, a pain, and they removed it from me, I don't have children, Dr. Clementina has two, I have none, Senhor Manelinho's wedding suit will tear sooner or later, don't twist your hands, mother, it's not worth it, the whole world knows about the cross you bear, the next-door neighbor, who didn't show hers
   —Everyone has their own
knitting with a speed that made you dizzy without taking off her clothes, just shoeless
   —Everyone has their own
if the wedding suit tears how will Senhor Manelinho get back to the kiosk, his wife
   —I told you so, jerk
complaining to a customer

—He doesn't listen to anybody

each time playing with the dog, disconnected from everything, sitting on a bench in silence, not paying attention to the women, the widower doctor who spent his vacation tending the hydrangeas took his temperature and auscultated him

   —You're not sick, my friend

and Senhor Manelinho put on his shirt disappointed that he wasn't sick, look at him wanting to pick up the fairy and my mother understanding him, despite her twisting hands

   —You can pick up the fairy if you want to, Senhor Manelinho, just don't drop it

the shoes of the next-door neighbor so obedient, immobile, they could get annoyed with each other, and they didn't show it, they could run on the beach and they didn't run, if the widower doctor observed them he'd find some problem

   —Pay attention to your prostate

in a room that I imagined to be full of organs in bottles that frightened me, they would be dead or waiting for me to come closer to do me harm, she doesn't know the difference between a bladder and an esophagus, they think, my co-worker

   —They don't think, silly

the ones who thought of her were her bones, they creaked when she got up from the sofa, maybe it was the springs, maybe I made it up, maybe it was my teeth that were mad at me

   —Why do you still come here?

my not deaf brother continued to ride in the military truck that scattered chickens as it drove through villages, my mother to the next-door neighbor, following the distribution of the wafers

   —Don't spoil them

if my older brother were here and I think he's not but who

can say for certain what the destiny of the dead is, at certain times they're so close that I can feel their breath, at other times so far away and you don't feel a thing, sometimes my father is with me, others, as much as I call him, at most a whisper
—I don't want to wander
probably with his father who praised him
—Boy
even after the bottles, my mother, the jobs that were ever more modest until there was no job at all, a microscopic pension, the unsteady steps
—You'll do well boy, whoever was born to conquer the world will conquer it
I haven't met many dead people, but I know the night in its various forms, for example a glass of water drunk in the dark in the kitchen, surrounded by familiar invisible objects and noticing the messages from the trees, for example insomnia next to a sleeping person, our irregular heartbeat, our shyness when we wake them up
—I'd just like you to keep me company for awhile
and we remain, without help facing death because if our heartbeat is irregular we die, if my older brother were here he'd keep Senhor Manelinho company, the way he keeps the firemen and the police company
—I'll find your gun and the handcuffs, don't worry
like when they brought him in from the beach you could see everyone was calmer
—It's not serious, don't worry
and the post office clerk, shocked
—Look, he talked
to the point that Tininha's mother got up from the lounge

chair and came to the gate, I know the night as if I had made it, believe me, during the day I can be fooled, I am human, but not at night, hours and hours at the window looking at the lights in the other houses, once, at another window, a man was crying, he didn't wipe his eyes with a handkerchief, you couldn't tell if he was talking, he didn't even shake, but nevertheless he was crying, my older brother to Senhor Manelinho

—Thanks for the company

the policeman rummaging with him through chests, trunks, closets with the

—Mendonça

thinking of the chief

—I don't understand what happened to them

and nobody understands, that's the malice of things, we think they're in one place and they evaporate, my mother's sewing scissors always moving from place to place, my mother calling them like a dog

—Where are you, you pest?

the scissors under the bed or in the fruit bowl, the sly thing, deceiving us, you pat yourself and don't feel it, you put your hand out and find it, that is you come across something hard, you look and there it is, my mother almost dropping it on the floor

—It's bewitched

hesitating when it's found, do I scold it, don't I, do I punish it, don't I, or is it us, I ask, losing our memory, things would like us to think that way, it's their ruin

—You're getting old, that's funny

pretending they break and remaining intact, pretending to say goodbye and they return, my co-worker

—Why do you spend so much time looking at things I'm here aren't I?

and I ask myself if you're there since there are times that, even in front of you, I can't find you, my mother to the next-door neighbor

—This child was always special

I who can already see her twisting her hands on the sofa as they give her the news, what bad thing have I done to God to have children like this or, then, when will I stop having to pay for my sins, or still, who has condemned me to suffer for all eternity, now in all seriousness I can't express what binds me to you and I can't figure out what it is, except for the afternoons we danced together what was there really between us, I am left with pines, blackbirds, the man who stops drying his tears on his sleeves becomes aware of my presence and recedes, my husband with the Sunday supplement and where am I to him, he's started to lose his hair, he's gained weight, I didn't marry that man, I married a young fellow who took me to the boarding house, so tense the two of us, losing nerve on the stairs, whispering

—And what if we left now?

imagining on the esplanade topics of conversation that made me fall in love, in a little while I'll say goodbye

—Adieu house

and I'll leave silently, as discreetly as I can, in the hopes that it won't notice my absence, my deaf brother agitated in Lisbon, rattling Dona Alice's relative, trying to open the door

—Shhheee

the father of the man who was crying was as dead as my father or in one of those places where they put sick people, they make them sit all day in chairs without pillows and they drink juice out of straws with laughter like hollow husks filling their gums, the butterflies remain in the yard undulating in the wind if we catch them they leave a little dust on our fingertips, I suppose the afternoon has begun since the sun is almost grazing the first treetops and there's a kind of blue glow in the yard, the tranquility that dilates inside the noise, the ocean sensing me, small bedrooms, a small living room, ants crawling tirelessly in the kitchen, in a year, poor things, they will walk on tiles, earth, some boards, our shadows that will remain by the well, I bet that my not deaf brother was here before me since there's a new footprint in the flower bed, did you look for us, brother, you will have to kill us if you see us, I felt the urge for my co-worker to embrace me, cover my eyes with her hands, blind me, Senhor Manelinho about me to my mother

—I didn't recognize her when she arrived on Friday

Senhor Manelinho's wife

—I thought I recognized her, but I wasn't sure

and I wanted to be Ândrea's friend, not Tininha's, rubbing her knees with her hands, so serious, my not deaf brother shouting into the deserted rooms

—You

convinced that since he had a rifle

—Show yourselves

and who can guarantee that my father didn't appear, with a last bottle that fell to the floor, advancing toward my not deaf brother and my not deaf brother

—Stay where you are sir before the others shoot you

the lieutenant unpinning a grenade not believing

—Is that one your father?

your father a black man who can barely move, look at his

stomach, look at his ankles, grabbing my not deaf brother, not grabbing me, a sigh, coming from the sewing box more than from my mother and that he didn't hear
  —Sorry
  while the rosary jingled until it deafened her
  —Take me Jesus from this bed
how the masses must have hurt her, how it must have hurt her not to take communion, my mother's mother
  —Aren't you even going to do confession?
and my mother silent or then
  —Confess what everybody knows?
if everybody knows, and considering the way people are, somebody got unstitched from God, the intern to the other intern
  —It wasn't that she was a bad person, so much wind, mother, I didn't understand her
  in each stone us, in each husk us, in my death us, I tried to see my house from up there and confused the gables, the rooftops, and the yards, a very old building facing the sea, the sea put them there, drawing in water during the years, after they demolished the village, and they put in a motor designed to roll up the waves, I won't insist on the storks, when I have time, if I have time, although I don't think I'll have time, I'll talk about them and the nests that seem to wake up, raising their uncombed heads from the pillows of the chimneys when they land, Tininha at the wall
  —It's a good thing you came
happy than Rogério, always taciturn and with a lowered head, who didn't even like himself, slipping away from the wall to escape us and landing in the grass on his back, legs akimbo, Dr. Clementina
  —Was the animal that weird?

and it's impossible that she doesn't remember, is she teasing or not, those memories last until the end of time, how many times did my mother mention them, my not deaf brother through the streets of Lisbon, between burning villages, and he burning with them, a cloth zebra, you turned a key in its bellybutton and the zebra gave uncertain steps toward my mother so she'd protect him, what was the zebra's name, ma'am, and not her voice, the voice of a child in a dream

—Leonilde

it was the zebra that mattered, not me, Leonilde my father's sister who didn't marry, a nun, they visited her at Christmas in a little room in the convent that had no windows or furniture, a rosary on the wall that didn't jingle and therefore they were excused from asking

—Do you think the kids will hear?

Aunt Leonilde, I don't have time to digress about storks, came in accompanied by the sound of an organ and the light of the cloister candles, to bless the three of them tracing a horizontal line on my mother's forehead

—Are you without sin?

pulling a square of marmalade out of her sleeve that my mother didn't dare eat, father calmed her, I know the night under all its forms and of this I will deliver a report when the moment comes, wait

—She doesn't have any sins, sis

and in that room without windows or furniture, almost bare, and why are the storks important, who bothers with them these days, who bothers with whatever these days, the intern doesn't bother with anything other than

—Faster

yellow pillows, red, lilac, multiplying to the ceiling covering the viola and the Moroccan drums, covering us, suffocating, immense, me thinking

—How are we going to breathe now?

while the ash from the incense stick curled and curled, Aunt Leonilde

—Sin comes from where one least expects it

with a resignation that the organ dissolved, if the organ stops there is no sound, pillows too and incense sticks instead of candles in the church, she meditated on her sins when you were with other men, mother, in the little room without windows or furniture, with the little square of marmalade melting in your palm, when your mother wiped your hand with a handkerchief

—You're sticky that's enough

warning

—Until you wash your hands don't touch anything

and she didn't touch anything, just to make sure she moved her arms away from her blouse, looking like the storks balancing on their nests, what use are intentions and strong compulsions, my mother, returning from Aunt Leonilde, careful not to step on the black stones on the walk, I remember seeing her as we went down to the beach, avoiding them and pretending not to avoid them, sometimes a large step, sometimes a small step, looking back, doubting

—Did I step on one?

my not deaf brother

—Is something wrong, ma'am?

there's nothing I can do, these birds are my fate, what blackbirds, what sparrows, what owls, what about those with the long tail whose names I didn't know and I lost forever, my older brother, although he's been dead for years, more than forty, I think, although smart and with a nose, those virtues don't pass, found the policeman's handcuffs in the pantry, stuck between the oil and the rice

—It's your gun that's missing, right?

and Senhor Manelinho willing to help but not able to help because of the wedding suit that, I don't know about the wind as much as I know about the night but I have a few ideas, wait and I'll get there, because of the wedding suit that turned him into a statue, he moved one leg ahead but fearfully, very slowly, alert to the resistance of the fabric, my co-worker peering through the peephole in the door, first, and then through a crack in the door

—After the grief you gave me with your death you have the nerve to visit Mama?

it wasn't that I had the nerve to visit Mama, it's that I had nowhere else to go, certain that another woman was with my husband, in the house next to the Thebes Bakery my mother was twisting her hands with a pack of people around her that my older brother pushed aside, now squatting, now standing, looking for the gun, followed by the policeman with his handcuffs in his hand to prevent them from escaping again, my older brother encouraging him

—You'll see, Senhor Mendonça, it's just a scare

while Senhor Mendonça's chief observed him from the squad car, Aunt Leonilde looked enormous to my mother when she was a child, if they dressed them like normal people and without the little room and the organ, you wouldn't notice her or if they did

—Yes, I have sinned, ma'am, and what's it to you?

a creature identical to thousands of creatures scurrying through the holes they lived in with a bag of groceries, struggling on the stairs, that in December, the sorry thing, wearing a man's overcoat, cheap galoshes, God indifferent to her, what can you give Him in exchange, a coin clanking into the alms box, healing for the leg that doesn't work, the landlord forgetting to ask for the rent

—I think you've already paid me, Dona Leonilde, I must look in my files

and with a little help from God, what does that cost, he didn't look, Senhor Mendonça's chief crossing his fingers, following my older brother in the squad car

—If he finds the gun, who will I torment?

my co-worker opening the door, the wind and I never got along, frightened me in bed rattling window frames and growling when it passed by, the blackbirds, sent off course to the beach, sobbing in fear, whoever says that birds don't sob is wrong, whoever argues that the stones don't become indignant don't know their souls, my co-worker, curious

—What's it like to die, tell me?

and there's not much to tell, we exist just the same just that nobody notices us, we are the middle of a table that buckles or a fold in a curtain, I can see from here my mother complaining about her children and my father on the step without extending his arm to me

—Girl

younger than I am now, Senhor Manelinho returning to the beach in the last bus, streetlamps lit along the road suddenly so long and those mountain shrubs with names I don't know, when he got off you couldn't make out the ocean, would it still be there or did they move it, Senhor Manelinho's wife, arranging the dishes

—The person who bummed around in Lisbon this late doesn't deserve to eat

if I had the little square of marmalade from Aunt Leonilde I'd offer it to him, but my mother didn't give it to me, Senhor Manelinho, discouraged by the memory

—I have an idea that it was the blonde daughter of the drunk on the stretcher, but my head doesn't work that well after all these years

that is, it's a supposition, he remembered his father's whistle in the orchard, he didn't remember his father, it was the whistle that watered the lettuce, and he propped up a vegetable with sticks, the whistle remained, not the whole tune, loose notes, without connection, he remembered a protest

—I can't stand this concert

from his mother or another woman, probably another woman because his mother was a mouth in bed refusing the broth

—I'm not hungry, leave me alone

and in a halo of wilted fever that visited him sometimes, he remembered humble fingers trying to hold on to the blanket and losing it, he remembered his motionless father next to the bed, taking off his cap, will I be returned to the storks, in silence, another woman changing the clothing of the dead woman and to live with them, it was the other woman who

—I can't stand this concert

the father, wearing his cap again, was still for a minute and started up again, the laces of the right boot different from those of the left, Senhor Manelinho's wife annoyed with Senhor Manelinho

—I've heard that story a thousand times

and Senhor Manelinho suspecting she was from the family of the other woman, a niece or a cousin, where do the storks go in

September, tell me, one day, with no warning, we find their nests are deserted, branches and mud that the first rains dissolve and make run down the chimneys, the accusation of my co-worker

—How did you die, then?

and a pendulum clock annoyed with me, in a recrimination of infinite hours, not seven, not ten, not twenty, the hundreds of hours of my life followed by the click of the tongue of the mechanism, imitating the displeasure of Dona Alice when a button was missing from a shirt or we hid her dust mop, why the plural, I never played with my brothers, each one of us alone, my deaf brother jealous of Tininha

—Shhheee

trying to pull off her princess earrings, he wanted to steal Rogério, still, the pines are going to speak, he even ran off a few steps with him and my older brother took it away from him, the pines are going to speak but I have stopped understanding them, what's happening to me, I always used to understand them, I leave here with as much care as Ândrea takes on the circus tightrope, go down the street without leaving the sidewalk because of the cars, pay attention to the crates in front of the grocery store, notice the barber with his scissors, not the doctor's pens, in his smock, the artisan craft store, clay vessels and wicker baskets outside and the owner waiting with crossed arms outside, the only taxi in its ruin of a garage, the driver not a peach, an old man in a shiny jacket stained with fat and blood talking with Senhor Leonel, my co-worker not kissing me

—Don't you realize how you made us suffer?

a cricket, without anything in common with me, who has anything in common with me, started up in the bushes and stopped right away, my co-worker

—Have you thought what my life is going to be like from now on?

or rather Mama's new year resolutions, the October of the house, the ground glass in her gallbladder shattering her with pain, the present so narrow that no hope fits inside although the hallways of the fort fit inside it, echoes of footsteps and her father clenching his lips trying to hide dozens of broken teeth in his mouth, Mama on the sofa, dirty tears of nests running down the chimneys all winter long, my co-worker blind to her chinoiserie, with the tea tray on her knees, the other intern to the intern

—What do old people do?

and what can they do, they sit alone, oozing all winter long, if we ask them something the shell in their ear

—Excuse me?

because they don't hear anymore, they answer

—Oh, yes?

without having heard us, they stop to think forgetting what they think, every so often my mother

—Did I say that?

surprised, trying to count us on her fingers

—How many children did I have?

getting it wrong and starting over, the oldest one fixing bikes or measuring boards with the *Manual for the Perfect Carpenter* guiding him, one look at the manual, a look at the boards, what decided to set fire to this house, if he paused to look at me, he said

—Mother

and disappeared down the stairs in the direction of people perched in a truck who were calling him, the deaf one pulling at my dress pointing at I don't know where or handing me a toy wooden truck so I'd play with him

—Shhheee

not softly, a howl without destiny, like the gulls when the tide rises, the same howl when my daughter, because I think it was a daughter, because I'm almost sure it was a daughter, because of the conviction it was a daughter, I had a daughter, as I climbed to the Alto da Vigia, hanging on to the weeds and the rocks

—Careful, Ândrea

balanced precariously on an outcropping of rock

—Remember your mother died this way

or maybe not my daughter, a girl who crosses, on a wire or a rope, I think a wire, who crosses a wire in the circus tent, there she is, I see her so well, my daughter crossing the circus tent on a wire, and I am silent

—We request absolute silence

so tense I couldn't applaud, suffocated with joy when, finally, she reached the other side, safe, and smiled at me.

8.

Every time Dr. Clementina walked by bed eighteen a princess earring fell off of her that she didn't know she wore, an orderly, a nurse, a doctor stepped on it without noticing it or my life with her, oh Tininha, I would like to, like to, I can't say it, I'm ashamed, don't pay any attention, I speak of the pines and the blackbirds so I won't talk about us, I lost you when I was eleven years old, I lost you and the empty house, no mother, no lounge chair, you weren't there, I wrote a secret diary that was different from the one in the wall, and in the secret diary, we stayed friends forever, promise, I was going to give you a wind-up rabbit, so cute, that a man, with a basket full of them, sold on the street, the rabbits jumped, dozens of them, here and there, going up and down the stairs until, suddenly, they froze in an attitude of surprise, I would have given you the sparrow eggs that my not deaf brother found in a fig tree or even, if necessary, my mother's fairy, so you would stay with me at the wall because your mother wouldn't let me in your house.

—My mother won't let you come in my house.

without understanding why, I wouldn't break anything, I

wouldn't make anything dirty, I wouldn't do anything stupid, your mother

—Trash

my parents were trash, my brothers were trash, I was trash, me thinking about what trash meant, today I know, my husband is trash, my co-worker is trash, the intern is trash, everything I touch or that gets close to me turns into trash, Dr. Clementina, when she grows up, will be just like her mother, to the patients in the hospital, for example, she considers them trash, she didn't address them as "ma'am" but with the familiar "you," the lives of trash are less important than, what a joke, a blackbird just went by with an insect in its beak, than hers, it's been awhile since I've seen a blackbird with an insect in its beak, it landed on a flowerbed to swallow it whole and its throat trembled for a moment, the black feet, the yellow beak, the wind-up rabbits jumping, jumping, if you'd seen them you'd smile at them or would suddenly stop, at the end of your cord, in an attitude of surprise, I liked to see them on the way to the beach, the man put them away in his basket without having sold one and I ask myself how many had fled, if I am still, when I walk into the living room, there will be a rabbit jumping in front of me

—Girl

and if the rabbit's in the living room, it could go into the yard, the well, the blackbird with the insect chasing it, not to eat it, how could it eat it, not just the hopping rabbit, the blackbird's hops as well, I tried hoping like they do and I looked ridiculous, ridiculous little trash hops, you to me

—My mother doesn't let trash in the house

and I understand her, don't think I don't understand, more than understand, I accept it, the people in the Lisbon bus, next to

the kiosk, trash, the man in the Café is trash, Senhor Manelinho and his wife are trash, the lady with the poodle, I bet that in bed eighteen, the people after me, more than trash, asking you fearfully
—Am I getting better, doctor?
and she wasn't, not dressed in silk, the shirt with the hospital logo, the throat, once fat, now just tendons, I'm sorry but you're not better, trash, the color of your skin doesn't lie, the swallows unearthed worms, the blackbirds butterflies, grasshoppers, equally things of the earth, little remains of food that nobody notices, you might not believe it, and it's almost certain you don't believe it, but a while ago I had the impression that a rabbit was with me, I didn't make any more friends, that is, I had Ermelinda and Dora, I liked them and everything, I almost forgot you but it wasn't the same, me and them grown up, if at least I didn't think of my fifty-two years, speaking of age my husband is fifty-four, how old would he be now, the blackbird with the insect skips a note of its song and then flies over the wall, I'll be happy if it comes back, I need everything around me before I go away, animals, words, family, my co-worker
—A kiss, princess
and I, immediately, give her a kiss
—Here
two kisses even, what difference does it make to me, a living body, near people, courage, the poodle lady to Dr. Clementina
—What did you say about my color, Doctor?
I don't know what Dr. Clementina said but I, who like to help, said that the circus is over and the caravans, incapable of hopping, rattling along from village to village. The Greatest Show on Earth, in letters that are no longer scarlet, but pink, anchored on an empty lot that they had to clear of reeds and weeds, and

throw husks into a heap, once there was a lion, once there were horses, now a donkey tapping its foot to count to ten, they hit him surreptitiously with a little stick, and even though it took a long time, he'd respond with the second lash, how much is three plus three, in a few minutes a heavy six, the lion, that limited itself to walking around the track and going through a hoop, so expensive to maintain, they had to give it to the horses to eat, his bones were enormous, almost no teeth in the mouth full of humble reproaches, the horses are trash

—Do you think the lion will eat us, Doctor?

and it almost ate us, it approached, tried a mouthful, and rolled in its cage in which it could hardly move, the lion is also trash, the blackbird with the insect didn't come back, a cousin came for him that looked at me from the wall, if I had the opportunity, I'd write in the secret diary, hoping you'd read it one day, we'll stay friends forever, promise, and we did, when I was released I switched my bag to the other arm and gave you the hand that you didn't see, how could you see it, I'm trash, you said, without stopping to take notes on a clipboard

—Don't miss your appointment date

and when I turned to leave, at the door, I found the princess earrings between two locks of hair, not as dark as before, dyed, we have to disguise ourselves, don't we, deceive ourselves, and still, we don't deceive ourselves, we know underneath, we know what's inside, the blood in the bathing suit stopped and, in compensation, the skin underneath the chin grows slack, where does this skin come from, these wrinkles, moles that weren't there before, no blackbird and the butt that gets flabbier, flabbier, no blackbird, and as for the pines, I don't even look at them, I look at the tide that starts to rise, my co-worker

—One more kiss and I'll forgive you for dying

and she almost forgave me first, and forgave me afterwards, the proof that she forgave me was

—I'll make you some tea

the little tea bag, on its string, sunk into the pot, the tag out so you could dip it up and down, candies, cookies, a dish of almost of different colors, what a luxury, when you licked off the sugar coating you didn't dare chew them because of your molars, right, you put them in the saucer, lips pursed and a hand in front of your mouth out of politeness, don't be annoyed with me but when you put your hand in front of your mouth you look like trash, it doesn't matter, I am too, us trash understand each other, I don't miss the blackbird, I miss the maid calling Dr. Clementina

—Come to the table, Tininha

and Dr. Clementina, instead of obeying, whispering into my ear

—I've fallen out of love with your older brother

because passions are waves that recede quickly and after a few moments you hardly notice their passage, my older brother walking in the direction of the bike and Dr. Clementina didn't even turn her head

—See, I didn't even look at him

and I saw she hadn't looked at him, that's the way we are, it's over, Dr. Clementina interested in the box holding the butterflies that keeps them from flying away

—Do you think they'll escape

and they might, I don't know, we put leaves inside and a thimble of water, every creature needs water, even the sparrows drink in the puddles left by the hose, one afternoon Dr. Clementina brought a cigarette from her mother's pack and a box of matches that we tried to strike and then threw into the garbage instead of lighting them, finally a tiny flame but we were too nervous, a tiny flame but the wind blew it out, I squatted on my side of the wall and tried to smoke the cigarette, I didn't cough or feel nauseous, the sensation of a locomotive that they stoked with wood in my stomach and connecting rods in my elbows, my legs were wheels, the fear that I'd end up like Senhor Leonel's niece in a bend of the road where mimosas, maple leaves, were unfurling in me and then, Vouzela, give me your blessing again, Father, while you fall, my mother, taking away the cigarette with a slap

—What is this?

and Dr. Clementina ran home, my co-worker

—Put the tea in your mouth into mine

wiping herself on the napkin because the tea was dripping down her chin, I promised to talk about the storks and I attempt to comply, unless, you never know, I hope not, I have to comply, how they get here, how they build their nests, how they avoid people, the burning wood diminished in my stomach but the smoke kept coming out in little clouds, look there's an very fat frog over there, the smoke is coming out of its nose and mouth

—Come on home, Germano

erasing my words

—It's nothing, ma'am

a week without, the frog is not just very fat, it's gelatinous, with pores, its fingers spread out with blisters on the tips, more yellow than green because the earth is yellow, while the rising tide isn't yellow, it's blue, a week without dessert, in fact it's always the same, a banana or a pear, I who preferred plums and the outrage directed at my father

—I caught your daughter smoking, can you believe it?

who didn't move from the step, my mother

—Plums, don't even dream of, it's a chore to take out the pits the next-door neighbor offered me wafers, my mother's sleeve between me and the vendor

—She must learn

Dr. Clementina, while my not deaf brother almost caught a grasshopper, didn't show up because of a black nail, the grasshopper on another trunk and he approached it slowly

—I put a lot of toothpaste on my tongue, and nobody noticed the smell

well, to begin with, I think that stork season begins in May or June, they spend a lot of time making ovals high up in the sky, one, then two, at different altitudes, leave, return, leave again, and they are gone for several days during which, I presume, they are flying so high we don't see them, they look down on us, spy on us, once in a while my mother searched my drawers for cigarettes and smelled my breath

—I hope you've learned your lesson

if it were a week without plums I'd learn better than if it were a week without bananas or pears, just one more hour to say goodbye to you, the grasshopper escaped my not deaf brother rubbing its legs on a branch where he couldn't reach it, sometimes we go weeks without seeing them, they try the olive trees, the oaks, they exchange us for the old forge, the stable at the old riding arena, for a little castle on a hill covered with mulberry bushes, always avoiding the waves, I'll give a sweet to anyone who shows me storks on a beach, purely and simply there are none, my co-worker wiping off my chin too

—How delicious, princess

a smidge younger, a smidge not as ugly, I still grieve your death, father, the world waiting to be put in a slipper and it slips out, so many memories in this house, and even though I'm alone, so many living presences, it's enough to call people and they appear right away, just as they were

—Here we are, girl

my mother not angry, smiling

—Do you remember when I caught you smoking?

because the stupid things that used to make us angry end up making us feel tender with time, fortunately she didn't notice Senhor Leonel's niece on the railroad tracks after the curve where the mimosas, maples, and I killed her, I ask myself if, had I noticed, she was still smiling

—Do you remember killing Senhor Leonel's niece in Vouzela?

Tininha's mother has no face, her enormous hands cover her eyes, horrified

—Holy Christ

pieces of clothing in her garden, a wallet, a shoe, a handkerchief, or that floating in the camellia and, with the enormous hands, gigantic red nails, how many centuries ago did they wipe my chin with a napkin, on certain occasions, even after I wiped myself

—I see a grain of rice there

taken off with the pincer fingers

—Look at this

as if a miserable grain of rice fascinated me, just like the blackheads that served as a pretext to martyr my nose

—Don't move

they insisted on exhibiting it to me on the pad of their index finger

—Look at the size of this

an insignificance that you could hardly notice, my mother incredulous

—Who did you inherit this skin from?

and the fact that I didn't know who I inherited my skin from bothers me, from which aunt in the album, from which very dead great grandfather in all the memories, not even the mustache floats around in alarm

—They killed the king

scratching my skin on the back of his neck asking himself

—What will happen to us?

Dr. Clementina

—My mother said that yesterday you were irresponsible

ready to consider me with respect and fear, every time she walked by bed eighteen, a princess earring fell off that she didn't know she had or she had become so used to it that she forgot about it, we just have teeth when a canine hurts us, we only discover our vertebrae when something presses on our back, when we're healthy we exist without a body, the storks, and I'm tired of the storks, legs of rusty wire, the king, in the photo in an almanac without a cover, dressed in hunting attire on a property in Elvas, with horsemen around him and a dozen pheasants with broken necks, or at least they seem to have broken necks, on a tarp at his feet, it could have been the king, it could have been the trains of Vouzela, what does it matter now, I calculate, it's a matter of faith, that the mimosas and the maples are still there, there are trees that last forever, if I had been born a tree I'd live on some plot of vacant land, or no land at all, losing my leaves in October and getting them back in March, monotonous, stubborn, Dr. Clementina to dissipate any doubts

—So, swear on your parents that you weren't irresponsible

although the shoe remained in the garden, accusatory, empty, probably the son of one of the lifeguards had thrown it on the other side of the wall, a shoe like the one the owner of the circus wore announcing with cadaveric solemnity

—Careful Ândrea, remember your mother died that way

and Ândrea, an orphan, a little bird, another little bird, I never saw her happy, I never saw her satisfied, squatting in the thistles wearing a shabby blouse, barefoot, her feet more adult than she was and covering her knees with her child wrists, the performer with the donkey was shaving outside with a little mirror, my co-worker

—Is there another kiss without an owner around here?

and there are dozens of kisses without owners around here, my husband didn't want to, my father, don't even think about it, my older brother escaped, I'm going to choose one with a lot of colors, fuller, but, for the love of God, don't sigh

—What would I do without you?

since you'll keep on doing what you do today, that is approach someone waiting for you in the dark, that you might just discover when you draw near to her, she will say

—Shall we go?

and the two of you go down the hall, in Peniche, talking about this and that on your way to the sea, the bolts clicking shut one by one, as you pass, first the echoes of your shoes, finally no echo at all, the woman and my co-worker in a last room and in this one the gulls were on the window sill, fighting over a piece of fish, mutilating each other with their beaks, their feet, their wings, it's my co-worker's body that falls, the doctor to the police, holding the flashlight

—They should have been more careful

and again, the blonde wife, the blonde children, crosses, cypress trees, the woman moving to another house, who can guarantee me that it's not this one, immobile, patient, it only talks with those it chooses to say goodbye, I presume I'll find her on the Alto da Vigia, hair blown by the wind, clutching her shawl around her, and she doesn't have to introduce herself

—Hello

so that I will understand her, I know, she will accompany me to the edge of the cliff, apologizing for abandoning me there

—It's best not to go any farther

and it's better you don't go any farther, ma'am, what is left is so simple, just a little step, with nobody to protect me, as soon as the wave advances there will be a sensation of cold, an immense light all around and the whisper of the bones that the currents separate, my mother, smiling

—Do you remember when I caught you smoking?

without my finding her, where she went, what happened to you, the king, with his pheasants, disappearing in Elvas, I went there one day, I remember an aqueduct, I remember a cat in the rain jumping into a window, there are memories that persist without one knowing the reason, the cat in the rain, the man drying himself on his sleeve, how strange that I never ran into him or saw him in the neighborhood, if I am still, when he leaves the house he's a different person, well dressed, dignified, without any worries, looking, at the bus stop, now at the corner, now at his wristwatch, what happened that night, friend, if I'm still, when I arrive at his house, the sadness rains down over it, the same furniture, the melancholy clarity of the lamp, the note from his wife, Sorry but I couldn't take it anymore, the man, reading it again

—Couldn't take what?

the note ended up in shreds in the toilet, and at the third flush, the spiral of water disappeared, there were one or two pieces that kept bobbing up, and to this day, when he goes to the bathroom, he is afraid he'll see them, to this day, on one of them, I can't . . . and on the second piece of paper that, praise God, disappeared immediately, one day he thought he saw it in a bookstore and his heart hammering, he walked away, turned back, checked again, it wasn't, or, it was, because in six years, what does time do, people change, he, who thought he was the same because every day he saw himself as he shaved, he had changed too, he noticed a weakness in his legs, he avoided stairs, it's not the lungs, it's the muscles, although it seemed that his lungs accompanied his muscles, since breathing was difficult, the man, with the furniture and the lamp around him

—What does all this mean?

without discovering any meaning, his wife attentive, calm, it was hard to believe that another, and then, there are times, what times, he had a hard time believing that another, impossible that there was another but what is the meaning of all of this, tell me, Ândrea is one more bird on the wire, taking care to step carefully, when she didn't step carefully she squatted in the reeds in her poor girl's clothing, she didn't say

—I want my mother

the way I feel like saying it, she kept silent, sometimes she'd gnaw at an apple, sometimes a flower, almost wilted, in her hand and what use was the flower, it wasn't straight, in fact, it was folded in her fist, what churned in my mind, hoping to understand what it meant and I don't understand, the certainty that, if I knew, my life would change I don't know in which direction, but it would change, I don't feel capable of imagining any direction, as for the rest, I'm identical to the man in the other window

—What does all this mean?

and what a useless question, it means nothing, if a meaning existed, I'd find it, except I don't know where it ends and I that terrifies me, therefore the hallways of Peniche terrify me and the gulls fighting with their beaks, feet, wings, the ferocity of their eyes

—We'll tear you apart too

I'm a fish moving my tail as they tear me apart, the fins, the back, what's left of the gills

—I couldn't take it anymore

and she didn't even take all her clothes, a small suitcase, you open a closet and clothes are in it, a drawer and clothes are there, you look into the washing machine and her clothes are inside, what does she wear these days, she looks at the furniture like he does or sits down relieved, content, the wife at the counter interrupting the gesture of paying as she scratches her elbow, it wasn't that one, fortunately, the itchiness belonged to the man, who kept scratching, gentlemen, during his entire life, this buttock, the shoulders, he examined the note for hours, not exactly a note, a piece of paper torn hastily from a three-ring binder with the holes still visible, where they wrote their grocery lists, you could see the indentations of the pencil, cabbage, detergent, socks, the day to day that we protest against and nevertheless provides us comfort, the man at the bus stop, in spite of being impatient, thinking it comforts him, the clouds in the mountains are not here, they're further north and not all together, one by one, they promise a grasshopper to my not deaf brother so I can see him at the gate

—What are you going to do, Sis?

and I satisfied at seeing him, when I was a train, I killed Senhor Leonel's niece, not in Vouzela, on the beach, what can a cigarette do, Dr. Clementina next to bed eighteen without paying attention to the X-ray

—It's not true, is it?

who held it in her wrist like Ândrea's flower, the end of which wasn't folded, not princess earrings, two little pearls with screw backs that don't stop turning, people turn, turn, and the screw and bolt turn endlessly

—It's not true, is it?

there's no screw that doesn't seem to turn endlessly, me to my co-worker

—Do you know of any screw that stops turning?

the cup between the saucer and her mouth, her eyes peering over the rim

—Pardon me?

probably, for her, a half dozen turns and that was it, I bet it's just with me that screws behave that way, small when you take them out of the package, and as soon as you put them in a little hole, kilometers of screw threads, how do they manage that, my co-worker freeing her eye from the rim of the teacup

—What's this story about screws, doll?

it's not a story, it's true, could my older brother, intimately familiar with these maneuvers, prove me right

—It's true

tracing the index with a nail so it would leave him in peace, an index by chapters and an alphabetical index, look in the alphabetical index if you don't mind, brother, you'll find the information there, my mother interrupting her sewing

—Screws, girl, you've got a screw loose

with her lower lip over her upper lip helping her not to miss a stitch, every time she had to perform a delicate task or when a strong emotion overwhelmed her there came the lower lip to cover the upper lip and my mother wasn't aware of it, when the thing that happened to my older brother at the Alto da Vigia she went around for months that way, when her two lips returned to their correct places her grief had subsided, Dr. Clementina handing the X-ray to her assistant, astonished at herself

—Bed eighteen thinks she's a train, what a crazy idea

and it's not crazy, Dr. Clementina, the train what did it do, it brought the cigarette, it brought the matches and the connecting rods of my elbows started to become dislocated, it noticed the mimosas and the maples around the curve, it saw my wheels and my effort to brake as soon as I saw Senhor Leonel's niece on the tracks, apprehensive

—You make up the strangest things

emerging as slowly from the teacup as the moon rising over rooftops, every time I looked behind the houses, in the morning because at night they didn't let me go out, buckets, hoses, a lady encouraging her daffodils however the moon was hidden, I think it was waiting behind the earth, in the dim light someone is dangling it from a pulley and there she is oscillating, the week that the moon didn't come my deaf brother was restless, looking for it in the yard, in the well

— Shhheee saaaills seea

my mother to my not deaf brother

—Bring his medicine bottle from the kitchen

my not deaf brother brings the bottle and my mother

—Do you want him to drink from the bottle and sleep for a month?

my not deaf brother made noises of things opening and closing, a clattering of dishes threatening to break, my mother

—In the third drawer, dope

more things opening and closing, more clattering, a soup terrine about to shatter, my mother in the direction of the kitchen

—You didn't even learn how to count to three

a last crash, silence, footsteps in the silence, finally the spoon, my older brother held my deaf brother, my mother poured the liquid into the spoon that looked like tar, ordered my older brother

—Bring me that, sorry kid

and even though she poured the liquid cautiously a drop always fell on the floor, a cat in the rain in Elvas, if I could draw he'd not be missing a hair, the useless things people learn by heart, for me it's the classification of insects and the tributaries of the Tagus, Almansor, for example, what a wonderful name, I'm going to write it again to give it the appreciation it deserves, Almansor, Almansor, probably a creek between little stones but what majesty in the syllables, the elegance of the sound, the drop on the floor grew, undulated, my older brother opened my deaf brother's throat the way you pry open a can of preserves that resists, my mother, I take off my hat to whomever invented that masterpiece, Almansor, threw the tar into a hole that screamed

—Shhheee

with a skill that I didn't think she was capable of, people, word of honor, will surprise me to the end, the restlessness and the

—Shhheee

diminished slowly and my deaf brother fell asleep on the couch, my co-worker

—Your eyes are closing, are you sleepy?

while the cat in Elvas evaporated in the window, my father

carried my deaf brother to bed, my mother, as she did every time my father picked him up, close to tears with the words
 —I'm sorry
 mute on her lips, Dr. Clementina
 —What is it your mother does?
 who can prove to me that she doesn't remember her mother
 —My peach
 stinking up the car with her perfume, smiling to herself on the lounge chair, whispering with her friend or getting dressed up for the Mexican actor, in case the person waiting for her proposed
 —Shall we go?
 the little snout of the Elvas cat appeared in the window frame, I remember everything before I lose it forever and I ask myself if I've already lost it since it goes with me, at least keep the cat, rejoice, when all else fails put it on your lap and promise that you'll calm down without the syrup, how long will it be until the new moon comes again, rising over the rooftops without my seeing it again, my deaf brother can see it for me with
 —Shhheee
 happy, Dona Alice's relative
 —There he is, having a good time
 and there he is, surely having a good time, four years older than me, fifty-six, is Almansor a stream or a real tributary, in spite of being fifty-six my deaf brother didn't grow, if I had him with me he'd keep chasing butterflies except more slowly, from Elvas you could see Spain, fields like these, little villages, a windmill, there's no difference between foreigners and us, consult the atlas and the Almansor is born there dripping from a rock, the same life everywhere, it's a good thing that we have Sundays to put an end to aimless pleasures and superfluous hopes, my deaf brother

now incapable of walking on his lame foot or putting his knee in his mouth, accepting without protest the tar syrup, the moon doesn't bother with him, it doesn't bother about anybody, it simply floats, it gets stuck in a chimney, it gets loose and bobs around, it insists, on dozens of occasions I found its rags in the pines that the wind gathers and places there, one night hanging from the trees, another, on the ground, Dr. Clementina to me, pulling the diary from the wall

—I shouldn't have been a doctor, I should have been an astronaut

tired of carrying pens in her pocket, of catheters, of sick people, my co-worker

—It's a good thing you woke up

I wasn't sleeping, I think better with my eyes closed, that's all, my co-worker

—Do you think when you snore?

and of course I wasn't snoring, it was the dishwasher changing speed, not me, me holding my deaf brother's hand helping my mother in the grocery store, you don't see me walk, you, you don't see me with the potatoes, I gave the bag to my deaf brother and he proudly, giving it to my mother wordlessly, of course, and nevertheless you could understand him

—I brought them, ma'am

I remained silent so not to spoil his illusion, why steal satisfaction from people

—He brought the potatoes, ma'am

my deaf brother without words

—Didn't I say so?

my mother feeling like hugging him, and full of dark memories, incapable of doing so, if I had been born in Spain what would

have changed in me, certainly co-workers and Alto da Vigias aren't lacking there, if I had become rich I'd be a peach, if I hadn't become rich then just old age would take me, peach or not the fate is the same, the woman in the dark waiting for us
 —Hello
wrapped tightly in her shawl without arranging her hair, a little pin that didn't prevent her curls from escaping, she was also fifty-two and looked like me, my co-worker mistaking her for me
 —Sit here on the couch
and the woman with her accepting the tea, the tide is almost ready, not a soul on the beach except the lifeguards collecting the tarps, the one with the cigarette smoking it down to a nub, fishing the tobacco from inside his mouth, his feet like those of an ox in a rice field, when I was little he was so big, they took out his guts and his legs got skinny, every August, a few years from now, he'll not climb out of his boat backwards near the wooden sheds, a little more time and the boat will be without him, nobody will rescue the lifeguards, gulls grazing the foam without smoothing their feathers, my mother, after taking the potatoes
 —Scram
wanting to see us from the back of her head, more my deaf brother than me, I remember her with the next-door neighbor
 —I carry a living sin inside me
and therefore more my deaf brother than me, the memory of the cat in the rain doesn't leave me, we were almost in the living room when I heard its footsteps, I turned and his little snout was so hostile that my deaf brother started to moan, not really moan, his breath ragged the way it gets before he moans, Almansor and Vouzela are mysteries to me, my mother turned and stood in front of us, I thought she might put us on her lap,

instead of that she said
   —I forgot to say thank-you
and she ran away covering her face with her sleeve.

9.

The house is quiet, and I am calm, I closed the window to my room slowly so my family would not hear me from the living room, and they didn't, my mother was scolding my not deaf brother for some stupid thing he'd done with the swing, I heard their voices without making out the meaning except Cousin Fernando who was saying I don't have any idea to whom

—Guess which hand has the candy

maybe to me, when I was little, and to the others in the room just that I didn't feel like choosing any hand, entertained with pushing lettuce into the cricket cage that wouldn't sing no matter how much we tapped the wire with our fingers

—So?

I crossed the hall avoiding the floorboards that tell on us and my mother immediately

—Who's creeping around without permission when it's time for dinner?

while she distributed the plates and glasses at the table, the next-door neighbor, buried in her crocheting, agreeing with her

—It's your cross

and it was her cross, in fact, four children and a husband clanking bottles in the pantry instead of putting the children, who need authority and firmness, in order, and since there was no authority or firmness they just do whatever they please and when they're adults, they drift, they're bums, the cricket gives a little squeak without music, elongating its antennae, if we ate lettuce we'd grow wings and you wouldn't be able to stand the symphony, my co-worker with her palms over her ears

—I can't stand the noise

at the beach house she, who only exchanged the chinoiserie for school, explained to my mother

—Your daughter and I have been friends for centuries

and the ocean was noiseless, discreet, it doesn't have floorboards that tell on us like the ones in the hallway, you step in the water and there's not even a vibration to show for it except for the toothed wheels that raise the waves, speaking of toothed wheels my molar stopped bothering me, I run my tongue over it and there's no hole, I drink soda and it doesn't hurt, the pines are entertained with the blackbirds and don't give a hoot about me and what remains of the flowers is inattentive, they think I'm helping my mother, putting the forks and knives on the table backwards

—Don't you ever learn?

and how can someone learn with a father like mine, he weighed like lead if you picked him up

—The rascal weighs like lead

who screwed himself, instead of the whole world, and he couldn't get out of it, from time to time a walk in the olive grove, from time to time a sit on the kitchen step, my co-worker to my mother

—Has your husband always been this way, ma'am?

unfortunately, he has been this way since, and my mother became tongue tied, Almansor, at first, I liked the word and now it annoys me, not one lifeguard on the beach, the last gulls over the lifeguard station, not on the rocks or on the cliff where the goat's knees start to shake, asking me

—Don't delay

and I won't delay, I promise, it's almost time, Dr. Clementina, disappointed

—The maid won't let me set the table she's afraid I'll wrinkle the tablecloth

ours is of cheap cloth, checkered, hers is white, with lace, if there's a wrinkle out of place Dr. Clementina's mother

—Trash

with resigned disdain, I hope that the building next to the Thebes Bakery doesn't lose more tiles and that the geraniums hold up, the way I hope that the palm tree grows and covers the whole neighborhood, in covering it, the night that I know it its diverse forms and the insomnia during which my husband moves position and drowns himself again, the mouth emerging in a few seconds accompanied by half an eye that looks at me blindly before disappearing forever

—Can't you sleep?

in the beginning, when I said the word husband, I swelled with pride, Dr. Clementina, on the other side of the wall, shrinking with respect for me

—Did you get married?

showing her the piece of tin that served as a wedding ring, my mother's perfume helped me be an adult, it was in a bottle with a gold top and I dabbed it behind my ears instead of wearing princess earrings, I was grown up, she had silver earrings, she had others with little stones and I was unsure if we were poor or not, my husband took a while to arrive, in the morning, inside himself, his body slowly filled up with him, shoulders, arms, throat, the neck of his pajamas tickling his nose, the house quiet, everything calm inside me, finally the eyelids, not at the same time, blinking one after the other, with the eyelids the voice that took a while to belong to him

—What day is it?

and forgetting what day it was, once

—Grandmother

and someone rolling up the fringe of the carpet escaping from the room, my husband not recognizing me, saying tenderly

—Darling

until he understood it was me and immediately pushing away the

—Darling

where is that shadow, trying to fold it, to hide it better, with stiff fingers, if I could I'd put it in my pocket so I wouldn't hear it, my mother holding up the perfume bottle

—Did you mess around with my perfume?

and why answer as she smelled my neck, she to my co-worker

—There's no way to convince her that she's nine years old and she hasn't gotten married yet

arriving at the gate I don't even look back at them, I go down the street, they are comfortable in the living room talking about me, only my father, on the step, talks to me for the first time

—Until forever

when he died not

—Until forever

an exhausted muttering

—Leave me alone please
   turned to the wall, my husband's grandmother here and there until she found the exit
   —How old were you when your grandmother died?
   my husband sitting on the bed feeling for his slippers, not even blackbirds are left, there is still the wind announcing the twilight and the trees are so clear, how things reveal themselves in the afternoon, my husband
   —Six
   he found his slippers, looked for the second one on his knees, with a piece of skin showing between his pajama tops and the bottoms, he looked like a child, and I felt so much love for him, surprised, it was enough for a little skin to show to bring us together again, if you told me I wouldn't believe it
   —A piece of skin what nonsense
   I didn't answer my father
   —Until forever
   I didn't answer anybody at all, goodbyes put needles inside my eyes, and I don't have time for sentimentality now, the owner of the Thebes bakery, despite being in Lisbon
   —Is today when you're going to abandon us?
   not angry at me, not sad, wearing the same apron, her thumb a little crooked from a fall at school, from the gate you couldn't see the ocean, the tricycle of the fish monger, bushes, the lifeguard stands with little kids whose bellybuttons showed and chickens, the same ones that my not deaf brother shot at in Angola and they ran over each other in confused flight, the urge to ask him
   —Come with me
   and even though it was impossible since the truck was calling him, the mountain was black now, me not understanding where

the night begins, I thought I knew and I don't not even a little just like I don't know the storks, I lied, I see them in the chimneys and that's all, they eat lizards, frogs, little snakes, Cousin Fernando, not caring about the candies

—birds of large stature

wearing a tie even on the beach, he was a warehouse clerk, my husband, in the middle of the room, noticed that I was thinking of his grandmother

—Do you still remember her

and the answer was a sigh that forced me to be silent, Dr. Clementina's mother lowered her sunglasses in Cousin Fernando's direction and put them up again

—A ghost

not a peach, a ghost, birds of large stature what an idiot, if I am still they won't notice my absence at the table and they won't ask for me, my glass will not be filled with water, my plate will be empty, my deaf brother pointing to my place

—Shhheee?

and my father crumbling the pieces of bread, how do you hide bad thoughts without saying a thing, my grandfather, displeased

—What's wrong with your nerve, boy?

commenting on my co-worker

—She's a bundle of energy, that young lady

making himself smaller, beaten, diluting himself in pictures that were not of him, of other relatives in the drawer, whose images appeared in front of the Roman Colosseum, tropical landscapes, fading away fleshless, my father's aunt consoling him

—Things will change, don't worry

the hell things will change, nobody changes, tell me the name of a single person who has changed, ma'am, Dr. Clementina pointing at a stain between other similar stains

—There's the tumor

a tiny tangerine and I wasn't even anxious, believe me, I was interested in a scorpion, its pincers raised, threatening a frog in whose mouth a beetle wing fluttered, walking down the street thinking of my older brother with the Post Office clerk, dancing around her and kicking cans, she married a solicitor, moved to Benavente, a place on the periphery of Vouzela, I imagine, what other places are there in Portugal, the mother of the Post Office clerk grabbed my arm on the street

—After your older brother died, I never saw her smile again

and therefore, spending an unhappy life in the provinces, between selling stamps holding a child in each hand which were two buckets of tears, everything calm inside me, this peace, my mother serving dinner

—There she goes

and Dr. Clementina, in a lab coat, alone at the wall, not just the black mountain, the Alto da Vigia was also getting dark, I'm exaggerating, I'm not exaggerating about the calm and the peace and even so I'm afraid, I exaggerate about the Alto da Vigia not getting dark, you can make out the thickets, you can make out the ruins, my older brother is up there without any cans, if Ândrea were in my place she wouldn't jump, she'd test the void with her feet walking over it, growing smaller in the distance, Ândrea was a little dot, Ândrea was an absence, my mother to my not deaf brother

—Don't eat so fast, the world's not ending yet

even without touching the swing it moved, one afternoon I found my father in it, going back and forth, convinced that my grandfather was pushing him and my mother peering at him from behind the curtain, when she saw me, her expression changed

—He's out of his mind

when that wasn't what I was thinking, I was thinking that the two of them, I was thinking maybe, I was thinking why delude myself, I was thinking it was too late, it's been so long since we've danced, ma'am, how long has it been since the thieving blackbird evaporated from your mind, before my not deaf brother took us out of the soup tureen and devoured all of us since, for him, the world was ending, a man with a pipe was left, a woman lying on the ground and rotten manioc on the floor, my father left the swing and my mother wanted to ask me

—If I sat on it, would you push me?

hitting pillows angrily, I love you, I love you not, what good is it to love you today, if a blackbird lands on that pine you love me too, she waited five minutes, she waited ten minutes, no blackbird landed, she waited five more minutes, she decided I don't care if you love me or not because I'm the one who doesn't love me, she looked at the pine tree a last time and shouted secretly

—Did you hear?

and although it was a secret my father

—I know

he who didn't talk answered

—I know

the Post Office clerk to my older brother, near the grocery store

—I'm six years older than you we should break up before my parents see us

a couple of women counting on their fingers, scandalized, the difference in ages to which Dr. Clementina's mother said

—My peach

she paid no attention, her eyes
—Come here, boy
without needing speeches, my older brother in a panic
—I don't know what will happen to me afterwards
afraid of disappearing into Dr. Clementina's mother, sucked in, shredded, there are insects that the female swallows whole, my mother looking for my older brother and my older brother listening to her dutifully but not able to answer, stuck inside Dr. Clementina's mother
—You won't get out of my stomach
the Post Office clerk
—We should break up
so that the can he was kicking hard was demolished, my older brother determined to marry the Post Office clerk and she said
—Aren't you a minor?

they didn't kiss, they didn't caress each other, just shyness and embarrassment, what do you do with your mouth to give a serious kiss, how do you hold another body close, the Mexican actor, before he kissed and held her, sang to the actress strumming a guitar, my older brother didn't have a guitar, not to mention the horse, the cactus, and a dozen barefoot Indians around, in black and white, not in color like in real life, and a bad sound track, first the lips and the melody afterwards or the melody first and the lips afterwards, I don't remember for sure, I remember, for example that the sound of a mug on the table preceded the mug on the table, you could guess the plot from the noises, a discussion in an empty room where the actors hadn't arrived yet, the noise of thunder preceding the lightning, if I am silent they will hear me fall from the Alto da Vigia, if I could throw myself off someplace less dangerous, I'd prefer it, the Post Office clerk

—Aren't you a minor?

my older brother pissed that he was younger

—They can change the dates on my birth certificate

and with some clout and an eraser the marriage would be possible, he in front of the post office building mulling over solutions, a bird on an agave plant not helping him, mocking him, he bent down to throw a stone at it, he missed and the bird, scornfully

—You can't even hit me

through the open window the boss of the Post Office clerk was stamping mail ceaselessly and the sound, by chance, coincided with his gestures, my husband extending a fist to me

—A button is missing here

not asking me to mend it, limiting himself to denounce my crime he let his shirt fall, the way soft things fall, without hurting themselves, it fascinates me, my co-worker to my mother

—Was your daughter ever a good housewife?

and the scar on my chest made movement difficult, my left arm was larger than my right because of the operation, the hair that took a long time to grow back, the discomfort of the prosthesis in my bra, the intern to her friend

—I didn't want to look at it and I stared at it the whole time

and although I was going down to the beach, I still hadn't passed the post office or the grocery store, my mother and brothers in a single file with me, as soon as we saw the grocery crates in the distance my mother said

—Watch out for the cars

not stepping on the intervals between the stones, identical to us at times, my older brother to her

—Watch out for the cars, ma'am

and my mother afraid one of us would pull her ear, the next-door neighbor to us
—Keep her from putting garbage in her mouth
a cigarette butt, a piece of paper, a dry seaweed, a little bone
—What's in your mouth, ma'am?
my mother, her mouth full
—Nothing
the cricket wouldn't sing no matter how much lettuce I gave it, I tried to teach it the thieving blackbird song and he didn't even get the first verse right, he walked around his cage in an obstinate silence, each foot a cane in relation to the others, try to give it a piece of candy, Cousin Fernando, see if it lifts its spirits, I could swear that Ândrea was on the Alto da Vigia with me with her poor girl's blouse and her dead flower, if I said hello to her
—Good afternoon
she didn't pay attention to me, leaning against the remains of a wall that protected her from the wind, how did they take seafood and drinks up there and how would the beer drinkers get down afterwards, the lifeguards aren't on the beach, they're in the foosball café Senhor Manelinho, while Senhor Manelinho's wife, after organizing the newspapers, locked up the kiosk with a chain, I thought it was easy, and I don't know why, it's hard, my mother
—If you think that's the only solution
and I don't think so, whatever it is, I limit myself to walking down the street watching out for the cars, a fragment of a billboard coming off a wall announcing a festival from last September, a parade, a dance, a raffle, my deaf brother, in Lisbon, incapable of pronouncing my name, the storks, birds of great stature since Cousin Fernando said

—Birds of great stature
protecting their nests, my mother laying the table
—You should know
and frankly, I thought I knew, and I don't, if I called my husband, I'd ask him
—Come get me
But nobody answered, a ringing in a deserted apartment, my husband talking about me to a woman I can't see
—She could show up this afternoon
and I won't show up this afternoon, I think, or I will, who knows the answer, if I asked my mother for advice and my mother was absent or leaning toward me
—What?
trying to understand, I
—It's not important, never mind
because it's not important, ma'am, seriously it's not important, the stairway to the beach, if I take off my shoes it's easier but I'll need them to climb the rocks so the sharp edges won't hurt me, even though the waves are so close I can't hear them, the sound comes much before like in the Mexican film or maybe there's no sound, Dr. Clementina
—What happened to the waves?
they're there, don't worry, throwing themselves against the sand, your mother, on the back seat, ordering the driver, conscious that he is trash and disdaining him for that
—Sit down the way you should, put your cap on and be quiet for a minute
without a lounge chair or a bathing suit and not even sunglasses, the friend, who had died from adrenal cancer, not in bed eighteen, between dozens of bed eighteens, the meal cart

squeaking in the ward and the morning that doesn't come, Dr. Clementina's mother

—An adrenal tumor?

remembering my older brother taking care of a pine tree, an adrenal tumor or some other thing what's the difference, what difference did it make to her, if I called my husband I'd say

—Come get me

or I might not even say

—Come get me

if he answered he'd hang up on me, I found a button for the shirt, I ironed it again, I ran my hand along the fabric, not a caress, why caress it, I ran my hand over it in a casual gesture, not noticing, and I put it away, one afternoon I caught my mother kissing one of my father's T-shirts, how ridiculous, I and I fled, I don't caress anybody's clothes much less kiss them, if the father of my father had known me he'd have said

—Even though you don't weigh like lead you'll make your mark on the world

and it's true, he returned to the album happy that he was right, tell your companions on the page

—It's like I said

and he'd stay there, in his hat, proud of me, crossing the beach with shoes on, at fifty-two, it was harder than I thought, Senhor Manelinho, in the foosball café

—I thought you weren't coming

he was thinking that the drunk's daughter, she who has someone to take after, it's not lacking in that family, just look at the older brother who went after the Post Office clerk who cheated on him, the older brother was respectful, the idiot, when for the girl, a bush was enough, we

—Lie down there

and then, I was thinking the drunk's daughter wasn't going to come, and she finally did, they owed the grocer, they owed the butcher, they were behind on the rent, not to mention the deaf boy

—Shhheee saaails seeea

and the one who came back nuts from Angola running after animals and an army truck that didn't exist

—They're calling me I've got to go

convinced everything was burning, my co-worker, intrigued

—Is that true?

and I don't know if it's true, I was little, that is I know, it's true, my father with the bottles on the step, his teeth clenched, my mother to nobody, drowning in bills

—What now?

she asked the next-door neighbor, after a few minutes of screwing up her courage, if you thought first before doing something stupid, ma'am, you even lost your dignity

—I don't know how to talk about this

she left her wedding ring as collateral at the bakery, she left the earrings that Senhor Leonel didn't want to accept at the butcher, and he finally did

—Let it be for the memory of my niece

I, who killed her in Vouzela, between mimosas and maples, if before going out I had noticed the yard beyond the wall I'd have found the shoe, maybe a bit of fabric from her blouse, maybe a scapular that God, without the obligation to notice everything, didn't have time to pick up, Dr. Clementina's mother made her deliver I don't know what, the maid to my mother

—You say it's the first and last time

I know because Dr. Clementina

—My mother gave some money to yours

while the working class doesn't rise to power, and it won't rise to power, others will rise for it, the working class is trash and trash don't protest, what good does it do, accept it, it will continue to accept it until the end of time, this house, sold, with lopsided window shades and leaves whirling on the floor and I along with them, what have I done but whirl around my whole life, my husband

—A button is missing here

my co-worker

What would I do without you?

the intern

—Fifty-two, seriously, my mother is forty-four

and red pillow moving away from me, the garage dismantled, stray cats and thorns, with the sea so close there were more thorns than flowers, you don't expect anything else since the salt burns everything, the last bottle on the step, knocked over, beyond the building with the tiles the owner of the Thebes Bakery on the balcony

—I'm sorry I can't give you any more credit

and I, taking from my salary, to pay for her, the first cliffs of the Alto da Vigia were easy, no moss, at first a kind of path, then no path at all, where did he put the candies, Cousin Fernando, where did you find them, what seemed like a path, weeds, reeds that you grabbed with your hands and scraped my knees, Cousin Fernando, outraged

—I have my pension

pulling a receipt from his wallet, looking like it had been in there for months, insisting

—I have my pension

or rather a relative who gave him clothes, a relative where he ate on Saturdays, a cheap room with access to a quick bath and the owner

—You've been using up gas for more than five minutes

twice a week, a ball of rice spreading leftovers on the sheets and even so officiously

—Birds of great stature

even so a tie with a shiny knot and the elbows fraying but lasting by some miracle, oh Tininha, forgive my indiscretion, Dr. Clementina, these are old habits, I don't consider myself to be your equal, my diary will stay here, I haven't shown it to anyone, I wouldn't compromise you, imagine a nurse showing it around to the others

—Look at the doctor's life

and now yes, the waves, at the vertex of the ocean, maddening the gulls, an albatross among them, two albatrosses and sea sparrows, I forgot about the sparrows for the whole book and now I'm not happy about the omission, I never appreciated their cries or the drops of mud that they let loose from their beaks, one of them on my deaf brother's head, one of them on my blouse, mud, leaves, moist earth, garbage, if I am still on the Alto da Vigia there was a cart driver because there was a platform on the rocks, not just the red cushion moving away, the blue one was between us, I pushed away the viola and it didn't make a sound, the roots helped me climb the remaining distance, almost as dangerous as the circus tightrope while the microphone warned

—Careful, Ândrea, remember your mother died that way

me with my knee on the top, tiles, troughs, contradictory gusts of wind, no donkey after all, they died over the years or

the gypsies took them and drive them in the mountains, in the mornings, rattling, in the direction of the border, the sparrows swoop over me, I apologize imagining there will be someone not yet born who will describe them for me, I end my story here, at twenty to seven on Sunday, I have nothing more to say, the edge of the cliff is twenty or so meters away, Senhor Manelinho
—There she is, look
and at that moment I saw my older brother sitting at a broken-down table
—Girl
and in fact, my older brother
—Girl
made me feel, how to say it, even though I knew the words they don't translate, if we could touch the hearts of others with our own, even though, as Dr. Clementina guarantees, it's just talk by trashy people and I don't feel like talking and I don't have time for trivialities, the fact is that my older brother being with me made me feel calm, it's obvious I'm afraid, or that is I think I'm afraid, or I'm not afraid and the waves are strong, but the drops of foam, but the approaching night, but my body down there, but the shimmer of the water, but the instants, and I've never seen instants that are so instantaneous as these instants, but the instants of silence inside the noise, but a waltz on the radio and my mother picking me up from the floor to dance with me, feeling like bending my head to lean it against hers and I don't, like putting my arms around her neck and I don't, resting my forehead on her shoulder and I don't, I remain straight, rigid
—Careful, Ândrea
while the waltz draws us nearer to the angle of the cliff as we twirl, my mother marking the beat

—One two three one two three

my older brother watching us from the broken table, I still had time to say

—Father mother brothers me

my dead older brother so long ago smiling a smile that bathed his face and mine, now you don't notice the waves anymore, you don't hear the foam, you don't hear the wind, my mother separating me from her and pushing me in the direction of the sea, and while she pushed me there, to lay me down, in the direction of the bed, the sheets, and the pillow coming closer to me and I was so content, so tired, so sleepy that, at the moment she let go, I don't know which one of us fell.

10.

—Shhheee saaills

Antonio Lobo Antunes was born in Lisbon, Portugal in 1942. He began writing as a child, but at his father's wishes, went to medical school instead of pursuing a career in writing. After completing his studies, Antunes was sent to Angola with the Portuguese Army. It was in a military hospital in Angola that Antunes first became interested in many of the subjects of his novels. Antunes lives in Lisbon, where he continues to write and practice psychiatry.

Elizabeth Lowe, born in New York City, has translated over thirty works by Lusophone writers from Brazil, Portugal, and Africa. She was one of the first to translate Jorge Amado, Clarice Lispector, Rubem Fonseca, Nélida Piñon, and António Lobo Antunes. She is the author of *The City in Brazilian Literature* (1982), and co-author with Earl E. Fitz of *Translation and the Rise of Inter-American Literature* (2008), along with many scholarly articles and book chapters. She is a recipient of an NEA Literary Translation Fellowship, National Science Foundation grants for language preservation projects, Fulbright fellowships to Colombia and Brazil, and recognition by the Brazilian Academy of Letters. Her memoir, *Translating from the Portuguese: A Life Translated*, is forthcoming in 2025. She lives in Gainesville, Florida.